Missing Persons

NICCI GERRARD

PENGUIN BOOKS

PENGUIN BOOKS

Published by the Penguin Group
Penguin Books Ltd, 80 Strand, London WC2R 0RL, England
Penguin Group (USA) Inc., 375 Hudson Street, New York, New York 10014, USA
Penguin Group (Canada), 90 Eglinton Avenue East, Suite 700, Toronto, Ontario, Canada M4P 2Y3
(a division of Pearson Penguin Canada Inc.)
Penguin Ireland, 25 St Stephen's Green, Dublin 2, Ireland (a division of Penguin Books Ltd)
Penguin Group (Australia), 250 Camberwell Road, Camberwell, Victoria 3124, Australia
(a division of Pearson Australia Group Pty Ltd)
Penguin Books India Pvt Ltd, 11 Community Centre, Panchsheel Park, New Delhi – 110 017, India
Penguin Group (NZ), 67 Apollo Drive, Rosedale, Auckland 0632, New Zealand
(a division of Pearson New Zealand Ltd)
Penguin Books (South Africa) (Pty) Ltd, Block D, Rosebank Office Park,
181 Jan Smuts Avenue, Parktown North, Gauteng 2193, South Africa

Penguin Books Ltd, Registered Offices: 80 Strand, London WC2R 0RL, England

www.penguin.com

First published 2012
001

Set in 12.5/14.75 pt Garamond MT Std
Typeset by Jouve (UK), Milton Keynes
Printed in England by Clays Ltd, St Ives plc

ISBN: 978-0-241-95006-7

www.greenpenguin.co.uk

Penguin Books is committed to a sustainable
future for our business, our readers and our planet.
This book is made from Forest Stewardship
Council™ certified paper.

ALWAYS LEARNING   **PEARSON**

Later, everyone who loved Johnny Hopkins had different ways to describe how what happened changed their world. Some of them experienced it like the silent collapse of a building – in one moment, when their backs were turned, something solid and familiar was gone, as if it had been a dream, and in its place was a terrifying nothing: a gaping absence, a blue blankness of uncaring sky. For some, it was slower, more dreary – not a violent break but a slow rust that gradually brittled the soul. Johnny's mother, when talking of it, always pressed her hand to her chest, as if without protection her heart would splinter into a thousand pieces. She talked in concrete, physical terms: memory was a knife, loss was an axe, and hope punched her stomach so that she would let out her breath in a painful gasp. Her thoughts were razor blades. Time was a corridor stretching away from her, empty as a nightmare of closed doors, a windowless eternity of footsteps echoing. Sometimes, though, suddenly at a loss, she would simply say his name – 'Johnny, my little boy Johnny', although it was a long time since he had been little – and it was as if she was still hoping that her soft, clear voice would carry over the world and down into the earth and he would hear her at last, wherever he was.

Johnny's father, long after, came across a photograph of a two-hundred-foot sink-hole that had suddenly appeared in Guatemala City. Houses and electricity poles and roads and human lives had been sucked down into its smooth-walled abyss and nobody could say quite why it had happened. He looked at it for several minutes, with his sore eyes. Then, putting on his reading glasses, he took the red-handled scissors that always lay on his desk, care-fully cut it out of the newspaper and stuck it into the scrapbook, as he had done with every single story, inter-view, letter and printed-out email about his son. Nobody else would know why this photograph was there, but it spoke for Felix Hopkins, a man who didn't always find it easy to put his feelings into words so some people didn't understand how deep they went. After all the noise and action, all the attempted explanations, the endless scrab-ble for meaning, this was what they were left with: a crater that was so big, so perfectly round, so sheer, that it had swallowed everything in its circumference. The hole was at the centre of the family. The hole was inside him. It plunged without end, so that feeling was vertiginous; being alive made him dizzy. He laid the scissors back on the desk, beside the little bowl of linked paper clips and the cracked green mug holding his pencils and pens, and gently closed the scrapbook. His Adam's apple bobbed. He took off his reading glasses and laid them on the desk. He pressed his slippered feet to the floor, gripped the sides of his chair, waited for this feeling to sink back down inside him.

Mia rarely talked about it. For a long time, she didn't have the words, and she didn't have the pictures – except for the particular one she carried in her head of Johnny that she had chosen from all the other images to remember him by: her brother Johnny, with his red-gold hair, the same colour as the fox that used to cross their garden at dusk, as silent as a shadow, and his freckles, which seemed to soak back into his skin during the winter but which in the summer were like muddy splashes on his face, giving it an asymmetry. Even when he was smartly dressed and his hair was brushed, he looked slightly slapdash and askew. Johnny, with his blue eyes and cleft chin. Strong shoulders, long fingers, muscled calves; at eighteen, half man and half boy, he had had a coltish grace. In this picture of him, he always wore a V-necked white T-shirt and an old pair of jeans, ripped in one knee, and was sitting on the small lawn with the sun slanting through the plum tree and falling on him, leaving one arm in shadow. His feet were bare, and his face was half turned towards her. He was smiling slightly. She didn't think there had ever been a picture like this, although later she had hunted for it, turning out drawers and rifling through the shoeboxes where her mother kept family photos, but there must have been a moment that she'd filed in her memory, or a reason that she had invented it. The smile, which made him look as if he were thinking of something secret and glad, the autumn sunlight lying across the green grass and the shadow approaching him. For ever young and sweet and mysterious. And she had another picture as well, one that she tried not to remember and that she woke, night after night, remembering. The day he had left and she had stood on the pavement waving until he was out of sight. His face, distorted through the car window, turned towards her, his funny little grimace – the rueful expression of farewell.

3

Later, people said: *He was so normal*, or *He was always such an easy boy. Who would have guessed?* They said, *Something must have happened.* They said, *It just goes to show. You can never tell. Out of a clear sky. The bolt from the blue and then the whole world changes.* They said, *How terrible*, and their eyes glittered with fear and excitement. No one knows.

Isabel

Chapter One

Isabel Hopkins arrived home early in the evening, when the light was just starting to thicken and the last of the summer swallows were lining up on the telephone wire outside the house. The driveway was empty, which meant that Felix was still at work, and the only light came from the kitchen, so presumably Mia was not back either. Isabel remembered her saying something about her first rehearsal for the school play, and she was relieved that, for a few minutes at least, she didn't have to force herself into the semblance of vitality. She felt spent: as empty as the car, which, this morning, had been crammed with all of Johnny's possessions and in which there were now only two paper coffee mugs and, on the floor, a single shoe, forgotten in the upheaval. Isabel undid her seatbelt and bent to pick it up. She held it on her lap and continued to sit there. It seemed impossible to move. Her legs were heavy and her neck ached from driving. Her throat felt sore and her eyes were tired from not crying.

The house looked lonely, she thought – one single bright eye staring at her and everything else blind and dark. For a moment, she let herself imagine returning from her journey to a populous city, layer upon layer of human life, crowded streets and open shop doors, steam rising from little cafés, and cars rolling past, with some dim music pulsing from them. Noise and dirt and the shove and hustle of other lives. It would feel easier to insert herself back into her life if she were living in some third-floor flat, others above, below and opposite, grids of lit windows where people could be seen cooking and dancing, kissing and quarrelling, and at night the darkness of the sky diluted by streetlamps. Here, the skies were so vast and so endless, great cathedral vaults of Godless silence. One person – one son – going made the space he left behind ring with his absence.

Isabel had grown up in Brighton, then moved as a student to London. She and Felix had lived the first eleven years of their married life there, in a small house in Brixton, where you could hear the neighbours' arguments through the thin walls, and where the garden was so tiny that there was no room for Tamsin to learn how to crawl, Johnny to kick a ball or Mia to do one of her straight-backed cartwheels – her legs would be in at the back door before it was completed. When they moved to East Anglia, she had assumed they would find a house in the heart of Norwich, not in a village over the Suffolk border, without streetlamps. It stood in a shallow valley and was surrounded by unbroken fields that curved over the flat horizon. Not far off was the North Sea. They weren't even in the heart of the village but at the far end of it. From one side they could see houses, a post office that was also a tiny shop selling milk and sliced bread, the pub, the primary school, which all the children had attended, the ugly bus stop where teenagers bought their drugs and drank their vodka, the old church with the broken spire, from which the lead had recently been stripped by thieves, and from the other only farmland and, in the distance, the long line of spindly poplars that in winter looked like delicate skeletons, every branch silhouetted against the sky. Yet they had fallen in love with their house, whose roof dipped in the middle and whose walls bulged, as if it was settling itself more comfortably into the earth, like an old sack of flour. And Isabel, who'd been appalled by the silence and thick darkness when they'd moved in, and sometimes missed the city with an ache that felt like homesickness, had grown to love the great skies, the keen winds, the grey seas and the slow shifting of seasons that she had never noticed in London.

A rickety shape hobbled past the headlights: the ancient mottled cat that was really Johnny's and had been his last thought when she'd left him this afternoon ('Remember to look after Digby. He should sleep on Mia's bed and make sure to get his flu jabs done'). Isabel switched off the ignition. She needed to go inside, turn on the lights and the radio, close the curtains, water the plants on the windowsills, plan supper. Something simple and comforting, she thought – pasta and pesto and a green salad, or buttery scrambled eggs. She wouldn't go into Johnny's room; not tonight.

When her elder daughter Tamsin had left two years ago, in a wail of tears, of banging doors and hysterical protestations of love and new leaves turning, it had taken Isabel several days to brave the room she had vacated. Tamsin had taken almost everything she owned with her, in splitting black bin bags and cardboard boxes. All the shoes she never wore, all the leaking bottles of makeup, all the shabby soft toys she had hung on to from her childhood, all the clothes that were too small for her but she vowed she would fit into after one of her binge diets – no carbs or no alcohol or no food at all except fruit. She had left behind empty crisps packets and half-eaten boxes of biscuits, cigarette burns and red wine stains in the shape of far-off countries on her carpet, used makeup wipes scattered like decaying petals, broken CDs, and a small pile of brightly coloured silky knickers in the laundry basket. Isabel, who had argued with Tamsin throughout her childhood and hated the mess she made wherever she went, melted at the sight of the debris. She had sat crosslegged on the floor and wept, bitterly regretting the harsh words, longing to have her big, wretched daughter here again so that she could hug her squashy body and tell her she was sorry. Now, whenever Tamsin returned home, usually after her generous, brimming heart had again been broken, she would bring half of her possessions with her, even if it was only for a weekend, and crawl like a wounded animal into the warm, muddled nest she had created for herself.

But Johnny had left without fuss. Of course he had. For all of his eighteen years, he had lived calmly in a house of noise. He took care of himself and made no demands. Quietness settled around him. This morning he had loaded three cases of clothes and shoes into the car, then a large box of stacked books, his tennis racket, bed linen and towels, his globe and one picture to hang on the wall – a black-and-white photograph of a man in tails jumping over a wide puddle, upright in his leap, his hands tidily behind his back and his face demure. For as long as Isabel could remember, Johnny had kept the peace in a house that at times had felt as though it would split apart under the force of their wrangling. He was the only person in the family whom nobody argued with. He seemed to absorb noise and tension.

Isabel had asked Felix if he thought it was healthy, Johnny's implacable quiet equability, and Felix had laughed in exasperation: 'You worry because Tamsin's overweight and hysterical, you worry that Mia's flat-chested and permanently embattled, and now you're worrying that Johnny always seems contented. For God's sake, be grateful for small mercies.' Felix was fed up with family dramas, and doors banging through the house. At the time, Isabel had wanted to ask: *Does being cheerful mean being happy?* Or perhaps that was later. You try to find a path through the horror; you lay blame with a frantic trowel, thick wet slabs of possible explanations that will later harden into cause. Even a rough road is better than no road at all. *Because he did not speak, I did not listen; I did not see what lay in front of my eyes all that time.*

At last Isabel got out of the car. She felt stiff. At the door, Digby wrapped himself around her legs, tail high and crooked, and she stooped to run a finger along the sharp ridge of his spine, feeling him quiver. What a quiet house it was going to be – except no place that had Mia in it could be completely peaceful. Mia was her own private war zone. Even when she was asleep, her thin, tense body wouldn't relax – she wrestled with her duvet and muttered wildly, eyes pulsing in dreams, or threw out her arms as if she were falling from a great height.

Everything was as it had been when they had left that morning, empty coffee mugs still on the kitchen table, a plate with a half-eaten piece of toast on it. The post had been pushed through the door, and Isabel leafed through it. Bills, catalogues that were already looking forward to Christmas, an invitation to a fiftieth birthday party, and then she saw she had a letter from her brother. His stiff italic hand hadn't changed since his schooldays. She slid a finger under the gummed flap and took out just half a page of writing, starting 'Dear Isabel' and ending 'Yours, Graham', as if they were formal acquaintances. When she thought about what they had been through together – but no. Don't go there. Not now, not today, when she felt frail and old and her hands, holding the letter, trembled slightly.

Dear Isabel,

Celia suggested that I write rather than phone, so that you have time to think about what I have to say and can make a reasoned response.

She winced: he meant that he wanted to avoid her reckless outbursts of emotion, her need to be shown affection by her only brother, who had long ago withdrawn it.

We are in the process of looking at our wills, and we feel that it is only fair to consider the family inheritance. As you know, you own the only painting of our mother and Celia believes that, although it was done by a family friend, the painter is actually of some import-ance in the art world and it may therefore be of value, quite apart from its obvious sentimental value. We were not aware of this at the time and clearly it changes things. I would like to send round some-one to give us expert advice and, if it should prove to be worth a lot, we should consider how to proceed. We could either sell it and split the proceeds or, more likely, you can pay me my half of its estimated value.

I look forward to hearing from you.

Yours,
Graham

Isabel stared at the letter. She crumpled it up in a ball and hurled it towards the bin, missing. Then she retrieved it, straightened it out, and reread it to find its meaning unchanged.

'Fuck. Bastard. *Celia suggests* . . . I'll bet she does. He looks forward to hearing from me, does he?'

Her internal voice – which she sometimes thought was simply Felix's voice, the voice of male reason – told her to wait for her anger to subside. She ignored it.

'Hello, Celia. Yes, it's Isabel here . . . Yes, that's right. Isabel. I'd like to speak to Graham, please . . . Yes, it is about the picture and, no, I'd rather talk to Graham directly. If that's all right with you.'

Isabel could imagine Celia holding her hand over the mouthpiece and whispering: *It's that sister of yours. She sounds furious. Don't let her browbeat you. You know what she's like.* Eyebrows raised.

After a few minutes, Graham came on the line.

'Ah, Isabel,' he said. 'I'm sorry to have kept you waiting.'

Since when had he talked like that, with strangulated pomposity, everything clipped, bitten off and swallowed? He sounded as though his mouth was full of marbles and bile. Or perhaps he was scared that if he didn't let his words out through a closed throat and carefully pursed lips, they would betray him: he would say something unintended.

'Yes, it's *Isabel*.' He used to call her Izzie, or Bel, but now he always used her full name, separating it out into its three distinct syllables. He used to tag along beside her, with his little hand in hers. He used to cry easily, wet his bed and have bad dreams that she would wake him from, cradling and soothing him. He would whisper hot secrets in her ear.

'I gather you've received the letter.'

'Yes. What the fuck do you think you're doing, writing to me like that?'

'There's no need to swear. And it's only fair that we –'

'No! You're talking about our mother. You can't write a constipated business letter about our mother.'

'A *picture* of our mother –'

'What's wrong with you?'

'I think we should be able to discuss this calmly.'

'Are you short of money? Is that what it is?'

'No.' He sounded offended. 'Of course not. This is a question of fairness.'

'Bullshit.' Isabel had often noticed that when she talked to Graham, she started talking like a drunkard in a Hollywood film, hurling obscenities. She sometimes even detected a faint American accent in her voice.

'Please. There's no need to make a scene.'

'When we moved Dad into the home, we shared things out.'

'But as I pointed out in the letter –'

'You took the dresser, the pearl necklace and earrings for Celia, the set of cut-glass glasses, the old carved chest –'

'You said you didn't want them.'

'I didn't. I don't. I don't care about them. I just wanted her books and the painting.'

'And the rocking chair.'

'Oh! It's worn and old –'

'Antique.'

'Antique! It's just a chair that wasn't made recently.'

'Let's talk about the painting. Celia thinks it might be worth everything else put together.'

'I don't care about the money!' She heard the quaver in her voice and hated it. Even when she was angry with Graham, she was pleading with him: she couldn't bear his aloofness, the way he had become impenetrable. She had always insisted to Felix, and to herself, that behind the reserve, the wincing dislike of sentiment, he was still the needy, affectionate boy she had mothered – but recently she had wondered. Perhaps if you behave in a certain way for long enough, the behaviour becomes the self. A cool surface chills the heart.

'Very convenient, when you happen to own it.'

'Graham!' Isabel heard her voice rise and crack, while all the while her brother remained efficiently correct. 'I'm not going to sell it to make some greedy profit out of it. Just because the artist might turn out to be someone well known doesn't alter it a jot. I wouldn't care if it was worth nothing at all. Don't you see? It's Mum, our mother. I love it.' She found she was nearly crying.

'I'm sorry you're seeing this in such emotional terms.'

'Well, of course I am! How did you think I'd see it?'

'Celia warned me –'

'Stop hiding behind Celia. If you didn't want to do this, you wouldn't.'

'I'm simply trying to redress any possible imbalance.'

'What? "Redress any possible imbalance"? Why are you being like this?'

'I'm not aware of being like anything.'

'It's me, your sister. You're not my accountant. You're my family, my little brother.' She heard a faint sigh coming from the other end. 'Oh, send round your bloody expert. Or no – don't. Just take the painting. I don't want to get in some horrible argument about what it's worth and who should have it. Just tell me when you're coming and I'll get some bubble wrap.'

'Now you're being silly.'

'I'm not being fucking *silly*. Look, today I've taken Johnny to Sheffield and now I've just walked in to find your cold little letter about Mum.'

'So that's why you're so upset, because Johnny's gone. I see that I've caught you at a bad time –'

'Don't you dare! Don't even think of patronizing me like that! It's odious. It makes me want to punch a hole in my own head. Or yours.'

'Well, I'm sorry.' Graham's voice was thick with distaste.

They were both silent. Isabel walked with the phone still at her ear and stood by the large window that looked out on golden stubble fields. At the bottom of the garden, in the tall ash tree, there was a small rookery – just four or five large messy bundles of twigs that hung there in the winter like blobs of mistletoe. The rooks returned early in the year, and woke Isabel each morning with their raucous shouts. They were ungainly, comic and sombre, and she loved them. Sometimes, when she was alone in the evening, she would sneak out with an illicit cigarette and sit on the grass beneath the tree, watching their dark shapes flap and veer towards their nests, crashing on to their perches and making the branches tremble. She looked at them now, coming home for the night, until she trusted herself to speak again.

'Sorry. I didn't mean to go off like that.'

'It's all right. I understand.'

'No – hang on. You're supposed to say sorry as well. That's how it works, Graham.'

'All right.' There was a pause. She could almost see him squaring his shoulders and swallowing hard, his Adam's apple bobbing under his shirt collar. 'I'm sorry if –'

'Oh no you don't! Not like that.'

'Pardon?'

'Sorry *that*. Not *if, that*.'

'I'm sorry that I offended you,' he said.

'It's OK.'

'But –'

'Let's leave it for now,' Isabel said. 'I'll talk to Felix. If it's worth a lot of money, of course we should somehow take that into account. The main thing is, we shouldn't fall out over it.'

Isabel went into the living room, where the painting of her mother hung. She sat on the sofa, moving a hairbrush embedded in the crack between the cushions, and examined the picture closely. It didn't seem a particularly skilful portrait to her. The shoulders were unintentionally lopsided and the hands were like sausages bunched together in her mother's lap. The background was brown and flat. There was, thought Isabel, a childish quality to the composition. Perhaps the naïvety was the point, but she didn't think so. Yet she had spent hours looking at it over the years, staring into her mother's brown eyes, which stared back as if she could see her. She was wearing a blue dress, the kind of soft, moderate blue that the Madonna always wore in Renaissance paintings, and the expression on her face was subdued and thoughtful, although her lips were quirked in a semblance of a smile. Her dark hair was tied back in an old-fashioned coiled bun, although Isabel had no living memory of her wearing it like that. She thought she could remember her mother leaning over her when she was lying in bed and her loose silky hair tickling her face. But that must have been before she became ill, bony and yellow with cancer, the funny smell in her room, and then the absence, hospital visits, holding the twig-hands and trying not to look into those eyes.

Isabel had always wanted to see her own face in her mother's: she wanted her lost mother to live on in her. Lately, however, she had realized that Mia most closely resembled her, or Mia as she would become, once she lost her awkward angles, her crooked teeth in their train-track braces, her skinny tomboy plainness. She had said as much to her daughter, who had stared at the portrait with scowling concentration, then pronounced: 'Far too pretty and well-behaved.' Had her mother been well-behaved? Isabel had no idea. She had never known Kathleen Cornish as a real person with desires and regrets. She was an ideal, remembered in soft focus. Once, when she was a teenager, she had plucked up the courage to ask her father to tell her something more, but he had made her feel that the question was cruel. His face had twisted and his moustache quivered; he had held up one hand, as if to stop oncoming traffic, and the matter had been closed. Isabel had never dared reopen it: she didn't want to hurt her father or displease him, so Kathleen Cornish had become a taboo, beloved and mysterious and, at the same time, an area of dread. The face in the picture gave nothing away: it just stared out from the dull background, contemplative.

After Kathleen's early death, when Isabel had been nine and Graham just seven, the portrait had hung in her father's bedroom, in the darkest corner away from the window, and the face had seemed shadowy and inscrutable. Isabel used to creep in there when Bernard Cornish was out and crouch in front of it, gazing up as if she was in a church, worshipping the relics of dead saints. After Bernard's stroke, when he had had to be moved from the down-at-heel family house into a nursing home, Graham had shown no interest in wanting it so Isabel had inherited it. It had been then that she had tried to track down the painter, a man called Thomas Loft. That was before the days of the Internet and Google; she had gone to the local library, looked up the name in reference books and, when that had given her no leads, resorted to ringing a few of the Lofts she had found in the Brighton telephone directory – her parents had been living there at the time the portrait was painted. But none of the Lofts she talked to were painters, or knew of painters in their family, and Isabel soon gave up. What did she want to know anyway? What Kathleen Cornish, who had died before she was forty, had been like? When you gazed at her face, what did you see? Were you in love with her? Would she have liked me? Do you think I grew up into the person she wanted me to be?

When they were courting, Felix had told her she was a hungry woman. Not for food, she often starved herself of that, but for love. He had laid his hand against her cheek and said she did not need to be hungry any more, and she had closed her eyes and leant against him. Work, children and love had filled the emptiness. Tiredness had obscured it. But in the middle of their lives, some people get lost. Dark woods and blind descents. Isabel knew this. She did not want to be one of them. She braced her thin, strong body against it, even as she felt herself begin to slide. She would not.

Chapter Two

The front door opened and then banged shut. Mia was home. Felix always closed the door carefully, with a click; Mia crashed it back on its lock as if she was a discus thrower, putting her whole weight behind the effort. Isabel heard her go into the kitchen. She could imagine her daughter pulling open the fridge, drinking milk straight from the bottle, eating a cold roast potato from the bowl, going to the store cupboard and snuffling through it like a badger. She waited. After a while the steps came back into the hall. 'Hello!' she called. She really should get up but she was too drained; her body felt limp.

The door swung open. Mia stood in the doorway and gazed in. Her cheeks were flushed and her hair ruffled, as if she had been raking her fingers through it. Her tights had wide ladders running up the left leg. She was sixteen and in her first year of A levels, but looked thirteen still: flat chest, narrow hips, knobbly knees, like the knees of a ten-year-old boy, the ridged braces that rubbed her gums, the dark hair that she insisted on keeping cropped short, the beetling brows. Her face was pale and small, her eyes brown and flecked with gold – just like Kathleen's eyes, thought Isabel, watching her carefully.

'What are you doing sitting in the dark?' asked Mia, taking a huge bite out of the apple she was holding and crunching mightily.

'Is it dark?'

'It's not day any more anyway. Here.' She switched on the light and the room lost its shadows and soft corners. 'Are you OK?'

'Fine.'

'You look odd. Have you been crying?'

'No.'

'I bet you have. Was it all right with Johnny?'

'Yes. It was good. How about your day? Tell me about the rehearsal. Later, we can go through your lines, if you want.' For she didn't want to revisit the feeling she had had as she had said goodbye to her son. The small damp room, the long corridor leading to it and the laughter heard from behind other doors he would probably be too shy to knock on. His carefully packed clothes put into drawers, his shirts into the wardrobe, his books stacked neatly on the desk. His picture hung on a stained wall. Johnny had smiled at her, his biggest smile. One chipped tooth; a tiny dimple in his left cheek. It was good he was going because she knew him too well and loved him too much, and everyone has to leave home in one way or another – and Johnny above all had had to do it like this: physically removing himself from her, marking a distance between them, taking his big, passive body away from her arms.

When Tamsin had left, she and Isabel had exclaimed over her new room, giggled, whispered to each other about her flatmates, tested out the bed and finally wept, Tamsin loudly and with gusto, her tears smudging her mascara and dribbling into her generous mouth. But perhaps this was worse: the sobriety and tact she and Johnny had exhibited. He had looked so forlorn and so obedient, standing there in the checked grey shirt in soft cotton that she had given him for his birthday. She had wanted to shake him, to take his arm, lead him back to the car and drive him home, sit him by a fire, give him rice pudding and a mug of tea.

She had a sudden memory, so long suppressed, of his first day at nursery, and how she had had to unpick his fingers from her skirt, one by one. How had she forgotten that, burying it under her other memories of Johnny blithe, Johnny self-possessed, Johnny tranquil? But there was that other Johnny, the one who had had night terrors and asthma and who had always put his warm little hand in hers, keeping close, dogging her footsteps, wrapping his arms round her like a koala bear. Had she pushed that tender soul away? She'd been so anxious for him to be happy that perhaps she had refused to let him express anything else, always loading the questions – 'Are you well? Are things fine?' rather than 'How are you?' – and telling him he was wonderful, he was beloved, he would do fine, anything he set his mind to. Look on the bright side, not the dark. That hadn't been for his good, but for her own self-protection, because she didn't have the courage to confront any misery he might feel. She was a coward masquerading as optimistic and brave. And now it was too late: she had left him behind in a rainy city, in a flat full of strangers. They'd hugged as she left, but constrainedly, each not wanting to upset the other, and he'd told her to take care of Digby. Then he'd asked her to send him recipes if she had time, but that was probably to give her something to do. He had always had an eye for other people's distress and an instinct for alleviating it. She'd send him one tonight, she thought, when everyone was safely in bed. Felix always went to sleep early, and rose long before her, padding softly down the stairs in his running stuff, then bringing her a cup of tea in bed when he returned from his six-mile circuit of the lanes.

'Why are you looking like that?' Mia demanded once more. She sounded impatient, even angry. Her brow furrowed.

For a moment, Isabel wanted to say that Mia should let her be sad for once – she was no longer a child but a sixteen-year-old, after all – yet the words lodged in her throat. It would just cause another argument. Mia would accuse her of loving Johnny best. She shrugged, and Mia left the room.

Felix returned. He came into the kitchen where she stood making a salad and put his arms round her without a word. So, he knew how she was feeling. She leant into him, grateful.

'All right?' he said at last, kissing the crown of her head.

'Kind of.'

'It will be.'

'Yes. I know.'

Isabel had met Felix when she was twenty-five and he was thirty-six. He had run her over. Flying off her bike, she had glimpsed his startled face through the windscreen, and even then she had thought he looked a bit like a hawk. He had screeched to a halt, but before he'd had time to get out of his car, she had picked herself up off the pavement and advanced on him in a limping hobble, screaming in a cracked voice, 'What the fuck? You idiot! You twat!' He'd unfolded his tall thin shape from the car and stood before her, apologizing, asking her if she was all right, saying it was completely his fault. 'I know it was your fault! You ran into the back of me. What were you thinking?' Apparently he'd turned in his seat to tell his children to stop quarrelling, taking his eyes off the road, and only then had she discovered that two small shapes were cowering on the back seat. 'You should have child seats for them,' she'd said. 'You'll end up killing them as well as any stray cyclist who happens to cross your path.' She had bent down to the two boys. One had started to cry and she had felt ashamed of herself and, briefly, sorry for their blue-eyed father, who was looking on helplessly. Then she'd climbed back on her bike, ignoring all offers of help, and wobbled off, only realizing when she'd got home how shaken she was, and how a large bruise was spreading up her thigh and her knuckles were nastily grazed.

Two days later, when she was about to go out for a drink with the man she thought would become her boyfriend, there'd been a knock at the door and Felix was standing there, a bunch of flowers in his hands. He'd told her that he hadn't been able to get her out of his mind. He had followed her after the collision that day and seen where she lived. 'My children liked you,' he added. Plunging her face into the flowers, Isabel had burst into tears, not knowing why. Then she had put the bouquet down and told him to leave. She wasn't going to get involved with a married man. (Again, she didn't add.) But he had told her he was separated from the mother of his children and had been for years. He had taken the flowers, unwrapped them and put them in a vase for her, carefully shaking the contents of the little sachet of plant food they came with into the water. Minutes later, they had been in bed together – though now it seemed inconceivable that Felix, who was so controlled and courteous, shy and morally upright, could have acted in such a way. Is that how my children behave, she wondered now, tumbling into bed with a stranger? The thought appalled her.

Anyone who met Felix for more than a few minutes would know that he was not an easy man – neither easy on himself nor on others. He was angular and severe, with thin lips, a beetle brow and a hooked nose, like a medieval saint painted in gold on a cracked wooden triptych. You could see the veins in his temples; when he was angry or upset, the emotion rippled through his face, like a squall over water, though his expression would barely alter. He was a puritan and a self-disciplinarian who rose at dawn and ran six miles most days, ten at weekends. Once a year he did the London marathon, taking three hours and ten minutes, give or take a minute. The family always went to see him: he would pound towards them, his head tipped back a bit and his narrow, muscled legs measuring out each stride, in his eyes a look of blindness, as if he was staring inside himself as he ran and could not see them waving their banner and shouting his name, or the crowds all around him. He played the violin in the same way, with a tense, fierce concentration, as though he was wrenching each note from the instrument. And when he worked in the allotment, he dug the spade into the loamy soil with the energy of a man who believed that only by back-breaking, self-punishing effort could he win his rest. He would come home with his palms blistered, his skin burnt by sun and wind, his eyes glowing with satisfaction.

Felix taught medieval literature at the university. He loved Chaucer, and Norse and Icelandic sagas; he could recite much of *Pearl* by heart. For the last three years, he had been struggling to write a book on pilgrimage literature. Isabel thought he was like a pilgrim himself: under this cloak of irony and sardonic wit, he was a dissatisfied, heart-sore man. Perhaps that was why she had married him: the rescue impulse, as Mia called it, mocking her. But, after all, it was true. Isabel had thought she could untie some of the knots inside him, the ones he thought held him together but that she believed kept him imprisoned in his own uptight English masochism. Mia said Isabel felt that about everybody she met — that she could see things in them that they didn't recognize in themselves and that could, in some mysterious way, free them.

Isabel wanted to talk about Johnny and about her conversation with Graham, but the phone rang and Felix went to answer it and then, holding it, went to his study and pulled the door shut. She poured them both a glass of wine, and put one on the desk beside him; he mouthed an acknowledgement to her. She could hear a high, angry voice coming down the line, imagined it was some academic wrangle he was meant to sort out, and left him to it. He'd be ages now. She put the dirty clothes from the weekend in the wash, cooked spaghetti with bacon and mushrooms for supper, cleaned out Mia's guinea pig in the dark, grubbing around with cold hands for the soiled straw, filling his bowl with food and his drinking bottle with water – Mia had been given him on her tenth birthday, and he had lasted far longer than any guinea pig was supposed to, singing like a canary from the bottom of the garden. Isabel moaned about doing Mia's dirty work for her, but secretly loved the plump, sweet-smelling creature. Sometimes she would even go out to sit in the run with him, letting him crawl into her lap and scurry under the folds of her clothes.

Tamsin rang from Southampton; Felix's mother called to arrange a time to visit; and Isabel had work to mark before tomorrow, which she'd let herself forget, and that bloody school trip to arrange, with all the health and safety forms to fill in and photocopy. Not to mention parents' evening coming up. And she needed to get a builder in to look at the crack running up the gable end of the house. Buy bulbs for the garden. Sort out Felix's birthday celebrations, though Felix wouldn't want to celebrate and would hate any kind of fuss – but you couldn't just let a birthday go past, could you? She'd have to get in touch with his two eldest children, her stepsons, and find out if they could come down for it. Tomorrow, straight after school, she would visit her father in his nursing home on the banks of the estuary. And, oh, damn, book the car in for its MOT, which it would definitely fail because it whined up hills and juddered down them – and write to Becky, whose mother had just died . . .

Very quickly, after a few hours of desolation, life ran into the spaces and holes left by Johnny, her quiet, careful son. Isabel let herself be carried on by its momentum, just occasionally feeling the undertow of her sadness. Which would pass, because everything passes: this was the lesson life taught her over and over again, and which she had never yet learnt.

But in the middle of the night she woke. Felix lay beside her, his body straight as a board and his face towards the ceiling. He had a Roman profile – aquiline and unyielding. Even in sleep he looked alert. He had the air of someone who was thinking, not dreaming, and who would at any moment open his eyes, sit up and tell you about the war in Iraq or imaginary numbers or allegory in Spenser. Isabel lay quite still, wondering if the owl that shrieked nightly for a mate across the flatlands had woken her.

When she was sure she would not go back to sleep, she rose and did what she had promised herself she would leave aside for a while: go into Johnny's room. In a house where it seemed a battle to impose any kind of tidiness, it had always been a safe haven. She loved its order: the files and folders and piles of textbooks; the folded clothes and lists with ticks next to tasks accomplished; the maps on the wall with highlighters showing where he'd been, pink snail trails winding through west and east Europe; the clock above his desk, which always told the correct time, the wall-calendar with appointments, marches, tennis matches, parties; the bookshelf in which his books were ordered according to subject (novels, poetry, campaign literature, travel, space, the stars, the moon and black holes, with mysterious formulae squiggled across dense pages). The sports bag under the bed, zipped up; the tennis and squash racquets beside the narrow wardrobe; the small mirror in which he could see just his face; the little basin with toothbrush and toothpaste, a smooth nub of soap, shaving foam, a razor, as if this were a room in a bed-and-breakfast. She liked the smell in there as well, sweat and soap, lived-in, yet clean and fresh – he often opened his window wide, even in winter. The curtains would billow and a few leaves scatter on the dull red carpet. Isabel thought that his room was like his life. It was functional, pleasing, with a sense of actions accomplished, days ticking past at a proper pace. If he had to work, he sat with his computer at his desk, which looked out on to the long, narrow garden. If he wanted to read, he would lie on his bed, with his pillow propped up against the headboard.

Mia's room was a mad jumble – work not done, clothes not washed, the bed not made, balled-up pieces of paper, ink stains on the carpet, half-empty mugs of tea or scummy glasses of orange juice on the bedside table, desk and floor, the primary-school recorder on which she had only ever mastered 'Three Blind Mice' and the violin from which she had never learnt to coax a sweet note and whose E-string was now broken, the computer with its grimy keyboard and chewed connecting cord, the small wooden easel she'd bought because she had briefly thought she would learn how to paint, a hobby that would lift her out of herself, a smeary full-length mirror that she didn't want to look into anyway, because each time she did, it stung her anew to see how different she was from the way she felt inside.

In Mia's room, Isabel was oppressed and agitated; in Johnny's, she felt her heart slow down.

It was empty now. Hangers rattled in the wardrobe, and the drawers, when she pulled them open, contained just a few T-shirts and jerseys. The posters had been taken down (she imagined him putting them up in his new room with drawing pins) and all the paper and pens had been removed from his desk. She knelt on the carpet in front of the shelves, which were now full of gaps. Dostoevsky, Kierkegaard, Roland Barthes. Books with strange titles that made her brain tingle with mysterious longing. *Fear and Trembling. The Scarred City. The Homesick Café.* They were like worlds she had never entered and like the shadowy, mysterious places inside Johnny to which she had no access.

She wrapped her arms around herself for comfort. Johnny has left and Tamsin has left; Mia is itching to go; their childhood is over and we can't get it back. Did we do well enough by them? And we're getting older. Time is like a river that carries everything away with it and, oh dear, what shall I do with myself now, what shall *we* do?

Chapter Three

The following evening Isabel went to meet Jenny and Leah to put the world to rights, or at least their little corner of it. She came back late from school, where there had been a drawn-out meeting with the social worker and GP of one of her children, a little boy called Mattie Jacques, who never talked, who always smiled, whose squinting brown eyes swam behind thick glasses held together by plasters. He had been in care since he was three, was disruptive at school and often tried to run away – though to where no one could work out. His foster-parents were on the point of giving up on him and teachers talked of him as 'that boy'. But sometimes, out of the blue, he would place his dry little hand, the wrist ringed with eczema, in Isabel's and her heart would melt.

People think that women dress up for men – but they don't. They dress up for other women. Isabel had a shower and rubbed herself all over with body lotion. She chose her apparently casual clothes with care: striped jeans, scuffed biker's boots, rust-orange shirt, black leather jacket, favourite necklace, given to her by Felix when she'd turned forty. She scooped her hair up, put on makeup that was invisible but softened the lines on her face, the brackets round her mouth, the shadows under her eyes, the worry furrows on her brow. These were her good, close friends – she bared her soul to them, exposing her fears and embarrassments – but she didn't want them to see her naked face, the way the skin puckered slightly round her mouth, or how her neck had become thin and scraggy, and her upper arms slack, hanging in – she winced – chicken wings. She thought of Tamsin's peachy radiance, the smoothness of Mia's pale face and the suppleness of her limbs, and she looked at herself in the mirror with a kind of surprised displeasure.

They met – as they always did – in the little bistro in town. Felix dropped Isabel off so that she could drink; she would get a cab back. Drinking was part of the point of their meetings – it loosened their tongues. They used to meet for afternoon tea and cakes, but that had been too sensible, and the time had been too proscribed – back home for supper, after iced buns and Earl Grey. In the evenings, however, time could spill over; they could play truant from their ordinary lives, returning home after their husbands and children were in bed, creeping upstairs and climbing in beside a snoring partner – or, in Jenny's case, to a space that had been empty for years, although she still slept on the right of the bed. On these nights out, they would become emotional, frank, confessional, nostalgic, shameless, giggly. They could surprise themselves with the things they said to each other. Leah was affected by half a glass of wine and tipped at once into tipsy girlishness, shedding her habitual irony, straight posture and thin-lipped elegance. For Jenny and Isabel, the process was more gradual – a slow unwinding of their carefulness.

Today the subject was – as it so often tended to be – the scandal of being middle-aged. They leant their heads (streaked blonde, highlighted brown and Isabel's black, showing single silver hairs that only occasionally caught the light to become visible) over the round table in the corner, near the window, which was spattered with rain. Isabel could smell their mingled perfumes, amid the waft of wine, garlic and ginger from their meal. They swapped anecdotes of outrage and humiliation, each trying to out-do the others in self-mockery.

Leah told them about an episode of a few days ago, when she had been on a crowded train and a young man had offered her his seat. 'But I was standing next to a woman who was *clearly* older than me!' she said. 'She had grey hair and a tweed skirt.'

'So what did you do?'

'What could I do? I said no. And he insisted. He was practically pushing me into his seat. And I heard myself saying, "Why me? What about her?" Everyone was listen-ing, and the young man – he was practically a teenager – looked a bit baffled, and the old woman was saying she didn't need the seat. Actually, when I looked at her properly, maybe she wasn't that old, she just didn't dye her hair.'

'So you sat down?'

'No. This is the ridiculous bit. I'd backed myself into a corner. I said I was getting off. So then I had to get off, didn't I? I dashed round to a carriage a bit further up, got on again there and stood up for the rest of the journey. Probably everyone saw me.' She shook her head. 'It was so stupid. I should have just taken the seat and been grate-ful. Who cares if he thought I was older than I am? I mean, if you're eighteen, anyone who's over forty is old.

But I did care. I felt cross and sweaty and undignified and ugly and close to tears.'

Jenny told a story about driving her fifteen-year-old nephew and three of his friends to a pop concert. 'They had this conversation about who they fancied and who they didn't,' she said, screwing her round face into a grimace. 'Including my daughter. They were talking about whether they'd want to grope Holly at a party. I sat there, holding on to the steering wheel with white knuckles and listening to this crap, and I thought, I'm invisible. That's what's going on here. It's not that they're being strangely rude or anything, it's simply that they can't see me. They don't register my existence, except as some kind of useful device that's getting them to their concert free of effort or charge.'

'Didn't you say anything?'

'That's the weirdest thing – I didn't. I was boiling with rage, but somehow I felt too embarrassed, as if talking would be inappropriate.'

'So you let them demean Holly and erase you,' said Leah, before twisting round in her seat and signalling to the waiter for a second bottle of wine.

'Yes. I was like an imposter in my own car.'

Isabel's story had a similar narrative: it, too, was about self-alienation and invisibility. 'I was in a big department store a few months ago. I was in a hurry, of course. I had to buy something for Mia, I think, and pick up stationery, and I was running late. I was in an anxious state anyway – probably about Mia. It was when she was being bullied, you know. When that kind of thing is going on, it's with you all the time. You can be at work or out with friends, and all the time it's like a fist round your heart.'

She stopped, thinking she'd mislaid the right tone, but Leah and Jenny nodded, made small sympathetic accompanying noises. Jenny put a hand on her arm. The waiter came over with the new bottle and poured some into each of their glasses.

'So, there I was, hurtling along an aisle hung with clothes, and suddenly this woman was standing in front of me, blocking my way. She was a thin, scrawny creature with untidy hair, in things that looked too dark and hot for her, and I remember thinking she looked a bit like a demented stork, and that she seemed wretched. I felt sorry for her. But she was still in my way, so I lifted up a hand and said, "Sorry!" And she lifted up her hand at exactly the same moment and her mouth opened, and I was smiling at her and she was smiling at me. And I thought, Fuck! It's a mirror! I'm standing in front of a mirror and that's *me*. That demented stork, that unhappy, scraggy woman is me.' She took a large gulp of wine and grinned ruefully at her friends who were grinning back at her.

'At least you weren't rude to yourself,' said Leah.

'And at least you felt sorry for yourself,' Jenny added.

'Here's to self-pity.' Leah raised her glass extravagantly, slopping wine over its brim. 'Very necessary.'

'To see yourself from the outside, though,' Isabel said. 'It's a shocker, isn't it? To know that you're middle-aged. Nobody warns you.'

'Well, at least you're not menopausal yet,' said Leah, who was four years older than Jenny and Isabel, and for the last year or so had been garrulous on the subject of the silent passage into barrenness. 'That's the real shocker. Sweats and nightmares and insomnia and weariness and panic attacks and the tendency to inexplicably break down and weep like a child.'

'Yes?' Jenny raised her eyebrows. 'So what's different? That's what I've been like for years now.'

'Maybe you've got early menopause.'

'Maybe I'm just a woman with teenage children.'

'You wait,' said Leah, ominously.

'I was at this dinner,' said Isabel, 'one of Felix's work things. Everyone seemed horribly clever and self-confident. They all had their areas of expertise – there were people there who knew about things like, I don't know, insoluble solubles or the Latin Vulgate Bible or the homing instincts of garden snails. No matter how irrelevant they seem, I've always thought that areas of expertise give people a kind of safety: a tiny fragment of solid ground to stand on. Whereas me, I'm just a primary-school teacher. I know about the two times table and blowing noses. Anyway, I was sitting between two men and I can't even remember what we were talking about and I suddenly started to cry. I don't mean gracefully weep – I mean really cry. I was sitting there looking down at my plate with my shoulders shaking and at first they didn't notice and then they didn't know what to do. I had to get up and go and sit in the Ladies for about ten minutes, just sobbing to myself. And then it was gone and I was OK. I couldn't work out what had set it off or what it was about. I never told Felix – he was at the other end of the table and so involved in a conversation that I doubt he'd have noticed if I'd taken

off my clothes and set fire to them. It was so odd, though –
that sudden sense of inconsolable grief.'

'Children leaving,' said Leah.

'Do you think?'

'Of course. We rush around being busy and needed,
and suddenly it's over. Like the wind going out of our
sails.'

For a moment, Isabel allowed herself to think of
Johnny yesterday, his nervous, smiling face, and then of
Johnny as a tiny child, plumping like a bag of flour into
her lap, and the sweet sawdust smell of him. She heard his
voice – then, now – saying, *Mama*. She felt all of a sudden
stone-cold sober.

'Well!' Jenny poured the last of the wine into their
glasses. 'At least we can talk to each other about it. We're
not alone. That's what makes it bearable. Even fun, in a
grim kind of way.'

They sat at the littered table, with their two wine bottles
and the shells of prawns scattered over the paper cloth.
Isabel raised her glass. 'Here's to being in the same boat.'

'Here's to rocking it.'

Chapter Four

Every two or three days, Isabel wrote out a recipe in her pointy handwriting and posted it off to Johnny: marinated chicken breasts, quick ratatouille, teriyaki salmon, red onion and goat's cheese tartlets, noodles in a spicy coconut sauce, bean stew. Sometimes she would wake in the night and think of a new recipe to send to him. Pumpkin risotto, like the one she had made far too much of the night before so the three of them had gazed at the heaped mounds with something like dismay; butternut-squash soup, now that it was October and Felix's allotment was full of different kinds of squashes and gourds; apple crumble with oats on top. She liked to imagine Johnny in the kitchen, cooking with painstaking precision from her inexact instructions, serving up dinners to the rest of his flatmates, ladling out spinach curry or fish with a bacon and crème fraîche sauce. Maybe he'd meet a girl – Isabel pictured someone with long, curly hair and a fresh, laughing face, the kind of frank, unthreatening girl a mother dreams of for her son and the son rarely falls for – and make her chicken with honey and five-spice dressing. She'd give him an apron at Christmas, she thought, and some sharp knives. She let herself imagine Christmas dinner – all of them, with her mute father and Felix's terrifying mother, maybe even Graham and Celia, and Felix's sister who lived in Ludlow with her new husband and always knitted itchy woollen socks for her Christmas presents. Oh, and their neighbour, of course: he had no family, only a large golden retriever that he walked along the lanes day after day, and that in the summer would eat Isabel's washing from the line.

Sometimes Johnny would call, and often there were noises in the background, like a party going on. He always sounded cheerful. He mentioned names – Lorrie and Fran, Seamus, Jose and Han, and someone called Phil, who was six foot six and played the accordion. He said he liked the work and was studying hard. Quarks and string theory and forces and billions of light miles of cold nothing and infinitesimal specks weighing more than the whole world. Yes, he liked his tutors, or most of them. Yes, he was eating well. He was playing football and had found a tennis partner. He had been once into the Peaks with a girl named Lil. And, no, Lil wasn't, before she asked. Lil was just a good friend.

Isabel loved to hear him but she rarely called him: she was determined not to be doting. Felix had told her she must not be one of those oppressively attentive mothers who smothered their children and made them feel guilty for leaving. No, the best thing was to wait for him to get in touch with them, and that was what she did, but she wrote him cheery emails full of trivial pieces of news from home – a bit of a cold but it's going now, rainy day today and the autumn leaves are piling up, horrible day at work with that little bugger Joey McCall making everyone's life a misery, Dad's book going OK but a bit slowly, what's new? Mia's fine, though school continues a bit of a misery and aren't girls cruel sometimes, but I think it's getting better after the gap of the summer and she had the part of Puck in the school play, her parents' evening approaching, and the Masons are coming to dinner on Friday. Graham's still going on about the painting but you know what? I don't even care any more . . . She was aiming to create a comforting background hum, like the regular tick of a grandfather clock or the chug of domestic appliances, so that he would have the sense of life running smoothly in his absence, of a house that wasn't missing him but would welcome him on his return.

At the beginning of December, two letters arrived, addressed to Johnny, from Sheffield. One looked official, and Isabel peered down the transparent window, peeling back the frame and trying to make out its subject. She could only get as far as 'Dear Mr Hopkins . . .' She held up the personal one to the light: it was square, and the address was neatly made out in round, looped handwriting, clearly a woman's. But why had she written to Johnny here? She shook it, feeling a card slide around inside, then redirected them both to Johnny's flat and posted them.

Their little garden filled with leaves. It was dark in the morning when they woke, and dark when they came home. Felix went for runs with a lamp on his forehead and a fluorescent yellow jacket. Isabel made rice puddings and went to bed early. She slept fitfully and had bad dreams. Her body felt as though it didn't belong to her. She woke several times each night and lay stretched out in the bed as if she had been dropped there from a great height, her heart banging. It felt like a balloon that had been pumped up too tight and might explode. Or like a bruise.

He didn't call so she rang his number. 'Johnny? Johnny, where are you?'

And then the next day, every hour or so, between lessons and in her lunch hour, standing in the playground watching children scatter round the yard like leaves.

But he wasn't there and he didn't call back. How many days was that now? Four? Five? That wasn't so many, after all – when he'd been travelling with friends, weeks could go by with nothing from him. Yet it felt like a lot to her. She was frail with anxiety; the pounding sense of unease against her brittle ribcage almost felt like guilt.

She crept from her bed and downstairs to the kitchen, where she made herself a cup of camomile tea and sat at the table, hearing the thick silence of the house and the whisper of the night wind against the windowpanes. A memory rose up in her, so vivid she could barely breathe. Johnny, Tamsin and Mia were cooking her a birthday meal and she was at this table with a glass of white wine, watching them: her tribe. Their flushed faces, their purposeful expressions. Scallops with bacon, then halibut with a spiced aubergine salad; a raspberry cheesecake; coffee and red chillies dipped in dark chocolate. Everything she most loved. The steam billowed from the hob. Tamsin wielded a wooden spoon and dropped an egg yolk on to the tiles in a viscous yellow splash; she over-whipped the cream and swore. Mia burnt the bacon and her face screwed up, like a bitter berry. They had made such a song and dance, those two girls, almost in competition with each other, advertising their efforts for her.

And Johnny – his shirt sleeves rolled to the elbow – had attended to the aubergines, following a recipe he'd printed off from his computer. He chopped them into cubes and rubbed them in oil, then roasted them in the oven with garlic, ginger and chillies. While he was waiting for them to cook, he set about cleaning up the mess his sisters were creating with such abandon. What Isabel remembered most was the look on his face: absorbed in the moment, very careful, a bit dreamy, almost tender. A motherly face, although it sounded ridiculous to think of your son in that way. It was a look he sometimes wore when he was reading, or playing the piano and thinking no one was watching him.

The memory twisted in her heart: the sharp blade of love.

She rang him again. Two o'clock in the morning. It rang and rang. Digby walked round her legs, tail high and stiff, brindled skinny body shaking with purrs.

'Where's your master?' she asked him, and he stared at her with his cool unblinking gaze.

She reached over and shook Felix's shoulder.

He muttered something and turned towards her. 'What is it?' It was amazing how alert he sounded at once: perhaps he, too, hadn't been sleeping.

'I'm worried.'

'What about?'

'I can't reach Johnny.'

'We've talked about this. He's probably busy.'

'He didn't remember your birthday.'

'I don't mind.'

'It's not like him.'

'Just because he forgot my birthday –'

'I've sent him emails and I've tried to phone him.'

'How long has it been?'

How long? Isabel tried to think. Days. A week, perhaps.

'Mia wants to go and visit him, but he hasn't contacted her either. It's out of character.'

'Why are you so anxious?'

'What if he's not all right?'

'If he's not all right, he'll tell us.'

'But if he doesn't –'

'If he doesn't, that's because he's working it out for himself.'

'How long should I wait?'

'Wait before what?'

'Before going to see him.'

'Isabel.' Felix sat up and turned on the bedside lamp and she blinked in the sudden dazzle, immediately comforted by the light. Felix looked at her intently; she'd always loved the way he could suddenly concentrate on a single person or idea. 'Johnny has left home. You have to let him go. He needs to feel free of us.'

'I've got a bad feeling.'

'What's the worst that could have happened?'

'I don't know. If he's unhappy –'

'If he's unhappy, you can't cure it, you know. Your children can't be happy all the time. Do you remember your first term at university?'

'Yes.'

She had fallen in love: that was all she really remembered. Robin, with long curly hair and torn jeans, one earring and a small tattoo on his left shoulder, long before

44

tattoos became popular. They'd gone on student demonstrations together, drunk warm wine in the park, recited poetry to each other. Three decades later, she could still recall the expression on his face just before he'd kissed her for the first time, and the first time they'd made love on her narrow iron bed with the homesick girl's weeping coming through the thin walls. She could still remember the exact words he had used when he broke off their relationship two terms later. And the way she had grieved – had she ever felt such pure grief since? A year or so ago, in a wash of sudden nostalgia for that time, she had looked him up on the Internet and found several Robin Calders of the right age, but she couldn't even tell which was him, and the photos of middle-aged men stirred no old memories. Perhaps they had walked past each other in the street. Yet it had been so sharp at the time, the heady love and then the heartbroken loss. She had believed she would never recover.

'So, then.'

'But if he's in trouble of some kind?'

'We would have heard.'

'Yes. You're right. I'm probably just being stupid. And it's a bad time to think about things . . .' The small hours of a cold night, when thoughts come like ill omens to keep you from sleep and an ill wind blows through your dreams.

Yet something was wrong. She knew; her body knew. Wind clattered against the window. Rain and leaves streamed down in the darkness. She rose and looked out at the black night. She padded down the hall and stood outside Mia's room for a few seconds. She remembered how when the three children had been small she would walk round the house when they were sleeping, like a sentinel keeping watch over those she loved. Now nothing felt safe.

Chapter Five

The following morning, Felix came to Isabel's school. For the rest of her life she would remember that she was reading one of her favourite books to the thirty pupils sitting in a circle around her, *The Mousehole Cat*. She had read it to her own children many times and almost knew it off by heart. Each time she turned the page, she held the book towards the class so that they could look at the pictures of a sea filled with pointy, white-capped waves, a sky full of swirling Van Gogh clouds, and the little glowing candles in the windows of the houses. She stopped often for their questions and comments, an eager hand stretched high in the air almost lifting the child from their sitting position. Sometimes it would take several minutes to read just one page.

It was twelve minutes past eleven by the large clock on the wall; she knew that Felix was giving a lecture that morning, so when she was called out of her class and saw him standing in Reception beside the life-sized, anatomically correct skeleton all of the children called George, a sickening pain went through her, as if a long knife had been inserted between her ribs and tugged violently upwards. She gave a small, terrified gasp, then walked swiftly across to him on her crumbling legs.

'What?'

'It's Johnny.'

But of course she had known that. Hadn't she always known?

'Tell me.'

'After what you said last night, I rang the university this morning. He's not there.'

'What do you mean, *not there*?'

'They haven't seen him for days. A week.'

'But –'

'He hasn't been to lectures or to his tutorials.'

'He had! He told me so. And he sat his exams. He said so. He said he did well.'

'He never went to his exams.'

'But –' She stopped, bewildered. 'Where is he, then?'

'He told his tutor he had to go home because of sickness in the family.'

Isabel remembered the letters that had been sent to him from Sheffield. If she had opened them, as she had wanted to, she would have known earlier. If she had listened to her fears. Days. A week. More. Her hand went to her throat, then to her mouth. It was full of bile.

'We have to call the police.'

'I called them on my way. We're going up there.' Felix was so calm. He stood so straight and the words came out of his mouth slowly, one by one, separated by considered thought.

'Yes. Yes.'

'Tell Marion you've got an emergency and somebody will have to cover for you. I'll be in the car.'

'Yes.'

She tried to run, but her feet tripped her up. The floor rippled. Her hand banged hard into the table that sped towards her and she felt the hurt as if from a great distance. A little tear of blood snailed down her finger. She caught a flash of herself in the school window as she passed, a thin little woman with wild hair, wild eyes and a jerky gait, like a puppet set in motion.

She sat in the passenger seat, leaning forward, as if she could push the car to Sheffield through the force of her terror. Felix drove too slowly. There were too many cars in front and behind. She wanted him to weave in and out of the traffic, accelerate into gaps, blare the horn and put on hazard lights, but he was careful and deliberate. Every minute made a difference. Every second. Her foot pressed into the floor; she bit her lower lip so hard it bled; she wrapped her arms round her body but found no comfort.

She kept ringing his mobile, thick frantic fingers pressing the numbers, saying in a small, harsh voice that didn't sound like her own, 'Johnny? Johnny? Ring me, Johnny.' Her mouth was so dry she could barely speak, yet she couldn't stop speaking – the same questions over and over again in her parched voice: how long did you say he'd been gone? What does it mean? What exactly did he tell them? Where is he? Did he plan to leave or did he just up and go? What's gone wrong? Do you think someone else is involved? Has he been in an accident? Is there nothing else they could tell us? What time will we be there? Who's meeting us? Can't you go faster? Isn't there a way round this traffic? I should have known; I did know. My boy; my son. What could have happened? It will be all right, won't it, Felix? Tell me it will be all right. Why didn't he say? Why?

At first, Felix answered her questions patiently, although

there wasn't much to add. Then, as they came round on a loop, a gabbled string of nonsense, he stopped replying, and after a while Isabel stopped asking. They sat in silence, except for small gasps and murmurs from Isabel, who couldn't keep quiet and couldn't sit still. She twitched, rubbed her hands against each other, rubbed them against her legs, sat on them to keep them still, curled her legs underneath her on the seat, pressed her face against the side window to feel the solidity of the glass against her skin. She turned the heating up because she was clammy, then down when beads of sweat sprang up on her forehead. Her body was swarming with fears. She kept seeing Johnny's face when she had left him, slack and forlorn.

On the motorway at last. The speed dial rose steadily and the old car vibrated beneath them. Eighty. Eighty-five. Felix was worried, too. Beneath that stern expression, terror was surging through him. Isabel looked at his whitened knuckles as he gripped the steering wheel. Ninety. Spray rose in great arcs from the wheels of juggernauts as they passed. The countryside flowed by in a blur. The last time she had driven this way was with Johnny. How had she not known and turned round with a screech of brakes and hurtled home with him? How had she been so blind, so selfish, so stupid? How was it that time only flowed in one direction, implacable and impersonal, dragging everyone with it, and couldn't be stopped and turned back to that one moment? If she shut her eyes and then opened them, if she prayed to a God she had never acknowledged since her mother had died when she was nine, if she held her breath until there was a red mist in front of her, if she pinched the skin of her arms very hard, if she gave up everything, everything she had ever wanted for herself – the memory rose in her of a drunken and euphoric conversation she had had with Jenny about going away with a rucksack and no children clutching at the hem of her skirt to hold her back. She almost screamed in hatred of such paltry, risible wishes. If Johnny was safe, she would never wish for anything again. If Johnny came home. Let him be safe, let him be safe. The words boomed inside her skull.

'We have to tell Mia we'll be back late,' Felix was saying.

'Yes.' Isabel peered at the clock on the screen, whose numbers couldn't be deciphered. 'She won't be home for a bit.'

'Don't tell her why.'

'No. Of course not. It might be all right by then.' She gazed in supplication at Felix's profile. 'Mightn't it? Felix?'

'We're not going to find him waiting for us, Isabel.'

'No,' she said. 'No. You're right. Of course. But he will be all right?'

Felix was silent for a few moments; Isabel could see the blue pulse jigging in his temple, the slight quiver at the side of his mouth. She thought she ought to reach out and touch him, but she couldn't make herself do so.

'People go missing all the time,' he said at last. 'I know this. Especially young people, who are so full of questions and troubles. They run away from something, or towards something. They almost always come back.'

That was what the police told them, almost word for word, when they sat in the room that had been set aside for them in the Science Building at the university. There were two of them. The woman, Constable Gillian Dover, was tall and slender with long hair held back in a severe ponytail; she had eyes of slightly different colours, which was disconcerting: Isabel didn't know which eye to look at. Next to her, Constable William Plowright ('Call me Bill') was short and stocky. His eyes were set widely apart, giving him a permanently startled look, like a deer on the alert for a predator. They had already spoken to the bursar and Johnny's tutors; they even had his college photograph, taken when his hair had been cut shorter than usual, which made him look younger than he was.

'These are better!' cried Isabel, rummaging through her wallet, pulling out a handful of photographs of her children that she carried around with her. They fell to the table and for a moment she and Felix stared, dumbfounded, at the three faces smiling up at them. Then Isabel extracted the picture of Johnny and pushed it across to the officers. 'This is more like him,' she said.

'Thank you.' The woman took it and slid it into a manila folder.

'What happens now?' asked Felix.

'We'll ask you some questions about your son, if that's all right, and then see where we are. Of course it's extremely worrying for you, we do understand that, but as far as we can ascertain, Johnny has left voluntarily.'

'That doesn't mean he's all right,' said Isabel. 'That doesn't mean we shouldn't search for him as a matter of urgency.' They looked at her. 'Does it? Does it?'

'He's an adult.'

'No! He may be over eighteen, but that doesn't mean he's an adult.'

'Let them ask their questions, Isabel,' said Felix, in his calm voice.

How old was Johnny? Eighteen.

What was his home address? They gave it.

When had they last spoken to him or heard from him? That was hard – was it about a week ago, maybe more? They couldn't remember when he had last called. He'd sent a postcard – here Isabel's voice faltered – telling them his exams had gone well. Though of course they now knew he hadn't done any, hadn't been to any tutorials.

Was he in a relationship? No. He'd never had one actually – but that wasn't relevant. No, as far as they knew, he wasn't in a relationship.

Did he drink? He's a teenager. Of course he drinks – but he doesn't binge drink or drink to excess, if that's what you mean, and he only drinks socially. He had always seemed very controlled about drinking, almost unnervingly so.

Or take drugs? Well, maybe the odd spliff (now Isabel felt she was sounding like an irresponsible liberal parent, careless about consequences, and her sentence trailed away; Felix finished it for her). As far as they knew, he had never been seriously involved with any kind of drugs. Though, of course, it was impossible for them to know whether or not he had been experimenting. Children keep secrets from their parents.

Had he ever disappeared like this before? No! No, of course not – he was so, so *stable*. And so considerate, Felix added after Isabel stopped. He'd never given them a moment's real anxiety. Briefly, his stern face crumpled. Then he regained his composure.

Had they any reason to think that he might – here, Constable Plowright's face became stiff with a kind of embarrassed distress – *might harm himself?* What do you mean? Oh. Oh, I see. You mean, you mean *kill* himself? No! No! You don't understand. You don't know who you're talking about. This is Johnny. He's level-headed, happy, popular – he comes from a loving family, he's never gone off the rails. This is all a mistake. An aberration. You just have to find him and bring him home.

She leant forward, urgent and pleading, but then saw the expression on both their faces and shrank back again.

Is there anything else we should know about your son? Anything that might help us?

There was a silence. Isabel thought about saying he was precious, beloved, special – but, even in her state of anguish, she knew that every mother will say that her child is precious, beloved and special.

Then Felix spoke. 'Johnny is a young man who is quite reserved but very concerned with – well, he's eighteen. He's concerned with the state of the world and the state of his soul. His conscience troubles him. He has an exaggerated sense of guilt.' Felix coughed miserably. 'I would say, anyway,' he added, not looking at Isabel.

There was a pause and then Gillian Dover spoke: 'Are you saying that you aren't surprised your son has disappeared, Mr Hopkins?'

Felix met Isabel's eye. 'Of course I'm surprised and upset and anxious. But I'm saying there are ways in which it makes a kind of sense to me.'

'How can you say that?' Isabel heard her voice fill the room, rough and angry, the voice of someone she barely recognized. 'It makes no sense at all! And what's this got to do with his disappearance?' Even as she spoke the words, she heard how unconvincing they were. 'Rubbish,' she added desperately. 'Nonsense!'

The three of them looked at her; she glared back.

'If he's done something he's ashamed of,' said Felix, softly.

'Then he'll tell us or find a way to make amends. But this is all ridiculous – we can find out why he went when we get him back. That's what matters at the moment. Until then it's just time ticking by. We need to hurry.'

And Isabel actually leapt to her feet, but she had no idea what to do next. She stared down at them. 'What should we do?' she asked. 'Where do we start?'

'We will go to his room, if that isn't too painful for you. And then his course tutor is waiting to see you. After that, the best thing is for you to go home and wait for news. In the meantime, we will make enquiries, circulate his photograph.'

'Is that all? Just – just *wait*?'

'Mrs Hopkins, I understand how distressing this is for you, believe me I do. But your son has clearly left of his own volition.'

'No.'

'He had stopped going to any lessons. He told everyone, including his tutor, that he had to go home because of a sickness in the family. There wasn't one, was there?'

'Well, no –'

'Young people often find it hard when they first leave home. In all likelihood, he will return in a few days.'

'Do you expect us just to sit at home and wait?'

'I know it's hard.'

'It's not hard, it's impossible.' Her voice had become loud again, against her will; it scratched her throat. 'He could be anywhere – out on the moors in the cold and dark, lying in a ditch, in a hospital and unable to remember his name – have you contacted the hospitals?'

'Not yet.'

'Well, then –' Isabel stopped, breathless.

The two officers stood up.

'Is that it? Is that all?' she cried.

'Shall we have a look at his room and see if anything's been taken?'

'Of course. Yes. Like what?'

'Did he have his passport with him?'

'His passport?' She tried to gather her thoughts and make sense of the words people were speaking. She had to concentrate, or she would be swallowed up in the maelstrom inside her. 'I don't know. Did he, Felix? He didn't say. I can look when I go home – I know where he keeps it. Do you think he might have gone abroad, then?'

'It's just a possibility.'

'But why? Why would he? On his own and without a word. It's ridiculous. Oh.' Isabel put her hands to her face. 'I'm so sorry. I'm so so so sorry.' Words were running out of her and she felt she had no control, as if her body was leaking them. 'I know I'm asking questions that you can't answer. I don't want to make everything more difficult. I want to help. Tell me what to do. I'll do anything. Just tell me. Please.'

'His room, then? We have the keys already.'

They left the main university building and set off up the

hill, Isabel practically running, welcoming the pain in her calves, and Felix keeping up with his long strides. They didn't speak to each other, and when they arrived at the block of student flats, Felix stood back and let the other three go on ahead of him. For an instant, Isabel saw that he was considering not going into his son's room and seeing all his familiar possessions there. He wasn't sure he could face the sadness of it, she thought, the tangible sense of Johnny's absence. She beckoned to him, and he squared his shoulders and followed her darting figure up the two flights of stairs and through the doors into Johnny's flat. Then, with a deep, steadying breath, they went through Johnny's door and into the damp little room.

Isabel stood in the centre. Her face was screwed up and her shoulders hunched over, like an old woman's. She held both hands against her heart.

Of course, Johnny's room was neat. His bed was made, and his striped drawstring cotton trousers, brought from Morocco a year ago, were laid on the pillow with an old grey T-shirt, emblazoned with the logo from some pop concert. His shoes were paired under the bed: his grey canvas ones, his trainers, his walking boots, his studded football boots. He had put all his books on the small shelf and his stationery on the desk; his pens and pencils were in a blue-and-white mug that he'd had since he was a child, with a small chip on its handle. The pieces were set out on the travel chessboard.

Isabel sank on to the bed, her face working. On the pinboard opposite were all the postcards she had sent over the past weeks, and also the recipes. She stared at them: the curries and marinades and noodle dishes written out in her neatest handwriting. She picked up Johnny's grey T-shirt and pressed her face into it. Then she stood up and stumbled towards the wardrobe. There were all the shirts she had given him, his two pairs of jeans on one hanger, his nice grey jacket. She put her hand into the pocket and found a bus ticket, a tissue and nothing else.

'Can you think of anything he might have taken?' asked Constable Dover.

'Oh.' She gazed around her like a blind woman.

Felix opened the drawers of the desk, one by one. 'There's no passport here, but it's probably at home,' he said, in a soft, hesitant voice quite unlike his own.

'His sleeping bag,' said Isabel, wildly. 'He had his sleeping bag and his winter fleece. I don't think they're here.'

She pulled open drawers, knelt to peer under the bed, and found nothing. She stared up at them from her crouching position, her face slack. 'But he wouldn't want to hurt us like this,' she whispered. 'He wouldn't just leave. I know him. He's so – so very considerate. No, that's not the right word. He's good. He's my good boy. A kind, good boy. This is all wrong. It isn't true. There's a mistake somewhere, a dreadful mistake.'

'Does your son own a computer?' asked Gillian Dover, from her position by the door. Felix and Isabel stared at her blankly, then Felix pulled open the thin drawers at the top of the desk and very carefully – as if it contained gelignite and might explode if tipped – lifted out the laptop he had given to Johnny just a few weeks previously, its connecting cord trailing from it. He put it on the surface of the desk, plugged its cord into the socket near the floor and lifted its lid.

Isabel leapt to her feet. 'That'll tell us where he is. It will, I know it. Felix?'

Felix pressed the small on-button at the top right-hand corner and there was a faint ping. They all waited and a white circle started rotating in the middle of the screen. Then it lit up, flat blue, icons appearing one by one.

'His mail – look at his mail. Quick.'

Felix double-clicked on the mail icon. Isabel huddled by his side and they gazed at the messages. The most recent had been received eight days ago but, as they looked, more started appearing: there were several from her, a few from Mia and one from Felix, several from Johnny's best friend Will, other friends, and official ones from the university. Isabel frantically opened the ones from names she didn't recognize and scanned them for clues.

'I don't know,' she said. The words seemed to be blurring in front of her. 'It's not clear.'

'We can take it with us,' said Felix.

'No. We have to find out now. There'll be something here.'

'Isabel –'

'Wait!'

She selected the 'Sent' messages with a thick, unwieldy finger and started scrolling through them. Behind her, she heard Felix asking the police officers if they could take the computer with them, and them agreeing that would be all right – as long as Felix got in touch with them if he found anything suspicious.

'I don't understand,' Isabel said, bending over the laptop, scrabbling among the recent trashed items. 'He can't just have gone. He doesn't say anything like that. He would have said something to someone. It doesn't make sense.'

'Mrs Hopkins.'

'It doesn't make sense.'

Felix leant over and turned off the computer. She watched it shutting down, messages disappearing, lights blinking, a blank screen. He closed the lid, wrapped the cord around it several times and picked it up, then took her elbow.

'Isabel,' he said, 'we can look through his computer properly later. We're not doing any good here.'

'His flatmates – we should talk to them. Ask them what they know.'

'Later.'

'And Will – why didn't I think of that?' Her face lit up with crazy hope. 'He'll be with Will! Visiting him. Of course! Felix, we have to get hold of Will in York.'

'Come on, Izzie.'

She struggled to her feet. She felt very heavy yet insubstantial, as though she might melt, dissolve entirely. She put a hand on the wall to steady herself. She felt the rough grain of its surface, and saw how her fingers pressed into it, and thought: This is me, Isabel Hopkins. I am here, alive, solid, real – and my son Johnny has disappeared.

'Where to?' she managed to say. Her mouth slipped round the words: the shapes of sounds wouldn't hold together.

'To see his tutor.'

'Yes. Yes, of course.'

'And then we're going home.'

'Home?'

'We have to tell Mia what's happened.'

'But – we can't. We have to do something!'

'Of course we do – but we're not going to start wandering around calling his name and hoping he'll just turn up.' His voice was harshly insistent. 'Don't you understand? He could be anywhere.'

'Anywhere,' Isabel echoed.

'You could telephone anyone you can think of who might have heard from him, Mrs Hopkins.'

'Yes. Yes, I will. But his flatmates – we should talk to them.'

'We can do that.'

'And we'll come back, Isabel,' said Felix. His hand was on her shoulder. 'We'll see his tutor and then we'll go home, make phone calls, have a plan. All right?'

'A plan,' she repeated. 'Yes.'

The police officers said goodbye, handing out numbers where they could be contacted, a sheet of paper with information on it, shaking them both by the hand, on their faces an almost identical look of sympathetic concern that made Isabel want to scream at them. She and Felix hovered uselessly in Johnny's little room. Isabel kept picking things up – a glass with the ancient dregs of red wine in it, a plastic bag containing a few items of dirty clothing – she couldn't resist taking out his brown linen shirt and holding it against her cheek – a pack of cards. It was hard to leave when traces of their son lingered in the room. She stooped and brought out a crumpled ball of paper from under his bed and straightened it out. On it was written, in Johnny's flowing hand, 'Wednesday'. What did that mean? She gazed at each letter as if some code was embedded there, then put the paper into her pocket. Everything he might have touched seemed precious. She picked up the pen on his desktop, ran her fingers over the pinboard full of recipes, sat on his bed again and picked up the pillow where he had – when? – last lain his tawny head.

'I keep thinking that if I concentrate hard enough, I'll know where he is,' said Isabel. 'I'll *feel* him.'

'I know. But we're doing no good here.'

Then they heard the door to the communal flat open, shut again, and footsteps in the corridor. Isabel lurched towards the sound before Felix could hold her back.

'Excuse me,' she said, to a young woman with a shaved head, wearing a baggy boiler suit. 'Excuse me, but I'm Johnny's mother. Can I talk to you?'

The young woman looked surprised. 'I thought you were ill,' she said.

'He said I was ill?'

'I think so,' the young woman said cautiously. 'I got the impression it must be serious, otherwise why would he go home?'

'When did you last see him?'

'I don't know.' Her eyes flickered to Felix. 'Has something happened?'

'Was it recently? When was he here?'

'When? I don't know exactly. But don't you –'

'A day? A week?'

'Oh, more like a week.'

'What's your name?' said Isabel. 'You aren't Lil, are you?'

'Lil? No. Kelly. I don't know anyone called Lil.'

'Do you know tall Phil who plays the accordion?'

Kelly took a step back from Isabel, as if frightened of

this small, quivering woman, but Isabel took her hand pleadingly.

'Isabel.' Felix joined his wife, putting a hand on her shoulder. He looked at the girl. 'Johnny's gone missing,' he said. 'That's why we're here.'

For Isabel, hearing the truth spoken out loud to this stranger made everything more implacable – like a nightmare that was gradually solidifying, becoming real in the waking world.

'No!' The young woman looked both appalled and self-conscious; her eyes darted around, in search of back-up. 'But that's awful.'

'So if there's anything at all you think might help us find him . . .'

'Missing. But we had no idea. We thought – well, he just left. No one knew anything. Why?'

'We don't know.'

'He was so nice.'

'*Is*,' hissed Isabel. She took a small step forward and even bunched her fists. 'Is nice. Is. Is.'

'Yes. I just meant –'

'Present tense. Coming home. But it's all right, don't worry,' she added, twisting her mouth into a four-sided smile, a rectangle through which her breath panted. She knew from the expression on Kelly's face that she was behaving in a disturbing manner. It was like being drunk, she thought, and trying to compensate for your drunkenness with your behaviour, but knowing all the while that your exaggeratedly articulated words will fool nobody.

'We know what you meant,' said Felix, reassuringly. 'We're not accusing you of anything.'

'Accusing?'

'We're not.'

'Did you notice anything?' asked Isabel, straining to keep her voice level. 'Did he say anything?'

'About leaving? Just that someone was ill – you, I thought it was you, but that might have been wrong.'

'When he was here? Was he all right? Did he seem all right to you? Were there signs that he was unhappy?'

Kelly looked at Isabel, then at Felix. She shifted uncomfortably. 'He seemed OK.'

'Were you his friend?'

'Well – not exactly his friend. But yes, of course we were friendly –'

'I tell you what,' said Felix. 'I'm going to leave you my email address. I want you to tell your flatmates what's happened, say that Johnny's disappeared and his parents are very worried. If there are things any of you think might help us find Johnny, or explain why he's gone, then you can write to us. And if there are other people you think we should talk to, then that could be helpful. Does that sound a good idea?'

'Yes,' said Kelly, with evident relief.

'Anything,' put in Isabel. 'You can tell us anything. Who his friends are, what time he got up, *anything*.'

'I'm going to leave you with my mobile number as well.' Felix took his notebook from his jacket pocket. 'And our landline too. The college will have all those, of course, but just in case . . .'

Johnny had mentioned his course tutor to Isabel: Dr Theresa Kessle. She was vast – broad and high as a landscape, wearing cascading clothes over her mountainous body, with long grey hair and a rolling chin. She had sharp grey eyes and a low, clear voice that would carry well in a lecture theatre. Isabel got the instant impression that she wouldn't suffer fools gladly. On any other day she would have warmed to her, but today Theresa Kessle's shrewd gaze seemed to pierce through her, making her feel small and vain, a kaleidoscope of blemishes. She felt that this woman could see into her depths, and make out her secret jealousies, her subterranean resentments, all her flaws as a woman and a mother. She would know, just by looking at her, that Johnny had run away from her, Isabel, from her tenaciously clinging, deadly love. She blanched and, in imagined self-defence, said in a tremulous voice, 'Did you notice nothing?'

'I noticed he was a quiet and reserved young man.'

'Is that all?'

'You must remember that I only met him on three or four occasions. He stopped coming to my class.'

'Why didn't you seek him out, find out what was wrong? Why didn't you tell us?'

'Of course, I now wish I had done all those things. I'm extremely sorry that I didn't. But many of our young students have trouble finding their feet. Several of them don't come to classes or deliver their work on time. It really isn't unusual. I contacted Johnny to ask why he hadn't attended the classes or lectures and to remind him his essay was overdue. I warned him of the consequences of dropping behind so early in the year and asked him to come and see me to talk about any problems.'

Her voice, like a river, flowed over Isabel; she felt that

she was drowning in this room. Her throat was clogged with her distress. 'And?' she managed to say.

'He didn't reply. He didn't sit his exams. Then I heard he'd had to go home because of trouble there. An illness, I think. That seemed to me to explain things.'

'I see,' said Isabel, dully. Then, wildly: 'But did you *like* him? Do you even *care*? That's what I want to know.'

'Isabel,' said Felix, warningly, 'this isn't going to get us any closer to finding Johnny.'

'No. It's a good question.' Theresa Kessle nodded at him. 'I found your son to be a singularly attractive personality, modest and generous to a fault, always wanting to praise others. And he was clever – he certainly shouldn't have had problems with the work. But he seemed . . . ' She stopped, not in confusion but because she was evidently searching for the right word. 'Full of care,' she supplied eventually.

'What does that mean?' asked Felix. He seemed to be settling lower in the chair. His face was propped in his hand, half covered by it.

'He appeared to me to be the kind of boy – young man, rather – who had an over-developed sense of his own lack of worth. It almost – well, is either of you religious?'

'Hardly.'

'It felt quite religious, to me. Like a feeling of sin. Perhaps it's more common in a subject like physics, which can reduce people to a sense of worthlessness and utter insignificance.'

'Sin! Worthlessness! You thought this though you only met him a few times?' Isabel's voice was scornful. She wanted to pound her fists against the woman's overwhelming bulk, her strength and certainty and calm rationality.

Theresa Kessle looked at her as if she knew exactly what Isabel was feeling. Her grey eyes were kind. 'I might be quite wrong, of course. Young people can be very precarious, very fragile.'

'Johnny was – he's a happy boy,' said Isabel. Her words felt very small and paltry. 'He makes us proud.'

Theresa Kessle startled them both by standing, with surprising grace and agility, and crossing to where Isabel sat shrivelled in her seat. She knelt and wrapped Isabel in her sweet-smelling, overflowing embrace, then pulled back and said, 'I'm not going to say I can imagine what you're going through. Of course I can't. I'm not even a mother. But I will do anything I can to help you, and I speak for the university and for myself as an individual. You are not alone.'

'Oh,' said Isabel. She clung to the woman's dimpled hands and stared into her grey eyes, until she felt that she was falling, unable to stop her spinning descent. She forced herself to sit back, wiped her hand across her forehead, which was beaded with sweat, and tried to breathe calmly. She didn't comprehend how her body could withstand the battering force of her emotions: how was she sitting in a chair, how was her mouth uttering words? She took a shuddering breath, and said, 'Sorry. But I can't – I don't –' She didn't know what she was saying. There weren't words any more.

'You don't need to.' Theresa Kessle turned to Felix, who sat still and unyielding as a stone in his chair. 'I will give you all my details and we will speak soon.'

'Yes,' said Felix. He stood up and it seemed to Isabel that he wasn't as tall as he used to be; that he was a man who was shrinking towards old age as she looked at him, and her terror, which had seemed boundless, grew greater, deeper. It stretched out on all sides, a shining black sea, and it sank deeper into her, into parts of herself that she had never even known existed. It cracked into her heart and twisted her guts, roared in her ears and put a thick muscled eel in her throat.

'We are grateful,' she heard Felix say. He shook Theresa's hand. 'Truly. Come on, Isabel. We're going home now.'

He picked up the computer, took her thin cold fingers in his and they left the room together.

Chapter Six

Mia was already asleep when Isabel and Felix arrived home. She was curled up in her duvet, one hand under her cheek and her black hair gleaming on the pillow. Her face looked ridiculously young, thought Isabel, and she was filled with cold anger against Mia that she should be alive, untouched, tranquil, cocooned in her warm bed while out there, somewhere, Johnny wandered. Then, as suddenly as it had come, the feeling disappeared and she was left with self-horror and an engulfing tenderness towards her younger daughter.

'We should leave her till morning,' she whispered to Felix, as they went out of the bedroom. 'Tell her then, and call Tamsin as well.'

'Maybe.' Felix sounded doubtful. 'She'll be angry with us for withholding information.'

'We might know something by then.'

'What will we know, Isabel?'

'Something. I'm going to ring Will's house and get his number. He might be able to tell us.'

'All right. If that's what you want.'

'Well, what do you want?' Again, she heard her voice rise and swell; she could imagine her face contorted with rage. 'Do you think we should – well, what? Have a bite to eat? Maybe watch a bit of telly to take our minds off things? Go to sleep? Is that what you want to do?'

Felix looked at her calmly. 'I am going to have something to eat, yes. So should you. We haven't eaten anything all day.'

'You go ahead. I'd choke on food.'

'It won't help to starve yourself.'

Isabel was leafing through the address book, looking for Will's home number, but she couldn't find it. She ran to the cupboard under the stairs and yanked out a pile of ageing *Yellow Pages*, started hunting through them for a Bolan, Grace, in Middleton Road. But the tiny letters knotted into each other. Her eyes burnt with sleepless fatigue.

'It's not here,' she said at last.

'Maybe she's ex-directory.'

'I'm going round there.'

'It's eleven o'clock.'

'So?'

'She might be asleep.'

'*So?*'

'He's been gone a week, Isabel. A night won't make a difference.'

'What do you mean? It might make all the difference. An hour might make a difference. A *minute*.'

'I'll come with you.'

'No need. No need.'

She hadn't taken off her coat, so now she grabbed the house keys and ran out of the door. She had thought she would drive there – Will's house was a mile or so away, five minutes by car – but as soon as she stepped into the cool windy night, she knew she couldn't get back into the car. She had to run. She had to pound along the pavements with her coat flapping behind her and her lungs sharp with pain and her breath coming in unsteady whooshes and her eyes watering. She couldn't stop. The faster she ran, the better it was for Johnny. If she sprinted. If she twisted her ankle but didn't stop. If she ignored the searing pain in her side.

At last she was standing outside Will's house, a small modern semi in a cul-de-sac. For a moment she stopped dead, feeling her heart pound like a witch-doctor's drum. Boom, boom, boom: bad things are coming. Then she rang, knocked, waited, rang and knocked again. The windows were dark, but after a minute or so of ringing and knocking, her fists hammering against the glass front, a light went on upstairs. Isabel stooped and peered through the letterbox, but saw only a patch of wooden floor. At last there were footsteps, the door opened on a chain, and one suspicious eye peered through the gap.

'Who's there?'

'Isabel Hopkins. Johnny's mother. Can I come in?'

'Hang on.' The chain slid back and Grace Bolan, in a towelling robe that she was holding shut at the neck, stood before her, her face grimed with old makeup and puffy with sleep. 'Isabel?' she said. 'What on earth's going on? I was dead to the world. Are you all right? What time is it?'

'I don't know.' Isabel was through the door and into the hall. 'Johnny's gone.'

'Johnny?' She seemed dazed. She rubbed her face with the back of her hand, then ran her fingers through her matted hair.

'I need Will's mobile number.'

'Johnny's gone?'

'I don't have time to tell you. Have you spoken to Will recently?'

'Just yesterday.'

'Can you get me his number? He'll know what's going on. I know he will. It'll be all right once I've talked to him.'

'Um – yes. Hang on. I'll get my phone. It's on there. You say *gone*?'

'Yes.' Isabel shifted impatiently from foot to foot as Grace extracted her mobile from the pocket of her coat, which was hanging over the back of a chair in the kitchen. She waited a hundred years for Grace to turn it on and then, with infinite slowness, to scroll down to Will's number.

'But what does that mean?'

'Gone, Grace, means just that. Gone.' Isabel had never much liked Grace Bolan. Now she loathed her – how was it that she had left Will to fend for himself through most of his teenage years yet Will was safe and sound while Johnny was not? 'He's missing.'

'That's awful. You must be so worried. Here it is – but I haven't got a signal.'

She read out the number and Isabel keyed it on to her phone. Her fingers had become cumbrously fat. She kept having to begin again. 'Thanks. I'm sorry to have woken you.' She heard the curtness of her voice and a part of her marvelled – she who had never been rude to anyone, who had always gone out of her way to win people over, make them feel better about themselves. 'Go back to bed.'

'Can't I do something?'

'I don't think so – I'll tell you if you can.'

'Let me know, will you?'

'Yes.'

'I'm sure it will be all right. He'll turn up.'

Isabel didn't answer: she could only have snarled. She was out into the cold night again. The moon was low and nearly full, and as it sailed between the clouds, it illuminated the empty streets, the snug houses where people slept and dreamt. She pressed Will's number as she walked. Her heart beat a ragged tune: 'Let it be good news, let it be good news.'

Fucking voicemail. He couldn't be asleep. Students didn't go to sleep before midnight, did they? They were up till dawn, taking drugs and drinking and dancing and screwing each other, talking about the meaning of life and writing essays for the next morning's class in a jumped-up caffeine-state.

'Will. It's Isabel, Isabel Hopkins. Call me back whenever you get this, day or night. It's urgent.'

She jabbed the phone off, stared at it, waited, rang again, got the voicemail, left no message this time. Her feet rang out on the pavement; a car drove past and she could hear music coming from it. She put the phone in her pocket, took it out again. There must be something she could do, someone she could call. She had to use this torrent of fear coursing through her body, divert it into a purpose. She reached home but continued walking up the street. How could she go in there to Felix, eating his dinner? How dare he be *eating*, as if nothing had happened? And Mia, sleeping? At the top of the road she turned and walked back again. Her phone rang.

'Yes?' She could hear music in the background.

'Isabel? It's Will, you called me – is everything OK?'

'Where's Johnny?'

'What? Johnny?'

'Is he with you?'

'No. I'm here, in York. What do you mean?'

'Do you know where he is? Has he called?'

'Not for a few days. I've left him some messages – what's going on?'

'He's gone missing, Will.' Isabel stopped by a lamppost, steadied herself in the pool of yellow light. 'No one knows where he is.'

There was a silence at the other end.

'I don't get it.'

'You mean he hasn't told you anything?' Hope dropped away. A deep, clean well: she couldn't hear the splash as it reached the bottom. 'He must have told you something.'

'No! I'd no idea – Jesus. But, look, it doesn't make sense. Last time I spoke to him he was fine. He would have said – wouldn't he?'

'I don't know.'

'When did he go?'

'I don't know.' Dull, dull, dull. The crashing tide had withdrawn, leaving her high and dry. She leant against the lamppost and closed her eyes. 'About a week ago. But he'd stopped going to lessons or anything.'

She heard an intake of breath, and then: 'He'll be OK, Isabel. He will. He's Johnny. He wouldn't do anything stupid.'

'So why's he gone?'

'Maybe it's just a whim – he's set off somewhere.'

'He wouldn't do that – he's not like that.'

'No. You'll see. I'll kill him for making us so anxious.' A laugh, too hearty, unconvincing, rang out at the other end of the line.

'What shall I do, Will?' Isabel heard herself say, though why would Will know? And when he spoke, she heard the panic in his voice that she should be turning to him in this time of crisis. It had always been the other way round.

'I'm going to ring round everyone, all the old gang, ask them what they know. We'll track him down.'

'Will you do that?'

'Right now.'

'Thanks. And you'll let me know – it doesn't matter what time it is. Any time.'

'Of course. And Zoë! I'm a numbskull. She might know something.' Zoë was Will's girlfriend, and had gone to Sheffield to study law – why had Isabel not thought of her? 'Though she would have mentioned . . .' His voice trailed off. Isabel could picture him, pacing round his room, frowning, bouncing on his toes. Was someone with him? There was still music playing.

'Will you call her for me?'

'Of course. I'll do it right now.'

'And you'll tell me anything you find out?'

'Sure. Of course. It's going to be fine, Isabel. I know it is. He'll turn up and in a few days we'll all be laughing about this.'

'I hope you're right.' I hope, I pray. She unpropped herself from her lamppost. Her legs felt unsteady beneath her.

'I *am* right.' His young voice trembled with fervour. 'This is Johnny.'

Now what? Isabel went back into the house. She saw from the plate on the table that Felix had made himself a sandwich but hadn't finished it. She went upstairs but he wasn't in bed. Of course, he would be sitting in his study. And, yes, there was a pencil line of light around the closed door. Isabel opened it a crack and peered in: Felix was sitting with Johnny's computer, his face in a frown of concentration. Isabel hesitated, but she didn't go in. What was there to say to him, after all? Nothing except more useless questions he couldn't answer, which carved new lines into his face. He was turning into a gargoyle of himself in front of her eyes. She didn't want to see that. But she couldn't just do nothing. She couldn't go to bed.

Of course she went into Johnny's room. Where else could she go? She stood in the depleted space and gazed around her, taking in everything that wasn't there: the books he had removed, leaving great gaps on the shelves, the picture on the wall, the notebooks on his desk, the shirts in the wardrobe, the smell of him, the shape of his head on the pillow. She lay down, and pressed her face into that pillow, whose case she'd removed and washed weeks ago. She stood up again and went to the window. The moonlight lay over the garden, where the trees were stripped bare for winter. She went to his desk and pulled open the drawers one by one. Old birthday cards, postcards sent by friends from abroad, a couple of adaptors, an old portable CD player with no CD inside it, a spiral notebook with his A-level history revision notes – pages of dates and treaties, names of modern dictators, causes and effects of wars and economic policies, all in his familiar writing. The nearest he got to self-revelation was the occasional doodle – always of complicated interlocking squares and triangles – in the margin. Other notebooks were full of incomprehensible formulae – jagged spikes and curves, like hieroglyphics, filling page after page. What had that woman said, his fat, majestic tutor? That physics is a dangerous subject, a lonely subject. She pulled open more drawers: a travel Scrabble set, a pack of cards, a list of things he needed to take to university, neatly crossed off. A packet of A4 batteries, a torch that didn't work, a bendy plastic ruler, a box of staples. No love letters, no condoms, no pornography, no stash of drugs, no diaries confessing to anguish, no message inviting him to join a sinister political organization: they were like the drawers of someone who knew his mother would rifle furiously through them.

And – she looked again, in all the places she had already looked, and all the places she knew it wouldn't be – there was no passport. That meant he must have taken it with him. His passport, his sleeping bag, his thick fleece. He could be anywhere, curled up like a shivering caterpillar in the streaming cold.

She sat at the desk, put her head on the grainy wood and closed her eyes. How would she get through this night, and if she did, how would she get through the next? There was a sound, a faint rustling, and her eyes opened; she leapt to her feet and stared wildly around, as if she would see him in the doorway, on the bed, smiling up at her. But the sound was the patter of rain on the windowpane and on the dead leaves stirring on the lawn; just the sound of wind blowing softly through bare trees.

Isabel went downstairs to the kitchen. Her mouth was dry so she opened the fridge, found an opened bottle of white wine and took a swift gulp, dribbling some down her chin and on to her neck. She walked into the living room and then out again. She looked at the clock, which said two a.m. When she looked again, it was two minutes past two. She rang Johnny's mobile once more, knowing that there would be no answer. She went to her computer and wrote him an email, because perhaps, even though they'd got his laptop, he would go to some Internet café, pick it up and read her words of love.

> Darling darling darling Johnny, where are you? Whatever's the trouble, why ever you've gone, just come home. Everything can be all right. Everything in the world. Please, Johnny, if you don't want to come home, if it's something about home that's sent you away, at least tell me you're safe. I can bear anything if I know you're safe.

She pressed 'Send', but now that it was gone, she needed to say something else, something that felt urgent:

> If you've done something wrong, or something you're ashamed of, just tell me. There's nothing you could do that I couldn't understand or wouldn't forgive.

She stared at the message, deleted the 'I' and put 'we' in its place.

It was eighteen minutes past two. Felix remained in his study, and Isabel remained crouched over her computer, waiting for a message back that she knew wouldn't come.

The house grew colder and outside the rain still fell, slant-wise now. She thought of moors and she thought of city streets; she thought of bridges and train lines, of ferries and rivers and rocking grey seas. She thought of wet ditches where water trickled and nettles grew, of dark canals. She got up and took the whisky bottle from its cupboard, unscrewed its metal top and had a fiery gulp. Her entire body felt transparent; her brain burnt with thoughts. She sat on the floor and hugged her legs, pressed her scorched eyes into her knees, waited for the morning.

Chapter Seven

Mia was warm in her bed, dreaming of being in a hot-air balloon that would only lift a few inches off the ground. She was sweeping through tall grass, hearing the swishing sound it made against the sides of her little capsule and feeling oddly untroubled by the wall they were skimming towards, when Isabel woke her. For a moment she lay quite still, squinting up at her mother's face until it came into focus as her dream receded and then was lost to her. She thought how odd it was that she would never remember the image she had just lost – she only had a sense of its brightness, its vivid and physical solidity. She was so cosy. Her limbs were heavy and Digby, in a curled ball at her feet, was faintly purring. Was he dreaming as well? It seemed impossible that in a few minutes she would be standing upright in the chilly morning, brushing her hair or pulling thick clothes over her skin.

'Mia,' Isabel was saying. 'Are you awake? Mia?'

'Mm. Be up soon, promise.' And she wriggled into the cocoon of her duvet for a last few minutes.

'Mia. Listen.'

Mia opened her eyes properly. What did she notice first? Her mother's face, chalky and small with dark, empty holes for eyes, or the fact that it wasn't fully light yet, and the gap between her curtains was grey? She turned her head and looked at the time on her mobile. Twenty past six.

'What's the matter? Why are you waking me?' And now she was sitting, her shoulders cold in the morning air.

Isabel was wearing her work clothes. Her hair was sticking in greasy lumps to her scalp and her skin looked ashy. Mia stared at her. 'What?' she said. 'Mum? Are you ill? Are you *dying*?'

Isabel sat on her bed and took one of Mia's hands. 'I have something to tell you,' she said. 'I'm sure it'll be all right. You're not to worry' – Didn't she know that those phrases just made things more worrying? thought Mia – 'but you should know. As long as you realize that it's going to turn out OK and there's bound to be an explanation . . .'

She didn't seem to be able to get the goal of her sentences out of her chapped and screwed-up mouth. Everything she said led up to a revelation that wouldn't come. Her hand was cold; a clutch of porcelain.

'What?' repeated Mia. 'What is it?'

'It's Johnny.'

'Johnny? Has something happened to him? Is he ill? Meningitis – he's got meningitis!' She'd read articles about it – students who had a headache and a rash and then were found dead in their rooms, or were rushed to hospital foaming at the mouth, too late to be saved.

'No, no. He's – well, we don't know where he is.'

'You don't know where he is?'

'He's gone missing.'

'Missing!' Mia's hand flew to her mouth. 'What do you mean, *missing*?'

'He –' Isabel's voice wavered. 'We've no idea where he is, but it is clear that he's chosen to go. I suppose that's a good thing. It means that he's not been kidnapped or hit over the head or anything. It means that he planned it. Maybe it's a jaunt.'

A jaunt. The word was like a tinny bauble.

'Johnny? Why?'

'We don't know.'

Isabel sat beside her and watched as half-thoughts tumbled and spun through Mia's mind: that her life had just changed, that she didn't know what to feel or how to behave, that she would be a heroine at school where she'd always been an outsider, and, tumbling over the heels of that idea, that such calculations made her into a cold, shallow and appalling monster who was incapable of real feeling, that Isabel looked old and wizened, that her skin was slack on her drawn face and wrinkled on her neck, like a turkey's, which in turn reminded her that Christmas was coming and would be ruined if Johnny wasn't back by then, that she was hungry and really wanted an English muffin with honey for breakfast but how could she eat anything? That now she had a good excuse for not doing very well in her French test, that Johnny might be dead, and why wasn't she howling and why did her thoughts jump and scatter like this? For one moment, she saw Johnny's face and was struck by such terror and pain that she felt her heart contract and a flame licked up her throat – but then it was gone, just like her dream, and she was left with dry, scraping, scrabbling preoccupations with what she should wear today, whether she should miss school, who she should tell, how her left foot had pins-and-needles.

'Mia?' Isabel said softly. 'Tell me what you're thinking.'

How could she? She saw her mother's hand on hers and wanted to pull away but couldn't. She saw that there was a stain on the carpet, where she'd spilt her tea last night. She heard sounds downstairs, then Felix's voice on the phone. This wasn't real. It was happening to someone else and she was watching to see how that person pretended to react. She wanted to be left alone to order her face and choose her words carefully, so that they would live up to the momentousness of the occasion, and at the same time she was disgusted with herself and determined to be authentic, in such a way that Johnny would approve.

Isabel was watching her face. 'I know it's a shock, sweetheart,' she said carefully, 'but we'll get him back. We will. I promise.'

Mia lay down and pulled the duvet over her head so that she was sheltered by the dim, hot cave of her own deceit. 'Wait a minute,' she mumbled.

She needed to get free of the garbage in her mind and think only of Johnny. She pictured his asymmetrical kindly face, but it dissolved and slid away. She put him at his desk, leaning over his work, frowning and concentrated, his mop of hair hanging over his eyes. She put him at the chessboard, facing a stern and ambitious Felix, wanting his father to win but unable to stop his own cunning pawns advancing and his queen bearing down on Felix's weakened army. She tried to see him as he had been the night before he had left, eating more fish pie than he wanted so that Isabel would be happy. Or with Will, tipping his head back and emitting that loud, clear yelp of mirth. He was always so well-behaved, she thought – so guarded, no cracks for anger and grief and doubt to erupt into view. Was that why he'd gone, so he could escape that obedient, charitable self?

'What are we going to do?' she asked, sitting up and rubbing the back of her hand across her eyes. Her stomach rumbled.

'You're going to school.'

'There's no way.'

'There's nothing you can do here. You'd just hang around feeling wretched.'

'I'm not going to school. I can't go to school.'

'You can.'

'Are *you* going to school?'

'No.'

'There we are, then. I'm not either. I can't. We'll find him.'

'Oh, darling. I wish we could.' For a moment, her mother's voice wobbled.

'Yes. We will.'

Mia flew out of bed. She pulled on her dressing-gown and ran downstairs. Her father was sitting in the kitchen and Mia momentarily halted: he looked so stooped and old. But she quickly regained her momentum, rushing towards him to hug him from behind, kissing the top of his head – how had she not noticed his hair was thinning before today?

'We'll find him,' she announced, pulling back a chair. 'He'll be back before the end of the day.'

Felix lifted his sore eyes to hers. Speaking seemed an immense effort. 'And how do you propose that we find him?'

'We're going to look everywhere he might be. Will! Will must know.'

'Will doesn't know,' said Isabel, coming into the kitchen

and sitting at the kitchen table, then at once standing up again, rubbing her hands up and down her legs. 'I called him.'

'He must have some idea.'

'No, he –'

'Or Zoë. Have you talked to Zoë?'

'Will has.'

'And?'

'Nothing.'

'There must be something. There must be. Where would he go? We have to make a plan.'

'I told Tamsin.' Felix stood up slowly, as if his legs were stiff. 'She's coming home.'

'When?'

'Now. She'll probably be on her way to the station.'

'Oh!' Isabel pushed her fingers through her hair. Now she looked even more dishevelled.

'Posters!' said Mia, suddenly.

'What do you mean?'

'We have to make posters – I'll find a good recent photo of him and we'll say, "Have you seen Johnny?" And give our phone number. We can photocopy multiple posters.'

'Wait,' said Felix. 'Where will you put these posters, Mia?'

'Everywhere. Here, Sheffield, London, I don't know. Why are you being so negative?'

'I'm not.'

'No. She's right, it's good,' said Isabel.

'And newspaper announcements,' continued Mia. 'In the local papers. They do it on milk bottles as well.'

'He's only been gone a few days,' said Felix. 'Do you think this is the way to proceed?'

'Only. *Only.*' Isabel turned on him fiercely. 'If he'd been gone a day, that would be worrying. *Only.* Don't you get it? And what do you mean, *proceed*? We're not in one of your bloody departmental meetings now, you know.'

'You should have a shower,' Felix said. 'Or, better still, a good hot bath. I'll get us coffee.'

'I don't want a fucking hot bath.'

'And something to eat,' continued Felix, as if she hadn't spoken. 'We have to conserve our strength.'

'We're not going on a march across the tundra,' said Isabel. 'I don't need a bath, I don't need anything to eat. I'd be sick if I put anything in my stomach.'

'Please,' said Mia. 'Don't. It scares me if you argue about this.'

'I know. I know. Sorry. I'm so sorry.' She gripped Mia hard by her shoulders and fixed her with a glittering eye. 'It will be OK. It really will be OK. Do you hear?' Mia nodded. Her mother's skin seemed to be quivering, as if an army of ants was teeming under its surface. 'I just feel I have to do something,' Isabel went on. 'Do you see? I'll explode. I can't sit and drink coffee or lie in a bath. What? You want me to relax, take it easy?'

'Isabel,' said Felix, in a quiet, stern voice. 'Listen to me. We are not going to find Johnny by plunging into the wilderness to look for him. We have to think rationally and carefully about where he might be. That's the only way to proceed.'

'You're right. Of course. I understand that.' Isabel pressed her hand against her stomach. Mia noticed that

86

she kept clutching at different parts of herself, as if she thought she had literally to hold herself together. 'But I feel –' She stopped. 'What the fuck does it matter how I feel?' she asked abruptly, in a voice of self-disgust. 'OK. I'm going upstairs to have a quick shower. You make coffee, Felix – strong, mind – and give Mia some breakfast if she wants it.' She turned in the doorway. 'The rest of the family!' she said. 'We have to call them. They might know something.'

'As soon as you come down. I'll list the calls we should make and other things to do.'

By midday, their house had filled up. Tamsin came home, spilling from the taxi that had brought her from the station in a sumptuous heap of bright clothes and dishevelled bright hair, tears gleaming on her flushed cheeks. She managed to combine radiance with grief, a kind of euphoric wretchedness that was oddly comforting, a rich stew on a cold day. She made endless pots of tea and kept hugging them all – at one point, Mia found herself squashed in an embrace with her sister and father, the buttons of Felix's cardigan pushing into her shoulder and Tamsin's perfume making her want to sneeze. It occurred to her that Tamsin had come into her own with this grim emergency: she had a role; she felt needed; she was no longer the hapless one of the family, no longer the problem. All her incoherent emotions, the gush and sweetness of her, seemed gathered together for the purpose of comfort. She mothered her mother and cradled her gaunt, resisting father against her breast.

Leah phoned three times and said she would come in

the afternoon but that – here, her voice became an urgent hiss – *it was going to be all right, did Isabel hear?* Jenny turned up, bringing with her a man called Benedict, who was a social worker and had experience of young people running away. He had a round face, a soft paunch and a gentle Irish accent, in which he told Isabel and Felix that people who went missing almost always turned up. At any other time, Isabel would have realized at once that he and Jenny were on the edge of an affair, full of middle-aged reticence and repressed excitement, but this was not any other time and she remained blind to it. Felix's teaching assistant, Connie Kramer, came round as well, and at any other time, Isabel would have seen that Connie was helplessly smitten with her husband: young, ardent and dangerous, she gazed at him as though he was one of his medieval saints and she a supplicant waiting for a miracle to fall on her from his outstretched hand. But Isabel did not see – and if she had, she wouldn't have cared. Felix seemed remote to her – she had no room in her for pity. He was simply an instrument to help bring home her son.

Mia rang Will and gave him an update, although she knew there was nothing new to say. She rang Johnny's other great friend, Baxter, to tell him – but he already knew. Will had phoned him that morning. And he'd called Jenna and Fran, Sam and Christo. And they'd called their friends, who in turn had called theirs. The word was spreading. A network stretching out, branch and twig, denser and denser – surely it would catch Johnny. Surely he couldn't slip through.

She found a photograph of her brother on the computer and cropped it so it was just his face. She wrote: 'Please help find Johnny!' in bold black print and increased the font size so that it stretched across the screen, with their phone number underneath and her own mobile number. Then she ran to the shop to get it photocopied. One hundred A4 posters. No, two hundred. How many? Every lamppost, every bus stop, every tree – like those posters for missing cats, dearly beloved, white bib and red collar, that owners were desperate to find. On the way back, seeing it was the school lunch hour, she called her friend Maud on her mobile and told her why she wasn't at school. Maud shrieked and gasped and moaned and said she would come round later, and was there anything she could do, and, oh! poor them, poor things, it would be all right, what a terrible, terrible thing to happen. She would tell people – not everyone, just the ones who mattered. And, of course, it would spread. Did you hear, did you? Mia understood, in one corner of her mind, that with this crisis she was to be fully accepted back into Maud's friendship and that when she returned to school everyone would welcome her: wholehearted sympathy, shining faces of understanding and affection, as if the last year had evaporated, leaving only a glazed shimmer in the collective memory. But she would neither forget nor forgive, only pretend.

Felix spent most of the day on the telephone. He had written out a list of people and organizations to contact and went through it methodically, putting a red tick by the side of those he had talked to. He spoke to the police, to the Missing Persons Helpline, to any of the teachers at Sheffield who had had any contact with Johnny. He started to receive emails from students there whom Kelly had talked to, and others he had contacted from Johnny's laptop whom he thought might have some information. He printed these out – beginning the collection of material about Johnny that would grow to such a volume he eventually had to clear shelves and drawers in his study to hold it.

> Dear Johnny's parents, my name is Claire Sedgewick and I am a first-year student at Sheffield. I was in Johnny's class and although I didn't talk to him very much because he was always quite quiet and I thought he was probably shy (I am very shy myself!). I liked him a lot and now I wish I had made more of an effort to be friendly. Perhaps we could have helped each other. I am writing this not because I have any idea where he might have gone, but because I wanted to say to you that you have my deepest sympathy and I can imagine what my parents would be thinking if I had disappeared . . .

'This isn't about Johnny,' said Felix. 'This is about her. Look, it goes on for ages.'

> I am a member of the Christian Union and our group is praying for your son . . .

> Hi. This is Charlie. I am one of the people in Johnny's flat. I'm writing this for all of us. We've talked a lot about what's happened and, as you can imagine, everyone is completely shocked, and also guilty that we didn't see that things were so bad for Johnny and so didn't help. But you wanted to know if there was anything we could think of that might help find him. I'm afraid there's not much to say. He kept himself to himself

90

quite a lot, though he did cook us a couple of meals quite early on – he said they were his mother's recipes. He didn't join in with much of our drinking and stuff, but he didn't seem obviously unhappy, although Kelly thinks he had an argument with someone shortly before he disappeared. She didn't think anything of it at the time, we all have arguments, especially when we've had lots to drink, but obviously now everything feels significant when it probably means nothing. He has one particular friend called Fergal who used to come round and they'd sit in Johnny's room and talk. I think they talked about deep stuff, like ethics and world politics and God and stuff. We're trying to find out who this Fergal is since he might have more insight. We'll let you know. He's very tall with round glasses and looks a bit odd, actually. We think Johnny went walking in the Peaks a few times. This probably doesn't help at all – but you said you wanted to hear anything we thought of. I'm really sorry we can't be of more help. We all like Johnny. (I played tennis with him once, in our first week, and he beat me 6–2, 6–1, and was really apologetic about it!)

Here's a question: do you want us to go through his stuff and see if we find anything? We nearly did last night, but then it felt wrong and we don't want to pry and stuff. Or maybe you're going to do it. If you are coming, let us know and we'll try and be there, because we want to help in any way and this must be very very tough for you.

Dear Mr and Mrs Hopkins, I am writing this separately because I didn't just want to put it in a group email. But I heard Johnny crying in his room one night. I went in and asked him what was wrong, and was there anything I could do. But he just curled up away from me in a ball and put his arm over his face and after a bit I went out because he obviously didn't want me to see him like that, but I stood outside his door and quite soon he stopped crying. I never knew why. We didn't ever mention it. I thought he was embarrassed that I saw him like that. I think of him all the time now. I feel I let him down. Cal xxxx

Felix handed the printouts to Isabel, who lowered herself blindly into a chair as she read. She sat bowed over for a few seconds, her hand wrapped round one side of her face, and then she started silently to sob. Her body shook. Occasionally a few choking rasps came from her. At last she turned her streaming face to Felix. 'He was crying by himself in a room, surrounded by strangers. No one comforted him. There was no one there who could help him. I should have known. I should have felt it. Why wasn't I there? Why didn't he tell me? What was so bad that he couldn't tell me?' Her face looked pulpy and raw; tears fell down it in rivulets.

'I don't know.'

'Where is he?'

'I don't know.'

That was all he could say, through the day: I don't know.

It was extraordinary how quickly word spread. Neighbours they barely knew slid notes through the front door, or knocked, standing at the threshold with solemn, anxious faces. Several girls from Mia's school arrived in a flurry, settling in Mia's room and bringing with them an air of excitement and festive unrest. Felix's sister, Suzanne, drove from Ludlow with a flask of soup and a cake tin full of over-cooked brownies, as though they were all in the Blitz. The head from Mia's school, who had always been devoted to Johnny, came by on her way home. Isabel's fellow teachers rang or emailed: they told her not to come back until things were resolved and, of course, if they could be of help, she should just say the word. Jim Gordon, a friend of Johnny's who was taking a gap year and working in a bar in town while he saved money for his travels, knocked at the door to stutter out his horror, his shock, until Tamsin took pity on him and towed him into the kitchen to give him tea and toast.

It was like a birth, a wedding and a wake; the house was the hub of constant noise and activity, and sometimes Isabel would fool herself that a machine was being set in motion that would bring Johnny home – only to realize that all the activity and busy rush were empty of meaning. Just words, bubbles of air. People were simply telling each other what they already knew, comforting each other and stirring the simmering pot of rumour and fear. And soon enough she wanted them all gone; she was tired of their noise and endless inane comfort.

As the day ended and darkness set in, the fact of Johnny's disappearance felt more real and far grimmer. The December nights were long and cold. Each of them imagined him somewhere in a black emptiness, alone and scared. Tamsin was making snacks as if Johnny's life depended on it. She rushed through rooms bearing plates of toasted-cheese sandwiches or hot mince pies. But Isabel had not eaten and neither had she slept. Every so often her eyelids would droop and her head nod forwards, but then she would jerk awake and her skull would hammer all over again with what, for a few seconds, she had forgotten. She would spring from her seat, pace the room, go into the garden and tip her head to the starry sky, sucking the cold air into her lungs.

Chapter Eight

At eight o'clock on that evening of the second day, there was a hammering on the door. When Isabel rushed to open it, wild with hope, she found Zoë on the doorstep, bundled up in a duffle coat. She looked past her, up the path, but no one else was there.

'What?' she said. 'You know something?'

'Can I come in?'

'You know where he is?'

'No. But I want to tell you something. I came from Sheffield as soon as I heard.'

'About Johnny?' Isabel laid her hand once more across her palpitating heart. 'Come into the kitchen, then.'

'Can I talk just to you somewhere more private, Mrs Hopkins?'

Zoë pulled down her hood and unwrapped her thick scarf. Isabel saw that she had been crying: her normally creamy face was creased, and mascara had smudged around her eyes.

'Of course. We can go into my husband's study. No one will disturb us there. I can even lock the door, if you want.'

As soon as they entered the room, Zoë sank on to the shabby sofa near the window and put her head into her hands.

'Please,' said Isabel. 'Tell me what you know.'

Zoë lifted her smeary face. 'We had sex.'

'You had sex? You and Johnny?'

'Yes.'

Isabel didn't know what to say or to think. She stared at Zoë, crouched on Felix's sofa. She had never much liked the girl: she was too handsome, too confident, with something impervious in her manner. And the way she patronized Mia and addressed Felix with a kind of off-hand flirtatiousness had always set Isabel's teeth on edge. But she was Will's girlfriend and had been for nearly two years now, and Will was Johnny's close friend, his best mate.

'When?' she managed to ask.

'About two weeks ago. A bit more. On a Thursday,' continued Zoë, in a flat voice. 'It wasn't meant to happen.'

How could she listen to this? Isabel wanted to put her hands over her ears to stop the words entering her and polluting her mind. She didn't want to know or imagine it. Her son with his best friend's girl.

'Is that why he's gone?' she whispered.

'I don't know. I just knew I had to tell you.'

'What happened? Why –'

'We'd arranged to meet up, just for a drink,' said Zoë. She wasn't looking at Isabel now, but speaking to the floor and reciting the words as if she had learnt them by heart. 'I hadn't seen him before that, except in passing – which was strange, if you come to think of it. For years, we'd seen each other almost every day, in the school term at least, and we'd all gone on holiday together, and then there we were at uni, living a few minutes from each other, and we didn't get together. I suppose that's what happens when you start at a new place – it was all so busy and confusing and –'

'Why don't you just tell me and get it over?' Isabel cut in.

'All right.' Zoë lifted her heavy gaze and Isabel saw a flash of hostility in her eyes. 'I'd just had a row with Will on the phone about when we were going to see each other. So I was a bit wired. And I'd had a few drinks. I wasn't drunk, though. And it was so nice to see Johnny, a face from home after all the bustle and strangeness of the first few weeks. I started crying about everything.' She stopped.

'Go on.'

'I don't know how much to say.'

'All of it.'

'I told him –' She gulped. 'You'll think I'm a slut and I'm not. I told him I'd been seeing this other guy on and off for a couple of weeks and I didn't know what to do about it or whether to tell Will. Long-distance relationships are hard,' she said, tears rolling down her cheeks.

Isabel bit back an angry retort, and then, startling them both, the phone rang and she snatched it out of its cradle. 'Yes?'

'Isabel. It's Graham. You rang me.'

'Graham – can I ring you back in about ten minutes?'

'Is it about the painting because if it is Celia says that she's arranged for –'

'No. It's not about the painting. You can have the painting whenever you want. And the rocking chair. You can have the car. You can have the house and everything in it.'

'Isabel, stop!' Felix had come on the other line now. 'Sorry, Graham. You'll understand when I tell you that –'

But Isabel slammed the phone down hard, not wanting

to hear the story again, or to hear Graham's shocked response. She turned back to Zoë, who was staring at her with her jaw slightly unhinged.

'So what did Johnny say?'

'He said if I didn't tell Will, then he would.'

'Good.'

'I said, what did he think Will would think of me, would he forgive me? And he said – he said that what really mattered was what I thought of myself and would I forgive myself. He said you had to be your own harshest judge. But then I asked him what he thought of me, to tell me honestly. I thought he would be understanding and he'd help me. I never thought of him as the kind of person who condemns anyone. And he said this really horrible thing: he said that he thought Will was too good for me and he always had. He said that in his opinion I had no empathy and that people like me don't get marked by the things that happen to them and people like Will get hurt. He said the good people were the ones who let themselves get hurt. He said it very calmly, as if he'd thought about it all in advance. I was so taken aback that I slapped him across the face and he didn't move, though it left a red mark on his cheek. So I slapped him again and he still didn't move. And then –'

'Yes?'

'Well – I just, you know – we had sex. It wasn't much, over in a few minutes. He just went along with it. As if he wasn't really there. I wanted to show him he wasn't so much better than me.' Zoë paused and Isabel waited for her to supply the end of her sentence, which she did: 'And he wasn't.'

'I see.'

'I do have empathy. I *do*,' Zoë said, sounding like a little girl. 'I know you've never really liked me very much. I've seen it in the way you act towards me —'

'I don't think that's relevant,' said Isabel. 'I'm not particularly concerned with your feelings just at the moment. I need to find Johnny. So I'm grateful that you told me about this.'

'After, he was sick. Yes. I made him physically sick. What he'd done made him sick. It made me sick as well. I wish it hadn't happened but it did. Do you think that's why he's gone? Was it me?'

'I don't know why he's gone,' said Isabel, hauling words out of herself with immense difficulty. 'I have no idea. But he sounds very unhappy, doesn't he?'

'Do you hate me?'

'Honestly?'

Zoë nodded.

'Honestly, I've no idea. I don't think I have room for things like hatred at the moment.'

'What will you do?'

'I'm going to find him.'

'Are you going to tell Will?'

'Oh, that. Why should I?'

'Do you think I should?'

'Zoë, I couldn't give a fuck.'

Later, she told Felix and he listened expressionless.

'What do you think?'

He shrugged.

'Felix?'

'I don't know, Isabel. I think you should have something to eat and sit down for one second.'

'Why?'

'You'll make yourself ill.'

'So?'

'Who's that going to help?' He took her by her scrawny shoulders. 'Now listen. You think that because Johnny is suffering, you have to suffer as well and as much – as if you can somehow take some of what he's going through on yourself.'

'That's stupid.'

'Yes. But it's what you think. You think it's immoral of me to put food in my mouth or close my eyes for one second while our son – *our* son, remember – is missing.'

'It's not that –'

'It is, Isabel. But this might not, this *will* not, be over in a day or two.'

'How do you know?'

'I don't. But I believe that Johnny is not going to suddenly turn up tomorrow, apologizing for having worried us.'

'But we're going to find him.'

'We're going to do everything possible to find him.'

'No, we're going to.'

'Isabel, dear heart –'

'Don't make me cry. If I cry I won't stop.'

'We're in it together.'

'No, Felix. We're not. We're in it alone. Both of us alone, and you know it. You with your terror and me with mine.'

'Yes, you're right,' he said, suddenly fierce. 'But you know what, Isabel? *Pretend*.'

'Pretend?'

'Yes. Pretend to the girls and pretend to me and pretend to yourself because that's the way you'll get through this, and if you don't pretend, if you let yourself feel what you're feeling, fear what you're fearing, we'll both go mad.'

Chapter Nine

So. It was ten o'clock on the evening of the second day. It felt as if those heavy, terrible days had lasted months, crawling years. Isabel closed her eyes and put her hands over her ears and concentrated. She tried to imagine being Johnny and wanting to run. Where would he go? Home, but he hadn't gone home. To Will's, but he hadn't gone there. To his half-brothers, but they'd heard nothing from him. So where? Would he simply walk out into the weather with his sleeping bag? Or maybe he'd go to London, but he didn't like big cities, even though he had been born in the capital. Of all of them, Johnny was a country boy. He knew the names of birds and trees; he loved searching for mushrooms in the woods in autumn; he'd had his own patch of soil in the garden where he'd grown courgettes successfully and failed to grow chilli plants. He would go for long walks with his parents long after Tamsin and Mia had refused, and off on rambles on his own, especially when he was in the middle of exams. When he was eleven, they had given him a telescope for his birthday and he had spent hours looking up at the night skies, which in their village in Suffolk were very beautiful, the stars thick and bright. Would he really go to London?

Then she had a thought: what about the little house near Woodbridge, whose green lawn spread down to the widening estuary, where they used to go sometimes for weekends? It was only a few miles from here, and it often stood empty out of season: the heating was unpredictable. Johnny loved it there. He and Isabel had often swum in the heavily tidal waters, sweeping out to sea and then battling back again, and he'd climbed the trees in the woods behind the house. Isabel could see his face now, between the tangle of branches, smiling down at her. Or kneeling on the mulch of the forest floor, scrutinizing mushrooms he would take home to identify. He had found fluted yellow chanterelles there once, and even cepes mushrooms that he and Isabel had cleaned and cooked in garlic. He had been so proud of himself, his face glowing. She could hear his voice as he'd held them out in his cupped hands: 'Mama, look! Are these what I think they are?'

So, of course, that was where he would go: home but not home. He would know she would guess where he was; he would be waiting for her and she could bring him back with her.

She didn't tell Felix, but went straight out to the car without even putting on a jacket or picking up her mobile phone, only remembering at the last minute to scrawl a note: 'Gone out. Back soon. Don't worry xxx'. It was dark and cold and the old Fiat spluttered and coughed before starting. But she was off, the car nosing its way along the narrow lanes, its headlights picking out small rodents that spun across the road.

After several miles and a couple of wrong turns, she was bumping down the potholed drive to where the little house stood, its front doorway facing inland, and behind it the windows looking out towards the sea. No lights were on so it was probably empty, but Isabel stopped well short of the house just in case, and eased her body out of the driving seat. Her heart was bumping painfully. It wasn't entirely dark because the moon was glimmering between light clouds. She walked along the drive, her feet crunching on gravel and mud, and stopped at the porch. She rattled the door, which was locked, of course, then pressed her face against one of the windows, straining to see inside. She made out the shapes of furniture, a sofa, a piano she remembered from when they'd been there, Mia picking out simple tunes with one finger, Johnny playing to accompany Felix on the violin. There were no sounds except the rasp of her breathing and the jolt of her heart.

She walked round to the back of the house, brushing against the plants in the borders. Once, the low-hanging branch of a tree stroked her cheek with a wet thick finger and made her start. The grass on the lawn was long and wet; she could feel water seeping into her shoes and she realized how cold she was, just a thin cardigan protecting her against the night air. He would go to the estuary, she thought, so she made her way down the lawn and then she heard the waves, so faint they were more like ripples, licking at the shoreline. On the other side of the wide estuary were the yellow lights of a hamlet: they looked so welcoming, glinting there and reflecting off the water in wavering lines. She could just make out the shapes of small boats at anchor, bobbing on the water, and just hear the sound of halyards chinking in the wind that blew in from the open sea.

Isabel stood quite still and waited. She knew, of course,

that Johnny was not here, she had always known he wouldn't be – and at the same time she expected to see his figure coming towards her down the lawn, or emerging from the massed trees beyond the neglected garden. After several minutes, she tried calling his name, quietly at first and then louder, until her voice cracked and the broken syllables hung in the air. Finally, into the reverberating stillness, she heard herself calling out so violently that her voice was just a frantic scratch of sound, 'Somebody? Anybody! Please help me! Somebody help!'

Johnny wasn't there. Johnny wouldn't come. He had gone to where she couldn't follow. He couldn't hear her call and her longing hands couldn't find him and draw him back. Her body hurt. She wanted to curl up in velvet blackness until the agony subsided. She inched forward to the river's edge, so that the toes of her shoes were touching the quietly slapping flow. It was high tide; there was grass under the shallow water, lying flat. Slack tide, she thought, and soon it would withdraw, leaving puddled mudflats, and the little boats would tip, and the lights from the other side would break up on the glistening greyness of the exposed estuary bed. The moon, moving out from a cloud, hung above her and glimmered at her from the water. It was a world of darkness and of drowning lights, and for a moment she thought how she, too, could ease herself into the waters and let go. It would be a relief, she thought, a great kindness.

It was not really a thought at all, just a wisp floating through her mind, like the leaves and twigs that bobbed past on the river's tide. And then she thought of Mia, her clever little closed face, her adolescent rages, her fierceness and her gallantry. She thought of Tamsin, so needy and so hungry to be needed, so generous and so often let down. She thought of Felix with his flinty blue eyes and his flinty sad face. She was ashamed of herself. She turned and walked slowly back to the car.

Chapter Ten

For a few hours, the four of them slept, each wrapped in their dreams that none of them would remember when they woke: a sea, a crowd, white faces like petals in the blackness, Johnny gone and Johnny coming home, a lurching fall upwards to remember afresh, then descend again into forgetting. Frost silvered the lawn. The owl cried. Wind sighed in the bare trees.

The following day, Isabel rose early, even before Felix, who was usually up hours before her. She was amazed that she had slept at all, but she had, though fitfully. She showered and washed her hair, then put on clean clothes, black jeans and a red shirt that was soft and long, and hung loosely off her. She went downstairs and cleared the kitchen, which was full of dirty pots and pans, and used plates. There were mugs on every surface and she collected them up and put everything into the dishwasher. She picked up clothes that were strewn on sofas and chairs. She rubbed a floorcloth over the hall tiles, which were muddy from all the people who'd entered the house yesterday. She tried to remember what day it was, and came up with Thursday – could that be right? Only the third day? Mia should go to school. Tamsin should return to Southampton, if not immediately then at least by the end of the weekend.

There were messages on the pad next to the phone, left yesterday evening while she had been out, and she picked them up, scanning them: Graham had called again, Jenny had called, Mary had called, Johnny's tutor had called ('Not with news!' Felix had written next to her name, sparing Isabel false hope), Will had called, Baxter, Felix's sister was coming again on Friday, so was Felix's second son, Ben. Countless people had phoned, written emails, put letters through their front door. Isabel didn't even recognize some of their names. Someone called Rosalie had left a small cyclamen in a patterned pot on their doorstep, with a card next to it, but who was Rosalie? Who was Shane?

She put down the message pad. It was seven o'clock and the sun had not yet risen. She made a pot of strong tea, waited for it to brew, then took a mug up to Felix and Mia. Felix was sitting on the side of the bed, staring at the gap between the curtains where the sky was just beginning to lighten.

'I'm going for a run,' he said.

'Right.'

'You probably think that's selfish.'

'No.'

'Then I'm going to get in touch with the local paper.'

'What for?'

'To run a story on Johnny.'

'Do you think it will help?'

'Maybe. The more people who know he's gone, the more people will look out for him. And perhaps Johnny will see it too.'

'Then of course we should do that.'

'Where were you last night?'

'Just driving.'

'Looking?'

'Yes.'

He nodded, as if to himself, and stood up from the bed. He was wearing blue striped pyjamas that were slightly loose on him and his left cheek had crease marks from where he had been lying. Isabel thought that he looked old. Very old and very tired. The ghost of pity stirred in her heart.

'Go for your run,' she said.

She left Felix. Then, stepping across damp towels and through more ranks of dirty mugs, she went to sit beside Mia. She watched her daughter as she slept, thinking that she looked a bit like a boy, with her emphatic eyebrows and her short hair lying in streaks across her forehead. At last, Isabel put a hand on her shoulder and shook it gently. 'Mia?'

Mia's eyes opened at once, and for a few moments she stared at Isabel without blinking. Then she closed them again and said, 'No news.' It wasn't a question.

'No.'

'What are we going to do?' She'd lost the fervour of yesterday; her voice was flat.

'I think you should go back to school today, Mia.'

'Is that possible?'

'What do you mean, possible?'

'I don't know. Nothing seems real. Can I actually go to school as if nothing's happened and sit in lessons and listen to people talk about their boyfriends and their spots?'

Mia sat up and Isabel handed her the mug of tea, which

she sipped at carefully before putting it down on the bed-side table.

'Of course it will be strange.'

'Everyone will look at me and whisper. There'll be this horrible sympathy. People who've been bitchy for years will suddenly be all nice and sweet.'

'Well. Does that matter so much?'

'You mean in comparison to Johnny going? Of course not.'

'I didn't mean that. I meant that perhaps it's not hypocrisy but kindness.'

'I don't want to be pitied.'

'Why?' Tears pricked in Isabel's sore eyes and she blinked them away before Mia could notice. 'What's so wrong with pity?'

'You make it sound like he's dead.'

'He's not dead.' The sharpness of her voice startled both of them. 'We're going to find him. I'm not going to rest until I find him – you have my pledge on that.'

To Isabel's surprise, Mia laid her head on her mother's lap.

'You smell nice,' she mumbled into the red shirt.

Isabel could feel from the dampness that Mia was crying. She stroked her daughter's silky black hair and rubbed the back of her neck. How long was it since Mia had let her do this?

'I had a shower,' was all she said.

'Mama?' *Mama* – each syllable equally stressed – was Johnny's name for her. Tamsin called her 'Mum' and Mia usually addressed her as 'Isabel' or, in mock sternness, 'Mother'.

'Yes?'

'I'm sorry.'

'What are you sorry for, my darling?'

'I've been horrible to you recently.'

'Oh – not really.'

'Yes, I have. I've known it but I couldn't stop myself. I feel lousy and then I hit out.'

'I don't mind. I usually understand. And I'm not so easy myself.'

'It shouldn't have taken Johnny going –'

And then she was crying in earnest, her body jolting on Isabel's lap and her snotty tears and dribbles seeping through her shirt and trousers. Isabel leant over her, murmuring, telling her that it was going to be all right.

'You promise?' Mia said, raising herself at last, her face swollen, her voice like a young child's.

How could Isabel promise? She knew only that Johnny had disappeared into thin air.

'I promise,' she said, making herself meet Mia's bloodshot eyes.

'All right, then,' said Mia, with a sniff. 'I'll go to school. You'll tell me if anything happens?'

'Of course. But listen – this might take ages.'

'You mean, like weeks?'

'Like weeks. Or months, Mia.'

'Months!'

'Probably not – but we don't know. We don't know where or why he's gone.'

'But we know he's not dead. Don't we?'

'The police haven't found anything. And there's been nothing from the hospitals either.'

No body had been discovered: that was the way they had put it to Felix yesterday. There were stories Isabel had read in the paper, not really paying attention to the details, about corpses discovered months and years after, but she pushed the thought away from her and wrapped an arm around Mia's shoulders.

'Up you get. Have a shower and I'll make some toast for you. Then I can run you into school for once. You're probably too late to catch the bus.'

'OK,' she said, with new docility.

Tamsin, who had always been such a copious weeper, blubbering into Isabel's lap, did not want comfort: today, she was the comforter. Isabel listened to Tamsin telling her how everything was going to come right. She let her elder daughter bustle around her, sitting her down at the kitchen table with a mug of coffee and a piece of toast and marmalade that Isabel couldn't eat – it felt like leather in her mouth – clearing up around her, leaping off to answer the phone when it rang. The ringing came like the peal of a miracle being born, and the shrill sound of despair. But each time, it was simply another well-wisher.

'Are you going back today?' Isabel asked.

'No!' Tamsin seemed shocked by the idea. 'Of course not.'

'There's nothing left to do here.'

'How can you say that?'

'I don't want you to put your life on hold, Tamsin.'

'This *is* my life. This is my home, Johnny's my little brother, you're my mother. What do you expect me to do?'

'How long will you stay?'

'Until we find Johnny.'

'This week, next week, next year?'

'Mum!'

The door opened and Felix came in, dripping from the rain outside. 'I'll be five minutes,' he announced, and disappeared again.

'You don't mean that,' Tamsin said. 'You mustn't say things like that.'

'On Sunday you'll go back to Southampton.'

'I don't want to!'

'Dad and I will find Johnny,' said Isabel. 'And if there's anything at all you can do, we'll tell you.'

'I want to help.'

'You have helped. You do.'

Isabel and Felix sat together in the police station. The officer in front of them had a livid cold sore at the corner of his mouth that he kept touching, cautiously, with his tongue, and a rash on his neck. He looked so young. How could a boy like him look for a boy who had gone missing? Isabel felt anger rush through her: they should have put someone older, more competent, authoritative and compassionate, in charge of the case – which wasn't really a case, of course, as this young man had already told them.

'Because we can assume from all we know that he went voluntarily,' he said, not looking at them but at his notes.

'Yes,' said Felix.

'But that doesn't make it less urgent,' added Isabel. 'It doesn't mean you shouldn't treat it as an emergency.'

'Mrs –'

'He could be in danger.'

'Mrs Hopkins.' He was young enough to be one of Johnny's callow friends, and speaking to her pleadingly, urging her to be reasonable. 'You must see, there is very little we can do. Johnny is eighteen, he left university of his own accord. He's a grown-up.'

'You have no idea what you're talking about.'

'Ssh,' said Felix to her. 'Have you examined CCTV footage?'

'In selected places. We can't do more than that. I mean – where are we supposed to be looking? And in what time frame?'

'Everywhere,' said Isabel. 'For the biggest time frame possible. We know when he was last seen.' Even to her own ears, she sounded ridiculous. She bit her lip and looked down at her tightly plaited hands.

'Apparently they've looked at the tapes from Sheffield bus and train stations over what seems to be the relevant period. Only one of the cameras in the train station was actually operative.'

'Nothing?'

'No.'

'But this is useless,' said Isabel. 'This is like pretending to look.'

'What would you like us to do, Mrs Hopkins?'

'What about stations in London?'

'All of them?'

'Have you checked ferry terminals and airports? He took his passport, you see – did I tell you that?'

'Yes. But he's not a criminal and he's not a minor. If he went of his own free –'

'Yes, yes. Own free will. But we still have to find him.'

'You have to see it from the police's point of view, Mrs Hopkins. Young people have lots of reasons for running away and not wanting to be found.'

'What? What are you suggesting? You think he's running away from *us*?'

'No, no.' His face had turned a blotchy red. He kept looking towards Felix for help, but Felix seemed to have stopped speaking: he was frowning as if in intense thought. 'I'm not suggesting anything. But there are rules we have to follow. Procedures. Priorities.'

'Oh, God.' The anger and energy drained from her.

'I'm sorry. His name and photograph have been circulated. He's on our computer. If anything comes up –'

'He's just a boy.' She tried one last time. 'Out there alone. Don't you understand?'

'I'm sorry.'

'Yes.' Isabel stood up. 'Come on, Felix.'

'Let us know if anything changes.'

'Daddy. It's me, Isabel. Bernard?'

His name must have struck a note in his memory. Bernard Cornish was nearly blind, but he turned his foggy eyes in her direction and aimed a befuddled look that fell on the half-closed curtain and the damp patch of sky. She took his mottled hand, the bruised skin loose under her touch.

'I have something to tell you.'

'Why tell him?' Felix had said before she left. 'What's the point? Even if he understands, he'll simply be alarmed and distressed, but then will forget about it, and you'll have to tell him all over again. Blow after blow falling on the old man, what's the purpose?'

'He's not demented, he's had a stroke. What if he can't communicate with us but he can still understand things?'

'He doesn't understand.'

'You can't be sure. If it was you lying in that bed or sitting propped up in that chair, shut into your own body as if it was a tomb, what would you want? Would you want to know? Or would you want people just to leave you in vegetable ignorance, treating you as if you were already dead?'

'But he doesn't know, Isabel. That's the point. Face it.'

'Then it doesn't matter if I tell him, does it?'

It was a discussion they'd had many times, in different forms. Isabel always insisted that her father could still be lucid, and that beneath his slipped face, behind his unfocused gaze, there might be an active intelligence at work. Felix felt that she spent hours of each week lavishing care on her unresponsive parent to no purpose except to punish herself.

'Think of yourself. You've looked after him all your life.'

'And I'm not going to stop now. This is his time of need.'

'It was always his time of need, and never yours. You've devoted yourself to his need.'

Now that she was in the small room whose window looked out over green fields and then, just visible over the brow of the hill, the open sea, she found that she couldn't bring herself to tell him about Johnny after all. Johnny had always been his favourite – the boy, the heir – and he was so very frail. He was propped against the bolster, the sheets lying over his body as if it was skin and air, his head lolling on his chest. Wisps of white hair lay across his thin, throbbing skull. His breath was hoarse and uneven, like a grumbling complaint rising from his deflating lungs. Once he'd been plump and his hair had been a gingery blond, like Graham's now. He'd had a moustache that would tickle her when she'd kissed his cheek, and he'd smelt of beer and tobacco and sweat. The room smelt of the hyacinths she'd brought him last week, and the talcum power the nurse used on his emaciated body, but he smelt of dust and decay, of things that crumble in cellars and attics, or underneath floorboards, invisible.

'Daddy,' she repeated, and sat down beside him.

The book she had been reading to him lay on the table and she picked it up and opened it at the marker. When he had first had his stroke and been moved to this nursing home, Isabel had spent hours having a one-way conversation with him: brightly informing him of all that was going on in her life, relating bits of news, telling him her opinions of things, never speaking her feelings or voicing her distress, but trying to jolly him along and give him a hold on the life he seemed to have fallen away from. These conversations always felt artificial to her, and she was sometimes overcome with a heavy self-consciousness that ground her to a halt mid-sentence. A year or so ago, she had decided she should simply read to him, leaving pauses in case – although she knew it would never happen – he should suddenly want to make himself heard. She had begun by reading to him the books that he had once enjoyed, although he had never been a great reader.

She'd ploughed through several by P. G. Wodehouse, but there was something utterly depressing about hearing her voice go through these sprightly, jocund comedies and seeing his eyes stare glassily in front of him, the sun shining too hotly through the windows. Quite soon she had switched to the books she herself loved, like *Villette*, *Madame Bovary* and *To the Lighthouse*. She knew that she was reading to herself: it felt sombre and dislocating to sit in her father's room, close by him, hearing his stertorous breathing, seeing the rise and fall of his hollow chest, and for hours read aloud words she already knew well. Sometimes she would almost fall asleep, then jerk awake to the clip of shoes in the corridor, to see him still there, unseeing eyes fixed on the wall, shapeless mouth drooling and the sun moving over the grass outside, evening shadows stretching long fingers down towards the sea. It had been Johnny who suggested she read children's books to her father, and this was what she now did. She brought the books she remembered her mother reading to her, a soft voice in the dusk, and that Isabel had read to Tamsin, Johnny and Mia, before taking them to her children at school. *Pippi Longstocking*, the Moomintroll books, *Winnie-the-Pooh*, childish ditties and rhymes, Dr Seuss. So, in the end room of her father's life, all these different childhoods were played out simultaneously to the unknowing audience of the ancient, frail man with thin white hair who had become like a child himself.

This morning she was reading Edward Lear. It was near enough to nonsense to be bearable. She was hearing the words, rocked by the rhythm, and thinking of Johnny, and she was watching the jackdaws outside, and surreptitiously fishing her mobile from her pocket to make sure it was turned on, which, of course, she knew it was, and to glance at the screen in case anyone had called, although, of course, she knew they hadn't, and she was also remembering the day that she and Graham had moved Bernard Cornish out of the house she had grown up in and he had grown old in. It had been as though her father had died: packing up his possessions, deciding who would get what, holding up small objects to remember previously forgotten fragments from their childhood. She and Graham had, for those insular few days, been close again, giggling and weeping over the selves they had once been: stupid things that brought them back to what they had lost – not just school reports, letters and diaries, leather-bound books, gilt-framed photographs, but the old biscuit tin, which had always been in the back of the cupboard, dented and rusting; the hopelessly soft-bristled hairbrush with the tapestry back; the sewing box, with needles pushed into its quilted lining and a silver thimble that had probably rested on her mother's finger – did anyone use thimbles now? Her father's old-fashioned shaving kit. Isabel remembered how, after her mother had died, she would watch him every morning in the bathroom while he shaved. She could feel now the way she had sat then, hunched with her back to the wall, her arms wrapped round her knees, nightdress pulled down tight, while he lathered foam over his cheeks and chin, his lips, eyes and wet pink mouth emerging shockingly from the whiteness, then run the sharp razor, stroke by stroke, over his skin. She could hear the satisfying rasp. Then he would scoop cold water over his face, pat on lotion and examine himself in the mirror over the basin.

Why was it that that self-examination had always made her feel tender and sad? Something about the mixture of anxiousness and complacency that stirred her heart, morning after morning. She had felt the same every time she saw her children, thinking themselves unseen, look at themselves in the mirror. Especially Mia during her worst times at school, when bitchy groups of girls had turned on her while friends had tittered and abandoned her: she had confronted herself in the long mirror in her room like a soldier going into battle, making sure she was defended, fixing a careless look on her small, vulnerable face.

'Daddy,' she said at last, closing the book and putting it beside his bed. She always felt like a little girl when she called him that, but she had never known him by another name. And yet she had never really felt like a little girl to her father, more like an inadequate replacement wife or a grotesquely tiny other, so perhaps she had used the word in a kind of appeal. He had been a testy, self-pitying, weak kind of parent, a collapsed figure who blamed everything that went wrong on the tragedy of his wife's death. He had felt that life had dealt him a bad hand; he had looked at his two children with an aggrieved air.

About three years after Kathleen Cornish had died, just as Isabel was entering her secretive adolescence in which all her torments and panics were kept under wraps, Bernard had met a woman called Alison Stowe and married her. She had been a boxy, mild-mannered, slightly ineffectual woman. She had never been unkind, or unfair, or even impatient, as far as Isabel could remember. But neither had she seemed imaginative or empathetic about what the two children were feeling about their lost mother and her replacement. There was something about her unruffled demeanour, like a Victorian housekeeper's disdainful calm, that had driven Isabel demented. Her silence and passivity seemed a particularly insidious kind of control, a self-righteous act of aggression. And she imagined her getting ready for bed with her father, just down the corridor and within hearing: unzipping her skirt, rolling down her tights, loosening her peppery-blonde hair, a woman stepping out of her disguise night after night. She had died nearly ten years ago, and it was only at her funeral that Isabel had allowed herself to think that perhaps her stepmother had actually been a kind-hearted and tactful woman. It must have been lonely for her, in a house haunted by the first wife, with two resentful yet demanding children and a cold fish for a husband, who wept easily for himself but shed no tears for others. What had she got in return? A home that wasn't a home, a marriage that was barely a marriage, children who weren't her own, other people's ghosts.

Her phone vibrated in her pocket and she dug it out with fumbling fingers.

'Hello?'

'It's just me, Felix. Ma and Helen and the baby are on their way. They'll be here in about an hour. When will you be home?'

'Why? Why are they coming?'

'It's obvious why.'

'They can't do anything. Helen's got to look after Lucy, and we'll have to look after your mother. She can't come, Felix.'

'But she is, and you know her, there's no stopping her.'

'Oh, God, Felix.'

'She said that this is the time for the family to rally round.'

'Fuck that.'

'She won't get in the way.'

'You know that's nonsense.'

'She wants to help.'

'She's eighty-four, Felix. What on earth can she do to help?'

'Nevertheless, she and Helen will be at the house within the hour. Helen's already picked her up.'

'So your poor daughter-in-law has driven all the way from Birmingham to Cambridge, with her baby, to collect your mother and bring her here?'

'Yes. Are you coming back soon?'

'OK, OK.' She knew from his voice and the dullness in her heart that there was no news but she couldn't stop herself asking: 'You've not heard anything?'

'No. I would have said. Just come home.'

Felix was tall and lean, with the faint stoop of someone who as a boy had been embarrassed by his height, but his mother was short, squat and solid on the earth, like a troll. Isabel was sure that every year she shrank a bit more. Used to being the smallest in a group, she found it strangely disconcerting to bend down to an adult to hug them. Miranda Hopkins stood with her feet apart, as if squaring up for a fight; her body was bundled up in layers of strange clothing, swathes of cotton and tweed, buttons and zips in odd places. She carried a thick walking stick whose studded tip she directed at people when she was making a point, and she was wearing a leather beret pulled down over her forehead. Beneath it, her eyes burnt in a face full of cracks and crevices; there was a wart on her cheek with stiff bristles sprouting from it. She looked as though she had been hacked from a rock, or dug up from the soil – a cross between a pumpkin, a fossil and a flint, magnificently dumpy and unyielding.

'Hello, Miranda.' Isabel felt how robust the old woman was through all the bulges and knobs of her clothes – so different from her father, with his ghost hair and twig hands, his clothes hanging over absences and collapsed spaces.

'What have you been doing to yourself?' Miranda Hopkins glared at her with Felix's eyes, Johnny's eyes. 'You look absolutely dreadful.'

'Probably.'

'Starving yourself, I suppose.'

As a matter of fact, Isabel couldn't remember the last time she'd eaten more than a dutiful bite of indigestible toast, one sip of unswallowable soup. But she didn't feel hungry at all. 'I suppose so,' she agreed. She couldn't face the tank charge, wanted to lie down in the drive and let Miranda roll straight over her, digging into her with her stick as she went, and on into the house. Tamsin could deal with her.

She turned to Helen, who had clambered out of the car looking slightly the worse for wear – a combination, Isabel supposed, of having Miranda as a passenger for the last hour and a half, and of her three-month-old child in the baby seat in the back, red face screwed up in frantic rage, gummy mouth open in a ceaseless roar, arms waving desperately, like a drowning swimmer about to go under for the final time.

'Hi, Helen. You'd better come in.' She knew she sounded ungracious but didn't care. She couldn't think why Helen – the partner of Felix's eldest son Rory – had driven halfway across the country with her tiny bawling baby simply to deliver Miranda to them to look after.

'Oh, Isabel.' Helen's eyes filled with tears. 'I'm so so so very sorry. I can't begin to imagine what –'

'I think Lucy needs changing,' Isabel cut in.

'Oh, God, she does.' Helen's face crumpled. 'But listen, Isabel, I'm not staying long. I'll go back after a quick lunch. I don't want to get in your way.'

'I've no idea what food there is in the house,' said Isabel. 'Maybe there are some eggs. Perhaps Tamsin can get you all something.'

Tamsin could. She cooked a Spanish omelette with chunks of spicy chorizo in it and a green salad. She'd been to the shops, she explained, and filled the fridge. Everyone sat round the table; the winter sun shone through the kitchen window, on the flowers that had been delivered that morning from Isabel's colleagues at the school, with a little card simply reading, 'Take as long as you like, with all our sympathy' – as if Johnny was dead, thought Isabel, savagely. She sat down and took a gulp of water from her glass, staring at the slab of omelette Tamsin landed on her plate. She'd be sick if she put it in her mouth, grease and salt and threads of melted cheese. She was suddenly boiling hot, and thought if she had to sit here for another minute she would explode.

'So where's this grandson of mine gone?' asked Miranda, in her too-loud voice.

Isabel put her unused fork down and stared at her. Felix gave a bleak shrug. The baby, lying beside Helen's chair in its tipped baby seat, woke and gave a loud shriek, then subsided again.

'And why?'

'We don't know,' said Felix.

'*Cherchez la femme*,' Miranda murmured.

'Please stop,' Isabel managed to say. She wasn't quite sure how she was still upright in her chair.

'Why? We need to face facts, not shy away from them.'

'Really? And what facts do you have to give us, Miranda?'

'You should eat some of that omelette. You look awfully peaky.'

'You finish it. I've got things I need to do. Urgently.' And she rose abruptly from her chair.

But, of course, there was nothing she needed to do, nowhere else to go. She blundered her way to the foot of the stairs and sat on the first step. Felix followed and sat beside her. He took her hand in his and held it on his knee.

'What shall we do now?' asked Isabel, after several minutes.

'I don't know.'

Chapter Eleven

Isabel had thought that the first few days of discovery must be the worst of her life, and that nothing could ever match them for the terror and surging grief. But perhaps this fourth day outstripped them. At the start of the nightmare, she had at least acted, even if her actions were furiously ineffectual: she had driven, run, searched, looked, hoped and howled out her son's name. Today she was becalmed in the foul standing water of her emotions.

When Felix retreated once more to his study, where he was waiting to receive phone calls from the local newspaper and perhaps from the police and the university, and where she knew he would be crouched over his computer and Johnny's, researching, collating, drawing up lists, ticking off tasks, underlining things that were urgent, trying to turn mystery and fear into grids and charts, she went to the bottom of the garden. The guinea pig hadn't been fed for three days and its porcelain bowl was empty, as was its water bottle, so she filled both, then went and sat by the run. The grass was damp and the trees were bare, just a few brown leaves clinging to the branches. She lit a cigarette. She was usually a secret, ashamed smoker but now she didn't care if Tamsin or Miranda observed her; she could see them through the lit kitchen window, still sitting at the table like allies. She wondered, listlessly, what they would be talking about. She didn't really care. She didn't care about anything – she was suddenly so weary and hopeless that it was almost possible to say she barely even cared about Johnny. Ash powdered from the end of her cigarette. The world seemed, at this moment, quite dead to her, or she was dead to the world.

Life returned in the form of Will, who, a few hours later, knocked on the door to stand in front of Isabel with bright eyes and the optimism of youth upon him.

'Isabel,' he said, impulsively kissing her on both cheeks, then flushing. She saw that he was shocked by her appearance.

'Will! What are you doing here?'

'I came up today. Of course. You didn't think I wouldn't, did you?'

'I didn't know. It's very nice of you. Come in.'

'Just for a bit.' He followed her into the hall, talking as he went. 'I've got lots to organize.'

'Organize?'

'It's not just me who's here. There are loads of us, or there will be – Baxter and Lewis and the gang. Baxter's dad's booked a mini-coach thing that seats about thirty people to take us all to London tomorrow. Mia's coming too with her friends – I've just been to the school and seen her.'

'I don't understand.'

'We're going to London tomorrow to look for him.'

'London?'

'It was Baxter's idea, really. He said that was the most likely place for Johnny to go – I mean, that's where most people go, isn't it, if they ... you know?' He stopped, embarrassed, and looked at her with tender concern.

'So about twenty of us are going with those posters Mia said you've got, and she's just gone to get some more done. She and Maud should be back here soon, though. We'll all spread out and go to the obvious places. You know, Centrepoint and down by the stations and things like that. Parks and stuff. Under bridges. We're working it out. The head's coming as well, and the librarian and his wife, and so is Mr Lowry, his old science teacher. Six thirty sharp we're leaving. We'll be in London by half past eight.'

'Oh, Will.'

'So, are you going to join us – you and Felix?'

'Yes. Well, I can't speak for Felix, but of course I'm coming. Maybe Tamsin. This is – well, I don't know what to say.'

'Don't say anything. We're going to get him back. You'll see. Ah, don't cry, Isabel. Please don't cry. You'll set me off too. You've always been so good to all of us. You were like my second home. Johnny's my best mate.'

Isabel smiled at him and, with the tip of her finger, wiped away the tears that were welling in her eyes. He didn't know about Zoë and Johnny, then: would he still be standing here like this if he did, so full of noble hope?

'We're bringing sandwiches for breakfast and lunch – it'll be like going on a school trip again,' he said, on a hiccupy laugh that threatened to turn into a sob. 'Except this time the teachers are doing what we tell them for once. The coach will be outside the school from six fifteen onwards, OK?'

'Yes. We'll be there.'

'Oh – and the weather forecast is for a cold day, so wrap up warm,' he continued.

She saw that he was excited by his new authority and stirred up by the desire to help. His eyes glowed. She touched his shoulder and said softly, 'Thank you, Will.'

'No. It's nothing. I mean, we've got to find him, right?'

'Right.'

The atmosphere in the house had changed. Will had introduced a sense of purpose once more, and everyone felt it, even Miranda who sat at the kitchen table, very slowly grating cheese for sandwiches, her rheumatic fingers twisted round the grater, her swollen knuckles catching on the blades. Tamsin made curried parsnip soup that she would decant into a Thermos flask in the morning. Mia came back with Maud and two other girls and they pored over the London *A-Z*, planning where to go, and making phone calls on their mobiles. Isabel called friends. Jenny said she would come with her daughter Holly and son Max, who were gutted, she said, absolutely gutted, and Isabel heard the tears in her voice; Leah would also come; another friend, Mary, who lived near Wimbledon, said she would meet Isabel during the day. The troops were being summoned.

Only Felix was the party pooper. He stared at Isabel. 'London's a vast city.'

'I know that.'

'Why would he be there, rather than somewhere – anywhere – else?'

'It's just the most likely place. And I think, I just have this feeling, that if we're all there we have to find him.'

'Do you?'

'Don't say it like that.'

'Don't have such high hopes. They'll be dashed.'

'That's defeatist.'

'Isabel, most people who go missing do return. They aren't found. They return.'

'So we simply sit and wait.'

'I'm doing more than that. I'm contacting the right people. I'm being strategic.'

'Oh! *Strategic.*'

'You say it like an insult – as if dashing around in the middle of the night is somehow better. As if going mad was a productive activity.'

'I didn't mean that. But I'm not going mad.'

'I know you – you feel you have to be physically active, out there, looking through doorways. Showing his photograph to whoever you happen to pass by. London is a city of millions of people. Britain is a country of tens of millions. By all means go and search the streets if it makes you feel better – but don't have insane expectations.'

'You aren't obliged to come. Stay in your study drawing up plans.'

'We all have our different ways, Isabel.'

'OK, I do know that. I'm sorry. I'm lashing out.'

'And don't be rude to my mother.'

'No. Sorry. She just shouldn't be here.'

'Where would you want to be if one of your children was in distress? She's here because she's my mother.'

'I know. But she can't help.'

'She can't go out and search, that's true, but perhaps it helps me to have her here – have you thought of that? And helps her. And she's not doing any harm, is she?'

'No. I'm sorry. I was wrong. I see that – I feel I should

be making an extra effort for her, that's all. And I can't. I simply can't.'

'Nobody expects you to make an extra effort, Isabel. People want to help you for once.'

'Yes, yes. Sorry.' Isabel was chastened. 'Will you come?'

'No. I'll stay here. I'll answer the phone, I'll pick up messages.' He tried to smile. 'At HQ,' he said.

Isabel tried to smile too. *Pretend*, he had urged her; *just pretend*. She could feel her mouth splitting open and her skin stretching tight. *I could tear myself up*, she thought. *I could fall into scraps and fragments of myself.*

'Yes. Good. We need that,' she said.

She rose the next morning, day five of a sentence whose end was undetermined, at half past five. It was still night, not even a faint band on the horizon where the sun would rise. And it was cold. When she pressed her face to the icy windowpane she could see that the grass was frosted. She went into the bathroom and washed her face, cleaned her teeth, then dressed in the clothes she had put out in the corridor the night before, so as not to wake Felix. Will had told her to dress warmly, so she pulled on a T-shirt, then a long-sleeved top, then a warm mustard-yellow jumper. *Layers*, she heard herself saying. That was what she had always told the children to wear when they were going out for the day. It had become a family joke – everyone would chorus it before she had time to speak. She made a pot of tea and took mugs to Tamsin and Mia, whispering to them in the darkness that it was time to get up. It reminded her of going on holiday when they were little – getting up before the dawn, lifting bags and bodies into the waiting car, driving off as the sun came up, handing squashy honey sandwiches and apples into the back seat.

She made a Thermos of coffee and heated Tamsin's soup, which she then poured into a flask. Upstairs, a lavatory flushed and feet padded along the corridor. Doors opened and shut. A cockerel crowed from three houses down, hoarse and loud. Tamsin came into the kitchen and sat at the table, yawning widely; she was wearing a red quilted jacket and was clutching a woollen hat with earflaps and a pair of mittens. Mia joined them, her hair in soft tufts. They didn't speak except about practical things – to remember the stack of posters that were on Felix's desk and the sandwiches that were in the fridge, to take their Oyster cards for the London Underground, not to forget their mobile phones. When they climbed into the car, Isabel had to get out again to scrape the ice off the windscreen. The steering wheel was cold enough to hurt her hands.

The coach was already waiting, and a few figures stood around outside it, hands thrust deep into pockets or holding mugs of coffee. The driver was smoking a cigarette, and when he saw Isabel, he must have realized she was the mother because he opened the door and, taking her delicately by the elbow, ushered her inside. Gradually the coach filled; young people Isabel knew or recognized clambering aboard in fleeces and hoodies, ears plugged up with music, faces raw with the cold and the early morning. Will walked up and down the aisle, ticking off names. Jenny arrived with Max, Holly and a box of warm pastries that she handed out. Leah arrived with hot chocolate and face wipes. Zoë walked down the coach in a group of four or five, heading for the back seat. She was wearing blue eye shadow, as though she was heading for a nightclub, and avoided Isabel's gaze. The head, Maureen Tench, was there, and the overweight librarian with his skinny, bright-eyed wife, and Mr Lowry, Johnny's science teacher, who must have been nearing retirement. They leant across to Isabel in her window seat, took her hands, murmured their sympathy. They loved Johnny. Everyone here loved Johnny, in their own particular way. The coach was crammed with people who carried him in their hearts, had their own bright memories of him – memories that some were sharing now. Isabel overheard Fran saying to Jenna, 'That time when he carried me piggy-back across the flood . . .'

The coach started. Will and Baxter took up their positions at the head of the coach; Will even had a mic that he spoke into self-consciously. They had planned the day: it wouldn't do just to spread out and randomly search; he and Baxter had allocated areas of the city, and everyone would be working in groups, but of course they could come to their own arrangements within those groups. In a few minutes, he and Baxter would be going down the coach, giving out maps of their particular zone and also the A5 posters with thumb tacks and tapes to fix them on doors or posts. They also had a few posters attached to sticks, to hold above their heads as they walked. If anyone discovered anything – he coughed here, his impersonal language faltering – they were immediately to ring the mobile numbers printed at the top of the page. In addition, they all had to give him their numbers before they arrived. The coach would leave from outside the station at

Stratford at nine o'clock that evening – that way they had the day and also the evening. Hostels for the homeless were marked on the maps, and also points where it was known homeless people gathered. He knew it was a long day, he said, so if anyone wanted to go back earlier or if they decided to stay over, they must make their own arrangements and be sure to tell either him or Baxter in advance.

Isabel was struck by how hard they had worked to organize all of this. They must have stayed up all night, she thought, though neither seemed tired. Will was bright-eyed, alert; he looked excited, almost happy. His hope made hers suddenly drain from her, turning her into a dull void. Even in the handful of days since Johnny had disappeared, she had grown accustomed to these violent lurches between euphoric optimism and flat-lining despair.

'So: any questions or suggestions?'

Mr Lowry – only today did Isabel finally discover his name was Walter – put up his hand, like an obedient pupil. He wanted to know if it would be a good idea to put posters up in the hostels that were marked; would they be allowed to do that? No one knew. A friend of Mia's, a sandy-haired boy called Lewis, asked about soup kitchens. Someone else, a girl with dreadlocks, said it was important not to make anyone they talked to feel threatened. The librarian's wife said that some of the homeless people they might want to speak to (though she called them 'vagrants') would probably want money: people had to decide for themselves what to give, if anything.

'OK,' said Will. 'Thanks. We've got an important job to do here.' His voice cracked. He looked young and anxious now. 'Listen, thank you,' he said. 'I mean, this is *Johnny*, right. He's in trouble and he needs us. But thank you all for being here like this.' He met Isabel's gaze and flushed to the roots of his hair.

Isabel listened as the talk rose and fell around her. She rested her head against the window and let it bump gently with the motion of the coach as it sped along the A12, sending up sprays of water from its wheels – it must have rained in the night. The sky was pale blue, streaked with pink clouds that were stippling to white. Fields spread out unbroken, and the few trees and isolated farmhouses rose from a thin fog, now dissipating in the morning light. Tamsin, sitting beside her, handed her a plastic mug of piping hot coffee, black and strong. Mia was with her friends a few seats back; every so often Isabel twisted round to see her. Jenny and Leah sat just in front of her, conversing in low voices. Isabel remembered their drunken conversation the day after she had driven Johnny to university: what had they said? Something about all being in the same boat. Well, that wasn't true now.

Isabel was going with Jenny and Leah to the West End, round Tottenham Court Road, Covent Garden, Holborn and down towards the river at Waterloo and Blackfriars. Mary would meet them there. Tamsin would go with Max and Holly to nearby Oxford Street, working their way towards Hyde Park. Mia and several of her friends were heading to Clapham and Stockwell. Isabel could see that Mia was anxious about leaving her, yet wanted to be with her mates. They were clustering round her, putting their arms around her shoulders, wanting to be the ones who comforted her the most. A few months ago, if Isabel had seen her daughter gathered into this protective circle of warmth, she would have been grateful and relieved; even today she felt a distant pleasure. So there was still a tiny space inside her for other people, she reflected – a hidden nook that the darkness hadn't reached.

At Stratford the group dispersed, even though most of them would take the Underground going west. Mr Lowry came up to Isabel as she climbed off the coach and took her hands. He didn't say anything, but raised each to his lips and kissed the knuckles. He was wearing a suit, shiny with age at the shoulders and knees, and a dark blue tie. Isabel wanted to tell him he was going to freeze for the wind was like a sharp knife, making her eyes water, but she couldn't form the words and he was gone, walking after the librarian and his wife with his bow-legged stride.

Jenny, Leah and Isabel took the Central Line as far as Chancery Lane and emerged into the bright, cold day blinking. Isabel looked down at the map clutched in her hand. They were covering a tiny square of London, but even that square was an intricate mesh of roads and alleys, of high office blocks and buildings they couldn't go into, of shops that in an hour or so would throng with young people, of cafés that were already open, steam rising from the counters, of empty churches, derelict shops and dim pubs that would fill up through the day, of theatres waiting for the matinée crowds, mile after mile of windows that shone emptily in the winter sun and doorways that were locked and barred. She stood paralysed, gaping at the road stretching ahead of her and the vans, cabs and cars that rumbled past. And then she thought of this scene multiplied over and over again, endlessly replicating and spreading out around her. And this was just London. There were all those other cities, other countries. Johnny was just an infinitely tiny speck in a crowded universe – yet he was her whole world, blotting out all else that existed.

'It's impossible,' she whispered.

Jenny hooked an arm through hers. Leah took the map from her and studied it.

'We need a proper plan,' she said briskly. 'We're going to walk along here.' Her finger traced a path. 'And circle around, then double back and go this way. That takes us to Holborn. We're going to put up posters on posts and on the windows of boarded-up shops.' She energetically shook the bundles of papers she was carrying. 'And we'll go into every single café and pub and shop we pass. We're going to work in a series of spirals around all the places Will has marked on the map. Like here, look. This is a hostel, just next to Covent Garden. And this one in Bloomsbury. And the day-centre run by the American Church. We'll get there by mid-afternoon, I reckon, although I've no idea, really – and after that, we'll go down towards Waterloo and the river. Right?'

'Right,' said Jenny, giving Isabel's arm a squeeze.

Isabel let herself be led by them. The day took on the quality of a dream. Under a sun that gave out no warmth and in a wind that rasped against her cheeks and ached in her ears, she was pulled down streets and into dark passageways that reeked of urine. Leah put posters up and marched into pubs. Jenny stopped to talk to every *Big Issue* seller they met, and accosted any stranger she thought – sometimes wrongly – might be part of the community of missing people who were swallowed into London every day and spat out at night, to end up under its dank arches or in its mysterious ruins. Leah bent down to alarming men in doorways, with dribbling Alsatians and cardboard placards proclaiming their desperate need for whatever a kind stranger could spare. They tugged her into a warm café and pushed a cup of tea into her hands, a rock cake that lay like studded granite on her plate, untouched. They spoke brightly and were practical, unflagging. They answered her mobile phone for her whenever it rang, speaking to Tamsin, Mia and then Felix. No news, they heard; no news, they agreed. They led her into small green spaces where men with weathered faces and tangled dirty beards sat on benches drinking their cider. They led her downstairs into a public toilet where a couple of teen-agers were sharing a joint. They interrupted buskers on corners, their guitar cases sprinkled with coppers, playing Bob Dylan or high, wailing folk tunes. Isabel stared into each face. She saw how the wind and the rain and the sun had cut grooves into them and roughened them, as if they were objects in an urban landscape, how drink or drugs had smeared their eyes, tobacco had yellowed their fingers. She noticed what they carried: blankets and sleeping bags, indeterminate items of clothing and fag ends, cans of cheap drink, but also sometimes books and music. Some were kind and eager to help, others suspicious or hostile, or simply befuddled with booze. They shook their heads, shrugged, made suggestions, turned away, stared uncomprehendingly, sometimes spoke words that were hard to understand, occasionally in voices that were middle-class or had that unmistakable private-school drawl.

How had she never seen them before, this crowd of forgotten people? Where had she been looking when she walked through the London streets? Once you were on the lookout, they were everywhere: scared teenagers and old people who had seen everything, and all the ones in between, in doorways and under awnings that did nothing to keep off the rain, asking for help. And passers-by passed by, curving in detours to avoid them, turning their heads so that they didn't have to see, fixing their gaze in that purposeful frontwards direction, as if they were blinkered by their busyness. The worst thing was to meet their eyes, acknowledge them as human and individual, one of us. Isabel gave money to each one. She handed out her cheese sandwiches, which they usually fed to their dogs. She made herself touch them, putting a hand on their arm or their shoulder. She made herself inhale, drawing in the stench of unwashed flesh, and breath that smelt like the rubbish bins at home on the day before collection – you lift the lids and warm fetid air hits you. Perhaps someone, somewhere, was doing the same for Johnny. And then always Leah or Jenny would draw her away again, calling thanks, continuing their corkscrew path through the streets.

Isabel thought, If there are hundreds and thousands of people who are lost on these streets, are there also hundreds and thousands of people like me, who are searching for them? Ghosts and ghost-hunters. She gazed around her at the faces of the people who passed. Everyone seemed to know where they were going, yet perhaps she, too, looked purposeful and assured, marching along between two friends.

At lunchtime they found themselves in Covent Garden.

Because it was a Saturday, not long before Christmas and, what was more, not pelting with rain, the place was thick with crowds of shoppers. It was hard to make their way through them, and impossible while linked together. They dropped arms and went singly towards the covered market. Figures dressed as silver-sprayed Roman soldiers, green-painted witches or whitened statues lined the route, motionless, though you could see their chests expand with their breathing. Isabel tossed coins in front of them. She saw a tiny smile twitch in acknowledgement on the statue's face. Christmas lights above her, a giant Christmas tree with huge red bows tied to it, shops belching out heat and carols. 'Hark! The Herald Angels Sing'. Her favourite was 'O Little Town of Bethlehem'. Johnny played that on the piano, and Felix on the violin. Sometimes – ironically but with a sentimental swoop to it – the women of the family sang along. Tamsin had a beautiful voice, although Mia and Isabel chanted like the rooks at the bottom of their garden. But it didn't matter: what mattered was the act of joining in. All together – and she could see herself in the living room, hand conducting wildly, face screwed tight, mouth a comic O, flat-sharp voice a constant source of surprise to herself, ludicrously happy amid her raggle-taggle crowd. Those were the days – why had she not known?

She couldn't see Leah or Jenny now, but it didn't matter. She let herself sit down on the kerb, in front of a man who was wheeling round on a monocycle, juggling cauli-flowers, his smile fixed in grim concentration. She put her head in her hands and waited. Soon she would get up again and trudge on.

'Here. Drink this.' Jenny's honey voice.

A paper cup was pushed into her hands. Hot against her fingers, steam rising and dampening her face.

'What is it?'

'Soup. Have some.'

Isabel took a sip and felt its warm goodness trickle down her throat. It made her stomach hurt.

'A bit at a time.'

She took another sip.

'It will help you.'

Isabel lifted her head and saw Jenny's blurred face. She remembered a day, not so very long ago, when they had had one of their wounding arguments: Jenny had accused her of never having time, of racing from task to task, child to child, friend to friend, as if a dog was snapping at her heels or as if every meeting was a kind of emergency. Isabel had been furiously hurt – it had been like having her gifts thrown back in her face and being told they were worthless. Now she wondered what the fuss and turmoil had been about.

'You're my friends,' she said to Leah and Jenny, and she saw they were crying.

Then she spotted him. She leapt to her feet, the soup flying from her grasp, and she saw in the corner of her vision the arc of flecked orange liquid fly through the air. She saw the man on his monocycle falter and fall, cauliflowers dropping to the ground. Straight as an arrow, she sped across the Piazza, past the tourists and the shoppers, bodies barging against her, people shouting. There he was, his floppy hair shining in the sunlight and there was no mistaking the way that he walked and she called his name. High and shrill it tore in the air. 'Johnny! Johnny! Wait for me!'

At last he turned. A man, not young, with a bony, startled face. She halted in front of him so now she was a living statue too. Then, slowly, she knelt on the ground and tried to protect herself from wave after wave of pain.

'Are you all right, please?' he asked. 'Are you ill?'

He wasn't English; his words held a foreign lilt, singsong and nearly comic. He stared at the woman on the ground in front of him and then around at the curious people who were gathering to see what was going on.

'She mistook you for someone. Sorry.'

Leah had arrived. She took Isabel's elbow and helped her to her feet, although Isabel stayed hunched over.

'Shall I call an ambulance?' someone was asking.

'Is she drunk?'

'Out of her head!'

'No, no, it's all right.'

Jenny and Leah herded her to the side of the square, arms circling her. She felt like one of those criminals who are taken from a police van with a coat over their heads. There was a church and they took her into its small yard and patted her, murmured endearments, told her that everything was going to be all right although, of course, they couldn't say that and neither could Felix, nor the police, nor all the young people on the bus this morning.

'What shall I do?' she asked at last.

'We're going to find a warm place to sit for a while. Then we can continue with the search. If you want.'

'No, what shall I *do*? Now. Next minute, hour, day. What shall I *do*?'

'What do you mean, Isabel?'

'How do I get from one minute to the next – how do I *live* through this?'

'Precisely like that – one minute to the next,' Jenny said. 'One foot in front of the other.'

'If I could do something, if someone told me that running to the top of a mountain, or sawing off my fingers, or shouting and screaming might help, then I'd know what to do. I could get through the time.'

'That's why we're looking.'

'Exactly. We're looking just so that we have something to do, so we don't feel so bad about doing nothing. That's all it means. Felix knew that. That's why he's at home – because he had the courage to stare the truth full in the face and not look away. Whereas I – I can't do that. I'll *die* if I do. I'll die of the agony.'

'Listen.' Leah was talking now. Her lemon scent was in Isabel's nose; her bright hair was blowing around them like a flag. 'We know it's hell. But Johnny might be here. This is not a meaningless search. And you have to look where you can. But he's only been gone a few days. Everyone says it: people come back. Almost everyone.'

'What did I do wrong?'

'Nothing. It's not you – you mustn't think like that.'

'I thought we were a happy family. I *told* myself we were. I insisted. I was lying because I so badly wanted it to be true. Things were wrong. I should have seen. I can't bear it.'

'Yes, you can,' said Leah, in a newly sharp tone. 'You can because you must. There isn't an alternative. You have two other children.'

143

'I know, I know. Of course.'

'So you keep going for them. Inch by inch. And you don't look down. You do not look down, Isabel.'

How did Leah get to be so wise? What had happened in her life that she knew what it was like to hang by your fingertips from a smooth rockface and feel in your stomach the sheer cliff falling away beneath you?

'Yes. Yes, you're right.'

Isabel straightened up. Her friends let go of her and looked at her uncertainly. She looked back at them. The cold had stripped their faces: they looked older than their years, hair undone and lashing round blotchy cheeks, eyes watering, noses red.

'Let's go,' she said.

The hostel near Covent Garden was Gothic. The lobby was full of dog shit and needles and the sound of men shouting and weeping. They weren't allowed to visit their rooms or leave a poster up, but they loitered outside for some time, speaking to the residents as they entered or left. As far as Isabel could make out, these people were the wretched outcasts of society, alcoholic and unhinged, with no family except the other misfits, no friends, no work, no purpose. She sat on the steps with a man in a thick, grubby coat that was belted at the waist with a piece of rope. He had streaky grey hair and a coarsely matted beard that grew up over his cheeks. His eyes were rheumy and there were nasty-looking sores at the corners of his mouth. His skin, where it was visible, was a fiery red and scored with wrinkles. His smell was of booze and fags, sweat and piss, wet dog and rank earth. His name was

Lawrence, and although he said he was forty-nine he looked seventy and his teeth were those of a man who had risen from the grave to sit beside her, with his rattling chest and stench of decay.

Isabel was a squeamish woman. Fastidious. She brushed her teeth after every meal, took a shower daily, loved clean sheets, shrank from picking up the dead birds that Digby used to bring in and lay, still warm and bright-eyed, at her feet. She was too easily disgusted by people chewing their food loudly, or leaving nail clippings or strands of hair in the bath, or sleep in the corners of their eyes. Yet here was undisguised mortality: nothing had been scoured with soap and hot water and washed away. He was possibly flea-ridden and crawling with lice. Probably he wore the same clothes day after day and was encrusted with his own filth. But, after all, he's no different from me, thought Isabel. It's just corruptible flesh, and underneath it, a man with a sore heart and bashed hopes and vivid memories. Once he was a baby, with pink gums and breath that smelt of hay, lying in his mother's arms. Or had his mother abandoned him? Was that why he was here now, lurching along the road and snaffling through bins for the remains of a hamburger or fag ends, fumbling in the dirt for a dropped coin?

Down by the river, the brown water lapped against the Embankment. The tide was up. The Thames was brimful, the day was dimming and then was gone. Such little snatches of day and such long stretches of darkness. London became a different city at night. Family groups dispersed, shoppers retreated. Long lines of tourists following a guide, holding a red flag high in the air, filed obediently out of sight. Now restaurants and bars filled, groups of young people flowing past. Girls in short skirts, thick jackets and shoes so high they stepped out like daddy-long-legs, youths in hoodies and jeans slung low over skinny hips. Men and women dressed up for the opera, coiffed, polished and gleaming. Taxis disgorging party-goers. A group of teenage girls, already drunk, tottering past, holding on to each other for support and giggling loudly. Lovers folded up together and held in each other's rapt gaze. All through the long hours, the city would heave and throb with the gaiety of a Saturday night. At midnight, people would spill out of pubs and queue outside clubs, ready to dance until dawn.

In corners, down small alleyways, hunched over braziers, rolled up under bridges in sleeping bags, swigging from bottles that might make the night go quicker and morning come again: hundreds, thousands of them. Where was Johnny? Where was her son?

The journey home was quiet. Nobody really wanted to speak. They were tired out and cold. Many of them curled themselves up to sleep, or rested their heads on friends' shoulders. Others plugged themselves into their music. Tamsin, seated next to Isabel, laid her head on Isabel's lap and cried softly. Isabel stroked her thick locks of hair, coiling them around her fingers and feeling their silkiness, until her daughter fell asleep. Across the way, Mia sat with Maud. She said she had a migraine, and she was very pale, with dark smudges under her eyes. Will and Baxter were at the front of the coach, drinking cans of beer. When Will came and talked to her, Isabel could see that he was already a bit drunk. He was treating the expedition like his personal failure, and was talking about how next time he would plan it differently, but they both knew there wouldn't be a next time.

'At least we've put up those posters,' said Baxter. 'We must have put up hundreds and hundreds between us. They might pay off.'

Mr Lowry was snoring, his head tipped back against the furry seat and his mouth slightly open. His Adam's apple was sharp and he looked cadaverous. The librarian's wife was eating a large floppy slice of pizza, taking the olives off first and handing them to her husband, who posted them obediently into his mouth. Maureen Tench was sending texts.

Isabel stared out of the window, eyes gritty with tiredness. London was disappearing, the lights and the crowds giving way to darkness, cold and space.

Chapter Twelve

At first it had been a matter of seconds and minutes. Then it became hours. Then they started to count in days, sliding by like beads on an abacus, clicking into the past. Three days since Johnny was reported missing, four, five . . .

On Sunday, Tamsin returned to university, getting the last possible train to London that would connect with another going to Southampton. She only had one more week of term, but Felix and Isabel insisted she should not miss it. She spent the last day making hearty soups for the freezer, cooking rescue snacks, and talking on the phone, retreating from rooms if anyone entered, covering the receiver with her hand.

Isabel drove her to the station and waited with her until her train arrived, sitting in the little café on the platform that sold flapjacks in individual wrappers and unripe, overpriced bananas. Tamsin, holding her mother's cold hands between her own, told her over and over again that it was going to be all right, that Johnny would be home soon.

'By Christmas!' she said. 'You'll see. And even if not then, soon.'

Isabel reflected again how their roles had switched: her eldest daughter had turned from the comforted into the comforter. She used a motherly tone with Isabel, as if her mother had become her child, and Isabel, seeing their reflections in the window, saw how little and shrivelled she looked next to Tamsin's overarching presence. It seemed to her that Tamsin was blossoming, visibly opening out, emitting warmth and generosity. As if she could see things with clarity for the first time, she wondered how much she was to blame for Tamsin's neediness and dependence, stoking it with her anxious vigilance. And yet, looking at her daughter's bright, tear-filled eyes, she also thought how much Tamsin still needed someone to take care of her. Tenderness tightened her throat.

'You haven't had any supper.'

'I don't need supper. I can buy something at Liverpool Street, if I want. Anyway, it won't do me any harm to skip a meal. The Worry Diet.'

'You never need to diet,' said Isabel – who had spent half of Tamsin's life telling her that she did.

'That's nice of you and a lie.'

'You've been fabulous,' Isabel said. 'And you're right, I'm sure you're right. But listen.' She sat forward. 'You're never to think that because we're so worried about Johnny, we're not there for you. It doesn't work like that – it's not as if there's only so much worry or love to go round and Johnny's using it all up at the moment. Do you hear?'

Tamsin nodded, biting her full lower lip with her white teeth, as one large tear rolled down her face.

'And now,' said Isabel, briskly, 'I can hear your train being announced. You are to go back to university, work hard and have a good last week. That's a command. OK?'

'Mm.' She couldn't speak; tears clung to her lashes.

'Let me know what day you'll be home. I can drive to Southampton to collect you, if you like.'

They went on to the platform as the train rounded the bend in the track, its lights shining like eyes, and hugged each other tightly, arms straining. Tamsin's body was full and firm; her breasts squashed against Isabel; her hair smelt of apples and her breath of peppermint.

'I love you very, very much,' said Isabel, against her soft cheek.

'I know. Me you too.'

'I know you do.'

'And, Mum?'

'Yes?'

The train hissed past them, rumbled to a halt, doors swung open.

'Well. There's something I wanted to tell you.'

'Yes?'

Tamsin giggled and gulped. She climbed up the step into the train and hung out of the doorway, her hair rippling, her face tired and sweet. 'Actually, now might not be the best time.'

'Is it something to worry about?'

'No! It'll wait till I see you.'

'Ring me.'

'I will. And tell me what's going on.'

'Of course.'

'Even if there's nothing to tell – or bad things.'

'Yes. Whatever I know, I'll tell you. I promise.'

A guard came past and slammed the door. Tamsin stood looking out of the window. She put her hand against it, fingers splayed. Her mouth opened in a soundless goodbye and she was crying properly now, great tears sliding into her mouth as the train started to move, gathered speed, slid from the station and into the tunnel beyond. Isabel watched it until even the lights were out of sight before she turned to go.

On Monday, Isabel and Felix returned to Sheffield. Felix had received an email from Charlie, the student from Johnny's flat who was clearly the self-appointed spokesperson for the rest of them, saying they thought they knew who Fergal was and where he could be found. Apparently he was an ex-student who had dropped out a few years ago and now hung around the campus, inserting himself into groups. He lived in Park Hill, under the shadow of the vast housing estate there, in a grotty condemned council flat. He was, Charlie said, a reformed junkie, an environmental activist, a committed vegan, and possibly someone with mental-health problems.

Isabel had agreed with her school that she would not return until the beginning of the next term. Her head had said that if she needed more time – for which read, *if Johnny still has not been found* – then she could of course have as much as she wanted. 'It would be helpful if you could let us know in advance,' she added. 'We don't want to be scrabbling around each day for a supply teacher.' Felix had only three days left of his term; there was no question of working until the new year.

Park Hill wasn't a housing estate: it was a surreal citadel of concrete and brick, a winding block of grey cement and glass that blotted out the skyline and towered over the city. One section of the vast edifice was clearly being renovated: it had been stripped back to its skeleton. The rest of the building seemed inhabited; Isabel could see bikes and pot plants and chairs on some of the myriad tiny, gridded balconies. She didn't know if it was beautiful or monstrous.

Fergal lived in a small block of flats about half a mile from Park Hill. Charlie hadn't given Felix the exact address, but it wasn't hard to find, for more than half of the flats were boarded up and abandoned, only a few still bearing signs of human habitation. Coarse, muddy grass grew up to front doors. A few of the flats had been set fire to and charred windows gave on to dank, empty interiors. Where the boards had been jemmied open by vandals or squatters, Isabel glimpsed some of the things people had left behind – an old table here, a standard lamp there, unwanted toys lying on a floor, a calendar still tacked to a wall, an ancient two-hobbed oven tipped on its side, torn pipes sprouting behind it, bits of crockery lying around.

Fergal inhabited this eerie landscape as if there was nothing dislocating about it. They saw him through the window and even before they knocked they knew it was him, for Charlie had told them in his first email that he was tall, with glasses. He came to the door in a leisurely fashion, drying his hands with a tea towel as he walked. He didn't seem surprised to see them.

'Yes?'

'I'm sorry to disturb you,' said Felix, in his formal, courteous tone, which made Fergal's narrow lips twitch with what looked like amusement. 'We're Johnny's parents.'

'Yes?'

'My name is Felix Hopkins and this is my wife, Isabel.'

He actually took a couple of cards, with his university and home contact details on them, and held them out as if they were ID. Fergal looked at them but didn't take them. Neither did he move from the doorway. He simply went on rubbing his long fingers with the tea towel and regarding them without curiosity.

'Could we come in?' said Isabel. She heard her voice, high and pleading. She found that she was trying to smile at him but his face remained expressionless. His glasses were thick and magnified his watching eyes. She hated him. She knew he could feel her hatred: it rose off her like steam.

He shrugged. 'If you like,' he said amiably.

They entered a tiny hall. Felix laid his cards on the windowsill, beside a hairbrush clogged with blond hairs and a clay pipe, and they followed Fergal into a room that had once been a kitchen but that someone had taken a sledgehammer to, splintering the internal wall and opening it up into the living room beyond. The effect was to make the space both grand and ruined, like a stage set.

Fergal was not alone. On the large sofa, a splitting and filthy affair that had been draped with stained, patterned blankets, sat a couple, with mugs of herbal tea. The remains of a large joint lay in the ashtray in front of them. There were several rubber plants in pots round the room, and they seemed to suck up the light. In the centre there was an easel on which was a portrait of a naked woman – the same woman who was sitting before them. Isabel looked at her, in her baggy pink jumper and her long striped skirt, and then at her picture, in which she was blue-fleshed and dead-eyed.

'Hello,' she said.

She didn't know whether to stand or sit, talk or wait for Fergal to ask questions. But Fergal didn't seem disposed to speak. He picked up his mug of tea, took a sip, then set it down on the wooden box that served as a table. He sat on the floor in front of them and crossed his legs. For a moment, Isabel thought that he would take up a lotus position and begin to meditate.

'We're Johnny's parents,' she began, looking down at him and feeling that he was deliberately putting her at a disadvantage.

'You said.'

'You know Johnny?'

'Johnny,' said Fergal, musingly. 'Of course. Young Johnny Hopkins.'

'He's disappeared. Did you know that?'

'Disappeared?'

'Yes. Didn't you know?'

'When you say "disappeared", do you mean that you don't know where he's gone?'

'I'm sorry?'

'What are you sorry about?'

'No, I mean, I don't understand the distinction. We don't know where Johnny is.' She waited. 'We're worried. We're frantic. We're trying to find him and we're looking everywhere we can think of. Someone gave us your name, which is why we're here – in case you know where he might be. In case you can help us find him.'

'Are you sure he wants to be found?'

'What are you saying? You don't understand! I'm his mother. I just want to know he's safe, that he's –'

'Do you know where he is?' Felix interrupted. 'For God's sake, tell us that at least.'

'If I knew –'

'Do you know?'

'If I knew,' continued Fergal, giving no indication that he had even heard Felix's interruption, 'then why would I tell you?'

'Do you want money?' cried Isabel.

'Aaah.' It was a soft, satisfied sigh, as if something had been confirmed for him. 'The entitled middle classes.'

'Please.' Isabel squatted beside him, trying to make some kind of human contact. 'Please. We don't know where to turn. If you know something, please help. Has he stayed here? Did he confide in you?' She reached out and touched his arm with her hand.

'He told me about you,' said Fergal, ominously.

'Oh!' Isabel felt her heart turn over – how could Johnny have talked about her to this creature, with his knowing smile and his cool eyes swimming behind his glasses?

'And you,' he said to Felix. 'He didn't want to be like you.'

Felix stared. His mouth opened but no words came out.

'Fergal persuaded him to be a vegetarian,' said the woman on the sofa admiringly. 'Didn't you, Fergal?' The man beside her had fallen asleep.

'Johnny?' Isabel remembered him cooking slow-roasted rib of beef shortly before leaving home. She remembered him frying bacon for Sunday breakfast, standing over the pan in his pyjamas. 'Does he still eat fish?' she asked stupidly.

'If he still ate fish, he wouldn't be a vegetarian,' Fergal answered, with a small smile.

'Maybe you think you'd be betraying his confidences,' said Isabel. 'Can you just tell us if you know where he went? Or why? And if he's all right?'

Fergal altered his position, untangling his long legs in their drawstring trousers. He considered her. 'I don't know where he went,' he said at last.

'Did you know that he was going to go?'

'Not as such.'

Felix frowned. Isabel could see that he was clenching and unclenching his fists.

'Do you mean he didn't tell you?'

'There's telling and telling.'

'Please. Please. Not like this. Can't you see —' Isabel knelt beside him and took his sleeve between her fingers. 'Just tell us: what do you know?'

'Your Johnny,' Fergal said, looking at her clutching fingers as though they were insects that had landed on his arm, 'is a seeker.'

Felix made a small, angry movement and controlled himself.

'Yes?'

'His background hadn't prepared him.'

'Prepared him for what?'

'Did you encourage him to go?' Felix's voice grated above them.

'Is he here?' Isabel asked suddenly. 'Is that it? He's hiding here.'

The man on the sofa opened his eyes. He blinked and sat up, then looked at Isabel. 'No,' he said. 'Your son isn't here. And Fergal has no idea where he is. He didn't even know he'd gone until a day or so ago. Did you, Fergal?' His voice was dull with contempt. The woman at his side shifted uneasily, looking between the two men as they stared at each other.

'So, you don't know anything?' said Isabel. The flat frightened her, and so did Fergal. She felt he was beyond her appeals and anyone's, that he was living in his own narcissistic world, manipulating other people like chess pieces, inflating himself with each petty victory. 'Nothing?'

Fergal looked at her. His eyes narrowed. 'I know he needed to get away from you,' he said, in a softly insinuating voice. 'Your love is like sleeping sickness.'

Isabel stood up. She felt Felix's hand on the small of her back.

'You are just a nasty little man,' she said, 'preying on the doubts and loneliness of vulnerable people who are worth a hundred of you, a thousand. I hate to think you even looked at Johnny, let alone spoke to him, poisoned him with your cold, empty words. He was homesick and insecure and you battened on to him, you crappy little parasite.'

She stopped, breathless. The man on the sofa was sniggering. Fergal crossed his legs once more, folded his hands in his lap and closed his eyes.

'Don't pretend you aren't listening. You're just a fraud!' She pushed him hard and he half toppled, put out a hand to stop himself. Anger rippled over his thin face.

'Let's go, Isabel.' Felix moved her towards the door,

past the naked portrait and the oversized rubber plants. 'We're wasting our time.'

'Yes, go,' said Fergal. 'You won't find him, though. He doesn't want you.'

In the car, Isabel doubled over, trying to breathe.

'You were right, he's just a fraud,' Felix said, although his hands were trembling on the steering wheel and his face was taut with distress.

'No.' Isabel bit her knuckles, forcing herself to think clearly about the encounter. Felix had remained above it all – he simply despised the man and was furious with him – but she, because of her fatal need to empathize and understand and make connections, felt besmirched by it, as if Fergal had put his long white fingers into the murk of her mind and nimbly stirred it. She felt his cleverness; she knew that he saw through her and understood her weakness. 'It's worse than that. He was saying something true, something I need to acknowledge. It's me that Johnny is running from. My oppressive love. He had to free himself from me.'

'Hang on, Isabel. He also said that Johnny didn't want to be like me.'

'Yes.' She didn't add: *and that's probably true as well.*

'And, anyway, don't you think that every child has to free themselves from their parents in one way or another? That's what it is to grow up.'

'Not this way.'

'No, OK. But don't make this a battle for who's most in the wrong here. We're both in the wrong, but so is every parent who ever lived.'

'He was disgusting.'

'He was just a creep.'

'A megalomaniac creep who got his nasty little fingers on Johnny and made him think everything about him was wrong.'

'At least we found out that he doesn't know where Johnny is.'

'That's no help, though. It's a step back.'

'It's an elimination,' said Felix.

He had taken out the notebook he always carried in his inner breast pocket and was writing. Since Johnny had left, he had been scribbling incessantly in it. It was almost full now, the pages covered with his small, neat writing; there were bullet points and numbers, and words underlined. That's how he gets through each day, thought Isabel. He orders things: he tries to impose a spurious control on this grief and mess.

She put her head on his shoulder, feeling how bony he was. They were both shrinking while the guilt inside them grew like a cancer. 'Are you all right?'

He didn't move. 'What does that mean?'

'Nothing. It's not really a question. I'm just – you know – saying I'm here.'

She sat upright again. Felix could talk to his mother – she had seen him at the kitchen table with Miranda, his head in his hands and his mother stroking his back gently as if he was a small boy again. She had seen him lift Digby off the sofa in the living room and put him on his lap, bending over the old cat, Johnny's beloved pet, with anguish on his face. She had seen him let Tamsin pull him into her soft embrace. But with herself he couldn't show what he was feeling. Perhaps he was being strong for her, or perhaps he knew that, deep down, hidden in the river-bed of their minds, they each blamed the other and were full of bitter anger that, if admitted to, might erupt in a tidal wave.

'What shall we do now?'

'His room. The warden's expecting us and can let us in.'

Felix had arranged with the Accommodation Office that they would continue to pay for Johnny's room. They were not going to move his possessions – except his dirty laundry, which Isabel insisted they had to take home to wash.

Snow was starting to fall, as they drove up to Johnny's building, settling softly on the roofs of cars and on the roofs of houses, melting on to the road. As they got out of the car, Isabel tipped her head back and looked up into the flakes. She felt as though she was falling upwards; the world had turned upside down and she was diving towards the tilted pelting sky. Then she shook her head, wiped the snow from her cheeks, pulled her coat around her.

It was the end of term. The flat showed signs of Christmas parties and late nights. There was a plastic tree in the kitchen, with flashing red and blue lights on it, and home-made paper chains festooning the fridge and freezer. The messy remains of a chocolate cake lay on the table. Crumpled beer cans were scattered everywhere, and several vodka bottles, empty. Bin bags sagged and split by the sink, which was full of encrusted plates and greasy water. The floor was sticky underfoot. Life, thought Isabel, with a flash of bitterness she knew was unreasonable, was continuing without Johnny.

His room was the same as it had been the last time they were there. But cold. Someone had turned off his heating. Isabel gathered up the few pieces of dirty laundry, then Johnny's pyjama bottoms and T-shirt from his pillow. Like last time she held them against her face to breathe in the familiar smell. But it was fading now.

Chapter Thirteen

And after grim Monday came Tuesday. A reporter from the East Anglian newspaper arrived at half past nine. Mia had left for school and Miranda was in the kitchen, eating toasted crumpets with Marmite and reading the papers with the aid of a magnifying glass. It was a frosty morning and she had wrapped herself in a quilt so that she resembled a tortoise, her back hunched and her grizzled head poking out.

The reporter was a young woman, in her mid- to late twenties, Isabel guessed. She stood on the doorstep with a sympathetic expression ready on her face, breath smoking from her mouth. She was tall and slender, with curly brown hair tied back from her narrow face, and brown eyes framed by thick-rimmed glasses.

'I'm Sarah Ingham. I think you were expecting me.'

'Yes. Come inside where it's warm. Let me take your coat.'

Isabel smiled. Her face felt odd, as if the skin was stretched too tight over the bones. Probably, she thought, this young woman was already sizing her up, thinking of ways to describe her. 'Distraught mother of three . . .'; 'Isabel Hopkins's face was probably once attractive but now it is gaunt and wrinkled . . .' She thought of parents who had faced TV cameras to appeal for the return of their children: their red eyes, their strained expressions, holding back the howls. Standing in front of the mirror that morning, she had stared at herself, wondering at how she still bore a close resemblance to the person she had been a week ago. How does a mother whose child has gone missing look? Does the face describe the pain? Of course not – how can it? Everything remains in place: nothing slides or cracks or ruptures. The mouth opens and words come out ('Would you like to come through to the living room? Felix has lit a fire'). The mouth stretches and a smile appears.

Felix had been for a ten-mile run that morning, setting out while it was still not fully light. His hair was still wet from his shower and plastered across his skull, showing its shape. His blue eyes glittered. He looked like a creature of winter, thought Isabel, flinty and colourless.

They sat together on the sofa, side by side but with a space between them. Sarah Ingham sat opposite on a chair and crossed her legs. She pulled a notebook out of her leather satchel, licked her finger, and flicked through until she got to the right page. She glanced down at it, then up at them, her eyes darting from one to the other. 'Is it all right with you if I use a tape recorder?'

'Of course.'

She placed it on the coffee-table, pressed a button. 'I'll just make sure it's working. Can you say something?'

'Um –'

'What did you have for breakfast?'

'Nothing. At least, I had two cups of coffee.'

'That's fine.' She pressed the rewind button and Isabel listened to her voice, which sounded unfamiliar. 'Right.' She gave a slight cough and Isabel realized she was slightly nervous. 'First of all, I'm so sorry for what you must both be going through.'

'Thank you,' said Felix.

'Um – maybe you can start by just telling me a bit about your son. You know, how old he is, what he's like, his hobbies, things like that. For colour.'

So they started. Felix sat upright on the sofa, hands on his knees, clipped and factual. (*Johnny is eighteen; Johnny is a talented scientist; Johnny has always been fascinated by astronomy – no,* not *astrology, astronomy, the study of stars and the cosmos; Johnny likes to play tennis and squash and he was in his school's football team; Johnny is the middle child; Johnny is musical.*) He had a folder of information ready to give her – fact sheets on how many young people went missing every year, photographs of Johnny as a young child and now, numbers people should call if they had any information.

Isabel leant forward. She gestured with her hands or wrung them together. She made sure she was looking into the eyes of the reporter. She was urgent, impassioned and garbled. (*He's beautiful and kind and everyone loves him. We just want him home. We just want him to be safe. He's my boy . . .*) She told Sarah Ingham about the coach trip to London to look for him, and saw her eyes light up: this was exactly the kind of story that would go down well with readers – parents' anguish, friends' loyalty and hope . . . She did not mention their meeting with Fergal yesterday, which was an ugly stain in her memory.

The tape recorder hummed and Sarah Ingham jotted in her notebook, occasionally making encouraging noises. 'Do you have any idea of why he might have gone?'

'No,' Felix said firmly.

'No!' cried Isabel, more wildly – Felix had told her not to go into any self-lacerating recriminations. 'No! It came out of the blue.'

'And can you tell me how you're feeling?' Pen poised, brown eyes alert.

Felix winced. 'How do you think?' he asked sharply, before collecting himself. He took a breath. 'Scared,' he said simply. The word hung in the air for a moment.

'And you, Mrs Hopkins?'

Isabel gazed at her. She made a supplicating motion with her hands, holding them out towards the reporter, palms up. 'I have hope,' she said at last. 'I must have hope. I would know if he was dead. I would feel it. He must be alive. Don't you think?'

Sarah Ingham nodded comfortingly. 'This piece will come out shortly before Christmas. So can I ask you, if it's not too painful, how you normally spend Christmas as a family, and what will happen this year – if he doesn't come home by then?' she added hastily.

Isabel described their Christmas, the rituals they had, the pillowcase at the end of the bed, the food they ate, the people who came and the songs they sang round the piano. She could see what she was speaking of: the cracker crowns, the golden-skinned turkey, the oranges spiked with cloves and hung on ribbons from doorways, candles and mistletoe and the Christmas tree clotted with decorations that used to hang on Isabel's parents' tree and had probably been bought by her mother decades ago: painted wooden figures, garish purple and green balls, a shabby angel for the top that always leant forward, precariously, as though it was drunk.

'And this year,' she said, 'I don't know. He'll be home. If he isn't home – how can we have Christmas? It's so cold outside.'

A man arrived to take their photographs. He made them stand in their doorway looking out as he snapped busily. Then he got them to stand in front of a framed family photograph. Isabel could tell that Felix loathed every moment, but he was obedient. And then they gave Sarah the email addresses of Will, Baxter, Mr Lowry and Maureen Tench. 'Just in case I need extra,' she said. 'Though you've been fantastic. Brilliant. Readers will love it. I'm so grateful. This must have been hard. Oh.' Pulling on her duffel coat and mittens, pushing her hair under the hood. 'Let me know if he comes back, won't you?'

'When,' said Isabel. '*When* he comes home.'

'Sorry.' She flushed and dropped her eyes. 'When.'

Two evenings later it was her night out with Jenny and Leah, arranged weeks previously. She had tried to cancel it, protesting that she didn't want to go out, she didn't want to eat or drink or talk, didn't feel up to it, wanted to curl up in a dark room, needed to look after Mia (although Mia was out that evening), but they had cajoled and insisted, and came to collect her in Leah's car just before seven. Jenny had cooked a dish of spicy noodles for Felix and Mia (Isabel didn't tell her that Miranda had already made a ferociously salty lamb stew) and Leah had brought a tin of chocolates that she left on the table. Isabel let herself be led out of the house. For the first time, as if by common consent, none of them had dressed up for the occasion – Jenny wore a turtle-necked grey jumper, black cords and no makeup, Leah was still in her office clothes, while Isabel had on the baggy blue jeans and cream-coloured cable-knit sweater she had worn for the reporter, hair tied back, no jewellery.

'Look at you,' scolded Leah. 'When did you last eat?'

'Lunchtime.'

'You look half starved.'

'I'm not, though.'

'You need a steak.'

'I hate steak.'

'Red meat.'

'I don't like red meat.'

'It won't help if you pass out from hunger.'

'I won't. I'm not hungry.'

'That's because your stomach's shrunk. Look at your jeans hanging off you. You worry about Mia starving herself, but how do you think she'll feel if she sees you wasting away in front of her?'

'OK. I'll eat something. Just don't nag me, all right?'

'We won't nag if you start looking after yourself.'

'Right.' She swallowed. Her throat hurt today and her glands ached. 'Thanks.'

'It's fine.'

'I mean, thank you for accompanying me.'

'Accompanying you?'

'On this journey. Being by my side.'

Risotto and green salad. Creamy blue cheese and thin poppy-seed crackers. Red wine, one glass making her thoughts fuzzy. Strong black coffee, twice. The bright restaurant wavered and blurred. Tables where people sat and laughed and complained about the kinds of things she used to complain about. What was there to say? She could say this: *I believe that Johnny ran away to escape from me. That is what I have come to think. I know you'll tell me I'm talking nonsense, but in my bones I'm sure it's true. That I loved Johnny too much, that I put too many hopes on him, that he couldn't bear to disappoint us and he was burdened by our pride in him, that I didn't trust him to be all right without me and therefore he wasn't.*

She didn't say any of this. Instead, she said, 'What am I going to do about Christmas?'

'If he hasn't returned by then?'

'Yes.'

'You mean, should you celebrate it?'

'How can I? It would be terrible sitting round the table together, reading out cracker jokes.'

'Have you talked to Felix about it?'

'Oh – he just shrugs as if it's not worth thinking about.'

'And is it worth thinking about?'

'I don't know. There's Tamsin and Mia.'

'They're not little children any more. Ask them what they want.'

'Do you think so?'

'Make the decision together.'

'Everyone was coming for the first time in ages – Rory and Helen and little Lucy, Ben and his girlfriend. My dad, Miranda, of course, Felix's sister and her new husband, our neighbour – well, he always comes. Even Graham and Celia and Celia's mother.'

'Ask your girls,' urged Jenny.

'I will.'

'And if you can't face doing anything, no one will mind. You could come to us if you want.'

'No! It's lovely of you, but I have to be at home. Just in case.'

'In case Johnny turns up?'

'Yes.' She sat up straighter in her chair and drank the last of the wine in her glass. 'But I think he'll come home before then. I feel it in my bones. Call it a mother's intuition. What? Don't look at me like that!'

Chapter Fourteen

Mia and Isabel walked along the coast in the teeth of the wind that blew in from Siberia, flattening the dune grass and sea kale that grew above the shore line, sending pieces of driftwood scudding towards them over the shingle and mud, whipping clouds across the great sky. Far out, Isabel could see the shape of a container ship moving across the horizon. The sea was a dark and frothing grey.

'I wanted to ask you about – ' began Isabel, but Mia was speaking as well, turning her face away so that the words streamed out behind her, inaudible.

'Sorry. What was that? You go first.'

Mia swung her head round and met her mother's eyes. 'I had sex last night.'

'Oh!' The bald statement almost stopped her in her tracks, but Mia kept going, head down, striding out with the salty wind scrubbing her pale cheeks crimson.

'With Will.'

'Will!'

'Don't look at me like that.'

Isabel stopped and gripped Mia by the upper arm. 'No, you're wrong, I'm not.' Thoughts jostled in her head. She had to do this right. 'First of all, my very darling Mia, thank you for telling me.'

Mia nodded and looked away, out to sea.

'Are you OK?'

'I don't know.' Her face crumpled. 'Oh, Mama.'

'Sweetheart. Tell me. Tell me anything you want.'

'You're not angry?'

'Why would I be angry?'

'I don't know.'

'Was it your first time?' Isabel asked neutrally.

Mia nodded.

'Let's just get this out of the way – before anything else. Did you, or he, take precautions?'

'No.'

'Right. In that case –'

'How could we? We had to pretend nothing was really happening. But I'm due for my period. I can feel it's about to start.'

'You're probably fine. There are pregnancy tests now that can tell you after twelve hours or something if you're pregnant. We'll get one on our way back home. OK?'

Mia nodded again. Her face was set but her lower lip trembled and Isabel saw how she bit it to stop herself crying. She put her arms around her daughter and for a few seconds Mia was stiff, and then, with a hiccuping sob, she yielded, tightening her arms around her mother's body and laying her head against her shoulder. They stood like that for a while, the cold wind whistling round them. Then Mia lifted her head and moved away. The two continued walking. The tide was out, and there were long-legged birds on the mudflats, shrill mournful cries lost on the wind.

'He texted me to say he was back from uni. He wanted to meet. To talk about Johnny and stuff. He'd been so nice to me when we all went to London, so sweet.'

'And you've always had a soft spot for him,' said Isabel quietly. Mia's face flamed, and she nodded a third time.

'We went to the pub for a drink.'

'When you said you were going to meet Maud.'

'Yes. Sorry. I don't know why I didn't want you to know.'

'It's OK. You don't need to tell me everything. You're not a child any more.' But she was, oh, she was: her youngest, her baby.

'We had a couple of beers and we talked about Johnny. It made it feel as if he was dead –' Mia's eyes welled with tears. 'He's not, is he?'

'No.'

'And Will said he and Zoë were over.'

'Are they?'

'Yeah. I thought they were strange last Saturday. He said he felt like he'd lost everything all at once. But that it must be much worse for all of us, and how could he be going on about himself like this with everything we were going through? He kept calling me Mimi – only Johnny ever called me Mimi before and then it was a kind of joke, but when Will did it I started to cry and cry. It was like someone had pressed a button at the back of my head, like that doll Tamsin used to have.'

'And that you scalped and buried in the garden.'

'Did I? I forgot that.'

'I didn't mean to interrupt. Go on.'

'And then he cried too. It was so odd, seeing him cry. It made me feel shivery inside.'

'Because he was your hero and now he was vulnerable?'

'I suppose so. I felt I could suddenly see inside him. Or

that I was in another world. It made me feel scared and happy at the same time, if that makes any sense.'

'I think so.'

'There's not really anything more to say. We did it in his mother's car. There was a crisps packet under me, scratching my skin. That's what I remember most clearly.'

Mia gave a dull little laugh, and Isabel took her hand to give it a quick squeeze. 'He didn't – well, force himself on you?' The words sounded ridiculous, something out of a Victorian novel or a bodice-ripper.

'No! It wasn't like that at all. It was more we were trying to comfort each other.'

'And did you?'

'Was it comforting, you mean? No. Not at all. It was over so quickly and we were both embarrassed and he kept apologizing and saying he didn't know what had possessed him. I'm nothing to him. I'm just Johnny's little sister.'

Isabel wanted to know if Will had found out about Johnny and Zoë – if this snatched act in his mother's old car on a dark lane somewhere had been a form of revenge. And if it was, if Mia ever discovered that, how much worse would this comfortless act of comfort seem to her, humiliating and nasty, erasing her even more? And she couldn't ask Will, because if he didn't know, the question would reveal it to him. But she could ask Zoë, she thought grimly, and stowed the knowledge away.

'Yes. You're Johnny's little sister,' she said. 'But not *just*. You're also Mia, whom Will likes, and you're probably a kind of stranger to him, a beautiful young woman, when he's been used to thinking of you as a child.'

'Pah!' said Mia, wiping the back of her hand across her eyes. 'I don't know about that.'

'I do. So of course he's embarrassed and confused. He must be asking himself who he had sex with – which of those people it was.'

'You're making it too profound,' said Mia, harshly. 'It was all very simple, really. He was upset, he'd had a few drinks, he fucked me.'

The word shocked both of them. They glanced uneasily at each other and then away.

'How did you leave it?'

'He dropped me back at the house and I said goodbye, and he said, "See you," and that was it.'

Isabel remembered hearing Mia's footsteps coming up the stairs. She had been lying in bed, wide awake, staring into the darkness, and she had thought about going to see her daughter but had stopped herself. Everyone needs their space, especially in a house so stifled with terror and grief. And Mia was like a cat – she needed to come to people in her own time, on quiet feet. Even now, Isabel felt the need to tread delicately, not to probe or be too emotional. Mia would clam up if she did that, retreat into a rigid hostility.

'You should have woken me,' she said.

'No. I washed my knickers in the sink and I brushed my teeth for ages and then I went to sleep as if someone had thumped a brick against my head. It's better like this. Out here in the wind. It doesn't feel so bad now.'

'Did it feel bad?'

Mia shrugged. 'Not even bad, really. Just not like it was meant to be.'

'How was it meant to be?' Isabel asked softly.

'I dunno – but it was meant to be about *me*. Someone looking at me and liking me, wanting me. Not just hiding away in me for a few minutes in the dark, in a car, as if it was a squalid, petty thing. I was just Will's way of shutting his eyes for a while.'

'And what about you? Did you want him?'

'Last year, when things were such crap at school and Johnny let me hang out with him and his friends, I had such a crush on Will – it makes me feel sick with embarrassment now. I remember once picking up a glass of water he'd been drinking from and putting my lips where his had been. I don't know why I'm telling you this – I'll regret it later. I think I probably regret it now.'

'There's nothing wrong with falling for someone,' said Isabel. 'Nothing to feel ashamed of.'

'Yes, there is – if he doesn't fall for you.' Mia speeded up, her dark hair whipping back from her face. There were drops of sleety rain in the wind now and Isabel could see from the gusting clouds that a storm was threatening. If they hurried, they might get back to the car before it came. 'It's all about Johnny, isn't it?'

'Is it?'

'Yes. Everything's about Johnny. Everything. Thinking of Johnny always made me feel safer. Does that sound stupid?' Isabel shook her head. She couldn't bring herself to say anything. 'He was always so nice to me, so reassuring. He made horrible things seem less important. Those times when I was being excluded, I don't know how I would have got through it without him. I always knew that whatever happened I could tell Johnny about it, and

even if he didn't say much, he would be comforting somehow. Oh, I know you and Dad would always have been
there for me – but it's different with parents. It's their
job. And you always seemed so anxious for me. Anxious
about me.'

'Did I?'

'It wasn't your fault. I'm not blaming you. But you're
always so – so *attached*. And Dad is so detached. But
Johnny was just, I don't know. Solid. And now –'

'Now?'

'Now when I think of Johnny it's like I'm falling
through space. It's horrible. He's everywhere and nowhere.
It's like the whole world is Johnny but he's not in it.'

'I know,' said Isabel. 'But –'

'Don't say but. I'm telling you how I feel. You always
try and find comforting things to say. Sometimes you just
have to listen.'

'Sorry.'

'If he doesn't come back – please don't tell me he's
going to, please, let me just talk. If he doesn't come back,
then I'm going to be Johnny's sad little sister for the rest
of my life. I'll never be able to be me. I don't know why
he's done it. I just want him to come home. If he doesn't
come home, what will I do?'

'I don't want to say things that may not be true just to
cheer you up. You're a strong young woman. You're honest with yourself. Whatever happens about Johnny, you
are going to come through. Do you hear? But having said
that, I believe he will come home. I do,' she repeated.
Though she didn't know any more what she believed: she

was simply saying the same words over and over again until they made no sense at all.

'Zoë?'

'Yes?'

'It's Isabel Hopkins.'

'Oh.' Zoë sounded nervous. 'Is there any –'

'No. I want you to tell me something.'

'What?'

'I know you and Will broke up. Did you tell him about Johnny?'

'That's private.'

'I need to know.'

There was a pause, and then Zoë said, 'Yes. I wasn't going to but then I did. I wish I hadn't. He said I disgusted him, and that he'd never forgive me as long as he lived. Satisfied?'

'No. It wasn't just you,' said Isabel. She was staring out of the kitchen window at the rain that was billowing across the garden, drenching the grass and running in rivulets down the path.

'Yeah, but Johnny's gone, isn't he? So he's a victim. A saint, even. And I'm just a scarlet woman.'

Isabel stood at the door to Will's house and rang the bell, then stood back. She heard footsteps, and when the door swung open, it was Will himself who stood there, barefoot and with a can of beer in his hand. His hair was wild and his shirt buttons done up wrongly; he looked exhausted. When he saw Isabel, his eyes widened. She could guess at the thoughts rushing through him – that she had news of Johnny, that she knew about him and Mia, that she didn't know and he had to pretend to be normal. His young face worked with the effort of keeping his expression under control.

'Isabel! Come in? Have you –'

'No.' She stepped inside. 'No news about Johnny. But I know about you and Mia.' She held up her hand to stop his expression of alarm. 'The thing is, Will, I also know about Johnny and Zoë.'

'Oh,' he said. 'Oh, Jesus, Isabel.'

'This has been agony for you, Will,' Isabel said. 'Your best friend going missing, all that searching for him – God knows, I appreciate it. "Appreciate" is the wrong word. I'll be grateful for the rest of my life. I'll never forget it. Then finding out that your girlfriend had sex with Johnny. What it must have felt like, finding that out, I can't begin to imagine. But.' She fixed him with her gaze and saw him wince. 'Mia is my daughter. If you and she have sex, that's one thing, it's not strictly my business, as long as it's consenting. She's still not seventeen. What I feel about it is beside the point. But if you had sex with her as a way of revenging yourself, that's something else. Then you were just using her. And I won't have it. Do you hear? Do you understand? She's vulnerable. She's got a crush on you. She's traumatized by Johnny's disappearance. I won't have her hurt any more by someone who's exploiting her hope and love and distress to punish those who've hurt him. Is that clear?'

'Yes,' mumbled Will. He looked ashen-faced, and in any other circumstance, Isabel's heart would have softened.

'You didn't even use a condom,' she added.

Will put his hands over his face. He muttered something.

'What? I can't hear,' said Isabel.

He took his hands away. 'I said, it wasn't calculated. It was just – it just happened. She was so sweet. And I was in such a mess.'

'Yet she's Johnny's little sister.'

'I know, I know. Or I don't know – I don't know anything any more, Isabel. Don't hate me.'

'I don't hate you.'

'Everything was certain. I knew where I was going and who I was. Zoë was my girlfriend. We were going to be faithful to each other. Johnny was my best friend. I knew he would be my best friend for the rest of my life. This –' He made a blind gesture. 'I'm sorry. I've always really liked Mia. Is she OK?'

'I don't know. She doesn't know about Zoë and Johnny, by the way.'

'Will you tell her?'

'Why? To make her feel even more worthless?'

'Everything's over, isn't it?'

'What do you mean?'

'Our childhood. We've destroyed it. It was only a few months ago that me and Johnny were sitting at your kitchen table and you were teaching us to make a white sauce. Do you remember?'

'Of course.'

'Well.' Will shrugged helplessly. His eyes filled with tears. 'Can you ever forgive me?'

'I don't think I've got anything to forgive, only to be grateful for. But can you forgive Johnny?'

'I don't know. He's got to come home and ask for it first, hasn't he? You can't forgive someone who hasn't even said sorry.'

'You're probably right.'

'Do you think that's why he's gone, because he felt so bad?'

'I'm sure it's something to do with it, but it can't be everything.'

'What a stupid fucking idiot.' Will groaned and rubbed his eyes with his knuckles. 'Of course I would have forgiven him in the end. He's my best friend.'

'Maybe he couldn't forgive himself.'

'That'd be Johnny.'

Chapter Fifteen

Tamsin came back the following day, the last Sunday before Christmas, on a train that was delayed by half an hour. She stepped out of her carriage, looking warm in spite of the chilly day, wrapped in a thick green coat. She was dragging two bin bags of laundry and a canvas sack of books. Isabel watched her as she glanced around in search of her mother: her plump, dishevelled, eager, generous daughter. When she saw Isabel, her face lit up and she started to half run towards her, her baggage bumping behind her, leather satchel slipping off her shoulder, her hair wrapping itself round her face. They hugged, Isabel's cold cheek against Tamsin's hot one, Isabel's undernourished body against her daughter's softness.

'No news?' asked Tamsin, knowing the answer. She had rung twice a day since returning to Southampton, in the morning before leaving for the library or lectures, and in the evening.

Isabel took the bag of books and the two of them went to the car.

'Are you OK?' Tamsin asked, as Isabel started the engine and backed out of the bay.

'Yes. Did you have a good end of term?'

'I did, in spite of everything. Does that sound bad?'

'It sounds good.'

Looking across at Tamsin, Isabel was struck by a new

kind of rosiness about her. Next to her, she felt wasted and grey. But she didn't mind – it was as though she was looking incuriously at herself from a distance.

'Mum, do you think we can pull over somewhere before we go home?'

'Yes, of course. Let me find a good place.'

They left the town and, after a few minutes, were travelling down a narrow lane, under trees that in the summer would form a green archway over the road but now stood bare, just a few dead leaves still hanging from their branches. Isabel turned in at a muddy entrance to a field and stopped. She took off her seatbelt and turned to Tamsin. 'Well?'

'When I said I'd had a good end to the term –'

'Yes?'

'– there was a reason for that.'

'Go on.' Though of course she had guessed long ago.

'I've met someone. His name's Jed. He's really nice, Mum.'

'I'm very glad, Tamsin. Really glad and happy for you.'

'I love him.'

'Do you?'

'Yes!'

'Does he love you?'

A whole history lay beneath these questions and answers: they both knew it. Tamsin was hungry for attention, insecure, sentimental, big-hearted and weepy. From the moment she was born, she had cried a lot, vomited a lot, made a great deal of noise. The flushed, bewildered face she had had as a baby had become the flushed, bewildered face of someone who is lost in the world but hoping that strangers will be kind to her. She wore lots of makeup and vivid clothes, binge-ate and binge-dieted, got into debt and got easily drunk. She wore her heart on her sleeve and never seemed to learn from experience. Ever since she was thirteen or fourteen, Tamsin had fallen passionately, wholeheartedly, self-abasingly in love with a series of boys and young men, who were often insensitive, emotionally withdrawn or downright caddish. Paddy with the strangely long neck and the tiny pupils, who had dumped Tamsin for her best friend; BK (Isabel never knew what the initials stood for), who had persuaded Tamsin to cut all her hair off a few days before leaving her; Leo, who had drifted off aimlessly; Goran, who had slept with her and then accused her of being easy. Each time, she would be radiant with belief that this one was different. Isabel thought of her daughter's trusting face, lifted adoringly to whoever she was currently smitten with, and felt fearful for her. The world would chew her up and spit her out, and she would land at her mother's feet, weeping and wretched, yet still ready to open her bruised petals to the world.

'Yes,' Tamsin was insisting. 'He feels the same way as me, Mum. I wish you could meet him.'

'Why can't I?'

'It's a bit complicated.'

'Why? Is he married?'

She said it without thinking, but before the question was out of her mouth, she could see she had hit on the truth. 'Oh,' was all she said now.

'It's not like you think, Mum.'

'How do I think it is?'

'You think he's a cheat and I'm a fool. I can see.'

'So tell me how it actually is.'

'He's lovely.' Tamsin's face turned dreamy. 'Just lovely.'

'But he's got a wife.'

'Kind of.'

'How do you have a wife kind of?'

'She doesn't live with him any more.'

'Because of you?'

'No! She doesn't know about me. No one does. Because they got married too young and it wasn't working. So he's not really married, you see.'

'How old is this – what's his name?'

'Jed.'

'How old is Jed?'

'Twenty-six.'

'How did you meet him?'

'Well.' Tamsin chewed her finger and looked out of the window at the blank sky, which promised snow. 'This is where it starts to get more complicated.'

'I thought the complication was him being married.'

'He's doing a PhD at the university and he teaches there.'

'You mean, he teaches you?'

'Only a couple of classes,' Tamsin said hastily, as though that made everything all right. 'Developmental psychology. He's *such* a good teacher.'

'I'm sure,' Isabel said drily.

'That's why no one can know. He would be in trouble if people knew he'd slept with a student of his – even though he's not really a teacher.'

'I'm sure he would,' said Isabel.

'But I finish in May,' said Tamsin, brightly. 'After that, it's fine.'

'It's quite a long time to wait.'

'Well, yes. I'm not sure we'll be able to, actually.' She met Isabel's eyes. 'In the circumstances.'

'Oh, no!'

'It's not a bad thing, Mum. Don't look like that.'

'You're pregnant?'

'Yes.'

'How pregnant?'

'Oh – hardly at all. A few weeks.'

'Then –'

'No! You don't understand. I'm happy. Really, really happy. I want to have it. So does Jed.'

'He wants it?'

'He's over the moon.'

'Let me get this straight: you're pregnant by a married man, who's your teacher, and you're pleased.'

'Well, if you put it like that,' said Tamsin, in an offended voice. 'You could have said, "You're in love and going to be a mother, how wonderful."'

'You're definitely going to have it?'

'Yes!'

'With Jed's support.'

'With Jed's support and love and pleasure. And yours, I hope.'

'Listen, you know you have my support, always and no matter what. But I want to make sure you know what you're doing.'

'You don't trust me.'

'It's not that.'

'It is. You think you can see things about my life that I can't because I'm poor, foolish Tamsin, who always gets hurt. You think he's going to let me down.'

'Because you've been let down before.'

'I know, I know. But this time it's different, it really is. Because he's different. I make him happy. I comfort him. He's been so miserable about his wife leaving, and now he's not – do you have any idea of how wonderful that makes me feel about myself? Me, Tamsin Hopkins, making Jed Selek feel that life is worth living again. We look after each other. He confides in me.'

She stopped, breathless, and waited.

Isabel was thinking how ironic it was that, in these last two days, her daughters had turned to her in their different ways, giving her their secrets and demanding her attention. Couldn't they see she was a ragged charade of a mother? A poor excuse, whose son had fled from her into some whirling darkness where she couldn't follow, and now all she could do was summon the last shreds of her common sense. They were leaning on her as though she was a pillar, not a scarecrow ready to tip into the mud. She put her hand on Tamsin's shoulder, and Tamsin gazed at her through swimming eyes.

'I am with you every inch of the way,' Isabel said.

Tamsin gave a loud sob.

'All I want is your happiness,' she added, thinking, *All?* I'm wanting everything.

'I know. He does make me happy. When you meet him, you'll understand.'

'Describe him.'

'I've got a picture. Do you want to see it?'

Isabel nodded.

Tamsin took her wallet from her satchel and eagerly pulled a photo from it. She laid it reverently in Isabel's hands. 'There!' she said, as if he was the most beautiful creature in the world.

Isabel stared at the face: thin, strained and sensitive, with a creased brow and an uncertain smile on his lips. He didn't look like a cad or a confidence trickster, but like a young man who had been treated roughly by life. Looking at his sandy hair, his sprinkling of freckles, Isabel could imagine him being teased at school, overlooked at university and abandoned by his wife. Suddenly, she could imagine him loving her kind-hearted daughter, and she warmed to his anxious, almost sad expression. 'He looks very nice,' she said decisively, handing back the picture.

'You're not just saying that?'

'No. I'd like to meet him.'

'You will.'

'So. I'm going to be a grandmother.' Isabel was trying to smile, but the pain of the idea was making her stomach cramp with longing for her son. To lose a child in one week, then find you're going to have a grandchild the next: she felt as though tectonic plates inside her were shifting and grinding. She put a hand on her own stomach, realizing even as she did so that she was imitating the actions of a pregnant woman.

'Yes,' Tamsin replied. The tears that had been pooling in her eyes now slid easily down her cheeks. 'And I know this is so hard, Mum. I almost didn't tell you. It seemed so unfair on you. But then I thought it was even more unfair not to tell you.'

'I'm very, very glad you did. Are you feeling OK?'

'Very.'

'Not sick or anything?'

'No. But I feel different. As if something's already happening inside me.'

'It is.'

'Will you tell Dad for me?'

'If you'd prefer.'

'He'll be furious.'

'He'll be worried.'

'And Mia – don't tell her yet. She'll look at me as if I'm a creature the cat's dragged in.'

'You may be surprised. But why does it matter what other people think, if you know your own mind?'

'It shouldn't, you're right.'

'Shall we go home now?'

'Yes. Mum?'

'Mm?'

'Can you be happy, even while you're so sad?'

'Of course I can.' She turned a bright, lying smile on Tamsin. Her stomach churned. Felix's word echoed in her skull: *pretend. Pretend.*

Chapter Sixteen

When the newspaper article came out, Isabel couldn't bring herself to read it. The headline blared out at her: 'Parents' Worst Nightmare'. And there were pull-out quotes: 'All I want for Christmas is for Johnny to come home' and 'We will never rest until we find him.' Had they really said that? Had they looked like that, standing with their arms slackly about each other's waist at the front door, on their faces an almost identical look of tense misery? Did she really look like that, so scrawny and worn away, and did Felix look so stripped to the bone, all sinews and nerves? Next to their photograph was the poster of Johnny, with 'Johnny, Come Home!' printed underneath in bold letters.

Isabel couldn't read it, but Felix perused it word by word, making sure that they had all the facts correct and had put in the right phone numbers to contact. Then, with his red-handled scissors, he cut out the article neatly and photocopied it several times. The original he pasted into a large scrapbook he had bought for the purpose of recording the investigation into Johnny's disappearance; it was already thickening with information he had gathered.

After the piece came out, the phone rang constantly. Felix, crouched in his study with the blinds down against the winter sun, would snatch it up on the first ring, pen already in hand, notebook open. Once or twice the call was from someone who thought they might have seen Johnny, although it always came to nothing. More often, it was an old friend or acquaintance with whom he and Isabel had lost contact long ago, but now wanted to get back in touch, full of sorrow and horror and a stifled, inadmissible curiosity about how the Hopkinses – that lucky and comfortable middle-class family – had come to such a pass.

Felix was still going through Johnny's laptop and following up anything that might conceivably turn out to be a lead. He had started with his emails, looking at everything in the inbox, even reading through the frantic and passionate letters Isabel had written when she had first discovered he had gone, making notes of names and email addresses, sending messages to every single person who had been in communication with Johnny in the last few months. He went on to the outbox and did the same. He didn't show them to Isabel – why should she read little notes, funny pieces of shared information, arrangements made or broken? Then he moved on to the trash, and after that he went through the junk mail. Now he was trawling through the websites Johnny had visited in the few days before he had gone missing, the only ones he could discover from the computer's history. Facebook was relatively new and only a few of Felix's students had started to use it; there was no sign that Johnny had. Most of the sites were YouTube ones, news sources, blogs, Internet banking. It seemed unlikely that any of them would yield new evidence but, nevertheless, Felix went through them all meticulously, recording them as he did so.

Quite often his mother kept him company in the study, taking up her place in the corner. She would sink into the deep old armchair – later she had to be hauled out of it – and take up her knitting, with the light of the standard lamp pooled around her hunched figure. She was not the peaceful presence that the act of knitting implied – delicate needles flying, the clicks ticking off the minutes, fine garments growing. She had taken up the activity just a few weeks ago, and could only make lumpy scarves, using huge, clunking needles and thick wool that rolled away from her, tangling up in the wheels of Felix's swivel chair. She couldn't see very well, and her fingers were thick and swollen, and no matter how large the needles, she always dropped numerous stitches, so the scarves – which she handed out with an air of triumphant generosity – had wavy edges and were full of holes. She sighed, muttered, breathed heavily. But she was the only person Felix would allow near him as he sat, a lonely detective, embroiled in his investigation. There was masses of information but not a single clue. Sometimes Miranda would stop knitting and stare at her son, and Felix, noticing the sudden silence, would meet his mother's brooding gaze and give her a half-smile before returning to his work.

Once, when Miranda was taking a nap upstairs, Isabel went into the study. She didn't sit in the armchair, but fidgeted by the door. She had just returned from one of her fruitless pilgrimages, looking for Johnny in places she knew he would not be. Today she had gone to a beach in Norfolk where they used to have picnics when he was younger. She had walked along the shining sands in the bitter cold, squinting into the wincingly bright light to make out solitary figures. That old man with a terrier, that couple entwined round each other and walking slowly along the hem of the sea, that pair of friends laughing at each other. She had gone to the tea-shop they had visited as a family and put up a poster, ducking away from the sympathy of the woman behind the counter. She could not bear pity: it pressed down on her and made her breath come in gasps. Yet at the same time she couldn't bear it if people didn't know, if they treated her coolly or with indifference.

'Yes?' Felix lifted his eyes.

'Sorry to disturb you.' Isabel noted how they were treating each other with a careful politeness.

'It's OK.'

'Have you found anything useful?'

'I don't think so.'

'Felix?'

'Mm.'

'Tell me what you're feeling.'

'I'm sorry?'

'We don't talk.'

'Do you want to talk?' He laid down his pen and waited, eyebrows raised, like an overworked businessman putting up with the petty enquiries of a minion. He cast an extra-ordinarily negative atmosphere over the room and over Isabel. She shivered and took a small step back from him. 'I don't mean that I have something particular to say,' she replied, with difficulty, forcing herself to remain calm. 'I mean, we're not accompanying each other.'

'And where would we accompany each other?'

'Oh! You know what I'm saying. When I'm with Tamsin, or with Mia, I feel we can somehow comfort each other. We don't need to say anything – but we can be together and that makes it a tiny bit better. And you and Miranda – she makes you feel less lonely, I can see that and I'm really glad you have it. But you and I, Felix, we're like barbed wire on each other's skin. We make things worse for each other – don't you agree?'

'I don't know what you mean.'

'Exactly that – that tone of voice, that refusal to recognize my feelings or expose your own. *I don't know what you mean.* You do, I know you do.'

'You want us to comfort each other?'

'Is that so impossible?'

'You don't even mean what you're saying. When we lie in bed at night, do you know what you do? You either screw yourself up into a tight ball, like a hedgehog, with your back turned to me, or you lie on the edge of the bed, as far away from me as possible. If I happen to brush against you by chance, you physically recoil.'

'I don't mean to.'

'You cannot bear to be touched by me. Do you think I want to have sex with you? Is that it?'

'No,' whispered Isabel. She was shocked by the fury on his face.

'Because I don't. It would be like having sex with a corpse.'

'We could just – hold on to each other,' Isabel said.

'You want us to hug each other?' Felix opened his arms wide. 'Come on, then. Let's hug each other.'

Isabel shrank from him. 'Not like this,' she said. 'It's horrible.'

'Everything's horrible. You don't really want to know what's going on inside my head, and I don't want to know what's going on inside yours. We could drive each other mad. So just leave it alone, Isabel.'

'If that's what you want.'

There was the sound of a stick tapping its way along the hall and the door swung open. Miranda, wearing an old dressing-gown over her clothes, entered with her bag of knitting. She made her way to the armchair, sinking into it as if that was where she belonged. Felix turned on his swivel chair back to his desk and Isabel left the room.

Tamsin and Mia both insisted that they had to have some kind of Christmas. They didn't want to cancel everyone who had been invited months ago, because they didn't want it to be just the four of them and Miranda in the house, waiting in on an empty day, hoping through the long hours, each of them locked away inside their own longing. Tamsin called Graham and Celia, Rory and Helen, Ben, and told them all they still had to come. 'But don't worry about presents,' she said. 'We're not really giving presents this year.' Mia went round to their neighbour, knocking and ringing on his doorbell, then peering through the letterbox while his golden retriever barked wildly at her from the other side. At last she saw him making his way along the hall towards her.

'Hello, my dear,' he said, and patted her hand. He still treated her like a small child; sometimes he would give her toffees that she put into her pocket to throw away later. She could smell the alcohol on his breath, although it was only three in the afternoon. His face was raddled under his soft white hair, which was thick and beautiful.

'Hello, Kenny – we just wanted to make sure you're still coming for Christmas dinner.'

His dog lifted its shaggy yellow head and licked her hand.

'If you still want me.'

'Of course we do.'

'Your poor mother. I see her in the garden. She looks like a ghost.'

'I know,' said Mia, wanting to be gone. 'It's hard.'

'When I think of your brother . . .' Mia shifted from foot to foot, edging back out of the door '. . . and how he always used to kick his ball over my fence . . .' Mia fixed a goodbye smile on her face, lifted a hand '. . . and such a friendly little chap he always was. I've known him since he was this high.'

'I have to go now but we'll see you on Christmas Day.'

'And I think to myself how you never can tell what's round the corner.'

'True,' said Mia.

'As my ma used to say, "Rain falls from the bluest sky."'

Isabel remembered a time when she and Johnny had visited the war graves in Normandy. There had been row upon row of white crosses marking the dead, as far as the eye could see, a peaceful and haunting field of mourning. Tucked away, almost unvisited, were the graves of the German soldiers. A great deal of thought must have gone into how to commemorate the dead on the defeated and disgraced side: instead of upright white crosses, they were horizontal black ones. Now when she contemplated Christmas Day, it was like turning the old, well-loved rituals on their backs, so that they were still there but in a sombre and muted form. So: a Christmas tree, but smaller than usual, with only a few of their decorations on its branches. No gaudy tinsel, but the same lights they had had since they were married – every year Felix carefully wrapped them around a stiff piece of cardboard and laid them in a box before storing them in the attic; every year, they mysteriously coiled up in the dark, forming into snarls and knots that took hours to unpick. And then some of the lights didn't work, and instead of going out and buying a whole new set, which hardly cost anything, he would test each bulb and when he found the faulty one, replace it – because they had always had these lights. No wreath on the door, because that would seem like a symbol of mourning. A stocking with bits and pieces for each of the girls, but nothing for Isabel and Felix, and nothing for their guests, except a bottle of whisky apiece. Turkey, but no crackers. Wine, but no champagne. They would still have carols round the piano, but nothing, Isabel told herself, like 'In The Bleak Midwinter'.

And then, secretly, she started buying small things for Johnny in case he came home. She bought a recipe book and a blue cotton apron and a collection of variously sized wooden spoons; a book of poetry; a pale yellow shirt; a red teapot. With each item, she allowed herself to imagine him – stirring food in a saucepan, pouring a mug of tea, lying on the sofa in his shirt reading, smiling at her, his blue eyes warm. She bought a new razor and some blades, because if he turned up he'd probably need to shave. She let herself imagine her happiness, the fresh and cascading river of joy that would run through her parched and cracking landscape, and then she wrapped each object in newspaper and hid them all at the back of her wardrobe, where no one would ever come across them.

She remembered how Fergal had said Johnny was now a vegetarian, and spent hours leafing through cookery books, of which she had many, though most she rarely used, trying to find a recipe that was special enough to welcome him home. She rejected the idea of stuffed peppers, a vegetable pie, Thai noodles or anything with lentils, because lentils seemed to have punitive connotations. She fixed all her turbulent longings on the meal, as if by cooking the right thing, she could bring Johnny back: food as magic, food as a spell.

'What do you think?' she asked Jenny, in whom she had confided. They were in Jenny's kitchen, which was full of the smell of baking ham.

'What do I think? I think you shouldn't make anything special.'

'I have to!'

'If he comes, he can have the trimmings. It doesn't matter. It's not important in any way at all.'

'Oh, but it is.'

'Listen, my darling Isabel. You're fixing on this, persuading yourself that Johnny will walk back in on Christmas Day, and you have to be ready for him or he won't come or something. He probably won't. You'll go mad if you behave like this.'

'Ravioli!'

'You do it all the time, in different ways. You tell yourself

197

he'll be down by the sea, up in the moors, with this friend or that, in a place you once visited. If you don't eat, if you don't sleep, or if you run somewhere until your lungs are exploding or hold your breath for long enough – I've seen you doing it – as if you can bring him back by the sheer force of your will. You can't.'

'Wild mushroom ravioli. Homemade.' Isabel fixed her red-rimmed eyes on Jenny, speaking over the top of her. 'That would be special.'

'Stop it.'

'I can make the pasta in advance and roll it out just before the meal.'

'Stop!'

'I've bought him Christmas presents.'

'Oh, Isabel.'

'You've given up on him. You think he's not coming back.'

'That's not true. I think he's probably not coming back on Christmas Day, though he might. I just don't want you to count on it and then go through the agony when it doesn't happen.'

'Everyone will give up. But not me. Not ever. I write him letters every day.'

'Yes.' Jenny sighed and rubbed her face. 'Well, I'd probably do the same if it was Max.'

'I haven't got anywhere to send them. I would write emails, but then they'd just go straight to Felix. So I write letters and put them in my desk. Sometimes the only time I feel all right is when I'm writing to him in my best handwriting, though he's always been quite good at deciphering it.'

'I don't know what to say.'

'There isn't anything to say. I'm going to make ravioli stuffed with wild mushrooms. I've never made pasta before. Felix once gave me one of those little machines with a handle. It must be around somewhere. It's probably a bit rusty by now.'

'I think you can roll it out by hand.'

'Really? Tamsin's in love, you know.'

'Oh.' If Jenny was surprised by the abrupt change of subject, she didn't show it. 'That's lovely – isn't it?'

'He's married.'

'Oh. Not so good.'

'And her teacher.'

'God.'

'Don't tell Felix.'

'He doesn't know?'

'Not yet. I need to tell him – Tamsin doesn't dare. But I can't find the right time. He's locked away in his study, and when he comes out, it's as if there's a wall around him with a big notice hung on it, saying "Keep Out". I have to tell him soon, because I think Jed is planning to visit us and it wouldn't do to have him arrive and catch Felix unawares. So the real bomb-shell is that I'm going to be a granny – not just a step-grandmother. The real biological thing. He doesn't know that yet, either, of course. I had to tell someone.'

'Tamsin's pregnant?'

'Pregnant and blissfully happy and guilty for being so happy.'

'Everything all at once. How do you feel about it?'

'In spite of everything, I have never known Tamsin so

contented. Of course I worry – that it won't last, that she's being deceived. But you know, if this had happened a couple of months ago, I would probably have been consumed by anxiety about it – what about her career, isn't she too young, will he actually stay with her, all those kinds of questions. Now, I just think that there are different ways of being happy and maybe this is hers and she should grasp it. I think we put our children on a road – GCSEs, A levels, university, a profession – and expect them to stay on it. But sometimes it's not the right road for them. I think I did it with Johnny and he didn't know how to get off it, except by running away. I don't want to make the same mistake with Tamsin. I can either support her or not support her – and supporting her means sharing her delight. So I do.'

'Good. That's good, then. A grandmother – wow!'

'I know. I'm not even fifty.'

'And what will Felix think?' Jenny asked cautiously.

Isabel shrugged.

'Is everything all right with you and Felix – I mean, as all right as it can be given . . . ?' Jenny waved her hands in the air.

'I don't know. No, probably not. We're locked in our own separate worlds. We don't meet. I don't care, actually. Does that sound awful?'

'Not awful – worrying, maybe.'

'Worrying? What's worrying, compared to a son disappearing?'

'Do you mean that nothing else matters? What about Mia and Tamsin?'

'They matter.'

'But not Felix?'

'He's not in my blood.'

'But –'

'He's not in my blood and my bones and my nerves and my epidermis. I can't feel him.'

'Isabel, do you think you need help?'

'Help?' Isabel gave a shout of miserable laughter. 'Oh – you mean counselling or something. Wouldn't it be more worrying if I wasn't going mad?'

'I don't know. Maybe.'

'I wish I could go mad, actually.'

'Don't say that.'

'What do you want me to say? That everything is going to be all right? OK: everything is going to be all right. Johnny will come for Christmas. Which is why I'm making him wild mushroom ravioli.'

'Have you cried yet?'

'No. Not properly.' Isabel thought of the racking sobs that had felt like a wild sea inside her, surging and battering.

'Why?'

'If I started to cry, Jenny, how would I ever, ever stop?'

She didn't time the announcement very well. It was twenty to seven in the morning and Felix was pulling on his running clothes, although the sun wouldn't rise for another hour. Isabel sat up in bed and watched him. She could feel the words forming, sticking together into a phrase. He stood in his boxers and his running socks, holding a top in his hands, his knees knobbly and his chest white, and she said in a rush, 'There's something you should know, Felix.'

Then, before he had had time even to turn his head towards her: 'Tamsin has met someone and she's very happy and she's going to have a baby.'

'What?' He dropped his top to the floor. He frowned. 'Our Tamsin. A baby?'

Why had she thought he would simply be angry?

He looked at her and stood up straighter, drawing in his stomach – an ageing man in his underwear, thinking about his daughter, worried but moved, a frown knitting his brow but his thin mouth softening in emotion. He sat down at the end of the bed. 'Oh, Izzie.'

'I know.'

'Is she fine about it?'

'Very.'

'And the father?'

'I gather he's delighted as well. His name's Jed.'

'She's very young – she hasn't even left university.'

'Yes.'

'Is he a student as well?'

She took a deep breath and tried to sound casual. 'A post-graduate student.'

'Ah.'

'He – um.' She found she couldn't tell Felix that Jed had taught Tamsin: she knew how his face would change, become stern and unyielding. He had very strong views on such things. She opted for the easier piece of news: 'He's married.' She spoke over Felix's exclamation: 'But not living with his wife, who left him before he met Tamsin, so don't look like that. Don't. We have to be happy for her. Felix?'

'Don't tell me to be happy.'

'If she's happy, we should be.'

'Is that your new creed?' He pulled his top over his head and stood up.

'I think it's my old creed as well.'

'It won't get you far.'

'Felix, let's do this together, shall we? Please. For Tamsin's sake.'

He put on his running trousers, pulling the drawstring tight. 'You're right,' he said, after a pause. 'Sorry.' He pulled the curtain back slightly and looked out at the dark, cloudy sky. 'Sorry for taking things out on you,' he added gruffly. 'It's not fair.'

'I do it to you too.'

'How long can we endure it?'

Will came to the house. From her bedroom window, Isabel could see him and Mia at the bottom of the garden. It was rainy and windy, and they stood among the wet, dishevelled undergrowth, talking. Will was animated. He gestured, pleaded. His face was mobile with expressions. Mia listened and watched him – and Isabel, standing to one side of the window so that they wouldn't see she was there, watched her. Her slight, strong figure, the way she lifted her chin. Gallant, unflinching, meeting the world head on. That was what she had always done. Mia turned away and Will touched her shoulder. She turned back. They stared at each other. Isabel saw Will take her fingers and then they leant into each other, foreheads touching. Will was still speaking. She thought they were both crying. She moved away from the window.

*

'Mum, this is Jed. Jed, Mum.'

They shook hands. His was thin and dry but his grasp was firm. He was a slight young man, with narrow shoulders and a look of translucency. Tamsin kept touching him – his arm, his knee, picking up his hand to fiddle with the slender fingers, whose nails were bitten to the quick. She wanted to tell her daughter to take care – but then she saw how Jed beamed softly at her, half awkward and half delighted, and how his tense frame relaxed at her touch.

'Where's Dad?'

'In his study, with Granny. Go and drag him out.'

'Is he – you know – angry?'

'Angry?'

'With me.'

'No. Of course not.'

'Is he pleased?'

'Give him time.' As Tamsin left the room, she said, in a half-whisper, 'I haven't told him yet about Jed teaching you.'

'Mum!'

'I will. I just thought we could wait a bit.'

They all drank tea in the kitchen, Miranda still knitting furiously, a lime green scarf, full of holes and knots, growing across the table like a convulsive snake. Isabel had never known how loud and unpeaceful knitting could be. Jed sat very upright and so did Felix, facing him. It was only when Isabel saw her husband with strangers, looked at him through their eyes, that she realized just how forbidding and how powerful he was. There was no mention of babies, or of previous wives, or of future plans. Instead

Isabel asked a few unthreatening questions about Southampton and then about where he had grown up, which turned out to be Wimbledon.

'Tennis,' thundered Miranda, from behind her needles.

'I don't really play tennis, I'm afraid,' said Jed, apologetically. His cheeks were pink and he kept darting looks at Tamsin, asking her to rescue him.

'No, but you run, don't you?' Tamsin turned to Felix. 'He's a really good runner, fast and unflagging,' she said. 'He's got the body of a long-distance runner, hasn't he? Thin but strong.' She looked at Jed with such adoration as she said this that Isabel had to look away. It was like seeing her daughter naked.

'Dad runs as well,' Tamsin said now to Jed, busily making bridges. 'He's done loads of marathons.'

'Have you done any marathons?' Felix asked Jed sharply.

'No. I'd like to.'

'He's done half-marathons,' put in Tamsin.

'What was your time?'

'Um, a bit under an hour and a half, I think.'

'Hmm. Under a seven-minute mile.'

'How fast do you run?' asked Isabel, who knew.

'Seven and a half minutes,' he said grudgingly. 'Or thereabouts.'

'So Jed is fast.'

'That's over twenty-six miles,' added Felix.

'I tell you what,' said Mia, who had come into the kitchen as the conversation began and now half sat on the kitchen table. 'Why don't you two have a race to decide who's the fastest?'

'Don't be ridiculous,' said Felix.

'All right, Dad. Arm wrestle him, then. Settle it like that.'

'Mia,' said Isabel, warningly.

'What?'

'You know.'

'I'm very sorry about your son,' Jed said. He had clearly decided to talk about what everyone was thinking; the muscles in his cheeks tightened and his voice was slightly hoarse. He took a sip of his cooling tea.

'Thank you,' Isabel replied.

Felix stared at him and gave a curt nod.

'And,' said Jed, 'I hope you know that I couldn't be more pleased about Tamsin.'

Brave, thought Isabel, and smiled at him. She could become fond of this young man.

Jed took Tamsin's hand and she looked at him with eyes full of tears. They were like an old-fashioned couple asking the parents for permission. Mia, swinging her leg, smirked and looked up at the ceiling.

'It's natural that you're anxious because of the way that everything has happened, but I love her very much indeed and I'm going to make her happy and I'm going to be a good father to our child.'

Miranda dropped several stitches and her puckered mouth opened like a fish's. Mia popped half a chocolate digestive into her mouth and chewed it noisily. Isabel stood up and went round the table to where Jed sat. She kissed him on one flushed cheek and then the other. 'Good,' she said. 'That's good. She's very precious.'

Tamsin joyfully began to weep.

Chapter Seventeen

She made the pasta dough on Christmas Eve. Felix had collected her father that afternoon, and he sat in his wheelchair at the table, watching her. His right eye stared at her and the left one drooped. She should sit by his side, hold his hand and listen when he tried vainly to speak, but she couldn't. She was getting ready for Johnny. Semolina and egg yolks and a pinch of salt, lots of pummelling until it was shiny and elastic. Then she wrapped the plump, tight dough in clingfilm and put it in the fridge. She soaked the dried wild mushrooms in warm water, shutting her eyes to breathe in their smell of Marmite and dark woods.

Ben arrived with his girlfriend, Gabriella, half a Stilton and a mass of flowers wrapped in damp newspaper. He lifted Isabel up in his arms when he hugged her and she felt like both a tiny child and a shrivelled old woman. There was flour in her hair and down her jersey. Gabriella had cascading dark curls with flakes of snow caught in them, and black eyes. She held on to Isabel's hands, looked into her eyes, and said she was sorry, so sorry. She smelt of musk roses and Isabel thought she was as beautiful as a receding dream.

But this evening everyone looked beautiful to her – beautiful and indistinct, like figures seen in a sea mist. Mia had decorated the tree and Felix had wound it round with lights, patiently unravelling the knots and tightening separate bulbs until the whole string glowed white. Tamsin had lit candles on windowsills and mantelpieces. The house was filled with a guttering soft light, and in it, people took on a mysterious quality, like half-remembered strangers, like ghosts in their own lives. She saw now that Tamsin was lush and lovely, because finally beloved. She saw that Mia had changed when her back was turned, no longer a tomboy but a slender young woman, clean-limbed, with black hair and pale skin, her brow stern over deep brown eyes.

Rory, Helen and Lucy arrived, bringing wine, chocolate and two boxes of crackers, as well as a travel cot, a high chair, a bouncy chair, a bag of nappies, several bags of clothes and a box of plastic toys. They would stay two nights, but their car was as crammed as those of emigrants in search of a new land. They had brought roses – everyone had produced flowers: the house was like a funeral parlour. Felix's sister Suzanne arrived with her new husband; she carried a tub of hyacinth bulbs in her outstretched arms, like a sacred offering – the shoots were just beginning to push up through the soil. The house was filling. Corks were pulled out of bottles; Lucy gurgled and wailed; Gabriella sang in the shower; Rory turned on the TV to watch some cheery pre-Christmas quiz show; the phone rang and was answered (each time Isabel's heart hammered against her ribcage and her eyes stung); the smell of cloves from the ham Tamsin was baking filled the air. In his study, Felix played adagios on the violin, and the sad, quivering sounds hung in the air.

At least with a crowd of guests Isabel didn't have to do anything except be in the background, attending to needs, pulling out mattresses for Mia and Tamsin, who had vacated their rooms for guests, putting out clean towels and making sure there was enough paper in each lavatory, ladling soup, cutting bread, sliding trays of mince pies into the oven, picking Lucy up when she started to cry, and all the time letting the animation wash over her. Every so often people came and spoke to her and she answered; they put a hand on her shoulder and she smiled and smiled and said, yes, of course she was fine; they kissed her cheek and she let them; they asked questions and she managed to answer. She knew they were watching her: she felt their eyes on her and sensed their protective concern. She knew that when she wasn't there, they would gather together in pairs and groups to talk about her.

Nobody mentioned Johnny but Johnny was everywhere – in the high, quivering notes of Felix's violin, standing beside her as she cooked, in the garden when she looked out of the window into the sleety and inhospitable darkness.

Johnny's room stood empty. Nobody was allowed to sleep in there, because it was waiting for his return. Everybody understood this without it being explained. The door was shut, and behind it lay an absence that was palpable, throbbing with loss. It was the still centre of the house and its vortex, nothing and everything. A terrible door, opening on to a void. When Isabel woke in the night, as she always did now, lying pinned and trembling in her bed with darkness around her, she rose and went into that room. The bed was made up with fresh sheets. A towel was folded on the chair. She had put a miniature cyclamen in there a few days ago and each day watered it carefully, making sure that the soil was moist. In the evenings she would close the curtains, and in the mornings open them again. The familiar anguish rose in her and she sat on his bed, patted the pillow smooth, and waited. Sometimes she shut her eyes and let herself imagine him beside her: he would put a hand on her arm and she would turn and see him there, that small secret smile, those blue eyes. Sometimes she slept in here, or at least lay down on the bed and put her head where his should have been; once, she had crept in and found Mia lying under the sheets, holding the duvet under her chin, her eyes wet with tears. Tonight she didn't stay long: when she was able, she stood up and went downstairs, hearing the creak of the steps under her feet, the rumble of the old boiler, the cry of the owl that called for a mate from the bottom of the garden, the ragged drum of her heart, the thump of her pulse in her ears.

She went into the garden in her nightdress and welling-tons and stood under the tree at the far end, near the guinea pig's run, near the owl's haunt. A few lights blinked on the horizon. She stood on trembling legs and waited. She didn't know what she was waiting for. She closed her eyes and wished, but didn't know what she was wishing for: for Johnny to come home, for herself to vanish into the comfort of nothing. At last, when her face was stiff with cold and her body shivering, she went back into the house and lay beside Felix – not touching him, not taking any comfort from his sleeping warmth – and stayed like that until sleep and fearful dreams sucked her under.

The next morning she woke early, when the house was still in darkness. Even Lucy was still asleep. For a moment, she lay quite still, feeling stunned after her crashing, brutal nightmares. Her sinuses ached and her heart felt as swollen and tender as a giant bruise. She rose and went downstairs. Felix's study, where Mia and Tamsin lay rolled in their sleeping bags, like giant chrysalises, was in darkness though his computer hummed, the little green light flashing. She swept the still-warm ash from the hearth, sending up sparks from the dying embers, then built a new fire for later. She stroked the knobbled spine of Digby and laid her face into his musty fur. She turned on the lights of the Christmas tree in the hall, cleared up the kitchen from last night and emptied the dishwasher. Then she boiled the kettle and made a large pot of tea for herself. There was a routine, year after year. Put the oven on for the turkey. Bring the Christmas pudding, tied up in muslin, out from the pantry. Potatoes. Brussels sprouts. Bread sauce. Radio 4. Background noise. Other people. Who cared? They all cared. The sense of life continuing. Like a motor carrying her along, whether she wanted it or not. Upstairs, she heard a child cry. The phone rang and her heart stirred. She bade it be still. Someone answered and she stood, rolling pin in hand, and listened. Nobody shouted or came running down the stairs with news, so it was nothing, after all.

She rolled out the pasta. The book said it had to be very thin, almost transparent. She worked away until sweat formed on her brow, leaning down on the rolling pin, dusting it with more semolina flour. The sheet of pasta grew.

Breakfast. People coming in and out of the kitchen. A kiss on her cheek, a hand on her back. She thought she replied. Morning smell of coffee and fresh bread. Marmalade. Toast. Ben made scrambled eggs. Lucy solemnly watched her still rolling out the dough, her eyes flicking back and forward, and then a plump fist knocked against a glass of milk and sent it flying off the table. It shattered on the floor. The milk spread in a river across the tiles. Her father sat at the kitchen table and his twisted mouth worked as he tried to form words. Graham and Celia and Celia's mother Anne arrived. Graham was anxious, too formal: his words came out of him in tense, prepared bursts. Celia was bossy. Her shoes clipped in the hall. Things were carried in and out of the house. The turkey was already in the oven. The tree lights kept flickering on and off, and Felix was on his knees, patiently studying them; she could tell from his stillness how nervous he was, how wretched. Nobody mentioned Johnny.

Rory prepared the sprouts. Gabriella stood at the sink with her glorious hair tied back, peeling potatoes. Graham opened bottles of wine he had brought and lined them up. Miranda played patience at the kitchen table, pushing cutlery and vegetables to one side to make room for her cards.

Mia stood beside her mother. She had washed her hair and brushed it back, and had put on a short black dress and red lipstick. Isabel thought that she looked a bit like a character in a club in Berlin in the thirties, starkly arresting. They didn't speak to each other, but at one point Mia took Isabel's hand in hers and gave it a tight squeeze before lifting it and pressing it against her own cheek. Isabel tried to smile. At least, she could feel the skin tightening around her mouth. Tamsin had put on a scarlet shirt. She kept putting her hand across her belly: now that everyone knew, she had started behaving like a pregnant woman. She found she didn't like the taste of coffee but made herself endless mugs of mint tea. She was taking care of herself. Every hour or so, her mobile would ring and she would take herself into the hall or living room and whisper into it, smiling her intimate smile, her eyes tender.

Isabel fried the mushrooms with garlic and added cream. She cut out rectangles of translucent pasta and put a spoonful of mushroom filling on to each one, then folded it into a neat parcel, pressing the edges together. They looked unexpectedly perfect, almost professional. She closed her eyes for a moment, before tears could form. Her father had fallen asleep in his chair, his head tilted forward. In the living room, his dead wife looked down on the flickering fire and the groups of young people and smiled at them. The television played. Christmas songs. Everyone smiling. Happy day.

Their neighbour arrived, hair carefully brushed and wearing a wide purple satin tie. He brought a crimson poinsettia and his dog, the slightly smelly retriever, who settled herself under the table and went to sleep. Digby watched from his chair, unblinking yellow eyes. Next year, thought Isabel, washing her hands, staring at herself in the unkind mirror, next year, whatever happened, she would work in a homeless centre at Christmas. She would be with people who had fallen out of the world, on whom the day lay like a cold shadow. She imagined the people she had encountered on the London streets now – staring in at the lit windows, at the sheen and hum of other people's merriment. Sometimes her life made her feel physically sick. She thought of the golden skin of the turkey bubbling and blistering in the oven and winced: how could she put that into her mouth, chew and swallow?

At last everyone had gathered. This was the time when her heart used to swell with a sense of completeness and, yes, with joy. That had to be the word. Something bright, quick and sharp, like a blade of light running through her body, which was now dark, cheerless earth. The Christmas lights were working. The turkey was ready. The potatoes were roasted and the spitting fat poured off into a jar. Tamsin was making gravy, every so often lifting the wooden spoon to her lips and taking a careful sip, nodding to herself appreciatively, grinding a tad more black pepper or pouring in a splash of red wine. Gabriella was carefully placing the triangles of brown bread and smoked salmon on a plate. Felix was sharpening the carving knife, scraping its blade against the stone over and over again. Miranda was talking to Bernard, very loudly and very slowly: she was telling him about the first time she had flown in a plane. Celia's mother was giving Helen instructions on which roses she should buy for her garden, though Helen only had window boxes. For some reason, Graham had been handed Lucy, and stood in the centre of the room, awkwardly swaying with her, and muttering under his breath in his version of a lullaby. Nobody had turned the television off next door and they could hear occasional splatters of studio laughter. Too much food, too much noise. Noise was better than silence, though, better than the clatter of everyone's hearts and the rasp of their breath. The table was being laid. There were crackers at each place. Fourteen people and then one more.

Isabel knew everyone had their eyes on her and on Felix, but no one said anything. The room seemed pressed full of a ghastly kind of embarrassment, a howling unspoken subject squatting in the room. They were all very careful and very kind. They filled her glass with the champagne she had asked not to be brought and she pretended to take a sip and she pretended to smile. She heard her voice and it sounded quite normal. The potatoes were on the table. The bread sauce was ready. The sprouts were in the pan. Clatter of plates. The candles were lit, and outside the day dimmed; little drops of rain pattered against the window. Felix drew the curtains and now Isabel could no longer see the lane, where he would come.

They took their seats. Celia insisted they pulled their crackers, although Isabel had said, please, no crackers. Crossing hands, links in a chain, everyone pull together now. Tiny dynamite pops and rustles of paper. Oh, merry days. How does one get through each moment? Head is just rushing wind. Eyes are just white light, red mist. Body just rotting fruit, splitting skin disclosing unlovely pulp. A paper crown on each head. Bad jokes shouted aloud and laughter: they had to laugh. What time is it when an elephant sits on the fence? Why do birds fly south? When is a door not a door? A door is not a door when it will not open. And a door is not a door when it is a mouth full of sharp teeth, spitting you out into the nothing that is waiting on the other side. And a door is not a door because, of course, Johnny won't come home.

She lifted her untouched glass of wine and held it high

until everyone fell silent. 'A toast,' she said, in a voice she barely recognized. 'To our beloved Johnny.'

Because they had to speak his name out loud. Because although she did not believe in prayer, somewhere, wherever he was, a ripple of love might reach him. For some reason, though, the wine was spilling from her glass onto the tablecloth and Graham was trying to take it from her. Someone was saying something, but she couldn't really understand.

Will and Baxter arrived as the meal was ending, the table littered with bones and crumbs and shreds of tissue paper, stupid cracker toys. Will only wanted to come in if it was really all right: he didn't want to intrude and he knew it might be painful, and if it was, they only had to say the word and of course that was fine, they'd just go – but he and Baxter both wanted to pay their respects. He spoke this formal phrase solemnly, as if he had rehearsed it. He had had his long hair cut quite short and had obviously shaved that morning: his cheeks were smooth and the tips of his now-exposed ears pink from the cold air. He seemed a younger and more innocent version of himself, full of self-consciousness and fear. His eyes flickered round the room, taking in all the strangers there. Baxter followed him, huddled in his coat and awkward. Isabel knew how hard this was for them both. She wanted to tell them she was grateful, but somehow she couldn't make her mouth form the words, so she just stared at them and saw they were trying not to cry.

Jenny came, with Max, Holly and Benedict. Someone must have rung her, thought Isabel, dully. Probably Tamsin. Tamsin has sent for reinforcements because she's worried about me. That would be it. Or even Felix – but Felix wasn't there any more. She had a very dim memory of him standing up from the table and saying, in his courteous and controlled voice, how he thought he would go into the study for a bit and would they think him rude? Of course they wouldn't – perhaps it was a relief for everyone when they no longer had to look at the straight-backed, rigid-faced man at the table, with his sore blue eyes. Miranda had followed him. She was probably in there now, in her chair, knitting. Or perhaps he was crying into her lap at last, and she was stroking his thinning hair and telling him to hush now, hush, because everything would be all right. Sons and their mothers.

Isabel saw how Benedict was holding Jenny's hand and how they both smiled down at her tenderly, concern in their eyes.

'I am happy for you both,' she said, but they didn't seem to understand her words. 'Cherish precious things.'

Leah arrived, alone and just for a bit, she said. Her husband was holding the fort with the assembled relatives. She looked fabulous, all painted and varnished and bright, with perfume wafting from her as she brushed Isabel's cheek with her carmine lips, then rubbed away the kiss. Everyone was protecting her. They couldn't protect her from what was inside her, ravenously consuming her, rat with yellow teeth, fat creamy maggot. Leah was talking animatedly to Tamsin. Mia sat on the floor near the fire with Will and Baxter. Helen was feeding Lucy. Gabriella was sitting next to Bernard and holding his hand. It was perhaps the first time in her adult life that Isabel let all effort and engagement drain from her. She was simply a figure in a chair near the fire.

Someone suggested charades – for charades was always played on a Christmas evening in their house. She felt everyone's eyes turn towards her and tried to lift a hand to wave away their anxieties, but it was too heavy.

'Please,' she said. 'I'd like you to. Is it OK if I just watch?'

So Felix and Miranda sat in his study together, and Isabel rested in the armchair, while everyone else – even Celia's mother, even contorted Graham – acted out charades. It was as though they were doing it for her sake, making clumsy, cheerful attempts to draw her back into life. They lifted their arms and waved them about, grimaced, hopped on the spot, all the time turning their eyes to her shadowy figure. Their audience of Isabel smiled at them. She smiled and smiled and hoped that that would be enough.

Someone took her up to bed. Perhaps it was Leah who laid her down and peeled away her clothes and turned off the light. She had Leah's deft fingers and her citrus smell. She had Leah's gift of knowing when not to speak. What friends she had, after all. Perhaps it was Tamsin who sat in the chair at the end of the bed until her eyes closed. Perhaps it was Mia who took her hand and held it between her own. She could hear voices from downstairs, Felix's sad violin. And then it was silent. When she opened her eyes, Felix was beside her. The curtains were open and the nearly full moon laid its quiet light over the room. Isabel thought that she heard a noise and she got up and went to the window and looked out. For one moment, she saw a figure there, standing beneath the tree and looking up at her, and she gave a tiny whimper. Then it dissolved and there was only moonlight on the grass.

She turned back to the room and saw him quite clearly. He was sitting peacefully in the chair where Tamsin had sat earlier, reading a book, even though the room was in semi-darkness. She moved softly towards the shape, not breathing. And as she reached it, she put out her hand and he looked up and he smiled his beautiful smile at her, and she saw the shape melt away and she was touching nothing but air. She knelt on the floor beside the chair and put her head on it.

She said: *Please*. She said: *I promise*. She said: *I didn't know, I didn't know, I didn't know*.

She wore baggy clothes. In the past, she had chosen tight-fitting ones, tight jeans, shirts that clung, something to remind her she wasn't just a mother. Now all she wanted was to look motherly, comfortable and comforting. Loose jumpers, men's shirts, jeans that she kept up with a rope belt, slip-on shoes in place of biker boots, shapeless warm coats rather than leather jackets or belted macs.

When she phoned friends, she would always say, quickly before they could ask or feel hope, 'No news.' And it reminded her of when she was pregnant and nearing or past her due date, how she would forestall excitement by saying the same thing: 'No news yet. Nothing.'

She found herself telling everyone she met that her son had gone missing. At the bus stop, in checkout queues at the supermarket, once just walking along the street and catching the eye of a woman who smiled at her and who, Isabel felt, with a surge of emotion, looked like someone she would want to have as a friend.

She resembled the Ancient Mariner, condemned to repeat the story until someone would take it away from her. She needed to be told – over and over again – that he would come back, and that it wasn't her fault. Each time someone laid a hand on her in sympathy and told her that they felt for her, she had a momentary sense of absolution that dissipated as soon as they were gone.

At New Year, she sat in the garden in the freezing cold, waiting for the year to turn. In the sky, fireworks exploded and cascaded in fountains of green and red and blue. When she shut her eyes, she could see them still. Perhaps somewhere out there Johnny could see them, too, lighting up the darkness, falling in ribbons of colour, dissolving in the velvet night.

Felix

Chapter Eighteen

If you walked into Felix's study, you would be struck first by the density of organization in it. In the days when they had laughed about such things, Isabel used to say that his study was a representation of his brain: all the things that obsessed and interested him were categorized and sub-divided, laid out in compartments, labelled, prioritized. There was a shelf for his sheets of music, a shelf for his books on running and cardiovascular fitness, an entire wall given over to medieval literature. In the corner – near the chair that Miranda would occupy over that hellish Christmas – there was a revolving set of shelves for the books he currently needed for his work. In the alcove, under the beautiful painting of *St Jerome in his Study*, which Isabel said was obviously a self-portrait as well, he kept his students' essays and reports, and any university bureaucracy he had brought back from his office to deal with at home. He stored the objects his children had made for him over the years in a small cabinet, behind glass: a small blue pottery elephant; Rory's clay hen sitting on a nest fashioned from chicken wire and filled with musty hay; a tapestry made by Ben displaying his inadequate grasp of cross-stitch, blanket-stitch and running-stitch; a poem Johnny had once written about Digby, in painstaking large handwriting that sloped down the page, and then framed; Mia's wooden shield, painted a nasty yellow with a blue splodge in the middle; Tamsin's rickety hand-made clock, whose battery Felix still replaced and whose time he regularly corrected.

There were also, on the top shelf, porcelain replicas of his children's hands, made from moulds, some outstretched, some curled, Mia's in a characteristic fist. Isabel had given them to him on one of his birthdays; you could see Tamsin's thumb ring; Ben's middle finger had broken off but Felix had Super-glued it back in place and you could hardly see the join. Five hands. Every so often he would stand in front of the cabinet and look at them. Once, when he was quite alone in the house, he had opened the door of the cabinet and slid his fingers inside the mould of Johnny's hand, as if he could roll back the years and have his youngest son a toddler once again, grasping his father's single finger with trust. But he quickly shut the door. He wasn't a man who made symbolic gestures, even to himself.

His desk was as orderly as his computer desktop, where each document was properly filed and each photograph named and dated. Everything that he had to do was written in a book that looked like an old-fashioned ledger, then neatly crossed off as the task was completed; it was like a diary of diligence. Every receipt was placed in the top drawer of his desk. In the second drawer was his collection of postcards that, in one way or another, showed people in the act of reading. He had stored them for years now and every so often would open the drawer and rummage through them, picking out this Dutch woman sitting by a window with a book, that black-and-white photograph of an old man on a bench with a letter in his hand, this doodled watercolour of a boy lying on a hill with a volume of poetry held above his head and W-shaped birds flying in the bluest sky . . .

His life was placed around him. If he sat in here, the window overlooking the garden, pencils in a mug Isabel had given him long ago and which was now cracked and useless for holding tea, his old-fashioned fountain pen lying on an even more old-fashioned piece of blotting paper, books in alphabetical order, the to-do list open before him, he could feel in control of his life.

Now, of course, that peaceful arrangement of his life into its disparate parts, each attended to in its turn, had shattered. Chaucer was neglected, his students' emails received an out-of-office automated response, his sheets of music gathered dust on the shelf, except the Bach violin cantata he played over and over again, only half aware that he did so because he and Johnny used to play it together. Instead, the study had become his headquarters; it was from here that he conducted his investigation into Johnny's disappearance, collected evidence, made phone calls and wrote emails, roamed the Internet in search of clues and new directions. He had bought himself a scrapbook, and in it he pasted everything he thought might be relevant to the case. In here were all the emails he had received from Johnny's flatmates and other students at Sheffield, the police reports, the letters from Johnny's personal tutor and the principal. He logged every phone call he received from people who thought they might have seen Johnny. He wrote down potentially useful phone numbers, email addresses and names. He put dates beside entries. He included heartfelt responses from parents or spouses of people who had also gone missing, and wrote beside them how he had responded. He had a list at the front of every police officer he had talked to, and of staff at the Missing Persons helpline, an organization he rang every few days.

He also wrote down thoughts – not articulations of his own grief, which he always avoided, even with his family, perhaps especially with his family, but reflections on the experience of loss. He jotted down quotations from other writers and thinkers, he responded to pieces in the news that seemed relevant, he followed ideas down what were for him new avenues. These entries, written between maps and printouts, sometimes just a few sentences and sometimes whole pages of meditation in his impeccable hand, came to resemble a twisted philosophy of sadness and responsibility: twisted because, if you were to read them in one sitting, it would become clear that Felix had become obsessed. Every thought he had, every desire, every purpose and inclination, was tightly coiled around the shape of Johnny's absence and his own failure.

That was how he started to look, as well. Isabel looked blown by emotion, buffeted and torn to shreds, hair adrift, skin slack, eyes wild, clothes hanging off her, hands fluttering in anxious gestures and holding her body together as if she would fall apart. But Felix channelled his emotions, ingested them. He became tauter, gaunter, harder; a chiselled, sculpted shape, skin over bone and muscle, eyes a blare of pale blue, tensile hands and thin mouth. He was pared down, oddly beautiful or repellent. People stopped and stared at him in the street. When he went back to university after Christmas, he became a kind of idol for students and, of course, news of Johnny's disappearance had spread like a bush fire even before the newspaper had come out with their story in it. His lectures were crammed; young women loitered outside his office and tried to think of an excuse to engage him in conversation. They wanted to save him – just as Isabel had wanted to save him all those years ago, when he had stood on her doorstep with his bouquet and his burning blue eyes.

But he didn't want to be saved. Colleagues tried to talk to him about what he was going through, but he only wanted to discuss strategies, ways of spreading information about Johnny – he had thousands of posters in his office, which he would hand to anyone willing to take them – statistics about missing people, and the need for vigilance.

Of course, the scrapbook filled up very quickly and he bought another, and then another, all identical, until they filled the shelf above his desk. He spent many hours on the websites about missing people, reading the stories of others. A few of these he printed out, because they seemed in some way relevant, or touched a chord deep inside him that he could not quite identify, like a tuning fork finding an answering frequency, a melancholy twang of recognition. He also took to leafing through newspapers and cutting out stories about young people who had disappeared. He stared at them for hours.

It didn't take him long to realize that almost all of the missing who got any coverage were middle class, from a happy family, white, preferably female and photogenic, but that few of those who went missing fell into these categories. If an adolescent black boy, with a broken voice and facial hair, disappeared, forget it. If a seventeen-year-old white boy from a rundown estate disappeared, forget it. If a black girl from a poor family vanished, there was little mention. Two parents were better than one. If the young person seemed blemished, they attracted significantly less interest. Of course, the pre-pubescent child was generally a cause of widespread anxiety, but if she was a girl, if she was white, if she had smooth skin, if she was pretty, if she had a photograph that showed her wide-eyed and with the bloom of innocence, then there was hysteria. An overweight, dark-skinned boy with fluff and spots on his face prompted a less frantic response. Any sign of drugs, or criminal activity, and the chances were the media wouldn't be interested. If the young person was in care, they were already invisible, missing from their own lives long before they had disappeared. Nobody searched for them, missed them, wept and ached for them.

Felix read about the boy of sixteen who had been in ten foster families before drifting away; the girl of fifteen who had been moved from home to home, constantly truanted from school, and then vanished. Drug addiction, alcoholism, problems with authority, attention deficit disorder, learning difficulties – there were lots of names given to their condition, which Felix came to see as a profound loss of self.

And, of course, there were all the young people not mentioned, who were no longer minors so were not the responsibility of any individual or institution. While most of the younger runaways were girls and returned quickly, most of the adults were men and often never returned. If they were traced, more than three-quarters of them didn't want to go home, and almost half didn't even want to make contact with their family, if only to tell them they were safe. And how many of them were there?

Felix read that two hundred and fifty thousand people go missing every year. He worked out that that was the population of a town like Brighton. Of course, most of them came back, usually very quickly. He read through police reports, and reports from Social Services and the Home Office (Research, Development and Statistics Directorate) that broke statistics down into categories of absence and grades of vulnerability, and talked about 'suspicious missing persons', meaning those who might be in serious danger, and 'repeat runaways'. But how many of those hundreds of thousands didn't return, but inhabited some underworld? The population of Stratford? Bath? Hereford? How many tens of thousands of people had dimmed and darkened from sight? It reminded Felix of those pulsing lights on sonar screens that go from brightly present to a fading flicker and finally – it's hard to pinpoint the exact moment – to unregistering darkness. They were still there but no one saw them, no one remembered. Missing but no longer missed.

He didn't understand how he had been so blind to all the ghosts who walked among us, and in his mind, his complacency became linked to the fact of Johnny's disappearance: as if his youngest son was punishing him for moral negligence. His scrapbooks became thick with newspaper cuttings that were in some way or other about the people we don't see and don't care about – as if one life is more precious than another, and this winsome ringleted creature deserves more from life than the scowling undernourished one. His archive grew. If he read that someone had been found, he would go back and make a note beside the cutting. If, as happened once or twice, he read that their body had been discovered, he noted that as well, writing 'Deceased' in his copperplate hand beside the newspaper gummed to the thick page. He cut out articles about the parents as well and noticed how they all – him and Isabel included – tended to speak a kind of stock tabloidese. *Shock, horror, terror, closure, just bring them back* . . . As if words crumbled in the face of such uncertainty. For what could you say when you didn't know? It seemed impossible to speak or feel anything precise or real; the formlessness of the fear and wretchedness became part of the horror. He saw how parents would even say, 'If we knew he was dead, at least it would be over and we would be able to put him to rest' – and, of course, they didn't just want rest for their son or brother or father, their daughter or sister or mother, they wanted rest for themselves and their turbulent unknowing.

Felix dealt with his uncertainty by trying to pin everything down. Numbers, dates, charts, records, grids, maps, statistics, locations, messages received and sent, time of call, all the possible sightings that, of course, turned out to be red herrings, the mood of Johnny when he had left, the names of friends, teachers, acquaintances, tennis partners, pubs he frequented, shops he used, websites he visited . . .

Soon there was a separate scrapbook for newspaper

articles that specifically mentioned Johnny – the first interview he and Isabel had given, of course, and then all the other features and news stories in which theirs resurfaced. It was amazing how once you were in print a first time it became like a contagion. Journalists called for a quote, a brief interview. Felix became adept at the soundbite, the cogent piece of information. He could reel off statistics. He could put them in touch with other organizations. Contextualize. In February, he was on local radio several times, then took part in a programme on Radio 4 about missing people after which emails and letters poured in. Early in March, he was on local TV – just for a minute or so but Johnny's face was shown. How many hundreds of thousands of people would have seen it? He tried to find out the viewing figures. He recorded each programme and stacked the CDs, labelled, on the rack by his desk.

On the cover of this new scrapbook, in large letters and indelible black ink, he wrote out a quotation he had found by Freud: 'I cannot think of any need in childhood as strong as the need for a father's protection.' Later, he added words by Tom Wolfe he had come across: the father is the 'protector, who would keep a lid on all the chaotic and catastrophic possibilities of life'. He was surrounded by images of Johnny but the framed photo that used to stand with other family pictures on the windowsill, showing him and Johnny in a small wooden rowing boat, suntanned and widely smiling for whoever stood behind the camera, he put face downwards in a drawer.

And, of course, he taught, lectured, ran, helped Mia with her coursework, ate meals night after night, sitting in his usual chair poker-spined and poker-faced, played the same piece on his violin over and over again, so that Mia and Isabel grew to dread it. But all the time his thoughts ran along the network he had so patiently laid down and which grew daily, capturing all in its intricate mesh.

Chapter Nineteen

On the morning of 14 February – Valentine's Day, although neither Felix nor Isabel remembered or cared about that – the telephone rang in Felix's study. He lifted it up and held it to his ear, all the while frowning in disgust at an email he had just received from a woman called Serena Flowers, who was a clairvoyant and had the strongest feeling that Johnny Hopkins was alive and living by water. She didn't know what kind of water: perhaps the sea, or a river, or a lake. It could even be a canal or an underground source. The spirit that moved her was more like a magnetic pull than a clear guide. Felix had been in his study since five o'clock, when the sky was still dark and frost glittered on the lawn; in half an hour's time he would go to the university.

'Yes?' he said. 'Felix Hopkins here.'

There was silence at the other end. The phone line crackled and he thought that perhaps he heard someone swallowing.

'Yes?' he repeated. He had received several prank calls recently, from people who'd seen the posters that still hung from lampposts and trees. Occasionally, Isabel answered them, and when she did, she would shout piteously at whoever was giggling at the other end, or try to explain why the joke was monstrously cruel. Her voice would break and she would gesture wildly with the hand that wasn't holding the phone, remonstrating, begging for kindness. Felix, however, didn't have her faith in humanity: he would just put the phone down. 'Who is this?' he said harshly.

'You don't need my name.' The voice was sibilant, with a curious accent he couldn't place.

'What do you want? Why are you calling?'

'I'm calling about your son. Johnny.'

'Go on. I'm listening.'

The swallowing sound again – he could almost see the Adam's apple bouncing.

'We met once. At Fergal's house. Remember? You and your wife.'

A feeling of foreboding rose in Felix, a cold wind. He closed his fist around the phone and sat up straighter. He seemed to be able to taste the memory of that horrible encounter, like iron in his mouth.

'I remember,' he said. 'You were the other man there? Is that it?'

A nasty laugh came down the phone, which seemed to break halfway through and turn into a strangled sob.

'The other man,' he said. 'That's one way of putting it.'

'Why are you calling me? What do you know?'

'I know you shouldn't let Fergal off so easily.'

'What does that mean?'

'It means there are things he's not telling you.'

'Hold on. It was you who said, that day, that Fergal didn't know Johnny had disappeared.'

'He had his hooks into your son. Good and deep.'

An image came into Felix's mind, of Fergal's long white

fingers, his uncut dirty nails sinking into Johnny's innocent flesh. He knitted his brow into a grimace.

'Is there anything new you can tell me?'

'Come and see.'

'What?'

'Come and see,' repeated the voice, insistent, like a snake coiling itself around Felix's guts. 'See for yourself.'

'See?' said Felix stupidly. 'See what?'

'Come now. He's not here now.'

'Come where? You mean to Sheffield?'

'He's out for the day. Him and her,' he added viciously.

'But –' He was going to say that he was in Suffolk, hours away, and that he was expected at work soon. But he swallowed the words because, of course, he knew he had to go on this wild-goose chase across the country. 'I can be there in three to four hours,' he said.

'I'll be waiting.'

The phone went dead. Felix did a call-back, but got a voice saying that the number he had called was not available. He sat for a few minutes, shading his eyes with his hand, as if dazzled by the light, although the day outside was one of gusting drizzles and low, dark clouds. Then he unfolded himself from his chair and went into the kitchen. Mia was standing by the fridge on one leg, like a stork.

'There's no milk,' she said.

'Oh.'

'And no butter. Or anything, really.'

'I see.'

'Dad?'

'Mm?'

235

'Did you hear?'

'Yes. No milk or butter.'

'Never mind. It doesn't matter.'

She shut the fridge door as Isabel came in, her shirt and hair damp from the rain. She had sodden slippers on her feet and was wearing her old gardening trousers.

'Mum?' said Mia. 'Where've you been? You're soaked!'

Isabel turned her bright, distracted glance on her daughter. 'Oh,' she said, and pushed her wet hair back from her face. 'Nowhere, really. Sorry. I meant to be back before you were up. What time is it?'

'Five to eight.'

Felix considered Isabel: her wet clothes and fluttering hands and darting, unseeing eyes. 'I'm off to work,' he said.

She nodded.

'I might be back a bit later than usual. Meetings.'

'Fine.'

'I'll call.'

'Yes.'

For a moment, he felt loneliness settle, a vast, oily bird on his shoulder. But perhaps he was just tired, so very, very weary from it all.

''Bye then,' he said, and she didn't answer, though Mia put a hand on his shoulder as he passed.

He set off during rush hour so it took him three hours and fifty-eight minutes to drive to Sheffield and park his car just down the hill from the tower blocks that seemed to shut out what light there was on this day of rain and saturated greyness. All the way, as the windscreen wipers swished back and forth in an arc, he thought about what lay ahead. He liked to have plans, to impose control over events, but he had no idea what he was going to discover in Fergal's house or what he should do. The day lay before him like broken glass. He tried to remember what the man who wouldn't give his name had looked like. He'd had a timid and greasy half-beard, he thought, and straggly brown hair, brownish clothes. But beyond that he couldn't remember. It had been clear from the ugly curl in his voice that he hated Fergal and had called Felix out of a desire to punish him for something.

Felix got out of the car and locked it. The rain fell on his bare head and trickled down his neck. His back was sore as he walked up the hill, and he felt old and rusty, out of tune with himself. He was like someone who had been programmed to put one foot in front of the other, no deviation, moving forward stiffly and implacably.

There was the flat, standing amid the wreckage of what had once been people's homes, nettles and weeds growing up against its front door and the rain streaking its smeared blank windows. It looked even more dreary and deserted than it had on his last visit, with Isabel: it was hard to believe that people lived in there, cooked and touched each other and lay in their beds at night. Felix saw that one of the windows had been broken and patched up with a thin grey blanket that looked exactly like the army blanket his father had carried around in the boot of their car. A cumbrous dead bird lay just by the entrance, a crow or a rook, he thought, but now just a ragged bundle of feathers and a sharp, useless beak. Felix's mouth felt parched. He stood up very straight, shoulders back, and rapped hard on the door for longer than was necessary, then stood back and waited.

At first he thought nobody would answer, and a secret worm of relief squirmed in his stomach. He had stepped out of his known world and felt that anything could happen to him. It occurred to him, uselessly, that he hadn't told Isabel – or anyone – where he was going; nobody would know where to look should he not return. Then the door eased open a couple of inches and an eye peered out, a segment of pale, unhealthy face with wispy beard and creased forehead. 'Yes?'

'It's me, Felix Hopkins.'

'Aaah. Yes.'

The door opened further, enough for Felix to step out of the rain and into the stench of the flat, strong enough to make him gasp.

'Thank you,' he managed, as he stood in the unlit hall, trying to make out the disorder around him – an old mattress, one spring poking out, heaps of empty bottles, many tipped so that thick liquid dribbled from their open mouths, a large paper bag that seemed to be filled entirely with cigarette butts. A stain spread out over the floor, greenish and dark. His eyes stung.

'What's happened here?' he asked.

'Happened?'

'It looks . . .'

'Oh, that. I'm not clearing up all the shit any longer, that's what. It's worse in here.' And he gestured triumphantly to the room with the splintered wall.

It *was* worse. It smelt of sweat and dope and sour wine and something sweet and rotten, as if a rat had died in the corner and was slowly decomposing under one of the piles of dirty clothes, old sleeping bags and scattered pages of newspapers. In the middle of the room the oil painting of the naked woman, whom he and Isabel had met, still had pride of place, but someone had slashed it savagely so that it hung in shreds. A purple breast trailed on a piece of canvas, stirring slightly in the air coming through the open door. Felix stared at it, feeling sick but somehow unable to look away.

'Oh,' he heard himself say. Then he clenched his fists, forced himself to look at the man in front of him, and said, 'What have you got to show me about Johnny?' Unable to stop himself, he asked, 'Did he come here a lot? Before he left.'

'Oh, yes.'

'You know him?'

'Know Johnny?' A flickering smile crossed his face. 'Yes, I know Johnny.'

'Why?'

'Because I was here.' The man shrugged.

'No, *why*? Why did my son come here?' Felix looked around him, at a room that seemed like a terrifying mirror image of Johnny's childhood home, everything smashed and corrupted and heaving with ugliness.

'Oh.' He paused and gave a smile that made his face look suddenly crafty. 'Fergal thought he'd be good for the group.'

'The *group*?'

'Yeah.'

'What group? What do you mean?'

'Our group.'

239

'What *is* your group?'

'We believe . . .' The man licked his cracked lips and stared at Felix. 'Shall I show you Fergal's room? That's why you're here, isn't it?'

'Johnny was part of Fergal's *group*?' Felix felt dizzy. He stared at the room, the unholy mess of it, with its rancid smell of things gone bad in the soul as well as the fridge. There were mouse droppings on the floor. There was a brown patch on the ceiling where water must have dripped through. There was a lace bra under his foot. Everything had unravelled.

He saw the man's small dry mouth open and shut, open and shut. Words – 'guilt', 'purification', 'atonement' – drifted past him. He stared, but he wasn't seeing what was in front of him. He was seeing Johnny, when he was a small boy, still delicate-skinned and knobbly-kneed. He was teaching him to play tennis in the local park court, sending him ball after ball over the net, shouting at him to run faster, to hit the ball lower, to use both hands on his backhand, to stretch wider, to leap higher. It had been a relentlessly hot and windless day and Johnny, who had just recovered from chickenpox, was tired: at one point, he had stumbled and fallen headlong, grazing both his palms and bruising his elbow, but Felix had been determined to make more headway. He had believed it was a matter of will-power, of mind over body and of cultivating the quality he most admired: endurance. Johnny's hair had been damp on his forehead and he had had a blind look to him now; his legs were spindly and his shoes too big and heavy for his feet. His forlorn patience had irritated Felix precisely because it was so touching. At last their hour was up; the four men who had booked the court after them were standing at the gate, so Felix and Johnny had made their way through the park and back to their house without talking. When they had got home Isabel had seen that Johnny's hands were raw with blisters from the cracked handle of the racquet he'd been using. 'Why didn't you say?' she'd asked him. 'You must have been in agony.' She turned to Felix. 'Why didn't you *notice*?'

Felix saw this scene as he stood in the havoc of the room. For a hellish moment, he thought he understood why Johnny had made his way here, why the uncomplaining little boy with blistered hands had become the young man with a need to expiate some sense of shame. He blinked rapidly and tried not to hear the words: 'entitlement', 'privilege', 'softness' . . .

'Why am I here?' he cut in, his voice slightly cracked.

'Fergal's out. With Mary too. A little day trip somewhere and I'm left holding the fort — though there's no one to defend it against any more. Everyone else's gone and I'll be gone soon as well. It's all over. I only stayed because of Mary and now she's gone off with that —'

'Why am I here?' repeated Felix. He didn't want to hear any more of this man's pathetic life, how Fergal had stolen his oil-painting girl.

'I got his key, didn't I? To his room. He never lets anyone in there but I got his key. I thought you might want to take a peek before he does a runner.'

'Why?' repeated Felix.

'He keeps things. Stores them for later use. You might find something. Might want to show the police.' He bobbed his head. 'I'm only trying to help you.'

Trying to get revenge, thought Felix, but he didn't really care about motives.

'Which one is it?'

'I'll show you.'

He picked up a set of keys. Fergal's door was secured with a large, rusty padlock, which the man unlocked and pushed open with a small grunt. Felix stepped inside a square, stale room into which all life seemed to have been sucked – as if it was the still heart of the flat's maelstrom. There was a bed covered completely with a fringed mustard-yellow throw, an uncurtained window looking out on to scrubland, a closed suitcase which, when Felix looked into it later, turned out to contain clothes that were neatly folded – and, stacked under the window, four or five cardboard boxes in various sizes, sealed with masking tape.

'There,' said the man.

'What's in them?'

'That's what you're here to find out.'

'Haven't you looked?'

'I haven't been able to get in here before, have I?'

'Are you going to look now?'

'Nah. I'll leave you to it.'

And he shuffled away, back down the stairs. The door swung on its hinges. Felix stared at the boxes: where should he begin, when he was pretty sure there was nothing to find, except things that would take him no nearer to Johnny? Probably he would only be grubbing through secrets he shouldn't discover, sides to his son that he wasn't supposed to glimpse. He felt no curiosity, only a kind of horror: he didn't want to dip his hand into the murk and slime of anyone's life, their shame or their roiling darkness. He left that to Isabel, with her quivering emotional antennae and attenuated sense of a person's distress and desire. Trawling through Johnny's laptop had been bad enough. This was something else. His skin prickled.

He lifted the first box on to the bed and, as he did so, saw out of the window that the man – he would never find out his name – was leaving. He carried a large, old-fashioned case in one hand; it was obviously heavy since it made him tip to one side, straining against its weight, and a splitting black bin bag in the other. He was wearing a long trench coat, whose hem dragged against the ground. He was half running, a stuttering jog, and his thin hair blew back from his pallid face. So Felix was alone in the flat, and perhaps even in this whole landscape of abandoned, boarded-up, burnt-out buildings, and cratered, gritty scrub. The rain blew against the window and, downstairs, a door banged.

The first box, only a third full, contained what seemed, to Felix's bewilderment, like a collection of essays in different handwriting and different-coloured inks, some quite long and others short. Each one was entitled 'What I Renounce'. Some had the name of the author at the top (Carl Fortune, Sanna Y., Wayne Fever . . .). Felix flicked through the bundle. Some of the essays were in looped, clumsy writing and were ungrammatical, littered with spelling mistakes. Others were pedantic, well structured, as if straining for literary effect. The renunciations ranged from obvious things, like alcohol, cigarettes, caffeine and meat – as if this was a particularly austere kind of Lenten exercise – to family, sex, intimacy, appetite, consumerism. Someone called Janey had given up 'choice'. Finn had renounced 'ease and vodka and useless things'. A set of initials, JDK, was going to make do without 'the ideas of others'. Felix thumbed through everything twice. There was nothing from Johnny. No scrap of his familiar handwriting among this strange jumble of tracts.

He turned to the next box, scraping the end of the masking tape free from the cardboard and then ripping it off, levering open the lid. In here there were several manila folders. He took out the first and opened it. On top was an A4 photograph of a naked woman, her breasts large, the nipples pale pink. The photo was cropped so she had no head, just a body. Under that was a sheet of paper giving personal details: name, age, sex, sexual predilections, education, family background, parents' occupations. There was a plastic bracelet in there as well, and a pressed four-leafed clover stuck to a piece of card. Felix lifted up the next folder and opened it. Another photo loomed out at him – the close-up, enlarged face of a young man with his mouth open, his nostrils dilated and his pupils huge. Not Johnny, although at first it was hard to be sure because the details were blurred and he was about the same age, with the same colouring, as far as Felix could see. He put it to one side and turned to the next.

'Found anything interesting?'

The voice was soft, friendly, slightly nasal. For a moment, Felix sat quite still, hand suspended over the box, the hair prickling at the back of his neck – and then he turned. Fergal stood in the doorway. He was wearing a poncho and a brightly coloured bobble hat with thick ear-flaps, one of which was turned up perkily. His arms were folded, and he was smiling.

'No,' Felix said dully, then added: 'Not yet.'

'Don't let me stop you.'

Another man, with cropped hair and heavy boots, and the woman from the oil painting downstairs appeared in the doorway behind Fergal. They stared down at him.

'I'm looking for my son,' said Felix, out of his rubbery mouth. His breath came up his closed throat in small painful spears. The room seemed to grow smaller and darker.

'Ah, yes. Young Johnny Hopkins.'

'I think you know something.'

'Do you?'

'That's Johnny's hat,' Felix heard himself say. 'Mia gave it to him one Christmas. He wore it for days, even inside. He wore it at meals. It was a family joke.'

And as he said it, he saw Johnny's face, fresh and sweet, under its stripes, and for a moment he felt courage stir under his thick fear.

'Is it?'

'Yes.'

Fergal took the ridiculous hat off his head and looked at it musingly. 'Perhaps it is. He was very generous with his possessions, was Johnny.'

Even hearing his son's name come from Fergal's mouth made Felix feel poisoned.

'Where is he?'

'Why don't you go on looking through the boxes, now you're here? We can wait.'

'Fergal . . .' the woman said anxiously.

'Go on, Mr Hopkins. Or it's Dr, isn't it? Dr Hopkins.'

'Do you know where he is? Do you have any clue?'

Fergal stared at him. He had a slight cold; his nose was red, and every so often he wiped it with the back of his hand. Silence thickened in the room.

'If there's nothing you can tell me,' said Felix at last, as casually as he could manage, 'then I think I should be on my way.'

He stood up. No one in the doorway moved, except the woman, who put a hand over her mouth, as if a catastrophe had already happened. He took a step forward and still they did not move. The man with cropped hair was opening and closing, opening and closing the hand that hung by his side.

'Fergal . . .' the woman said again. Then, to Felix: 'He doesn't know where your son is. You shouldn't be here. You made a mistake.'

Another step. They would be able to smell his fear. Johnny's face under that mad child's hat, his candid smile: it flickered inside him like a candle flame. *My boy: I will get you out of here.*

One more step. The man with heavy boots put out his twitching hand and pushed him, very gently, back into the room.

Felix stepped forward again. The touch had liberated him: suddenly he was no longer afraid. He wanted the fist in his face, the boot in his body. He wanted to be punished: pain would be welcome.

'You don't know anything at all, do you?' he said, in a voice he barely recognized. 'That's your real secret. You have no power. He got away.'

There was the hand again, lifting, opening, stretching forward. Not so gentle this time. It pushed him down on to the floor. He could see pieces of lint and dust on the grubby carpet. The boot was on his fingers now, pressing down. It was scuffed and in need of a good polish, he thought. Cleaning shoes used to be his job, when he was a father.

'He got away,' he said again. 'From you, from me, from all of us.'

A gob of spit landed on his upturned face. Something sharp against his cheek; something hard against his stomach, his thigh, his groin. Muffled grunts. Again, again. He stared up at the three faces and they stared down at him and he smiled and smiled.

'You lost him, didn't you?' he said jubilantly, and closed his eyes, opened his body up to their blows. Didn't they understand how much he wanted to be punished?

Felix walked very slowly down the hill; with each step, pain tweaked and tugged at his body, now in his ribs, now up his side, like an electric shock. The rain had stopped and a faint sun was breaking through the thinning clouds. He looked at his watch and discovered only forty minutes had passed since he had parked his car: how was that possible? He felt he had been away for hours, days. Turning, he glanced back at Fergal's flat and now it seemed merely drab and dejected, no longer monstrous and reeking of terror. Perhaps they were looking at him as he made his way from the place, limping slightly, and he tried to square his shoulders and walk more briskly.

His thigh and stomach ached and his jaw throbbed, although when he put up a hand to touch it, it didn't feel too bad. He was having slight difficulty in seeing things properly – his vision blurred, cleared and blurred again. Puddles glistened underfoot. He was carrying Johnny's hat: he had snatched it up when he left, as if he was rescuing a piece of his son's soul. He would wash it clean of all traces of Fergal and hide it somewhere that Isabel wouldn't see it. He wouldn't tell her what had happened today. He wouldn't tell anyone, not even the police. There was nothing to tell. They didn't know where Johnny was and there was nothing in the boxes except scared young people's confessions: no one should look at those. He briefly closed his eyes and felt the rough carpet against his cheek, smelt its musty odour. All the fear and elation had drained away from him and he felt only a great weariness pressing down on him.

He got to the car and eased himself in, laying Johnny's hat reverently on the seat beside him. They'd taken the money from his wallet, but that didn't matter. They'd spat on him, but that didn't matter either. The only thing that mattered was that they'd laid their grubby hands on Johnny's soft soul but that Johnny had got away. And that he, Felix, still had to track him, although he felt further away from his son than ever before: they were just two specks in the universe, separated by infinite space.

Chapter Twenty

Johnny's birthday was in the middle of March: spring time, and indeed, after a long, cold winter, the daffodils were out, the trees were in bud, and birds flew past Felix's window with twigs in their beaks. Before long, the swallows would arrive. In the streets, people wore lighter, brighter clothes, lifted their faces towards the blue warmth and walked with a bounce in their step.

(Johnny would be nineteen years old. Isabel had bought him nineteen little gifts – a striped cotton scarf, an anthology of poems, socks with coloured heels and toes, a glass lantern, a packet of sparklers – which she wrapped up and laid, alongside the Christmas presents, at the back of her wardrobe. She bought nineteen birthday-cake candles as well, and found the recipe she would make if he came home: ginger cake with black treacle and ground almonds. He loved ginger; used to. She had gone back to work part time; on her free days she went either to Sheffield or to London and wandered the streets. She no longer handed out posters or followed any route, just tacked aimlessly up alleys and down cul-de-sacs. She was hardly even looking any more – crowds blurred past, individual faces dissolving – she was simply walking. Perhaps it was her act of hope.)

Felix went to work on Johnny's birthday, leaving early in the morning after his six-mile run round the country lanes, cars splattering him with muddy water from the puddles as they passed. He had four classes and a tutor group, then went to a meeting about budget cuts. Afterwards, instead of going home, he went back to his small office and sat at his desk, which looked out of a first-floor window on to a small courtyard. The twilight sky was grey, but the shape of the cool sun, low on the horizon, could be seen behind the cloud covering. Felix turned on the computer and waited for it to load up, but even when it was ready for him, he didn't move. He felt frozen to the spot. He saw that he had emails from both his older sons, doubtless acknowledging the melancholy nature of this particular day, but couldn't make himself open them. He saw that the light was winking on his answering machine. He told himself he had to make an effort and not give in to the paralysis that seemed to have gripped him suddenly, but still he kept sitting there, staring at the glowing blue of his screen and the winking light on the phone and the faint fuzz of the sun in the sky. His hands felt like icicles on the keyboard and his face was stiff, like a piece of metal. For a moment, he let himself imagine splintering into hard, cold pieces, his heart a rusted knot.

The door opened but he couldn't turn around.

'Felix?'

It was his young teaching assistant, Connie Kramer. Still he didn't move.

'Are you all right? I thought you were going home after the meeting, but then I saw your light on.'

'Fine,' he managed to croak.

She stood over him and put a warm hand over his cold one. 'I know what day it is, Felix.'

'Fine,' he repeated.

'Look, I've made you some tea.' And she put the mug on his desk, beside the stone with a hole in it that Mia had given him. She had said that stones with holes brought luck, but both of them knew that wasn't true.

He didn't drink the tea or show that he was aware of it. The room was filled with a distress so palpable that Connie let out a little sigh in sympathy. She had never dared touch him before, or speak to him in anything but a formal tone, always about work or his students. But the room was waiting and something needed to happen. She hesitated, then stepped up to him, her shadow falling across his. Putting her hands on his shoulders, she paused to see his reaction; there was none, either of acceptance or recoil, so now she gently rubbed his rigid muscles, trying to soften them. Felix closed his eyes.

'You poor thing,' she said, in a tone she would never have dared to use with him before, speaking to him like a child, not the formidable Dr Hopkins, who strode around the corridors like an omen.

'I can't imagine,' she went on, still massaging his shoulders. 'So painful.' She could have been talking about his seized-up muscles or his frozen life. It didn't matter.

Felix didn't move; he went on sitting bolt upright in his swivel chair, which rotated very slightly as Connie rubbed his aching neck. His eyes were still closed, but in his mind he was seeing Isabel as she would be now, racing round the house, that expression of jumbled distress on her face, her clothes falling off her wasted frame. He knew how she would look at him when he came in – with a distracted indifference, perhaps even hostility flickering across her features before she pushed it away. He remembered her when he had come to her that first time, holding his bouquet, his heart racing, his mouth dry. She had opened the door and he had felt suspended in a moment that he knew would change his life, if he let it. She had seemed so slim and true, from her seeing glance, which appeared to understand him in that single moment, to her deep brown eyes and questioning smile. A small woman with a big heart. But now that heart was blasted. Her brown eyes were indifferent to him.

It all seemed so long ago: him and Isabel, him and his first marriage; even Mia and Johnny and Tamsin were tiny figures on the distant horizon, and he was here, in his study, letting Connie press her fingers into his sore flesh. He knew what was going to happen, and even before it did, his self-disgust bit into him. He thought of Johnny letting Zoë seduce him and wondered if his son had felt the way he was feeling now. It was going to happen. He would betray his wife, his children, himself, and even this lovely young woman with coppery curls standing beside him, her eyes wet with tears, turning his chair so that he faced her at last, pressing her mouth to the hard line of his. Soon he would have crossed a line and become the person he didn't want to be because, for just a few minutes, he might feel alive, his blood stirring and his mind forgetting. Suppressed despair rose in him, and for just this moment he could bury it in Connie's welcoming body, in her pity and infatuation.

Afterwards she put her arms around him and he stroked her hair.

'Listen, Connie,' he said.

'No. I don't want to. I know what you're going to say.'

'You need to understand –'

'No, Felix. Don't you think I already understand? I'm not a naïve young student, you know. You're going to tell me you're married, which of course I know and have known from the first day I met you. And that you're my boss and have taken advantage of your position. And that you're an old man and I'm a young woman and it's a mid-life-cliché and I could do so much better, et cetera, et cetera. And that your present circumstances are no excuse for what you've just done. Oh, and finally that it was all a terrible mistake and it's entirely your fault and you're very sorry. What have I missed out?'

'Nothing . . .'

He thought that actually Connie had left out the most important things on the list: that fucking her had been an act of self-loathing and self-punishment, and that she could have been anyone. He would have had sex with a student, a stranger, a middle-aged woman or a teenager, whoever had come in through the door and rubbed his neck and murmured words of sympathy and let their hair fall over his rigid face.

'And, of course, it's all true,' she was saying, but cheerfully.

'. . . nothing – that is, except that it can never happen again.'

'Ah, I forgot that. I don't accept it.'

'Connie –'

'I've got a boyfriend, you know.'

'I didn't.'

'Well, why would you? What I mean, when I say that

I've got a boyfriend, is that you're not to categorize me as a victim and use that as yet another fact to beat yourself up with. I've got a boyfriend, he's really nice and we're good together. We're thinking of buying a house soon. I won't tell him what happened. I won't feel guilty and nor should you. I wanted to comfort you. You needed to be loved – you were crying out for it, whether you knew it or not – and as it happens, I love you very much.'

She did up the buttons on his shirt, then kissed him on the mouth. Felix was baffled by her mixture of heady romanticism and cool pragmatism. He thought of Isabel, who was so very different from Connie, and at that moment his mobile vibrated in his pocket. He knew it would be her ringing him. He didn't answer it. He thought she would be able to tell from the sound of his voice that a woman's hand was stroking the side of his face, or that she would somehow be able to smell Connie's perfume over the phone. Felix had never been unfaithful before. He had always regarded himself as the kind of man who never would be: his will-power, his sense of duty and rectitude were stronger than any desire he might feel. When his first wife had slept with his friend, the gale of rage and moral disgust he had felt for her had blown him out of their marriage, out of his settled fatherhood, before he had had time to think about it. Yet when it came to him, how easy it had been, what a short time it had taken. From the moment Connie had come into the room to the moment he had come into her, his face screwed up and a tiny groan escaping him, about twelve minutes had elapsed, according to the time shown in the top corner of his computer.

His phone vibrated once more.

'I must go.'

'Of course.'

He stood up, feeling awkward, and tucked his shirt more firmly into his trousers, making sure everything was fastened and buttoned and in its proper place. 'I don't expect you to forgive me . . .' he began, not knowing how the sentence would finish, or what he wanted to say, just that he needed to draw some kind of formal line under the episode.

'Oh, for goodness' sake,' said Connie. She laughed and took his face between her hands and kissed him on the mouth and on the eyelids, then on his neck, and he didn't stop her. 'There. I'll see you tomorrow,' she said.

'No.'

'For work, Felix.'

'Oh. Yes. But —'

'Go now. Everything will be all right.'

'No. It won't.'

'Give yourself permission to be human.'

He stared at her, his mouth an ugly sneer. 'Don't be stupid,' he said harshly. 'Permission to be human? You don't know what the fuck you're talking about. Where did you get that from? Some crappy self-help psychobabble book you bought at the airport?'

'There's no need to be cruel. Or does it make it easier for you, if you can tell yourself I'm just a silly little thing who thinks in clichés? Does contempt allow you to feel less guilty?'

'No.'

'Maybe you think that if I'm stupid and platitudinous

I can only have shallow feelings. Because that's how you think, isn't it? You think that only clever and complicated people, who love poetry and subtle ideas and are cultured and precise and tasteful, can really have deep emotions. All those messy, inarticulate people out there, who don't read Chaucer or love Bach – they don't suffer like you.'

Felix smiled thinly at her. 'Is that what you think of me?'

'Maybe.' She softened. 'No. Really, I think you're in pain and lashing out at anyone who comes too close.'

'Hmm. I liked it better when you were insulting. At least you were being authentic.'

An hour ago, Felix had paid little attention to Connie Kramer: he had been polite to her and grateful for the way she helped to organize his life; after holidays, he would always ask if she had had a good time. But he had known nothing at all about her life. Now they were snapping at each other like rowing lovers and he was regarding her with a mixture of hostility and desire.

He strode from the office, leaving the door open and Connie standing in the middle of the room. He climbed into his car and drove away, but after a mile or so he pulled over to examine his face in the rear-view mirror, checking himself for tell-tale signs, although he knew that Isabel – in better times hyper-alert to other people's distress – would probably not notice and perhaps barely care. His reflection stared back at him, apparently unchanged. He bit his colourless lip, rubbed an imaginary lipstick mark from his cheek – had Connie been wearing lipstick, though? He didn't think so. Actually, it occurred to him that he had no idea what she had been wearing; he couldn't even remember if she had had a skirt on, or trousers, or a dress. He didn't even seem to be able to recall the actual event in any detail. Had he embraced her, undressed her, called out in his self-hating arousal? He knew what had happened but his mind had erased the pictures. He looked at his face, blue eyes staring unblinkingly back. Car headlights shone into his mirror, then passed and he was surrounded by darkness again.

What had become of him? He was a father whose son had gone missing, a husband who had just betrayed his wife. He thought this, but he didn't feel it. It was as though it had happened to someone else, to a man he didn't like and barely recognized.

He readjusted the mirror, turned off the internal light, started the car again and drove home.

Chapter Twenty-one

He saw at once that Isabel had made some semblance of an effort this evening. She had washed her hair, which was still damp, and she had made a simple supper of sea bass and fennel, avocado and apple salad, which he knew she wouldn't really eat, just pick at. There was a bottle of white wine in the fridge. Her face was gaunt and her eyes looked sore, but she tried to smile at him as he came in and even laid a hand very briefly on his arm, withdrawing it at once as if she was scorched by the contact. Felix didn't look at her. He waited for guilt to surge through him but he felt very detached from himself. Everything was happening through a telescope. When he washed his hands in the sink, they seemed impossibly far away. He looked down at his feet, which were also a long way off and placed on a floor that seemed to be sloping precariously downhill. He thought he might fall over and imagined himself crashing forward on to the kitchen table. Perhaps he was coming down with something.

'Would you like a glass of wine?' Isabel was saying.

'Whisky,' he managed, though he never drank spirits – just wine, in controlled doses. Nobody had ever seen him drunk.

Isabel looked at him, then fetched two tumblers from the cupboard and took down one of the whiskies from its shelf – over the past few months they seemed to have been given dozens of bottles of whisky by friends and acquaintances; it was the drink of comfort, full of dark-golden lights and the smell of mulch and medicine, to be tipped down the throat in a trickle of fire. She poured them each a slug and put the cap back on. She lifted her own glass and held it up.

'To Johnny,' she said. 'Nineteen years old today.' She had learnt to speak his name without weeping, or even without that husky catch in her voice.

'To Johnny,' said Felix. He couldn't look at her, staring instead through the window.

'Mia's out this evening.'

'Where?'

'She didn't say – she just called to say she wouldn't be home till ten or so.'

'Oh.'

'I think she just can't bear to be at home, Felix. That's the truth of it. Home isn't home to her any more. It isn't safe.'

Felix stared at his whisky, which rippled in the glass when he moved it as if it was slightly viscous. He swallowed it, feeling it burn but remaining horribly clear-headed and removed, then unscrewed the cap on the bottle to pour himself another couple of inches. Isabel didn't say anything, but watched him as he drank it.

'We've got to do better,' she said. 'That's what I've been thinking today. Among other things.' She gave a spluttering laugh, like a car engine turning but not catching into life. 'You lock yourself away in your study and hardly notice her, even when you're talking to her, though I know you've made an effort to help her with things like work, and that's good. And I've been . . .' she hesitated, searching for a proper word '. . . chaotically wretched,' she said. 'Sometimes there for her and sometimes unable to function.'

'Mm.' Felix took another drink, wanting the whisky to dissolve the edges of his strange mood and scorch him back into consciousness.

'You told me, when it first happened, to pretend,' Isabel was saying.

Had he? He didn't remember that. He didn't really remember what he had felt or thought or said then.

'We've both been pretending but it isn't working. We've got to do better than that. We've lost one child. We mustn't lose two.'

'No,' said Felix.

'And we've got to go and see Tamsin and talk to her about her baby and her finals. She needs us to be thinking of her, not just of Johnny.'

Felix nodded. His head jiggled on the stem of his neck and pieces of his brain seemed to be coming loose. He wrapped his hand around his tumbler, feeling the cold glass against his hot, slippery fingers. His face felt stiff but rubbery, like a surface in a feverish dream. He put a hand up experimentally and touched his lips, his cheek. He poured a bit more whisky into himself and felt it dribble down his chin.

'Felix?'

He had to get up and go into his study. Something terrible would happen if he didn't. Everything would come tumbling down on top of him. He watched his hand pour another whisky. Near the top, why not? How many was that? Three? Four? He lifted it up and the rim of the glass bumped against his teeth and the whisky sloshed over the edge, making his gums sting. His lips felt blistered. Isabel's face seemed to be advancing, then drawing back. Her mouth was opening and shutting; there were sounds coming out of it that distorted before they reached him. He leant forward, trying to concentrate. He thought of telling her what he had just done, but before he could wrap his mouth around the shame of the words, Isabel had turned her back and was doing something with the fish. And he remembered Connie's lips on his skin, like suckers, in an underwater world.

'I have . . .' he said, too loudly. Have what? I have sinned. In thought and word and deed.

The phone rang, startling him, jangling in his skull.

'Do you want to get that?' Isabel said.

The days had long gone when the sound of the telephone had made them both go still with hope and terror, when they would look at each other, holding their breath until one of them answered.

Felix started across the kitchen towards the phone, which lay out of its cradle on the surface near the window. It seemed an awfully long way and the floor was swaying, like a wooden suspension bridge. Out of nowhere, a clean, clear memory rose up in him of an early holiday with Isabel, and of watching her as she walked before him across such a bridge, above a ravine. How she had turned her face to him, laughing, the wind whipping her hair. Very beautiful. Eager for him. Those days were gone. She would never look at him like that again. He bumped into the table and his legs seemed to get entangled with the legs of a chair.

The phone stopped ringing but he tried to keep going, to get to his study. He would be safe if he got there, to his chair, away from Isabel's eyes. But she was in front of him. How had that happened? She was putting out a hand; it loomed up in front of his face. Its weight on his shoulder sent him spinning. His glass was like a ball turning in front of him, gathering momentum, an arc of golden liquid flying from its mouth and scattering droplets of whisky over his upturned face. In the end, he thought, it was easier to let go. It was easier to give up. It was easier to admit that he couldn't do it any longer and step off the tightrope and plummet through the endless drop. There was a terrible noise, screeching, tearing, grinding metal, and it jagged up his throat and ripped the air around him and his head was bouncing on the floor while the light from the bulb in the ceiling skinned the membranes of his eyes, and through the blinding whiteness of pain he saw Isabel's face slowly crumpling as a paper bag crumples before it catches fire.

Perhaps he half woke several times; later he had jumbled recollections of a man standing over him and a thin, sharp beam of light being directed into his eyes, of hands laid on him, voices saying things. It was like a crime-scene investigation – but he was the crime and the victim, the clue and the answer. These became part of his dreams, which were thick and noisy, coming at him from all sides and pressing down on him. When he finally woke, he was lying in bed in the semi-darkness. He had an ice pack on his head, where pain swung like a wrecking ball through the chambers of his brain, reducing thoughts to grey rubble and toxic dust. His shoulder throbbed, and he had a nasty taste in his mouth, which was parched and sour; he could barely swallow. His tongue felt thick, and too big for its normal space. His cheeks stung as if someone had scrubbed them with a scouring pad.

'Try to drink,' said a female voice he dimly recognized. A hand slid under his head and lifted it slightly; a glass was fitted against his lips and a trickle of water slid down his throat. He blinked and tried to focus on the face that swam in and out of his vision. It was Leah, he realized. Elegant, ironic Leah. Isabel must have called her for help. He wondered what time it was, what day even, and tried to turn his head towards the radio-clock but it hurt too much: his head was too heavy.

Anyway, it didn't really matter. Hours, days, years were just the slow sift of time, the gradual gathering of a life into its paltry heap of things done and not done. Perhaps a week had passed, perhaps a month, in this twilight room of fugitive shapes and muffled sounds. If he never moved again to lift a hand, form a word, make a plan and carry it out, he wouldn't grieve. Somewhere in his memory, he saw himself running, pounding along mile after mile, and he felt sorry for that driven figure. So much effort, just to keep the demons at bay. They weren't at bay any longer: they had pounced on him, tearing at his flesh with their teeth, and he had finally lain down to let them devour him. It hurt less than he had expected: the real pain had been the torment of trying to escape, hearing them always at his heels and smelling the meaty stench of their breath.

'You've got concussion,' said Leah. 'You gave everyone a fright, passing out like that. But the doctors say you'll be all right. We need to wake you every hour or so to make sure you're OK. I'm part of the rota, while Isabel is seeing Mia's teachers for her parents' evening. Are you OK?'

'Hnnh,' said Felix.

'Good,' she said, taking this for assent. 'You must hurt.'

'Nnn.'

'Don't cry,' she said. 'Please don't cry.'

Was he crying? That must be why his cheeks stung so and why his pyjama jacket was damp against his neck.

'There's nothing to worry about. Everything's in hand. Isabel's rung to say you won't be at work for a bit and they're completely fine with that, as they should be.'

Felix closed his eyes. Even the faint light in the room hurt him. He wanted complete darkness, like layer upon layer of thick black velvet over him: not to see and not to be seen; not to think or be thought about; no sound except the sound of his own breathing. Not to be touched, except like a child who can't attend to his own needs.

'Mia and Isabel should be back soon. Do you want me to leave you alone or sit here?'

He couldn't reply. She dabbed a tissue against his face, then bent down and put her lips on his cheek, very gently, before clipping out of the room. Felix thought that perhaps he could stay there for ever, splayed limbs under warm covers, and that gradually life would recede, the baying dogs fade back into the undergrowth. He remembered being ill as a small boy, feverish with bad dreams and waking nightmares, and Miranda moving softly round his room, her feet solid on the tipping floor, her hands steadying the walls.

He was alone and that was what he wanted – alone, but

with the sounds of life going on elsewhere. A vacuum cleaner, a dishwasher, an indistinguishable hum of voices from downstairs. He could be carried along by life without having to make an effort himself, like a stick in a flowing river. A car passed by, its headlights striping the ceiling, but didn't stop.

Another car and this time it slowed. Headlights slewed into the room again and stopped, then were extinguished, and his room fell back into soft darkness. He heard doors slamming. He didn't want to be looked at – not by Isabel and certainly not by Mia. A daughter should not have to witness the disintegration of that once-impregnable figure her father, or see beyond the frown, the glare, the ironed shirt, the clipped address, the show of strength and certainty to the shame and corruption that lay beneath. He inched further down in the bed and pulled the duvet over his head. Isabel always told him that when he was in bed, he lay stiff as a board, at attention even in his dreams, but now he huddled into himself, wrapping his arms round his hollow chest, pulling his knees up. If either of them came in, he would pretend to be asleep. Soon it would be night-time anyway – but that thought scared him, like the dark waters that make you dizzy with their depths and in which were alien life forms, spooky mutants with their tentacles and slimy suckers. No, he wanted it to be neither day nor night, but somewhere in between, a limbo of faded light and suspended purpose. A radio turned on, but so low the voices were just murmurs. A smell seeping up from the kitchen – fresh bread or hot chocolate or vanilla custard – nothing that was fierce or fried, only the sweet and the bland and the infinitely reassuring, taking him back to that world before terror had begun.

He heard footsteps on the stairs. Leah's voice called in farewell and the front door opened and closed. He was so scared of Isabel and Mia that he actually heard himself whimper in protest as the door was pushed open and a shaft of light from the landing lay across the carpet. He could make out both their shapes silhouetted there and he winced, squeezed shut his eyes again and retreated into the burrow he had made for himself. He was in hiding, a coward who was literally pulling the covers over his head. What would Dr Felix Hopkins make of this? What would that upright and stern arbiter of morals and good judgement have to say?

'Felix.'

Isabel was beside him now. He lay quite still. His face was sticky with old tears.

'Felix? Leah said you were awake. Are you awake?'

She put a hand on his shoulder. He didn't move.

'Felix?'

'Mm?'

'Can I get you anything?'

'No,' he murmured, not emerging.

'Are you feeling any better?'

He gave a meaningless grunt. At her kindness, tears were sliding slantwise down his face, into his mouth, and he made an effort not to cry out.

'Dad?' Now it was Mia's turn. Her voice was high with anxiety. 'Dad, are you OK? I've been so worried. Dad? Please say something to me.'

He really should speak: his daughter needed him. But it

was like hauling a vast boulder up a hill. The words were too heavy and the effort it would require was too much for him.

'Is it something we've done?' she was saying. 'Something *I've* done? Dad?'

A small whimper escaped him and she pulled the cover back slightly to see his streaming face. He couldn't stop himself: he was crying now in a steady rhythm, like a muffled machine-gun, five broken sobs, then a breath for reloading, and five more. On and on and on. He marvelled at how the body could just take over, and at how much salt water there was in the tear ducts. Surely it should run out at some point, but at the moment it seemed inexhaustible and neither would the sobs cease. He yielded to them. Mia knelt on the floor and laid her head on his bucking body, begging him to stop. Isabel sat on the other side of the bed – her side – and laid a cool hand on his clammy forehead.

'It's all right, Felix,' she said, and he could hear from her voice how weary she was with it all. He had become just another burden she would have to carry. He recognized that she was stronger than him, because she could bend and therefore would not break. She was like those sea grasses that would lie flat against the earth in a storm but gradually straighten when the wind died down. She was crushed and broken, but she endured and she would never give up. She had absorbed grief and fear into her body and made it part of her flesh and blood, but he had held it at arm's length, made it into a problem to be grappled with and thrown to the ground – and it had thrown him, and now she'd have to go on alone. He could see this now, as he lay curled up like a foetus in the bed, his wife and daughter at either side, trying to comfort him.

'I'm going to bring you some soup,' said Isabel. 'You need to get something inside you. Butternut-squash soup – I made it from the last of your squashes from the allotment. You just stay there. You need rest. It's all been too much, I know.'

She left but Mia stayed, crouched beside him, holding his hand now. She was crying too. It was like being on his death-bed, except he knew he wasn't going to die. He would just stay there and wait for a very long time. Somebody else would have to take over now. He couldn't do it any more.

Chapter Twenty-two

In the kitchen, Isabel heated the soup and Mia tried to cut slices from the wholemeal loaf to toast. She was uncharacteristically clumsy. Her hand slipped on the knife. Isabel turned off the gas and went across to her, taking the knife out of her grip and laying it to one side.

'It's going to be all right,' she said. She wondered how many times she had said this to other people or heard them saying it to her in the last few months.

'What's happened to him?'

'He fell over and got concussion.'

'No! I don't mean that. What's wrong with him? He just lies there and cries. He never cries. I have never in my whole life seen him cry. Except a tiny bit when he reads poetry to us.'

'Perhaps that's why he's crying like this now. All the things he's never cried about.'

'But what *happened*?'

'He came home, he seemed a bit – odd. I don't know. He drank several glasses of whisky in quick succession – he doesn't even like whisky much – then fell over and bumped his head badly. Mia, you know what happened. It was Johnny's birthday. Perhaps he just couldn't keep himself together any longer. It was all too much. He keeps everything so under control, I think he'd become like a ticking bomb. It was the trigger.'

'But he'll get better?'

Isabel looked at Mia. Her eyes were bright and her face pinched with anxiety. She suddenly noticed she had a new ear piercing. When had she had that done? What else had she not noticed? 'This is awful for you,' she said.

'Will he get better?'

'Of course he will. Maybe in the end it's good he's let everything out like this. He needed to cry.'

'Mama?'

'Yes, my darling.'

'If Johnny never comes home, what's going to happen?'

Perhaps for the first time, Isabel prevented herself from protesting that of course he would come home.

'Happen to us, you mean?'

'I suppose so. I mean, how will we be able to bear everything?'

'Truthfully, Mia, I don't know. But I do know this: we will be able to bear it. You are going to be all right. Whatever happens, you will be OK. You are going to have a wonderful life and you are not going to be wrecked by this – hurt, of course. Sad, how not? But you are not going to be wrecked. You have a year and a bit left at school and you are going to do your exams and go to university and do all the things you ever wanted to do. Johnny will come home, but if he doesn't, it will still be all right.'

'Do you cry?'

'Sometimes.' Isabel looked attentively at Mia. 'You mean am I going to collapse like Dad and lie in bed in the dark weeping? No, I am not. I give you my word.'

'You can if you want. I'm an adult now, pretty much.

You don't have to be all strong just for me. I can cope on my own.'

'But I don't want you to cope on your own!'

'Well, I have been, haven't I?'

'Have I been so neglectful?'

'I'm not stupid. You've been going through the motions. Who cares if I'm doing my AS levels in a few weeks? Who cares if I fall out with friends or have a fling with Will or can't sleep properly or miss Johnny? Who cares? It's nothing, is it, when you put it next to what's happened? Everything in my life's just trivial.'

'No!'

'I'm not blaming you, I'm just saying, that's all. It's obvious. How can I tell you about stuff when I know what you're going through? And now Dad's lying there blubbering like a baby. It sounds selfish, I know – I feel sorry for him. I really do. I can hardly bear it, if you must know. But at the same time it's not fair.'

'Oh, Mia.'

'Now I'm sounding like a two-year-old, as if it's all about me. Nothing's fair, is it, and nothing's about me. It's all about Johnny.'

'Oh, God.'

'Don't look at me like that – as if I've stabbed you. Because then it's *still* not about me, it's about you and your suffering.'

'I didn't mean to.'

'Oh, forget it. I shouldn't have spoken. It wasn't kind. But do you have any idea of what it's been like for me?'

'I'm sorry. I'm sorry about everything.'

'It's not your fault. It's Johnny's fault. I hate him.'

'Don't.'

'I hate him, I hate him, I hate him.'

'Please.'

'I wish he was dead. At least I could get on with my life then.'

'You don't mean it.'

'I fucking do.'

Birthdays

Birthdays

Chapter Twenty-three

On Johnny's twentieth birthday, Isabel bought him a painting of a tree in spring, and put it in his bedroom, face to the wall, still in its bubble wrap. She invited close family and friends to the house for a small gathering. Mia, just two months away from finishing school, brought her latest in a sudden string of older boyfriends, a spiky twenty-three-year-old called Lachlan, who was a student in Norwich and had once, for a few weeks, been taught by Felix. Mia treated him in a peremptory fashion, often curt or even cutting, but he didn't seem to mind. He watched her longingly and Isabel, following his gaze, saw Mia with the eyes of a stranger as someone mysterious and coolly sexy, with her slick black hair and her unfathomable eyes. Tamsin, Jed and Merry (full name: Meredith Clarissa Hopkins-Selek) came for the weekend. They collected Miranda on the way, and inserted her into the back seat, among the nappies and the buggy and the bottles and the soft toys and pre-prepared Tupperware boxes of baby food. Tamsin was living with Jed now and they planned to marry as soon as his divorce came through. They seemed very happy. ('Nauseatingly happy,' said Mia, who hated the way they held hands at the dinner table, called each other 'sweetheart' and 'darling', and baby-talked to their daughter in identical cooing voices.)

Rory and Helen arrived, with Lucy; Helen was pregnant

again, beset by morning sickness, and Lucy had entered the tantrum years with a gusto that filled Isabel with admiration: to be so small and so angry. She was hectic and blotchy and strident. She stomped round the house with thunderous steps. Ben came, but alone and subdued: he and Gabriella had just split up because Gabriella had fallen back in love with her ex and, after months of tears and indecision, had moved out of their flat. Will came down from York (which was probably why Mia had dragged Lachlan along). He had cut his hair brutally short and wore drainpipe trousers and tight jackets – but he still blushed when he saw Isabel and stammered when he talked to Mia, his glance sliding over her body, then away again, with a mixture of shame, knowledge and desire. Baxter came from Brighton, where he was still living even though he had dropped out of his course. He had brought a pot of his mother's newly made marmalade for Isabel, and for Mia a hyacinth in a pot.

Leah couldn't come: she had been diagnosed with breast cancer and was going through her first bout of chemotherapy. She was making a great fuss about the weight she would put on with Tamoxifen and had acquired an outrageous wig for when her hair started to fall out; she pranced around in it and her precariously high-heeled shoes, looking like a drag queen. In her bravado and self-mockery, Jenny and Isabel sensed her fear. Jenny was there for both of them, with Benedict beside her, a softly spoken, crumple-faced man with a gentle paunch and a slightly pigeon-toed walk. Every so often they would touch each other's hands reassuringly or catch each other's eye to smile a private smile. He had moved into Jenny's house a month ago, along with his beehive and cookery books.

Isabel had made a vast pot of paella and bought bottles of Spanish wine to go with it. She had filled the house with spring flowers and put on a green dress and lipstick. She had had her hair cut shorter recently, so that it framed her face, and although she was still visibly thin, she no longer had the haggard, unhealthy gauntness of the previous year, or the brittle manner, a kind of attenuated quivering tautness that had made everyone step so carefully around her, as if one wrong word might crush her. Instead, there was a weariness about her, something subdued and worn, as if her edges had been rubbed away. She had been so bright and alert, vivacious and visible, and now she was slower and more patient. She sometimes looked at you as though she could barely make you out. Jenny called it her gone-away look.

There were too many people to sit round the table, so she pushed it back against the wall and put the paella in its centre for everyone to help themselves. The smell of saffron and prawns filled the air. She opened several bottles and found an assortment of glasses. Felix had said he would be there as well, but he hadn't emerged from his study yet. No one knew what he did in there any more. He wasn't working; neither was he playing his violin – he hadn't picked it up in months. It lay in its case, lined with blue velvet, gathering dust, the strings loosening. He had never quite recovered from his breakdown. That's what everyone said. It was a shame, but not surprising – after all, how would any of us deal with a thing like that? Although who could say what had finally pushed him over the edge, so that he had lain in his bed like a toppled statue, unnervingly still, tears cascading down his weathered cheeks.

Isabel could have told them. Two weeks after Felix had collapsed in the kitchen, Connie Kramer had come to visit her. Isabel knew her vaguely, having met her at various university functions and on the few occasions that Connie, with others, had come to their house. She had instinctively liked her self-deprecating humour, her sharpness and bounce. But as soon as she had opened the door and seen Connie on the threshold, wearing a stiffly self-conscious expression and her hands tightly braided together, she had known what the woman had come to tell her. She had sat her down at the kitchen table, given her a cup of tea, shut the door to make sure they weren't overheard – but who could hear them, except Felix, lying upstairs? – and waited for her to confess.

Connie, trying not to cry, blamed herself for seducing Felix, especially when he was so vulnerable, and sending him into his present state. She felt like a criminal, she said, and then, resorting to hyperbole under Isabel's calm stare, like a murderess. Ever since she had heard he was ill, she had agonized over what she should do, but she had decided Isabel should be in full possession of the facts. Isabel nodded. Of course she should. It was what she had always said she believed in: she had told anyone who cared to listen that you had to know what was going on in your own life in order to have any kind of autonomy. Autonomy had once been a very important word to her: she had used it all the time. She had passed it on to Mia and Tamsin. It meant having access to yourself, having your own unique voice, being in control of your life. It was a word women used, because women above all knew what it was to be denied autonomy. She and Jenny had discussed it at great length after Jenny's husband had left her all those years ago. Jenny had hated the fact that other people had had knowledge about her life that had been assiduously hidden from her. So, Isabel had nodded at Connie as if it mattered. She hadn't said she really didn't care that Connie had had sex with Felix. She had felt at a great distance from the news; it was just a dot on the horizon. She had understood that one day it would mean something and she would have to deal with it – but then, with the fact of Johnny's disappearance lodged in her like a tombstone, it had seemed insignificant.

Even now, it held no power over her. She felt sorry for Felix, and treated him gently, but she had never properly confronted him with what he had done, although she had let him understand that she knew. When Jenny, in whom she had confided, asked why, she had replied, after a long pause: 'I couldn't make the effort to care enough. That's the truth of it – I felt burnt out.'

Now she poured wine into glasses and summoned her guests, who were standing in groups around the kitchen and living room. She wanted to propose a toast, she said, and held her glass high in the air, and steady. She could see that there were several people who didn't really want to be there, and were uncomfortable and embarrassed. Some were even angry.

Isabel knew that Johnny's friends were beginning to let him go from their lives: what had once been a living catastrophe had now settled into a sad story from their past, and they were moving forwards without him. She didn't want that to happen. When he came home, she wanted them all to be waiting.

'Happy twentieth birthday, Johnny, wherever you are,' she said, in a clear, insistent voice.

And everyone dutifully repeated the words. She was demanding that they held him in their hearts and kept him alive. She wouldn't give up.

Isabel spent Johnny's twenty-first birthday with Graham, clearing Bernard's room of his possessions. Their father had died ten days previously. She had been there when the nurse pressed his eyes closed and wheeled away the machines that had surrounded him, leaving Isabel sitting beside him in a heavy silence. But Graham had arrived too late. It had been months since their father had spoken to them or shown any signs of recognizing them, but that Graham hadn't been present to witness the moment at which the old man had passed almost imperceptibly from a shadow life to a final death had undone him. He had been inconsolable. He had adored his mother, Kathleen, clung to her all her short life and never got over her death, but he had shrunk from Bernard after she had gone. The resentment he had felt towards him when he was a bullied and anxious child had hardened in adulthood into a kind of derision that Isabel believed was a form of self-defence against his feelings of abandonment and self-pity. Graham hated self-pity, and was contemptuous of anyone who displayed it. It was a weakness, a soft and shaming narcissism. He talked about Bernard in an off-hand, even callous, tone, and clearly regarded him as a burden – an unsatisfactory father who, as he grew old and weak, sucked more and more money and time from him, which could have been better used elsewhere. Isabel saw that by the end Bernard had disgusted her brother – his smell, the dribbling, his slack flesh and lopsided body, his disintegration and his mortality. Graham could hardly bear to look at him.

But now Graham cried over him, while Isabel – who had tended him so faithfully – could not. He had sunk to his knees beside the bed and picked up the hand that flopped over the sheets, pressing it to his streaming face and sobbing. What was he crying for? wondered Isabel. For the death of a father who had never been fatherly, for the death of a mother he had barely known, for the death of that needy and affectionate little boy whom he had buried beneath the prim and self-righteous man he had chosen to be, for the fact that he had no children and now nothing to bind him? He was a link with no chain, alone but for his wife in a world that had always terrified him.

He had cried at the funeral as well – he, and little Merry, puce in Tamsin's arms, filling the crematorium with her shrieks. Everyone else had been subdued; it had been a muted ceremony for an old man who had had few friends and who had disappeared from his life long before he had left it. They had collected the ashes the next day, but not known where to throw them. It seemed like a symbol of Bernard Cornish's life that they couldn't think of places that had been precious to him, just as at the funeral they had struggled to find readings that would express the kind of man he had been. In the end,

Isabel had taken the ashes – placed in what looked like a Tupperware box – back home. They rattled slightly when she shook them, so they weren't just powder but tiny pieces of bone, she imagined. She put the container on the lower shelf of her bedside table. It should have seemed very odd to be sleeping next to her father's ashes, but she quickly forgot about them.

Now they sorted through his paltry belongings. He had lived so long and left behind so little at the end, a life that had been reduced to this simple room, painted in neutral colours, in a corridor of similar rooms. They threw all his underwear away, the pyjamas and most of his shirts, as well as his shabby black shoes and his worn-out felt slippers, a few shapeless jumpers and a cardigan that the moths had feasted on. A few clothes – his one suit, which he had insisted on taking with him to the home and which Isabel had never seen him wear there, a good white shirt and a nice striped one she had given him, a woollen jacket whose pockets were still sewn up – they would give to a charity shop. Isabel rolled up one of his ties – blue with a thin red stripe – and put it into her pocket.

There was a photograph of Kathleen and Bernard, taken on their British seaside honeymoon, that Isabel insisted Graham take – she still had the portrait of her mother, after all; Celia and Graham hadn't mentioned it again. There was a family photograph of the four of them together, when Graham was still a baby, and she said Graham should have that as well. There was nothing she wanted: not the little chair with the tapestry upholstery, not the few books, including an old King James Bible, with thin silky pages, a set of handsomely bound, hopelessly out-of-date encyclopedias and Palgrave's *Golden Treasury of Verse*, which she remembered her mother reading from when she was a child – she was quite sure her father hadn't opened it in years – not the shaving kit in its leather case that Bernard had had ever since she could recall, or the silver hairbrush that still had wisps of his hair in it. Why did that suddenly make her feel so sick and so sad? She didn't want the nice glass jug she had put flowers in every week since he had arrived here, or the digital radio she had brought for him, or the portable CD player, or the television and DVD player. Or the fountain pen, though she hesitated over that before passing it across to Graham, who wanted everything, as if the things his father had owned might fill some emotional void.

She did take the mug that Mia and Johnny had painted together several years ago, at a local ceramics shop where people could decorate their own pottery. They had drawn peaky blue waves round it and splashed blue droplets inside it, and then written 'storm in a teacup' on the rim, in very wonky writing, a fine brush dipped in navy blue. Johnny's writing. Her storm. She wrapped it carefully in one of Bernard's towels, although there was already a hairline fracture running down its side and it would never hold liquid. She would put pens in it, she thought.

One of the helpers brought them tea, very milky in plastic mugs, and they sat on Bernard's bed (stripped of sheets and with a large stain the shape of France on the mattress).

'Now I can never tell him,' said Graham.

'Tell him what?' She wasn't used to this kind of conversation with Graham and she was aiming for the right kind of tone – interested and sympathetic without being too intense or urgent, which might close him down again, send him scuttling back into the fortress of himself.

'I don't know. I just thought that one day we'd have The Conversation.'

'You can't have thought that after he'd had his stroke.'

'He always liked you more than me.'

He sounded so like a little child that Isabel almost had to laugh. 'I hardly think that's true.'

'Of course it was true. I was a disappointment.'

'Oh, Graham, it wasn't like that. He just couldn't show his feelings. He didn't have the vocabulary.'

'Do you think I'm like him?'

'You?'

'Yes.'

'No. I mean, in some ways you are – I'm sure we both are,' said Isabel, cautiously. 'But not really.'

'He's why I didn't want to have children. I didn't want to turn into the kind of father he was. It seemed safer just never to take the risk. Now?' He shrugged. His eyes filled with tears.

Isabel resisted the impulse to lean forward and hug him; he looked so like the little boy he had once been, trembling chin and watery eyes. 'Now?' she prompted.

'Now I don't know. Maybe it would have been good.'

'To have had children?'

'Maybe. I used to look at you and think, Why is it so easy for her? Happy families and all that.'

Isabel felt suddenly cold. 'You used to, and then Johnny disappeared, you mean?'

He grimaced. 'Sorry. I shouldn't have said that.'

'It doesn't matter. It's true. We turned out to be not such a happy family after all. Today's his birthday.'

'Oh. I didn't know. I should have remembered.'

'Twenty-one. I bought him lots of poetry books.'

'Oh.' He looked embarrassed, constipated with awkwardness. He didn't want to know about Isabel's distress, and certainly didn't want to hear about presents she hid in the back of her wardrobe, or placed on Johnny's bed, ready for him to come home to.

She leant forward and kissed him lightly on the cheek. 'It's all right. I can mention his name without crying.'

But suddenly she found that wasn't true. Tears welled in her eyes. Her son, her only son, her beloved child, was twenty-one on this day: who was with him to wish him all good things in life, to put candles on a cake and presents on the table and smile at him with love? She wiped her eyes and sipped her milky tea. But she hadn't cried over Bernard, or even been close to it. Dry as a desert. She didn't even feel sad, if she were honest. Or anything. Her father was dead; she would never see him again. She would never again sit in the warm, square room and hold his unresponsive hand and read children's books to him, or tell him things she knew he couldn't understand. Bring him flowers. Be his mother as well as his child. Look at his face and see the face it used to be. She thought these things yet they didn't touch her. It seemed to her now that for all these years she had been simply playing the part of the good daughter, and had never actually cared. Did that make her a monster?

'When did you last have sex?'

It was Johnny's twenty-second birthday, and Isabel and Felix were sitting in a poorly lit room in the Civic Centre. They were on a wooden bench-like sofa with a wide gap between them, and the Relate counsellor – a large woman with wavy chestnut hair and bright eyes – was sitting opposite them, with a table in between. On the table, there were daffodils in a small carafe and a large box of tissues. In case we cry, thought Isabel. And she remembered how for months Felix had done almost nothing but cry, until the drugs had dried up his tears. But his face had never recovered from that period: his cheeks were like rock down which water had flowed for so long it had made permanent grooves. His grief was carved on his face.

'When did you last have sex?' repeated the counsellor, cheerily, as if instructing them not to be embarrassed. Her name was April Marlowe. She smelt of astringent soap, perhaps like the alcohol hand-gel Isabel had in the car for long journeys that evaporates on your skin.

'I – I can't quite say,' stammered Felix, staring at her.

'I think she means you and me,' said Isabel, gently, to her husband. 'Don't you?'

'Well, yes,' said April, looking surprised.

'I don't know,' said Felix. He kept passing his thin hand over his high forehead, as if he was brushing something away.

'About three and a half years ago,' said Isabel, in a brisk and clinical tone, as if she was talking to a hairdresser about the state of her split ends. 'Late November, it would have been.'

'I see.'

'You probably don't.'

Isabel didn't like April. She was irritated by the way she kept smiling at them. She was already regretting that she had suggested this to Felix and that he had, to her surprise, agreed.

'Would you like to tell me why it has been such a long time?'

'Because . . .' Isabel stopped. Why was it so hard to say the words out loud to this woman? Her irritation was like an allergic reaction. She looked at her plump fingers (wedding ring and thick engagement ring on the fourth finger, signet ring on the pinkie), and at her plump knees, firmly pressed together, and a wave of contempt passed through her, followed immediately by a wave of self-hatred. Who did she think she was, judging someone like this? She made an effort, sat up straighter.

'Because our son, Johnny, disappeared shortly after.'

'Oh!' April's face lost its smile. Even her gleaming brown hair seemed to become less bouncy. 'That's terrible. Is he –'

'Still missing? Yes. He's not dead. I know he's not. If he was dead, I would feel it, here.' And she pressed her hand to her heart.

'Oh,' repeated April. She seemed at a loss for words.

This wasn't in her training, thought Isabel, half sorry for her and half furious.

'It's his birthday today,' she continued. 'He's twenty-two. Before he went, we were fine, weren't we, Felix? . . . Felix?'

Felix moved his head slowly up and down in willed agreement. He looked like one of those nodding dogs in the back of a car, thought Isabel.

'Not just with sex. With everything, more or less. Don't you think, Felix?'

Felix nodded again, even more slowly, as though the momentum was running down. Isabel resisted an impulse to swipe him with the back of her hand.

'I can see that something like that – so terrible . . .' Again April ground to a halt. Presumably, she was used to dealing with couples who talked about numbing familiarity, domestic wrangles and resentments, maybe an affair, a mid-life crisis. But how do you start talking about respecting the other person, attending to them, remembering what you like about them, in the face of something like this? Poor April, thought Isabel, who was breathless with rage, toxic with bad feelings. However far away she was sitting from Felix on this nasty sofa was too close. She shifted a bit so she was right up to the armrest.

'You seemed to suggest,' said April, carefully, 'that there had been sex, but not with each other. Is that right?'

Isabel waited. Felix made a small sound of assent, like a rusty door opening a crack.

'Felix?' said April.

Felix nodded.

'This is not about blame or judgement,' said April. 'You're here to talk about your relationship with each other. You can walk out if you want. I'm only here to help you speak to each other.'

'I had sex with a colleague,' said Felix, with obvious difficulty and staring off to one side. 'Three years ago.'

'To the day,' supplied Isabel. Her mouth was trembling as if she were about to start giggling.

'And that was it?'

Isabel waited. She was interested to hear what Felix would say: he wouldn't lie, she knew that.

'Yes.'

'Listen. We're not here about that,' said Isabel. 'It's a red herring. You might think that's – what's the word? – false consciousness. That I mind without realizing I mind or something. I really don't mind. I never did. It was just something that happened amid the horror of what was going on. One moment was all it took. One brief moment – and, God knows, Felix has paid for it with his guilt and self-loathing. Maybe I would hate him if he didn't hate himself so much. He's a man of integrity. I've always thought he's a much better person than I am. Actually, I feel sorry for him.' Felix visibly winced. 'Sorry for both of us. I don't know why I'm here. I can't think now why I even thought it was a good idea. I don't care he was unfaithful – which isn't how I think of it anyway. I don't care that we haven't had sex in years and barely touch each other. I don't think I want to have sex – with Felix or anyone – ever again. I don't feel I have a body like that any more, or a heart. I'm too tired.'

'So why are you here?'

'Good question. Why am I? I guess I'm just doing the things I think I ought to do. I'm setting rules for myself and then obeying them. In a kind of far-off and disconnected fashion, I want to do what's best for all of us, or want to want to do, or think I ought to want to. Et cetera. I have two daughters and I have to keep the home safe for them, and for my grandchildren. I need things to be all right for Johnny when he returns.' Same old same old. Parroting words that were so hollowed of meaning now that they were just sounds hanging in the air. 'But although I'm here, I can't actually believe you'll be able to make a difference to us,' she finished, fixing April with her gaze. 'No criticism of you, I'm sure you're good at what you do. I can't even get to the first stage of wanting things to be better. I'm under water.'

'Under water?'

'Yes.'

'Like – drowning?'

'I don't know. Is that what I mean? I think I just mean I'm under water. In a different world from you, sluggish and drifting, not able to make out the sounds that reach me from above, waiting to be washed up. Maybe you can pull me ashore.'

'I can try,' said April, bravely, as if she was a trainee life-guard standing beside a tidal wave.

Isabel nodded at her. Her anger had gone, replaced by torpor. 'Thank you,' she said. 'We appreciate that. Don't we, Felix?'

Felix gave a murmur of assent.

Mia spent Johnny's twenty-third birthday night sleeping in a doorway. She had done the same on his last birthday, and several times since then, not telling anyone about it in advance, or ever saying afterwards what she had done. It was her secret, her lonely descent into a darkness of grief that nobody else knew about, however much they chose to confide in her. She implied to her housemates – two English students, one history and a medic – that she was going to be with her boyfriend. She told her boyfriend that she was out with friends. She let friends think she was working late at the library: finals were in a couple of months' time. She left her mobile phone behind, and her iPod, dressed in warm, dark layers of clothing, tights under jeans, two T-shirts under a thick jumper, pulling a hat down over her spiky hair and putting on two pairs of socks. Quilted jacket, with gloves in the pocket. Scarf, wrapped twice round her neck. She felt swaddled in clothes but she knew how chilly it could get, even in March when the buds on the trees were stickily unfolding and the dawn chorus woke her before six. Cold from the pavement seeped through outer garments and into your aching bones. She rolled up her sleeping bag tightly and stuffed it into her canvas hold-all.

At the corner shop she got two more packets of cigarettes, although she still had several left. At the little supermarket she bought several past-their-sell-by-date sandwiches, some iced buns and several bars of milk chocolate. It would soon be dark: the sun was sinking towards the horizon in a rippled glow of orange and pink. The air was already losing its early-spring fragile warmth, and in the shadows it felt cool.

Mia walked quickly from her shared house in Camden towards central London. She was brimming with an emotion that she usually tried to keep tamped down inside her, but which every so often she let rise to the surface. She had felt heavy with sadness for days now, knowing she would be spending this night on the streets, among the missing people, and each day the sadness had thickened, so that now it was a powerful pressure pushing up through her chest, her throat. Her body felt too fragile to contain it; she didn't understand how her skin didn't split and her features didn't break up.

Last year she had slept near Waterloo. She had been kicked in the head and she had been embraced by a woman covered with urine, and had kissed her shiny wet face. She had watched the couple next to her cook their heroin on a spoon. She had watched darkness fall, then day breaking, and in between, time had stretched in front of her like a dreary dark plain and plummeted away underneath her, like a precipitate cliff. It had been a bit like going mad, to imagine how these people sat here night after night waiting for dawn. No wonder they drank and injected themselves and fought and fucked. No wonder they looked at you as if you were an alien, or as if they had arrived from a different land themselves, red-eyed and aghast, crusted lips and shaking hands.

Once, on a family camping holiday, she and Johnny had slept under the stars. She remembered how they had lain on their backs and gazed up at the clear sky, with faint skeins of the Milky Way showing. Johnny had told her that only about two and a half thousand stars were visible to the naked eye yet there were at least two hundred billion stars in our galaxy. Then he added, triumphantly, that if she thought that was awesome, she should consider that there were about a hundred and seventy billion galaxies in the observable universe, and a galaxy could contain from ten million to a hundred trillion stars. Mia hadn't really listened to what he had said. She just knew it meant inhumanly vast, crazily unimaginable. She was drifting in and out of sleep anyway, dizzy with the sense of the inconceivable space but anchored by the tangible certainty of Johnny beside her, Tamsin in her little tent behind them, her parents in theirs a few feet further back, then the other tents and caravans and communal showers, and the road beyond that, which led back to home.

Sleeping on the streets of London was very different, for her at least. You didn't feel the existential loneliness of a tiny individual in the vertiginous hugeness of the universe: you felt the tormented loneliness of the human mind. The black hole was inside you, sucking you into it and extinguishing you entirely. You were nothing and you were everything, as light as a particle, as heavy as a dying planet. Dark matter and empty space.

She wasn't even sure why she felt compelled to do it and why she could never tell people what she did. It was an act of remembrance. It was an act of self-punishment. It was the power of magical thinking (if I do this, you will return). It was a lowering of the self into the nightmare world, like a bucket into an inky well, smooth slimy walls and ghostly echoes, waiting for the splash, the pull up to daylight again, surviving for now. Once, she had seen someone she knew passing by on the other side of the street and had recoiled, her heart racing. She didn't want to be seen or known; she had the strongest sense then that these people of the doorways and underpasses, the invisible ones, belonged to a different world entirely from the one she normally inhabited.

She took up her place in a small garden just off a road near Trafalgar Square. She had planned it in advance. She knew that in the daytime, people sat in there with their gathered fag-ends and cans of white cider. At night, it became a place where men and women curled in their bags or sat nursing their bottles and their memories. Nearby was a hostel for the homeless – Isabel had visited it on that first trip to London, all those years ago. There was a soup kitchen a few hundred metres away where lines of ragged people queued. There was a churchyard where sometimes a brazier glowed in the darkness. The little garden, which really consisted of three wooden benches round a patch of soil where daffodils grew in the spring and a single rosebush flowered in the summer, was still empty and Mia took a seat on a bench and pulled out her cigarettes. She lit one and drew her breath in slowly and deeply, then let it out and watched the blue smoke curl and dissolve in the air. She used to think that one day Johnny would come and sit beside her. She had played through the scenarios in her mind: how he would take his place, not saying anything, hand her a roll-up, and they would sit together in the darkness, the tips of their cigarettes glowing, not speaking for a while, because what was there to say? But they would be glad. That was as far as she had got with her imagined narrative – it went into a cul-de-sac and stopped dead. Where do you begin with someone who simply walked out on his happy family (she put the two words into quotation marks in her mind) and disappeared? Which comes first? The relief or the consuming rage?

The night crept forward. She wandered to the soup kitchen and watched the figures there. A couple of men were scuffling near the front of the queue. A sad-looking youth with a thin, scarred face sat by the side, put his head into his hands and wept. Some people were clearly drunk and others were so sluggish it seemed they could barely force themselves to move, to speak, to take a mug of soup and wrap their hands around it for warmth. But also people laughed. They made jokes. They swapped stories. Mia heard one of them talking about the football team he supported. A woman was comforting another woman, putting an arm around her shoulders and telling her everything was going to be all right. 'Dry your eyes,' she said, in a lovely voice, a Somerset accent. She sounded as though she should be standing in an orchard.

Mia walked. She went down to Trafalgar Square, then cut her way through side-streets towards the river. Every so often, she handed out a cigarette or a sandwich, though she felt fraudulent and self-disgusted: acting Lady Bountiful for a night. Normally she would be cautious about walking alone at night, but this was different: in her woollen hat, her loose jogging trousers and her quilted jacket, she was just a shapeless, sexless, anonymous figure, and nobody looked at her. She went on to Waterloo Bridge and stared down at the water beneath. There was a moon – nearly new and floating mysteriously between thin clouds – and its fugitive light reflected on the rippling surge. She stared across at the Houses of Parliament and the Eye, still lit up though unmoving. She wasn't really thinking, or feeling, even: she just gazed and let images gather in her mind. Her father with his staring blue eyes that didn't really see her. Her mother with her jumper on inside out. Herself as a young child, tagging after her brother. Herself as a teenager, walking with Isabel along a beach and calling his name. Will, crying in her arms. Johnny. She let herself, just for these few minutes, remember her brother as he once was.

She looked across at Big Ben. It was nearly midnight. In a few minutes, it would no longer be Johnny's twenty-third birthday.

It had been four years and three months since he had left.

'Mr Loft, as I said, my name is Isabel Hopkins.' She sat in an armchair that was so soft and sagging she had almost disappeared into it and wondered if it would ever release her. He sat across from her, on a much more upright chair. He was very thin and very old. His skin was weathered, lined, cracked and fissured, like a landscape that had been through many storms. His hand, when she had shaken it, had felt as brittle as bird bones, and was covered with liver spots. But his grey eyes were shrewd and he sat very straight in his chair. The room was quite dark, pools of light thrown by the standard lamps; dark furniture – polished-wood coffee-tables and upholstered armchairs – and heavy curtains, half drawn against the weak sunlight. It was an old person's room. Several paintings hung on the wall: she wondered if they had all been done by him.

'But before I married, my name was Isabel Cornish,' she continued.

A silence settled on the room. The old man leant forwards slightly in his chair and scrutinized her. 'You look like her,' he said at last.

'Do I?'

'I should have known.'

'My younger daughter looks more like her, I think.'

'You have her bone structure, the eyes.'

'Really?' This, of course, was what Isabel wanted – that she was her mother's daughter and that her mother lived on in her. 'I have the portrait you painted of her,' she said. 'I've often wanted to meet you.'

'Kathleen Cornish,' murmured Thomas Loft. 'Goodness me, her daughter. Well, well, well.' He gave a soft, sad chuckle. 'Who'd have thought it?'

'You know she died a long time ago?' said Isabel.

He nodded.

'When did you paint her? Was she already married?'

'No, no. She was Kathleen Farraday then.'

'How did you know her?'

'She lived near me. Her friend had a brother who knew my brother. Something like that. I don't quite remember now. I just knew her.'

'Why did you paint her?'

'I liked her face,' Thomas Loft said, simply. 'It was a face that spoke to me. Soft brown eyes. She was a very kind young woman, your mother. I am sorry for your loss.'

He spoke as if Kathleen had died a few weeks ago and Isabel was still in fresh mourning for her.

'Thank you. I wish I'd known her better. I suppose that's why I'm here. That probably seems stupid to you – it was all so long ago.'

'We don't leave things behind,' he said. 'We carry them with us. You think I'm an old man but I'm a young man as well. A young man who once knew your mother. Did your father ever mention me?'

'No,' said Isabel. 'What would he have said?'

'Nothing good, I'm afraid. We didn't see eye to eye on many things.'

Isabel hesitated. She didn't know what questions to ask to unlock an answer she couldn't guess at.

'Tell me about her,' she said. 'Apart from being kind. What else do you remember?'

'She had a lovely laugh,' he said. 'And she always smelt nice. Fresh, like honey. Her hair was always clean, as if she had just that minute washed it. She liked to dance. She and I would dance the foxtrot and the waltz. I was a good dancer, in my day. Nifty.' That soft reminiscing chuckle once more. 'Do you remember her dancing?'

'No. No, I don't. I didn't know she danced.'

He had made it sound like another age – one of tea dances and oil lamps and hands touching in the dusk.

'She once told me she liked my smile,' he said, smiling now.

'You loved her.' It came out too bluntly, an assertion not a question.

'I asked her to marry me,' said Thomas Loft. 'Mrs Kathleen Loft.'

'But she said no?'

'As you can tell.' He spread his hands around him. 'Here you are, her daughter. Here I am, in my son's house. I have three sons, eight grandchildren and one great-grandchild, with another on the way.'

'How lovely.'

'Do you have children?'

'I have two stepsons, two daughters and a son,' replied Isabel. 'And grandchildren as well, though I can't quite believe I'm a grandmother already; it wasn't how I'd imagined things.' Something was happening to her eyes. They were stinging and it was hard to see properly. 'My son is twenty-four today. Johnny.' She made herself say his name, although nowadays it was getting more and more difficult to do that.

'I'm sure your mother would be very proud of you,' he said.

'I wish that was true. I'm afraid I've done things that I shouldn't have done. I haven't always been the person I wanted to be.'

'My dear,' he said, with the smile that her mother had liked and she could see why. 'My dear, which of us with honesty could say any different, eh?'

'I don't know.' She wanted to fall at his sharp knees, put her head on his lap and weep, so that he would stroke her hair and tell her she had done well. 'Maybe you're right.'

'Wait there a minute.' He took the walking stick that was hooked over the side of his chair, and raised himself with slow care. Then he made his way out of the room. Isabel listened to the tick of the grandfather clock and the sweet repeating call of a bird just outside the window, but out of sight. Some minutes later, he returned, holding a flat, rectangular shape in his hand, about the size of a paperback.

'I would like you to have this,' he said. 'If you would do me the honour of accepting it.'

Isabel turned over the small picture, framed in plain wood. It was a painting in oil of a pair of hands, folded together, fading at the wrists into darkness.

'Those are your mother's,' he said.

'My mother's?'

'The painting I did – the hands aren't very skilfully done, are they?'

'Well, I –'

'I did this a few weeks later. I think they're better.'

Indeed they were. Peaceful and composed, holding each other.

'You're sure about this?'

'Who else would want to have a painting of the hands of a woman I once proposed to, and who turned me down?'

'I don't know what to say.'

'Then don't say anything.'

'Thank you, Mr Loft. Thomas. Thank you very much. I don't think anyone has ever given me something that means so much to me or that I could value as highly as I will value this. Always.'

'Good. I hope that soon you will not be so sad.'

'I have an announcement!'

It was later that day, and Jenny, Leah and Isabel were sitting in the bistro together. They still met up for their regular evenings, though for a shorter time, leaving early enough for Leah to get a proper night's sleep. She was always tired nowadays. She walked ploddingly – she who had had such a purposeful gait – and sometimes she fell asleep in front of them, waking with a jerk.

'Go on, then,' said Jenny.

Leah put a hand on each of their arms, consoling them in advance. 'It's spread.'

She spoke in such a cheery tone, almost triumphant, that it took them a few moments to adjust to her words.

'Oh, God,' said Jenny at last. Her eyes filled with instant tears. Leah patted her hand.

'Oh, Leah,' said Isabel.

'Yup. I thought you two should be the first to know.'

'I'm so, so sorry.'

'When did you hear?'

'Two days ago.'

'Where?'

'At the hospital. I knew as soon as I walked in that it was bad news. You know the solemn kind of face people wear when they're about to break something to you? I almost felt sorry for the doctor. I had to stop myself trying to comfort him.'

'No, I meant where has it spread?'

'Oh – my poor old bones. That backache? It wasn't just from picking up a box of books.'

Isabel looked at her. 'What does it mean?' she asked.

'You mean, what's my prognosis? That's what people usually say. They mean, are you going to die? Yes.'

'Yes what?'

'Yes, I'm going to die. Well, we're all going to die, aren't we? I just know it. That's not much comfort, actually. Months, a year or so. Wine, I need more wine.' She waved at the waiter.

They leant in towards her, touching her, saying inane, tender things, telling her they loved her, they would always be there. She was gay, sprightly, sarcastic and unsentimental. Angry, perhaps. They cried and she was dry-eyed and acerbic, but she regarded them fondly.

'We've been through such a lot,' said Leah, an hour or so later, after a second bottle of wine. Her words slurred, and she looked smudged with exhaustion. 'Good, bad, terrible. That's why I can tell you. So.' She tipped the last few drops in her glass down her throat, assumed a businesslike air. 'You're going to have to cheer me up over the next few months, OK? Dying takes precedence. I don't want to mope and I don't want to be pitied and tiptoed around. I want to have fun. And I want to know that someone's going to look out for Peter and the girls once I'm gone. They might be grown-up but they're still my girls.'

'How are you being so – so amazing about this?'

'It won't last. I'm drunk, and I feel quite excited at the moment, if you want to know. Uplifted. As if I'm going in to battle and haven't quite accepted I'm going to lose. Actually, I hate it when people talk about their battle with cancer: I'm just the battleground.'

'Life's a bugger.'

'And one other thing.' She bared her teeth and practically wagged her finger at the two of them. 'I don't want to die alone.'

Three days later, when Isabel was at work, a letter arrived. It fell with all the other post – junk, bills, an invitation to a fiftieth birthday – on to the doormat, where it lay face down.

Isabel came home at five o'clock. She saw that Felix was already back, but he had shut himself into his study and she didn't disturb him. It was a balmy spring day and she thought she would spend an hour or so working in the garden before it got too dark. She had delphinium seeds and sweet-pea plugs that she had bought at the weekend and needed to plant. She unlocked the door and pushed it open, stooping to gather up the bundle of letters without properly glancing at them. She went into the kitchen and tossed them on to the table while she took off her jacket and then put the kettle on. She would take a mug of tea to Felix and change into her rough clothes, she thought. She picked up the birthday invitation. A couple they knew were jointly celebrating their fiftieth birthday: Felix, Isabel and family were invited to a barn dance in three weeks' time. Tamsin and Mia were far away, and at the best of times, Felix wasn't a barn dancer, but maybe she would go alone.

She put teabags into two mugs as the kettle started to boil. She was just turning towards it when she glimpsed the corner of the envelope, lying underneath an appeal to donate to the Red Cross. Only two letters – the *n* and *s* of 'Hopkins' – in blue biro, were showing, but something stopped her dead in her tracks. Everything slowed around her. Outside she could see the blackbird on the wall. Its yellow beak was open and its beady eye stared at her, brightly knowing. She took a tiny step towards the envelope, then another, and reached out her hand. Her breath was sore in her throat. She touched the corner, took hold of its tip with her forefinger and thumb, and closed her eyes.

'Please, God,' she said. 'Please, God. Oh, please, please, please.'

She wanted to die with the agony of hope. She tugged the envelope, still with her eyes shut, then squinted them open a crack, barely able to see through the fringe of her lashes. She opened them a tiny bit more. She couldn't breathe at all any longer and her heart was a galloping torment, an engine that was about to explode.

'Oh, God,' she said. 'Oh, God. Oh, God. Oh, my God! Oh, Jesus Christ. *Felix!* Felix, come here, come here! *Felix!*'

For it was Johnny's writing on the envelope. There was no mistaking it. Crooked, slightly larger than usual and written in a blue biro that was obviously about to run out – but his. Yes, oh, yes! Isabel put her hand against her chest, her stomach. She lowered herself on to a chair and held it against her cheek.

'Johnny!' she whispered. 'Oh, dear Lord.'

She saw there was a foreign stamp in the right-hand corner and a smudged place of postage. She tried to make it out but for some reason couldn't see properly. Everything was misty.

She pushed a finger under the flap and slid it carefully along; it seemed important to keep the envelope as intact as possible. When it was open, she saw there was a postcard inside, and she lifted it out. She thought she might be sick. There was a picture of a stone bridge over a river. She licked her dry lips and turned the card over, blinked to clear her vision. The writing was messy, as if he had been in a hurry when he wrote it:

> *I am sorry. Very very very sorry. I just had to. I am all right. Don't worry about me. Sorry.*
> *I love you.*

That was all. Isabel stared at the words as though they were written in a foreign language. She traced them with her fingers, as though she might feel her son among the shapes of the letters. Then she jumped to her feet and charged from the kitchen, flew wildly along into Felix's study.

'Felix!' He looked up. 'Felix! Look.'

She ran to the window and pulled open the curtain that he'd closed against the bright evening light, which flooded into the room. Felix winced, putting one hand to his eyes.

'Johnny's written! He's safe! He's alive! He's written! Look, look, look.'

She thrust the card into his hands and stood over him to reread it herself, snatching it back before his eyes had had a chance to adjust themselves to the dazzle. Felix stared at it unseeingly. His face was a ruin of itself.

'He's *alive*! Say something. Get up. He's not dead. We're going to be all right. Oh, God, I thought he was dead and he's not dead. He's alive,' she gabbled.

'Where?' Felix managed to say.

'I don't know. Here. I've got the envelope. It's from somewhere in France. I can't make out the place. But look, look at this. He sent it in January. January! He sent it nearly two months ago. How's that possible? All that time. God. He was thinking about us, not wanting us to worry. He's not dead. He will come home. One day he will. Nothing else matters, nothing in the whole world. Felix? Say something, anything. Jesus, my head's spinning.'

Isabel hurtled over to the window and flung it open, letting cool fresh air enter. She leant out and saw the sun. She sank to her knees and hugged her body. She got up again and went to Felix, taking his hand between hers, then peered at the envelope again. She felt wild, elated, mangled by emotions. Her stomach churned and her forehead was suddenly clammy. She had to run from the room and only got to the lavatory just in time before she was sick, retching until there was nothing left in her stomach and her throat felt torn. She threw cold water over her face. She looked at her white cheeks and her dark eyes, like holes, and for a moment she was frightened by herself. She had to tell everyone immediately; every second counted and her heart was a drum beating out the time.

Then she returned to Felix, who didn't seem to have moved, with his head propped in one hand, his eyes staring unseeingly out on to the fields. She went over to him and he turned to her, and his eyes filled with tears that he didn't move to wipe away. Isabel watched as they trailed with agonizing slowness towards his mouth, which was stretched in a grimace.

'So when's he coming home?'

Mia

Chapter Twenty-four

Mia stood by the open window, smoking a cigarette and watching the day begin in the street below. Metal grids rattled open and shopkeepers put out the racks of newspapers or shelves of fruit that already looked past their sell-by date; cars drove through the gleaming puddles; men and women walked by, early risers holding furled umbrellas or coffee in cardboard mugs. When she was a child and living in the countryside, dawn came in a gradually widening band of light on the horizon, before the sun rose into view. Here, surrounded by blocks of flats and tall houses that had long ago been divided into apartments, dawn was more surreptitious, coming in the slow gathering of light.

There was old Mrs Juniper – you could set your watch by her, plodding along the road whatever the weather – with her cocker spaniel, which scuttled sideways and always stopped to pee against the lamppost just below the window. There was Paul, with his stained sleeping bag and tatty plastic carriers crammed with bottles and fag ends and who knew what? Mia knew that he slept in the underpass near Hyde Park most nights, then made his way to the West End for the day. Sometimes she took him to breakfast in the café at the end of the road, where he ate bacon, eggs and fried bread and drank mugs of sweet, milky tea, muttering things she couldn't really understand and continuously wiping his mouth with the back of his dirty hand. He smelt bad and probably had fleas, and his skin was leathery and nicotine-coloured; his hair was thickly matted and his eyes bloodshot and yellow. But if you looked carefully at his ruined face, you could see that he was still quite young, perhaps only in his thirties. When she saw people like Paul, she imagined them when they were babies, with clean pink mouths and sweet-smelling necks, cooing and stretching out dimpled hands towards a face they loved. Like Merry when she was tiny, or like Seamus now. She had once asked Paul why he didn't sleep in one of the hostels round here, but he couldn't tell her. Surely they must be better than sleeping in an evil-smelling concrete tunnel in the freezing cold, with people walking past your bundled-up body as if it were a piece of garbage, if they noticed you at all. Or maybe not; maybe she was missing the point and Paul was beyond all of that now – the walls, doors, barred windows, narrow beds and other people thrashing in their dreams beside him; the rules of conduct, the human contact and human disgust; no more hope and no more desire, except the oblivion of whisky or white cider, and the warmth of the sun in spring. Mia wondered when he had last touched anyone, or been touched. She dropped coins into his outstretched palm. When she gave him cigarettes, she made sure their fingers didn't meet. What must it feel like to have become someone whom people shrank from touching? She didn't even know if he was really called Paul. Perhaps he no longer owned a name. But he was still a man for all that.

A flock of starlings rose in a sudden chatter from the plane tree just a few feet from where she was, making her start. She loved this time of day, this time of year:

mid-May, when the air was soft, the sky delicate, and everything seemed clean and blue. She inhaled again and blew out a plume of smoke, so that for a moment the figures in the street below softened, like figures in a fog, like figures in a dream – and, indeed, she felt she was in some kind of dream: behind her the cool room and the unmade bed, and beneath her people melting in the haze of her cigarette smoke.

She was wearing an oversized man's shirt. Its cool fabric rubbed softly against her bare legs. Behind her the shape stirred beneath the flung sheets; a hand flopped over the edge of the bed. Near it was an empty wine bottle and a pile of discarded clothes – his, hers. She turned towards him and felt his eyes on her, only half awake yet speculative and full of last night's desire. She had a clear sense of herself from the outside, as he was seeing her – the shallow curve of her breasts under the shirt, the little purplish vein in the crook of her elbow, the thin feet and bony wrists, the golden down on her tanned legs, a slender woman with spiky black hair and bony wrists; a tattoo on her ankle and a stud in her nose; a woman who was cool, self-possessed. And she felt herself on the inside: the hollow boom of her heart and the thundering rush of her blood.

She could speak now. She could draw the curtains half closed so the room became dim and protective, cross the space between them and, sitting on the bed, say, 'There is something I have to tell you.'

She could almost feel the words forcing their way up her throat, into her mouth. How often had she practised them in her head? 'There is something you should know . . . There is something I need to say . . .' Now casual, as if they had just occurred to her; now more momentous, spreading out in an echo, like the muted boom of an aftershock. Then nothing would be the same: just saying it out loud would be an act of declaration. She would be heaving open a door into her life, into the cellar of her past, the thing that more than anything defined her. And she would have to watch very carefully to see how he reacted: it was a test.

She finished her cigarette, stubbed it out in the geranium pot on the windowsill, noticing it needed watering, then let the stub fall into the street. In a week's time, Ben was getting married to Gabriella, with whom he'd been in love for most of his adult life and who had left him for some years, then returned to him six months ago. Mia was almost scared by Ben's happiness. He was so transparent and unguarded. His face was lit with joy; his voice trembled with emotions that he couldn't hold back. When he looked at Gabriella, he did so with an expression of such beatific gladness that Mia had to turn away. It made her uncomfortable. She preferred things to be hidden. But now she had to make a decision: Ben and Gabriella had asked her if she wouldn't like to bring someone to the wedding, which was going to be in Suffolk, with the party afterwards in Isabel and Felix's garden, if the weather held out, and in the house if it didn't. Did she want to bring anyone? Did she want to bring Lex? If she did, she would have to tell him about her family; he couldn't just discover for himself, and Isabel would be bound to mention it, if Tamsin didn't get in there first. Those two were liable to tell their stories to whoever they came across, fixing them with their tearful glance. And, anyway, the house was full of the evidence: Johnny's picture was everywhere, but Johnny wasn't there. Johnny's bedroom was a museum, a shrine even, and no one could drag their sleeping bag in there without permission, even when all the other rooms were crammed with guests. Felix's study was an archive of Johnny's disappearance.

She turned and looked at Lex. She liked him. They had fun together. They had laughed and gone to art exhibitions and on long walks through London. Sex was good. What was more, he would be great about it, she knew, full of understanding, and also glad that she was at last confiding in him – and at the thought of his readiness, her soul winced. She wasn't going to say it. She couldn't. He wasn't the right person to hear the story she had never told anyone.

Because, of course, nobody was the right person. With every man she met, when she got to the point at which she had to consider whether or not to disclose herself, she balked and walked away. It was the reason why she never brought anyone home, and rarely went herself (if, indeed, 'home' was the right word for a house so full of a past self she didn't want to meet). It was the reason she had had so many affairs and flings, and why it was invariably her who finished them. Closeness, the hint of any real intimacy, heralded the end. Happiness terrified her.

A week later she found herself at Ben and Gabriella's wedding alone. She woke early, as she almost always did. Her flatmate, Vicky, also studying part-time for an MA, had come home very late last night and would be asleep for many hours yet – Mia could imagine her in the warm huddle of her duvet, her luxurious curls spread around her like another cover. She was the messy one of the flat: dirty clothes heaped in the corner of her room and stuffed into the washing-machine, washed ones draped over chairs and hung on every available hook to dry, wet towels on the sofa, dirty plates in the sink. Mia cleared up after her. It never used to be this way: when she had been a teenager and living at home, she'd turned her room into conditions of almost unimaginable chaos: layer upon layer of clothes and clutter piled on the floor and on every surface. She had never put anything away in drawers or cupboards, and when she wanted to get dressed or find a piece of work, she would scrabble through the detritus around her like a dog digging in the soil for a bone. That had changed after she'd left home: it was as if she had decided to become a different person. She had learnt to control her temper, which used to erupt without warning, and to hide her possessions. It was as if her room was like a demonstration of her mind, and her mind had become orderly and secretive. She wasn't giving anything away.

She had a quick, hot shower, washed her hair and left it to dry – it was so short it would take only a few minutes – and then she made herself an espresso from the machine that Vicky's father had donated, and took it back to her room. She sat at her window with her thick black coffee and the first cigarette of the day. She always smoked eight cigarettes each day, at appointed times – most of them towards the evening, but always one first thing in the morning and last thing at night, when she would sit in the dark and watch the ember glow with each drag she took.

The day was warm, the sky a tender turquoise-blue, just a few trails of cloud on the horizon that would burn away as the sun rose. All the work Isabel had been putting into the garden was going to pay off. She stepped out of her cotton robe and pulled on her red silk shift dress and her black shoes. Stud in her nose, studs in her ears, little chain round her ankle, no makeup except the red lip gloss she chucked into her bag for later: she was ready. Lex used to say he had never met any other woman who could so quickly prepare herself for the day. Mia was one for the quick getaway, the emergency exit.

She put on her old blue mac, which she'd had for years and loved beyond reason, picked up the present she had bought for Ben and Gabriella and wrapped in brown paper and string. She had pondered for a long time over what to get them. She was very fond of them both, and sometimes worried that she had transferred a little of what she used to feel for Johnny to them: sometimes, without warning, she would turn up on the doorstep of their small house in Lewisham and they would take her in without question, casually introducing her to whoever happened to be there at the time, laying another plate for dinner, putting clean sheets on the spare bed. She'd met the boyfriend she'd had before Lex there – she hoped he wouldn't be at the wedding today, although he probably would. In the end she had chosen for their present an old-fashioned oil lamp, and the entire set of the Moomintroll books, which she knew Felix had read to the sons of his first marriage just as he had later read them to her, Tamsin and Johnny. It wasn't meant to be a hint to Ben and Gabriella about having a family themselves: she just thought that everyone should own the books they had loved when they were young. Whenever she was tired or low, she would read Dr Seuss or *Alice in Wonderland* or *Winnie-the-Pooh* and feel comforted. Instead of giving them a card, she had printed one of her favourite poems by Louis MacNeice on to a sheet of silk and threaded it on to a slim metal rod so it could be hung on a wall. She was maladroit with a needle: the silk sheet hung askew and the stitches were uneven, puckering the delicate material. It looked as though it had been sewn by an impatient child in primary school.

She took the Underground to Liverpool Street, then a train going east. It was such a familiar journey, looking down at back gardens, hidden canals where rubbish and ducks bobbed, light industrial units and storage centres, and finally out into a kind of countryside – though one cut through by dual carriageways and constantly interrupted by towns. At last the train was rolling past the widening estuary. The tide was low so some of the boats tipped on the mudflats and seabirds stalked by on their long legs, disdainful. Soon she would arrive, and she started to feel anxious, in the way that she always did when visiting Isabel and Felix. Her skin prickled slightly and her mouth was dry, chalky. She started counting the hours until she would be able to leave again – the wedding was just before midday, an in-and-out job at the register office before they would return to the house for a lunch that Isabel and Tamsin had prepared; Gabriella had no family, no mother to make her a wedding feast. Then the speeches and the tears; the couple would leave in a shower of flung confetti and ribald cheers and it would all be over. Three hours, perhaps, probably four, and then she could return to London.

But Isabel would expect her to stay longer; she was probably assuming she would be there for the night and maybe the next day as well – that the three of them could clear away the remains, talk over the event, sit around the kitchen table with their mugs of tea and swap stories in the way they used to do, while her father hid in his study, the way he always did when he wasn't at one of the bloody Quaker meetings he'd started to go to – him, the one who had always derided religion and cursed God – and Tamsin's children played on the lawn with Jed, or on the swing or hanging from the tree at the bottom of the garden. But she had to get back. She'd say she had a prior arrangement – even in her own head, the words rang hollow. She had known about this wedding for weeks and months.

The train arrived with a small backwards jolt. She picked up her awkward-shaped packet and her small bag (no night things or toothbrush in it) and descended on to the platform. She had not told anyone what time she would arrive so no one would be waiting for her, yet still she found herself scanning the faces and was bizarrely disappointed and at the same time relieved not to see anyone she knew. She hailed a cab and asked the woman driver to take her straight to the register office. The day had got warmer and she took off her mac, ran her fingers through her hair, applied her red lip gloss for bravado. What did she dread? Stepping back into the bosom of her family, fending off Miranda's brusque attentions, being hugged too hard by Isabel and seeing how her father stared off to the side with his glazed blue eyes? Tamsin would gush and coo, Rory would pick her up as if she was still a small child, Graham and Celia would tell her she was too thin and too pale. She knew in advance how she would behave – surly, brittle, guarded, and allergic with irritation to people's assumptions that they knew what was good for her, and at their claims of intimacy. She didn't like being looked at. She didn't like sympathy. She would smoke at the bottom of the garden and scowl and feel dreadful later. The thought of her mother's unspoken disappointment made her feel physically sick.

She paid the fare and stepped out. The register office was set back from the road, with a small bald lawn in front of its door. There were already people gathering and Mia hung back so that she wouldn't be seen, and squinted in the light to make them out. Her heart banged. There were Helen and Rory, with Lucy, Greta and Dan. Helen was wearing a broad-brimmed hat and under it her face looked warm and pink; Rory had put on weight, she thought. His shirt was tight over his stomach. He was only in his early thirties but she could suddenly imagine him as middle-aged. Lucy was wearing a bright yellow dress and child's sunglasses; she was holding Greta's hand tightly, with a look of solemn duty. Who was that beside them? It was Jenny, of course, with Benedict hovering in the background, balder than she'd remembered, and shorter – or perhaps that was because Jenny was wearing high-heeled shoes and her hair was swept up in a flouncy bun. She had always been so kind to Mia, like the best type of aunt. They were all arriving now, stepping out of cars and cabs, walking along the road in a vivid straggle. Reds and oranges, blues and greens – brightly coloured clothes for a May wedding. People she recognized and others she didn't. There were Graham and Celia, dressed in muted clothes that looked too warm for the day, and Mia felt a surge of unwanted pity for them. And, fuck it, there was the friend of Ben's she'd had that affair with. The last time she had seen him, his face had been contorted with rage. Now he was holding the hand of a woman with apricot-coloured hair, who moved as gracefully as a ballet dancer, and he was smiling down at her with love.

Reluctantly, Mia stepped out from the shadows and moved towards the thickening group. People raised their hands in greeting. Lucy ran towards her, tugging Greta. She moved into the crowd, nodded, grinned, kissed cheeks, suffered arms to be wrapped round her shoulders.

'You look sumptuous, as usual, in a starved-waif kind of way,' a man with a rose in his buttonhole said to her, and she stared at him glacially. Had they met before? The way he was leering at her made her wonder if he knew something about her that she didn't. And the way he uttered the word 'sumptuous', dragging it out unctuously, made it sound as though she was some tasty side dish. She frowned and moved away from him.

Jenny came up and gave her a hug. Her perfume was the same as it had always been – rose water, but not so sweet it caught in your nostrils. Her face was more lined, though, and her hair thickly streaked with grey.

'How are you, Mia?' she asked.

'Good. Fine.' She searched around for the words that would carry them over the awkwardness of the moment. 'How are Max and Holly? I haven't seen them in ages.'

'It has been ages,' Jenny agreed, and Mia felt she was

accusing her, but her eyes remained warm. 'Talking of which –'

But then they arrived. They came round the corner slowly, going at Miranda's pace; she was on Felix's arm, and with her other hand she held her stick, which she cracked on to the pavement as if it was her enemy and she was thrashing it into submission. Felix bent sideways towards her, listening attentively to whatever she was saying. His suit was old and he himself had a worn, moth-eaten look, as if he had recently been pulled out of the store cupboard and dusted down. Tamsin walked in front, pushing the buggy, while Merry hung off Jed's hand as if she was trying to grapple them both to the ground. Seamus was on his shoulders, but leaning forward with his face pressed against the balding crown of his father's head. And behind them came Isabel. She was in a pale green dress and a funny cloche hat, set on her head at a rakish angle. Mia would have recognized her just from the way she walked – upright, determined, pressing her feet firmly against the pavement as if she was going up a steep hill. She wore a vague, bright smile as she approached – one meant for everyone, a general welcome until she got close enough for the crowd to separate into individuals. Mia felt her eyes prick with tears at her mother's gallantry. I should be with them, she thought, not watching them like an outsider.

Isabel's eyes were sorting through them now, searching, and at last they came to rest on Mia and her face broke into a proper smile. She quickened her steps, swerved past Miranda, and came straight up to her, ignoring everyone else.

'Darling,' she said, like a sigh, her thin hands gripping Mia's sharp shoulders. 'You're a sight for sore eyes, for my sore eyes.' She kissed Mia first on one cheek then the other, then whipped a hankie from her bag and rubbed Mia's cheek in a gesture that was so familiar to her from her childhood that she was back there again, marked by the print of her mother's mouth and pulling away from the licked tissue. 'I was anxious you wouldn't be here.'

'Of course I'm here.'

'You know me,' said Isabel, making a joke of it, yet dragging a whole history into her words. 'I worry.'

There wasn't time for anything more. She turned to greet someone; Felix arrived with Miranda and gave her a bony, fierce hug; Tamsin stroked the red silk of her dress wistfully and told her she looked so glamorous and thin. There was a small posset on her shoulder. She seemed to have grown taller and plumper while Jed had become smaller, drier and sandier.

Then Ben arrived with his mother on his arm and a cheer went up. He beamed and waved bashfully. He shook his father's hand, then clasped him briefly to his chest, and everyone cheered again, jostling forward to greet him. It went quickly after that, Gabriella stepping out of the cab with her best woman, a cascade of dark curls; she was like a warm fresh breeze that first of all blew the crowd back slightly as they watched her, then sucked them forward. They gathered round her, formed a circle that she walked through. Ben held out his hand and she gripped it, winking at him. A blue dress. A blue, blue sky and warm pushing bodies.

A set of chairs in a long, light room, a sensible woman

with glasses on a chain swinging at her chest presiding over the cheer and bustle that suddenly set into something quieter and more solemn. The sense of everyone holding their breath; a tightening and concentration of goodwill. She sat next to Felix and held his hand. She felt her mother's presence, though she was obscured by the tortoise bulk of Miranda. Ben couldn't get his words out for emotion – he got stranded on 'solemnly declare'; Gabriella couldn't force his ring over his knuckle. Isabel would be thinking of Johnny and of Leah; she would be leaning forward, her hands in her lap and her eyes fixed on Ben and Gabriella.

The garden was rich with sweet peas, lush peonies and early roses. The lilac tree was in bloom, and the dogwood. The herb bed near the kitchen door had been weeded, and clumps of oregano, marjoram, chives and thyme were neatly set apart on the crumbly soil. Isabel had put jugs of flowers on the tables that were set on the patio. Sparkling wine was being opened, cheerful pops going off amid the chatter. She took a glass and drank it. 'It's not lemonade, you know!' someone said, in a bossy, jovial voice, but she ignored it and took another. Her shoes sank into the soft grass. Goat's cheese tartlets, home-made gravlax on thin slices of rye bread and bowls of green salad. She tried to avoid people she knew, but they found her. 'You've changed . . . You haven't changed at all, I would have recognized you anywhere . . . Do you remember . . . Iraq . . . tsunamis . . . floods . . . tuition fees . . . governments . . . betrayals . . . Facebook . . . the Gauguin exhibition . . . your poor mother . . . your dear mother . . . your dear father . . . What are you up to nowadays . . . Another drink? . . . What a feast! Did you help to cook it?'

'No,' said Mia, shortly. 'That was Tamsin and my mother.' She had to stop herself calling Isabel 'Mama'. She could always see her out of the corner of her eye, wherever she stood in her soft green dress, slipping silkily between groups of people.

Jenny had probably helped as well, she thought. The three of them in the kitchen, in the fug of warm and spicy smells, clattering pans and rolling pastry, stirring the pot. But not her. She made her way to the bottom of the garden, away from people, and took a cigarette out of its packet, her third of the day so she had five left – she thought she would probably smoke them alone, sitting at her window and watching the evening settle in the street outside. She lit it and inhaled deeply, closing her eyes for a second and tipping her head, feeling the sun on her face. When she opened them, she almost expected to see him there, by the lilac tree, in the shade. A shimmer, a trick of the light. Always.

'Mia?'

She turned to see Isabel coming towards her down the grass, keeping her cloche hat on her head with one hand, and holding a glass of what looked like water in the other.

'Oh – hi.' She gestured at the party. 'This is nice. You've done well.'

'It *is* nice, isn't it? Have you eaten anything?'

Mia frowned. 'No. Have you?'

They stared at each other, feeling the tension in the air. Then Mia shrugged and held out her packet of cigarettes. 'Fag?'

Isabel gave a small, relieved laugh. 'I shouldn't. Nobody knows I ever do. Oh, OK, then. Who cares?'

She took one and Mia lit it for her, shielding the flame of the match with her cupped hand. Their two heads bent together. Probably, thought Mia, if I'd asked her to inject heroin with me, she would have said yes, just to salvage this moment of intimacy. 'How's Dad?' she asked.

'Busy,' said Isabel. 'He buries himself –' She stopped herself saying any more. 'Better than he was. Don't you think?'

'Maybe,' said Mia, doubtfully. She was always shocked when she saw Felix: she carried a different version of him in her memory – someone younger, straighter, more solid and vigorous. This ageing and cadaverous man was a husk of the real Felix.

'He still goes to his Quaker meetings. I think it's the only place where he can be truly himself.'

'I can understand that,' said Mia.

'Mm. Well. I thought you were going to bring what's-his-name.'

Mia knew Isabel was pretending not to remember what he was called. Every piece of information she ever gave to her mother about her personal life was squirrelled away. 'You mean Lex.'

'That's the one.'

'No.'

'I would have liked to meet him.'

'I'm not seeing him any more.'

'Oh!'

'It's fine.'

'Is it?'

'Yup.'

'Was it you who ended it?'

'Does that matter?'

'Well, yes. I think so. It makes a difference to the meaning.'

'OK. Then yes. It was me.'

'Why?'

Mia shrugged.

'You're so guarded,' said Isabel. Her voice was full of concern and her face sorrowful.

Mia felt herself tighten with an irritation so intense it made her head ache, as though a band was being tightened around it. 'I don't think so,' she replied curtly. 'It was never a big deal.'

'That's all right, then,' said Isabel. 'Are you staying?'

'I can't.' Liar, liar, liar.

'What a pity.'

Isabel kept her tone light and her face carefully expressionless. She had learnt not to put pressure on Mia. She had grown accustomed to the fact that her daughter didn't want to come home often, and instead would arrange to see her in London – usually for lunch, or a meal in the evening. Sometimes they went to an art gallery for an hour or so, then sat over coffee discussing it. It was easier to talk about Rembrandt's self-portraits or Van Gogh's drawings than their own feelings. Mia understood that her mother was waiting for her to make the first move: that she was making it known she was ready. Every so often, she said as much ('You know, if there's ever anything you want to discuss . . .') but Mia's desire to speak and her revulsion against doing so were like the ends of two powerful magnets throbbing against each other, pushing each other apart. She usually ended by treating Isabel in a stony manner, hating herself all the while, feeling almost physically sick at the look on her mother's face. The metal shutters clattered down and the locks slammed across; she was in a state of lockdown. Sometimes she was her father's daughter.

'I'm working in the café tomorrow.' She was pretty certain that Isabel knew it wasn't true. 'I couldn't get out of it.'

'Another time. We could go swimming in the sea.'

'I'd like that.' Mia looked away. She couldn't bear to see her mother's face, with lines that were deeper than they should have been, shadows that were darker, a sense of something starved. It was Johnny who had done that, she thought, and for a moment there was a furnace in her belly and its flames roared up her, scorching her throat and making her eyes mist over.

Something rubbed against her bare leg and she looked down. There was Digby, Johnny's cat, improbably ancient now, all bones and yellow eyes and tattered ears, hardly able to make his way on spindly crooked legs. Mia bent down and ran her finger along his spine, the way she always did. Someone called to them. A friend of Ben's was clinking a knife against his wine glass.

'Speeches!'

'We'd better go,' said Isabel.

'Mama?'

'Yes?'

'Sorry. It'll be all right.'

She didn't know what she was apologizing for, or what

would be all right, only that it probably wasn't true, but Isabel's face relaxed. Hand in hand, they walked up the garden together, and for a moment, as the hum of chatter reached them through the trees, and the sun fell through the branches and lay in dappled puddles on the soft grass while Isabel's hand held hers firmly, Mia thought she could be as a child again, and trust.

Chapter Twenty-five

Mia sat on the shabby brown divan. Her back was already hurting and she had only been sitting like this for about a minute. It wasn't just her back, either: her neck ached, her legs felt slightly cramped, the sole of her foot, encased in its laced-up shoe, was horribly itchy – so itchy she thought she was going to have to take off her shoe and sock and rub it along the rough wooden floor.

Worse than her body, however, was her face. For some reason, it felt very odd and unnatural. Her mouth had settled into a thin, lop-sided line and she was reminded of her grandfather, Bernard, after his stroke. Her eyes were sore and she kept having to blink. She had the urge to reach up a hand and touch it to check everything was in its proper place, and to massage away the rubbery sensation in her cheek. But she wasn't supposed to move at all.

A couple of evenings ago, she had been in a bar with an amorphous group of friends, and friends of friends, drinking sangria. She had not met Lucas before, and didn't really notice him on that particular evening. She was preoccupied and a little tired. It was a Wednesday evening, the flat middle of the week. But as she was leaving he had come up to her and said abruptly, 'Could I please paint your portrait?'

'What?'

'I'd like you to sit for me.'

'Are you an artist?'

He had shrugged. 'I'm a part-time art teacher and a part-time bartender and I also paint, when I have the time. Will you?'

'Why?'

'My project at the moment is to make quick water-colour portraits of friends, over a short period. Six portraits over a couple of weeks, say. Your face will change. I'm creating moments in time.'

'No. I meant, why me?'

'I've been looking at you. You've got an interesting face.'

Mia had drawn away from him and his dark-eyed stare. She hadn't been seeking a compliment and now felt both self-conscious and irritated.

'I don't think so,' she had said coldly.

'That's a pity,' Lucas had said. 'If you change your mind –'

'It's not likely.'

Yet here she was in his flat in Dalston on a sunny morning when she should be in the library. He sat a few feet away from her, on a rickety wooden chair that was higher than her divan, staring at her like a hawk fixing a motionless fieldmouse in its sights. There had been no small-talk. He had told her to make herself comfortable, and try not to move, then had set his easel up to one side, filled a jam-jar with clean water, wiped his paintbrush on an old rag, and examined her for several minutes. At first, Mia tried to play the same game, scrutinizing him, assessing him as she felt she was being assessed. He wasn't tall, and he was slim, yet seemed solid. He had rolled up his shirt sleeves and his forearms were muscled. He had curly dark hair and thick brows, white teeth, one earring, long slender fingers. His face was mobile; as he considered her, he frowned, nodded, bit his lower lip.

But, very quickly, she found it impossible to out-stare him. Painting her had given him the right, it seemed, to stare at her mercilessly, as if she were simply an object in a room full of other objects – this sofa, that chair, the easel, the table, the mugs on the windowsill. He dipped the brush into the water, dabbed it into some paint, mixed it, made a bold stroke on the paper pinned to the easel. He looked at Mia, then away, repeating his searching, incurious glance over and over again. After about ten minutes, rigid and appalled on the brown divan, Mia felt she was going to have to abandon the project. It wasn't simply the acute physical discomfort that had turned her body into a series of aches and irritations, it was the sense that his glance was pinning her to the spot, as if she was a butterfly impaled on a sharp pin.

She had never been stared at like this. Every time anyone looked at her, they did so with the eyes of a friend, a relative, a colleague, a teacher, a lover. They looked at her with love, desire, affection, hostility. Their feelings for her were in their glance, which was altered by the way she returned it.

Lucas stared at her without mercy. He had no feelings and made no allowances. He was a scientist and she was his experiment, a specimen on a Petri dish, neither adored nor resented, simply seen. But what did he see? His eyes flicked back and forth. The brush moved over the paper. The sun shone through the open window, and occasionally small gusts of wind fluttered magazines on the table. Mia felt it on her hot cheek. She wanted to scream. It wasn't possible that she should continue. There was a small clock on one of the shelves. Its minute hand moved with agonizing slowness. He had said it would take no more than an hour, but an hour spent under this cruel stare had been stretched into a thin, arid torment. Like being in a desert, she thought, under the blowtorch sun. Peeled skin. His gaze like a scalpel. What did he see? What terrible secrets was he observing, laying down on the white space in front of him? Her real self, in overlapping layers of paint.

She looked down at the divan she was sitting on. Its brownness and its patches of baldness from where innumerable other bodies had sat filled her with disgust, a nausea that made her forehead clammy and her vision misty. She loathed it. She loathed the way it contrasted with the green shirt she was wearing today – something about the combination of colours revolted her. Rage crackled through her, a forest fire of anger against Lucas, with his intent, speculative face, his dark and pitiless eyes.

Now there was a tic, just to the left of her mouth. She could feel it twitching and jumping. Surely her whole face must be jumping with it. Her mouth was being brutally tweaked as if by a doctor's needle, piercing her flesh and stitching her up. Or like a fish being pulled ashore by its gaping mouth. She tightened her lips, then loosened them, but the tic wouldn't go away. Soon, her whole face would be juddering, like a metronome that had been set at a certain speed. Couldn't he see it? He could see everything else in her, why didn't he notice that?

Now there was a line of ants under her skin. She could feel them tingling there. Millions of them crawling just under the surface. This was stupid. She should just stand up and say she'd had enough. It didn't matter what he would think, or how her face would look, unfinished on the page. She imagined herself rising to her feet in one fluid movement, shaking her head clear of these horrible sensations, striding out into the clean blue day. Yet she continued sitting, and enduring his quick, flicking glance, like a lizard's tongue. She hated him. Could she not cover her face with her hands and hide?

'There,' he said at last. 'You can move.'

Mia got to her feet. Almost immediately, her body was returning to normal – the blood could flow freely again. She rubbed her face, ran her fingers through her hair.

'Do you want to see?'

'I don't know. Do I?'

But she moved round and stood by his side to look at what he'd done. He had made her face into a storm of dark hair and wild eyes and sharp bones.

'Is that how I look?'

'You don't like it?'

'I don't know. I look as though I was facing a firing squad.'

'Mm. Is that how you felt?'

Mia gave a short laugh. 'Maybe.'

'You were uncomfortable?'

'It's hard to sit for a long time without moving.'

'Is that all? I don't think you like being looked at. Not really. I could feel your resistance.'

'I've got to go.'

'You don't want a cup of coffee?'

'No.'

'Come on. I'll make a pot and we can arrange the next sitting.'

'I don't know that there'll be a next sitting. Sorry.'

'Was it that bad?'

Mia noticed he had a small scar in his upper lip and that there were flecks of lighter brown in his dark brown irises. 'Can I have a cigarette in here?'

'Sure. I'll make us that coffee.'

She lit one and stood by his open window, looking out at a small patch of garden, with a broken wooden bench at the end. Beyond that was the canal; she could just glimpse its brown, oily waters. She blew plumes of smoke out and watched them disappear, feeling her own turbulent sense of disquiet dissolve as well, though it had left her tired and shaky, like a convalescent.

'Here.' Lucas came back in, carrying a tray. 'I toasted a muffin as well.'

They sat at opposite ends of the divan with their mugs. Mia was still slightly revolted by the balding brownness of the sofa: it was like the memory of a feverish dream.

'Tell me,' she said. 'What do other people say about being painted?'

'It varies. Quite a lot of people enjoy it. They say they can relax, just sit and think of nothing for an hour, let their minds wander.'

'Oh.'

'And some people like nothing more than to be looked at and drawn. It flatters their vanity – though sometimes they don't like the end result much.'

333

'I understand why that would be.'

'But you didn't like it at all, did you?'

'No.'

'Why?' He leant forward. 'What were you feeling, Mia?'

Something about the way he said her name, separating it out into its two syllables with a small space in between, moved her. It was as though someone had touched her very softly on her head, or put a warm hand over hers for a moment.

'I felt exposed,' she said simply.

'And you hate that.'

'I guess so.'

'I can see that.'

'What can you see?'

'That you wear armour. That you're scared of being found out.'

'You don't know me,' Mia said, with sudden sharpness. 'So you can't say that. And now I really should go.'

'Because of what I've just said?'

'No. I've got things to do. Thanks for the coffee.'

'Will you come again?'

'I don't know. It might not be a good idea.'

Yet two days later, she returned and took up her position on the abhorred divan, with Lucas sitting opposite her on his high wooden chair, staring at her. Not just at her, but into her. Down the mine shafts, into the terrible darkness, where all the pulpy, tender, shameful parts of her lay curled. All her fear and all her dread. He looked at her, then looked away, and his paintbrush bristled across the rough paper. She could hear its rasp, and hear, too, the blackbird outside in the small garden, and the tiny tick of the clock on the shelf, and the occasional infinitesimal sigh of Lucas as he found the right line. Hear her heart beat, hear her blood pulse, hear the silent scream screwed down inside her.

'Thank you,' said Lucas, laying down his brush, and then, standing up, he took her hand and pulled her to her feet. 'Come and see what you look like to me today.'

She looked stricken. Her eyes were black pools and her skin was bleached.

'Oh dear,' she said, trying to laugh.

She went to the window that showed her snatches of the canal, and smoked her cigarette while Lucas made coffee, bringing it over to where she stood. Today he was wearing a blue T-shirt and had shaved, so his face was smooth and he looked younger than he had last week. Neither of them said anything for a while. Then she asked, 'Can I see some of the other portraits you've done?'

'Sure.'

'But I don't want you to show mine to anyone.'

'OK.' She could feel him examining her, but she went on staring out of the window. There was the blackbird, pecking its yellow beak into the grass, its glossy body shining.

'This is my sister,' Lucas said, holding up a succession of candid faces, half-smile on the lips, cheerfully assenting to Lucas's gaze. 'This is my father': an old man with a beaky nose. 'My friend Cora': cool, knowing, ironic, humorous. 'My friend, Alvin': looking sideways at Lucas, sly and intimate.

'You're the one with the power,' said Mia.

'I suppose you could see it like that.'

'You do – we let you have power over us.' She gave a small shiver.

'And you hate that.'

'I seem to. Both times I've very nearly fled. I find it almost unbearable.'

'I'm glad you didn't flee.'

Their eyes met – this was a different kind of looking: it was looking and being looked at. Mia felt that she was standing on the edge of a precipice and she was about to step over it. *There is something you should know* . . . She took a deep breath, then let it out again, defeated. Why was she thinking of baring her grubby, scared soul to Lucas when she hadn't done so to anyone else? She didn't even know him. She might never see him again, after her sittings. She turned away, feeling the moment pass. He must have felt it, too, because after waiting for a few seconds, he started putting away his paints, swishing his brush in the jar and wiping it on the rag, using a tissue to clean the palette.

'The day after tomorrow any good?' he asked, as she picked up her bag, and then, as she hesitated: 'Please?'

'OK. Same time?'

'It's good for me.'

'See you then.'

She went out of the door without looking back, raising a hand as she went, and walked down the little street so quickly she was almost running. Her heart bounced in her chest like a rubber ball. When she got home, she went into the bathroom and locked the door so her flatmate wouldn't burst in. She leant her forehead against the cold mirror, trying to get her breath even. Then she drew back and stared at herself for several minutes. She had the sense that she was gradually losing a grip of herself, like a boat bucking in a storm and finally about to break free of its moorings. What would happen then?

Chapter Twenty-six

At the end of her third sitting with Lucas, Mia didn't stand up to look at what he'd made of her this time. Instead, she bent forward and put her head on her knees. Through her half-closed eyes, she could see the grainy floorboard and her feet in their sandals. Crimson toenails.

'Mia?'

She didn't want to answer. It was all too much effort.

'Mia, what is it?'

'Wait a minute.'

'Can I get you a glass of water?'

'All right.'

He left the room and she heard the tap running in the kitchen, then his rapid footsteps coming back. 'Here.'

He didn't touch her. Good. If he touched her, she would explode into splinters, or melt. Yes. Her body was loose and boneless, and she felt something warm on her knee, where she was resting her head. The floorboards and her painted toenails shimmered and distorted. She was crying, and she couldn't remember when she had last cried. She didn't want Lucas to see and pity her. She would just stay like this and wait for the tears to cease.

'Mia?'

'Please wait,' she said.

At last she felt safe enough to lift her head. He was

sitting on his chair, looking at the painting he'd just made, a frown on his face. Then he looked towards her. 'OK?'

She nodded, liking the fact he wasn't making a big fuss of it. If he had tried to hug and comfort her, or press her for an explanation, she would have been out of the room and down the stairs into the street like a shot. Instead, she stood up and went to the window for her fag. He didn't join her and didn't talk, staring at her portrait rather than at her. A bicycle lay on the grass today, its wheel slightly spinning in the breeze. She watched it dreamily for a while, then stubbed her cigarette out and put it in the metal bin near the divan.

'Are you running off again?' asked Lucas, still busy making tiny alterations to the portrait, carefully dabbing at it with the corner of a tissue.

'I don't think so, no. Not today.'

'Good.'

'Shall I make us coffee?'

'All right.' He seemed pleased, slightly amused. 'I keep it in the fridge.'

'OK.'

She went into a kitchen that was small and cluttered. It didn't have any units, only a strange assortment of rickety furniture – a narrow dresser, painted green, a set of drawers, a table with four unmatched chairs arranged by it, and a few more stacked by the wall. There were rows of flowerpots on the windowsill, with small shoots poking through the soil.

'What are the plants?' she called through to Lucas.

'Chillies.'

'Wow.'

She filled the kettle, found the coffee and rinsed out the cafetière. This was the third time she had visited this house, but the first time she had stepped out of the living room, except for the first day when she'd used the tiny downstairs loo. She looked around, noticing jam-jars full of paintbrushes, clothes draped over the chair, a woman's coat.

'Who else lives here?' she asked, as she returned with the coffee.

'There's Alvin — the one whose portrait you saw. But he's travelling with his girlfriend at the moment. He comes back in a week or two, I think. And Kathy.'

'Where's she?'

'She's at work. She's got a job with some kind of graphic-design company. I don't really understand what she does — it's all about logos and rebranding.'

'Is she an artist too?'

'Whatever that means — I met her at art school. Her and Alvin. But Alvin works in a bike shop now, and I work in a bar and do bits of adult education.'

'And paint.'

'When I can. And you're doing an MA?'

'After a fashion.'

'What does that mean?'

'Part-time student, part-time waitress. I'm doing my dissertation on the twentieth-century memoir. I don't know why. I seemed to just find myself doing it. Because I didn't know what else I wanted to do, probably. It's a way of not making up my mind, putting off the day when I have to be a proper adult with a real job.'

'Will you have lunch with me?'

'Now?'

'It's after midday.'

'Where?'

'Here. I can make us something. We can sit in the garden.'

'I don't know. I ought to get back.'

'Why?'

'Work,' said Mia. She put down her mug with a click on the table and stood up.

'I only suggested a sandwich in the garden.'

'Well . . .'

'Brie. I have some really nice Brie and some bread I made myself.'

'Just a snack, then.'

He grinned at her. He had a faint dimple in one cheek. It reminded her – She turned away from the thought.

'Only a snack,' he agreed.

They sat on the grass beside the bike. The bench was too rickety to risk. Lucas had made a tomato salad and mashed an avocado with sour cream in a version of guacamole. He couldn't find a rug, but he laid down his jacket for Mia to sit on. It was only the start of summer – this balmy weather could go on for months, thought Mia, and she took off her sandals and stretched out her bare legs, feeling herself uncoiling in the warmth.

Lucas asked her about her flatmate, and then about her family. Her heart raced. She told him her father was an academic, part-time now, and her mother a primary-school teacher. Safe enough. Then he asked if she had siblings. She licked her dry lips and took some water, playing for time. 'Yes.'

'How many?'

It was always tricky.

'I've got a sister, a brother and two half-brothers,' she replied. She heard how her voice speeded up; had Lucas too?

'Where do you come?'

'Youngest,' she said.

'And are you all close?' he asked.

'Oh.' Her skin was prickling in the heat; there were sudden uncomfortable patches of sweat gathering between her breasts and behind her knees. 'In a way. You know what families are like. We've drifted apart a bit recently, nothing big just, what with one thing and another . . . but what about you? Do you have family? You have a sister and a father, I know that.'

'My mother is dead,' he replied. She let out a small sigh: she was past the danger point now. The dread abated, like a tide going out, and she heard Lucas telling her about his Spanish mother, who had died when he was a teenager, and his father, who had married again just a few months after to a woman Lucas disliked intensely, who had been fiercely possessive of his father and had bullied his younger sister. She thought how astonishing it was that people talked so easily about their past: you asked them a question and it was like pressing a button. Words poured out. They had neatly shaped stories of their lives prepared, anecdotes to tell, narratives that summed up whole slabs of time.

She finished her sandwich and lay back. She was

exhausted; somehow the hour spent sitting pinned and frantic on that sofa with Lucas looking at her had emptied her of energy. She didn't want to make any effort. She didn't want to speak or smile. She closed her eyes, still seeing the sunlight through her lids. The grass was soft. Lucas's jacket smelt of him, and if she reached out her hand she would be able to touch him where he sat, and run her fingers along the golden skin of his strong arm. But she was too tired to do that.

'Mia. Mia.'

She opened her eyes. He was blocking out her sun, leaning over her, his dark eyes staring into hers.

'Yes?'

'You fell asleep.'

'I fell asleep,' she muttered. 'I never do that.'

'I didn't like to wake you, but I thought you'd want me to.'

'How long?'

She touched her skirt to make sure it hadn't ridden up while she had lain on the grass and he'd watched her. Had she snored? Dribbled? Called out names?

'Just a few minutes. Don't worry.'

'Oh,' she said. The garden was coming back into focus; the veins of branches and blades of uncut grass.

'You looked very peaceful.'

'Did I?'

'Yes.'

'I was dreaming,' she said.

'What were you dreaming?'

'I don't know.' She didn't let herself think. She reached up and pulled his head down and kissed his lovely mouth.

He tasted like he smelt: of paint and soap and the summer. She put her fingers into his tangle of dark hair and pulled him closer. Then she pushed him away and sat up. 'Now I really must go,' she said.

She knew when she returned that she would have sex with Lucas. Her body tingled and thrummed with the knowledge. She almost wanted to put off the day so she could live for a while longer with this sense of thrilled anticipation, when every inch of her skin throbbed, when her stomach was loose and her blood hot and fast in her veins.

On the day, she woke early and spent a long time getting ready. She stood in the shower until the water ran cold. She mooched round the kitchen in her towelling robe, making herself a breakfast of fruit and yoghurt and honey. She painted her nails bright orange, rubbed lotion into her arms, her legs, her stomach, pulled on a pair of khaki shorts and a sleeveless white top, ran her fingers through her damp hair, stared at herself in the mirror. Her eyes were bright and her skin, usually so pale, had a faint tan. She looked strong and alert, and she felt alive.

She sat on the sill of her wide-open window and smoked her cigarette, with a mug of strong coffee that had surely never tasted so good. People flowed past. Everyone looked different in the sun, even Paul who wasn't called Paul, with his carrier bags of other people's litter. For a moment, she thought she saw another face – but it was a trick of the generous light; her imagination at work again. She stubbed out her cigarette, slid off the sill, picked up her flip-flops.

Cycling along the tow-path to Lucas's house, she took her time, free-wheeling, once halting to look at the messy moorhen nest on the bank, and the scrabble of tiny chicks making their way towards it in the calm wake of their mother. Everything was conspiring to make her happy. Life seemed to gush through her unimpeded, and it made her realize how clogged up she had been for months, years, like a riverbed that had been silted up with shit and debris and strange slimy weeds, until only the smallest sludgy trickle could find its way through. That sense of blockage would return, of course – she knew it – but today she didn't feel it.

First, she had to endure the sitting, but even that wasn't too bad. Whereas previously she had felt her body was broken down into its constituent parts, and each part had its own particular aggravation of pain, today she felt whole, of a piece. She didn't ache or itch. It was no longer such a trial to feel Lucas's eyes on her, although she was more aware than ever of the change that came over him when he painted – how sternly assessing he became, how speculative his glance was. Today, he had put on music – she didn't recognize it, something ambient and insidious, worming threads of sound into her brain – and instead of her thoughts being frozen into the silence of the room, only the soft swish of his brush interrupting it, her mind wandered. Without moving her head, she noticed things she hadn't seen before: the photos on the wall of family groups and single faces, the titles of books on the shelves, the habit Lucas had of sometimes laying down the brush and blowing against his fingers, as if to unstiffen them.

'There,' he said at last. 'Thank you.'

'Can I see?'

'No. Not yet.'

'What, then?'

He crossed the room to her and with one finger traced the outline of her face. 'This?' he asked, and kissed her. She put her hands under his blue T-shirt. His back was warm and firm; she could feel his ribs.

He loosened the belt of her shorts and then, without hurrying, undid the buttons and let them slide down her legs. He took the hem of her white top and eased it carefully up and over her head. She lifted the T-shirt over his head and let it drop to the floor.

'You're sure?' he asked.

'Sssh.'

'No. Tell me you're sure.'

'I'm sure.'

She kicked off her flip-flops and he laid her on the brown divan that she had hated so much. Its fabric scratched her bare skin, leaving faint burns along her thighs. He wouldn't let her close her eyes, which was what she always did during sex, blotting out the face above her. He watched her as she watched him, and she saw her face reflected in his eyes and she saw herself call out and she heard him say her name, with that odd little break in the middle: 'Mi-a.'

He moved away from her, though the divan was narrow and they were still joined at hips and knees.

'Now we can have coffee,' he said.

'Mm.'

He pulled on his jeans and went into the kitchen, a barefooted pad. She heard him singing softly to himself as he ground coffee and boiled water. She put her knickers on and then his T-shirt, which held his summer smell.

He came back in with two mugs of coffee. 'Are you hungry?' he asked.

'I don't know.'

It was now, she thought. This very moment. Take the plunge. Her throat was blocked.

'We can go out for lunch – or I can cook you something. What do you like to eat? Or what don't you like? Apart from Brie.' He smiled at her. He was happy, and she thought, I did that, brought that gleam to his eyes.

'Lucas.'

'Yes.'

'I have something to tell you.'

There: she had spoken. The words hung in the air between them like a thick drift of smoke.

'Oh.' He sat down beside her. 'That sounds serious.'

'Yes.'

'There's someone else?'

'In a way.'

'I see.'

'But not in the way you think.' She took a deep, unsteady breath. 'I have a brother.'

'Hmm.' He gave a grimace. 'That's not quite what I was expecting.'

'His name is Johnny. He's two years older than me. I'm twenty-three so he's twenty-five. When I was growing up, he was my hero.' Mia wasn't looking at him, but into her coffee. Her voice was flat and factual; she wasn't going to stop now. 'Not just my hero. He was my refuge. I looked up to him and I felt safe with him. He made me think I was all right when I didn't feel all right at all. I was bullied quite a lot and he protected me from all of that. I was a bit of a tomboy, and a late developer – and I tagged after him and his friends and he let me. He never made me feel unwanted.' She heard her voice give a dry catch, something sticking or coming unstuck. 'I could talk to him about stuff that I couldn't tell anyone else. Dark, nasty feelings. I think I always knew he was a bit – I don't know. A bit unsafe in himself, if that makes sense?' It was a question, but she still didn't look up to see Lucas nod. Her voice sounded hollow and thin, as if it belonged to someone else. 'But I also thought he was the best person in the whole world. So. Anyway.' She gave a cough, then a small, nervous laugh. 'Ooof. Here we go. So, one day, nearly seven years ago, he disappeared.'

Now she did lift her eyes to meet Lucas's. He didn't speak, but waited for her to continue.

'He was at university. And he just went missing. It was clear that he had gone voluntarily – he hadn't fallen off a cliff or been abducted or anything – and I don't know if that made it better or worse. At first, everyone thought he would come back quite soon – after all, young people go missing all the time and they usually come back within a few days. I know all the statistics – or, at least, my father does, and I mean *all*. I told you he was an academic, but his real special subject is missing people. Missing Johnny. Of course, we were frantic. It was like a bad dream, the kind of thing that happens to other people, not to a family like us: middle class, comfortably off, apparently happy. We didn't fit the usual picture. My mother – I can't tell you. It was like seeing someone wiped out. And my father, he went off the rails and never quite got back on again.

'We told the police, we searched, we got in touch with

newspapers, we put up signs, we contacted the Missing Persons Helpline. We did everything we could think of, and in the end there was nothing to do but wait. That was the worst. Waiting and not knowing, always this pit of fear in your stomach. But he didn't come back and he didn't come back. After a bit, I think people started to assume he must be dead. But not my mother. She was completely certain he was alive – she said she would know in her blood and in her bones if he had died.' As she spoke, Mia could hear her mother saying those very words; her voice rang out strong and impassioned. 'And then, after years, he sent a card. He was safe. But still he didn't come home. Since then he's sent a couple of letters, saying he's all right but not where he is or how we can contact him. All three were from abroad. Europe. And he's still missing and we're still fucked. All of us, in our own special ways. And I love him and I miss him and I hate him so much for what he's done to all of us that sometimes I think I'll go mad with hatred.'

She stopped, breathless. She had told her secret to someone she knew almost nothing about. Now what?

Lucas put his mug down on the floor and took her hand, holding it between both of his as if he was trying to warm her. For a few moments, he didn't speak. There was a small furrow between his brows.

'There's obviously so much to say about all of this,' he said at last, formal in his desire to be sincere and not get things wrong. 'But before anything else, I want to tell you how glad and honoured I am that you've told me. Thank you.'

'You're welcome,' she said, her voice shaky. 'It's no big deal.'

'No? I get the impression that you don't tell many people, do you?'

'No one.'

'No one?'

'Everyone tells me I'm a bit guarded.'

'You poor thing,' he said. 'Really – no one?'

'Don't get the wrong idea. I'm not asking anything from you – it doesn't mean anything. It was probably just the way I was feeling. That's why I told you.'

'No. Listen. Don't do that.'

'What?'

'I can feel you closing down on me. You're like one of those anemones in a rock pool, shrinking when they're touched. Or a mollusc.'

'Mollusc – thanks.'

'I'm saying you don't need to do that. You've told me and I'm glad you've told me. Really glad, Mia.'

Mia ducked her head and muttered something. She felt slightly dazed and everything seemed unreal to her – the sex she had just had with Lucas, the story she had told him after all these years of not telling it, the way he was now sitting beside her, holding her hand, as if she was an invalid.

'Well,' she managed, 'now you've got to tell me something.'

'What do you mean?'

'Tell me something.'

'I can't match you, Mia.'

'Tell me what you don't tell other people. It's only fair.'

'I get it. You think you've put yourself in my power and now you've got to reverse it.'

'Come on.'

'It's not like a debt, you know. It doesn't work like that.'

'I'm serious.'

'So am I.'

They stared at each other. Then he said, 'OK. Here's a secret. I think about you all the time.' Mia said nothing and he went on, almost angrily, 'Is that enough? Does that give you back your power?'

'Yes.' She raised his hand and put her mouth to his knuckles. 'I keep thinking I see him.'

'That's understandable.'

'At first I saw him everywhere I looked. In every crowd, looking down from the top of buses, at stations, across streets. Sometimes I'd be quite sure he was behind me, that I could feel his eyes on my back, and I'd whirl round to catch him and of course he was never there. But bit by bit that faded. I stopped seeing him. I don't think my mother ever did and my dad – well, I've no idea about him. But I stopped. I almost didn't want to – it felt that I was giving up on him and letting him go. As if I didn't care enough. But recently he's come back. He's like a ghost that returns to haunt me. Sometimes I think I'm going mad.'

Chapter Twenty-seven

'How many, then?'

'I'm not saying!' Mia gave a laugh, trying to turn it into a joke, but she was disconcerted.

'You have to. You tell me and then I tell you.'

'Or vice versa. Surely it should be the other way round.'

'OK. I don't mind. I'll tell you and then you tell me.'

'This is stupid. I don't see why either of us has to say.'

'Because we're a couple.'

'We're not a couple!'

'We're a couple and that's what couples do. They swap confidences about their sex life.'

'What if I don't want to?'

'Do you really not want to?'

'I don't know. It makes me feel a bit . . . oppressed.'

'I won't mind.'

'What do you mean, you won't mind?'

'If you've had hundreds.'

'Why should you mind?'

Lucas shrugged. 'Men do, I've heard.'

'You mean, if you've had hundreds, that would be OK, but if I have, it wouldn't?'

'That wasn't me speaking. I was just saying men mind. Not me.'

'Well, good for you,' Mia said sarcastically.

'Are we actually having an argument about how many

people we've had sex with, without actually telling each other how many people we've had sex with?'

'It's the basic premise I object to.'

'That we have to tell each other?'

'That – and the fact that there's a gender difference.'

'But I was saying there's not – in my case. Anyway, we don't have to tell each other. It doesn't matter. Leave it.'

'OK.'

'Good. That's settled. We won't discuss it any further.'

'Fine.'

'Seven.'

'What?'

'Seven. I've had sex with seven women. Six of them were long-term girlfriends, who I'll tell you about one day, if you want me to.'

'Oh.'

'It's OK. You don't have to tell me. Goodnight. Sleep well.'

'Night.'

She waited until he was asleep, then softly got out of bed again, pulled on his shirt, then padded on her bare feet past Kathy's closed door, down the stairs and out into the little garden. The earth felt cool and damp and there was a bite to the air. Night-time in London – the lights of the city glowed on the horizon and she could hear traffic in the distance. In the countryside, it would be completely dark now, except for the stars, and the only sounds would be the wind in the leaves, the whisper of the far-off sea and perhaps an owl, perhaps your heartbeat. Everything secret and silent and under wraps.

Mia sat on the broken bench, which swayed lightly and

gave a moan that sounded horribly human, then lit a cigarette: her ninth in an eight-cigarette day. She closed her eyes and calculated and smoked, digging her toes into the earth. Up there, behind that unlit window, Lucas was sleeping. She pictured him, the duvet pushed half off him, his chest rising and falling, his long lashes on his cheeks. At last she stood up and went back inside. She crept into bed next to him and he murmured something and turned towards her, his body warm against hers. Such trust. She put her mouth against his ear. 'Twenty-three,' she said.

His eyes flickered open.

'Except I'm lying. To make it more even with your seven. Thirty-one. Nine of whom were what you would call boyfriends.'

'Thank you,' he said composedly, closing his eyes again, his hand resting against her thigh. 'But you really didn't need to say.'

'And that's not counting the first: Will. Who I will tell you about one day, if you want.'

'OK.' He kissed her on the forehead. 'Go to sleep.'

But she couldn't sleep. Her heart was galloping with all the disclosures she had made to Lucas since she'd met him. She wanted to shake him awake again to tell him that she'd always ended the affair – had never let anyone come really close to her, and if she thought they were getting close, she would bang the door shut. She should warn him against her and drive him away.

'You've missed the turning.'

'You didn't even say there was a turning.'

'Sorry. It loomed up on me and took me by surprise.

You'd better take the next one and see where it leads us. There doesn't seem to be a map in the car.'

They were on their way to see Isabel and Felix – Lucas had the use of Alvin's car while he was away; its passenger door wouldn't open and its back seat was torn, disgorging grubby slabs of foam. Its brakes seemed too tight, so every time they stopped, it was with a violent jolt that threw them forwards in their seats.

'Who's going to be there?'

'Just my parents, I hope. And I bet my mother's friend Jenny comes round. And Maud said she might be visiting her parents, and if she is, maybe she'll pop over.' Although that would be odd, she thought, so many introductions to her past, all at once: it made everything seem too official and public and she didn't want that.

'Maud?'

'My closest friend when I was at home. Maybe my only real friend.'

'You didn't have many friends.'

'I had friends, just not close friends. Stop the car.'

'What? Now?'

'Yes. Pull over.'

Lucas pulled over and turned to her. 'What is it?'

'I'm absolutely petrified.'

'I'm the one who's supposed to be petrified. Meeting the parents and all that.'

'Are you?'

'Petrified is putting it too strongly. I'm anxious. I'm trying to think up conversations we can have if it gets too awkward, opening gambits.'

'What have you come up with?'

'How about "This is delicious, how did you make it?"'

'She'll just make salad and put out cheese.'

'Or "Tell me about Mia when she was little." Don't scowl, it was a joke. Tell me why you're petrified.'

'I don't know. For the last hour, I've been thinking I'm about to tell you to turn round and drive back to London.'

'Please don't.'

'It's stupid.'

'Why are you so nervous of me meeting your parents?'

'I don't know. My mother will be so happy it'll make you want to run away –'

'No, it won't. I'll be pleased.'

'And my father will look at you as though you're some creature who's come into his crosshairs.'

'That's all right. You're his daughter, after all. He's protective.'

'Jed – that's my brother-in-law – told me that after he'd first met my father, he felt so upset he needed to lie down in a dark room. I remember it, actually.' Mia snorted at the memory. 'It was horrible.'

'So you're worried for me?'

'I'm more worried for them. I don't want you to judge them.'

'All right. I won't judge them. That's not why you're scared.'

'What I really mean, of course, is that I don't want you to judge me.'

'How would I judge you?'

'I'll be someone you don't like. Who I don't like.' She shuddered. 'Or at least, who I don't want to *be* like.'

'Because of what you went through?'

'And I don't want to judge you either.'

'Am I on trial here? It's getting horribly complicated, Mia. We're just going for lunch.'

'Yes. And we can leave straight after, if you want.'

'Fine.'

'We can just stay an hour.'

'Shall I drive on, now that you've infected me with your fear?'

'Yup. OK.' Mia put her sunglasses on and sat back in the seat. 'It's just a few miles.'

Chapter Twenty-eight

Mia could tell at once that Isabel was nervous too: she had put on lipstick, which she never wore in the daytime, and a loose white top with sheer sleeves that Mia had never seen before. She must have washed her hair that morning, because it was soft, almost fluffy. She came out to greet them, talking before they opened the car door and could hear what she was saying, smiling, holding out her hands, palms up, in an effusive gesture Mia recognized from long ago. She wanted to like Lucas and, more than that, she wanted him to like her; she wanted Mia to be pleased with how she was behaving, which made her self-conscious, and above all she wanted to consolidate this relationship she knew nothing about, rather than doing anything to destabilize it. She would have thought about how to behave in advance – just as Lucas had thought about it. No gushing, she would have told herself; no inappropriate probing into Lucas's personal life; no hint that this meeting felt important. Casual, welcoming, discreet, not embarrassing. No revelations about Mia as a child or, even worse, a teenager; no sudden gusts of emotion; no mention of Johnny; no tears. She was keeping her eyes on her daughter, trying not to look at Lucas yet.

'How lovely,' she said, putting her hands on Mia's shoulders.

'Hello, Mama,' said Mia, and kissed her soft, powdered cheek, smelling her perfume. 'This is Lucas.'

Isabel held out a hand. 'Nice to meet you,' she said. 'You've chosen a good day for it.' She gestured at the sky, as though she was responsible for its turquoise light.

'I'm really glad to be here,' said Lucas. He suddenly sounded slightly Spanish, thought Mia; a certain clip to his words. Perhaps nerves brought his dead mother out in him. 'It's beautiful.'

'Let's go into the garden.'

They sat at the wooden table, drinking the lemonade that Isabel had made. The garden was beautiful at this time of year, newly green. This could have been so nice, thought Mia, sitting back and sipping her drink, letting Lucas and Isabel tentatively approach each other, finding comfortable subjects, each ready to be pleased with the other: this garden, this house, this family, all seem made for welcome and safety. Generations gathering, the old and the young, presided over by Isabel and Felix. As it was, it seemed to her like a poisoned Eden, a place full of sadness and fear.

'Where's Dad?' she asked.

'In his allotment, of course. He should be here soon.' She gave Lucas her bright hostess smile. 'With the first of our asparagus.'

And there he was, coming along the little alley by the side of the house with a laden string bag. He was wearing baggy canvas trousers and walking boots clogged with mud, and there was a smear of dirt on his neck. He didn't at first realize they were there, and his face was frowning and intent. He looked old, thought Mia, with a rush of anxious tenderness. Old and worn out. When she was a child, she had thought Felix invulnerable. He had been the voice of authority in the house. Where Isabel was volatile and subjective and full of doubts, always changing her mind, unpredictable in her enthusiasms, he had been rational and apparently objective. He had known answers to her questions (or so she had thought at the time). Politics, religion, morality, science, literature, music, history – he had known what he thought and presented it as truth. God did not exist, hard work was its own profound pleasure and far more important than talent, free will was an illusion to which we must necessarily give ourselves up (and so was falling in love), the gulf between the rich and the poor was the abiding scandal of the country against which all right-thinking people should fight, depression was beaten back by strenuous physical exercise and not lazy little pills, Chaucer was a hero, the royal family had to go, music could save you, especially Bach's, sentimentality was a sin, celebrity was a curse, wealth rotted and power corroded. Shakespeare's greatest sonnet was Sonnet 29 ('When, in disgrace with Fortune and men's eyes . . .'), red wine was greater than white, vegetarians were mistaken and pets were a mistake, mint sauce did not go with wine, a foetus was not a baby until the moment of its birth, holidays were generally a waste of time . . . and so on and on, laid down with such an unyielding sense of his rightness that for many years he had been Mia's gospel. The Gospel According to Felix Hopkins. Even up to Johnny's disappearance, Mia had clung to her belief in him.

It is painful to see your father fall from such an elevated pedestal. And Felix had crashed, smashed on the ground: those terrible months when he had lain in his bed with the curtains half closed and a sour smell hanging round him, the rancid odour of failure and self-disgust. His famous blue eyes veined with red, his proud face crumpling, his stern voice broken.

She rose and went towards him, putting her arms round him and kissing his cheek. Did he smell of alcohol? She frowned into his shoulder and drew back to look at him. 'Hi, Dad,' she said, hating how she still talked to him as if he was ill, or a small child. 'What's in the bag?'

'Come and meet Lucas,' called Isabel. 'I was just asking how you two met.'

'Through a friend,' said Mia.

'I painted her portrait,' said Lucas.

Mia glared at him and he smiled imperturbably back. He seemed ominously relaxed and cheerful, she thought.

Felix and Lucas shook hands. Lucas took the bag from him and peered at the contents.

'You painted Mia?' asked Isabel. She was almost rubbing her hands: this was what she liked – a story, something symbolic and romantic.

'Many times,' said Lucas.

'You haven't got any of the pictures with you?'

'No!' said Mia.

'Sorry,' said Lucas. 'I'll bring them next time – or you can see them when you visit.'

Mia banged her glass down on the table in a surge of childish rage.

'I can see why she'd be a good subject,' said Isabel, wistfully.

They both considered her.

'Right. That's enough,' Mia said. 'I'm going to wash

these lettuces; you can talk about my face when I'm not here to listen.'

Through the kitchen window, she could see them still talking animatedly, while Felix sat at the end of the table with his glass of lemonade and a faraway look in his eyes. He didn't seem unhappy, just disconnected. She ran the leaves under cold water, then laid them on a tea towel to dry. When she returned to the garden, they barely raised their heads. They were talking about the early death of their mothers: Isabel's eyes were shining, and Mia thought she might cry but she didn't, though her voice quivered with emotion. Lucas barely glanced Mia's way: he was focused on Isabel and what she was saying, nodding every so often, his soft dark hair flopping over his forehead, his hands on the table, their slender, flexible fingers curled. Without looking at him, she put out her hand and laid it over his, felt him take it, and a little shudder went through her, as if she was letting go of something. She slid off her shoes, stretching out her legs and letting herself relax in the windless heat.

They had watercress soup for lunch, then bread and cheese, with salad from Felix's allotment. Jenny arrived with Benedict and they all drank coffee together. When the sun is shining, you don't need to make an effort to have unbroken conversations. Silence is plumped out by the warmth.

'Let's go swimming,' Isabel announced suddenly.

Felix had gone inside by now. They could see his figure seated at the desk in his study, bent over something. He probably wasn't doing anything, but had taken himself there by habit, which no one questioned any more. It was his bolt-hole, his refuge, the place where he could let his body slump and close his eyes, pressing his fingers to his temples.

'Swimming?' echoed Lucas.

'In the sea.'

'Oh! But I have no swimming things.'

'We can lend them to you.'

'Mia?' He turned to her.

'All right,' she surprised herself by saying. 'If you want.'

And so it was that she found herself in the North Sea, far out and watching the four figures nearer the shoreline. She squinted in the dazzle of the sun on the water: there were Jenny and Benedict, still standing thigh-deep amid the skirt of waves and squealing like children at the cold; and there were Lucas and Isabel, side by side, holding their heads above the waves. She lay on her back and looked at the flat blue sky, let her arms float on either side of her. She flipped on to her front again. If she turned and swam out through the glinting ripples, how far would she get before she could go no further? How far before she could no longer be seen from the shore? Was that the kind of thought that Johnny had been tempted by before he let himself be swallowed by emptiness?

She trod water, looking out at the horizon. Two container ships were moving very slowly across it, great blocky shapes, like small modern towns floating past. A hand touched her shoulder. Their legs briefly tangled.

'You OK?' Lucas asked, and she nodded. 'You're not angry?'

'Angry? Why would I be angry?'

'Do you have to have a reason?'

'Am I such a bitch? Don't answer that. No. I'm not angry. I'm thoughtful.'

'Do you regret bringing me here?'

'No.'

'I like your mother.'

'I can see that. She obviously likes you.'

'She seems a very lonely woman.'

'You think so, do you?'

Mia moved away from him and made for the shore, doing a thrashing crawl that left her breathless. Her eyes stung with the salt and her body tingled. She rubbed herself dry with a towel, turned away from Lucas and the rest of them.

'We've got to go,' she said abruptly.

'Really? I made a cake for tea.'

'Next time.'

'Oh – well, take it with you. Please? It's your favourite.'

She's a very lonely woman.

'No. Let's stay,' she said. 'Of course we can stay, can't we, Lucas?'

'We can,' he said carefully. 'Whatever's good for you.'

Only at the end of their visit was Johnny mentioned, and then not even by name. They went inside as the sun got lower, and Isabel stopped in front of a photograph that had been taken of the whole family a few months before he had gone off to university. He was wearing a white shirt and the summer had lightened his hair and brought out his freckles. She said, 'Did Mia tell you?'

'Yes.'

'I'm so glad.' Then she said, 'I wonder what he looks like now. My boy.'

*

On the way back to London, Mia said, 'When you said she was very lonely . . .'

'I noticed your reaction to that.'

'You think it's my fault.'

'Not your fault, no.' He had laid a light emphasis on 'fault'.

'I could see what you were thinking. That she lost Johnny, and then she half lost me – isn't that right?'

Lucas didn't glance over. He drove with his hands resting lightly on the steering wheel, his eyes on the road ahead, and the sun sinking in the sky.

'In a way, yes.'

'So you're seeing it from her point of view.'

'I'm not sure that I'm seeing it from any single point of view,' he replied.

'You are. I can see why. She and Dad – of course they're the ones who lost the most. To lose a brother is hard, but to lose a son, that's something you can never get over. Do you think I don't understand?'

'I know, Mia.'

'But you've no idea what it was like.'

'I know. I'm not criticizing you. I feel sorry for them – that doesn't mean I feel less about what you went through. It's not a zero sum game.'

'It sounds stupid – no, worse than stupid. Babyish and callous. But I want someone to be on *my* side. To see *my* story. You can't understand what it felt like to be in that house, just me with Isabel and Felix, once Johnny had gone. Tamsin was OK – she was in love and pregnant, happy for the first time in her life really, and although of course she minded, she went on being in love and pregnant and happy. Rory and Ben – they always had a whole separate life, they never lived with us and it just didn't mean the same to them. Johnny's friends . . .' She frowned, was silent for a few moments. 'They were gutted, properly gutted, and they felt guilty and rallied round. For a bit. That's the thing. For a bit. They could leave. They could forget. They didn't have to spend day after day and night after night with their father lying in bed weeping and their mother wandering round the house like a bat that's lost its radar, with her clothes inside out and her hair flying, and her eyes wild and looking at you like she couldn't quite remember who you were.

'It wasn't her fault, or his, I couldn't even blame them, though God knows I tried. But Johnny was always their favourite – or, at least, he was the model son. Poor sod, no wonder he had to flee. When he was at home, I was in his shadow, and after he'd gone, I didn't stand a chance. St Johnny and crosspatch Mia. Who went off the rails, just to prove them right. I tried to kill myself in my first year of university, you know.'

As she was speaking, Lucas slowed down, then pulled over into a lay-by. He turned off the ignition and undid his seatbelt. Mia stared ahead, her face set and tears in her eyes.

'Mia,' he said.

'Ignore me. I'm being stupid. This is why I didn't want you to come home.'

'I *am* on your side.'

'There are no sides. I know that, really.'

'You tried to kill yourself?'

'Oh. Probably not. Probably it was just a cry for help.'

'A cry to whom? Did your parents know?'

'No. I called my half-brother Ben, and he took me to hospital to have my stomach pumped.'

'All the things you don't say to people.'

'All the things I'm saying now. Scary.'

'It doesn't scare me. Was it just once?'

'Yes.'

There was a pause. He stared at her and she stared at the fields outside her window, a rich green darkening in twilight.

'Don't regret telling me,' he said.

She gave a little smile, still not turning towards him. 'You're not stupid, are you?'

'And don't go cold on me just because you've told me things you usually keep buried.'

'I'll try.'

'One more thing, now we're here.'

'What?'

'Will.'

Will. Mia tried not to think about him very much, although sometimes she knew she still dreamt about him. She never remembered the dreams, but she recognized the sensations they left her with upon falling awake with a horrible lurch – a mixture of desire, humiliation and grief. It could take hours for the after-effects of the dream to fade; on some days they didn't diminish, but sat in her chest like a huge, hairy spider, scratching its bent spindly legs against her lungs and her heart. On those days, she couldn't sit in one place. She had to walk for miles, or swim dozens of lengths in the local pool, up and down, up and down, trying to exhaust her body and wash her polluted mind clean. The counsellor she had seen after her attempted suicide – a woman she had found so oppressively irritating in her amorphous, melting concern that Mia used to want to jump through the large glass hospital window to escape her – would have said that Will wasn't a real person for Mia, more a locus for all sorts of unresolved emotions. But Mia had never told her about her brother, or about his friend. The thought of the counsellor's understanding, her wise, nodding appreciation of Mia's suffering, made her crackle with rage. And, of course, she knew perfectly that what she felt about Will was hopelessly entangled with Johnny's disappearance. Any fool would recognize that.

People often said that there was nothing like your first love – however brief, however doomed, the intensity of emotion was rarely repeated in later life. It was certainly true for Mia. She had had a violent crush on Will when she was fourteen or so – an under-grown tomboy, whom people actually sometimes mistook for a boy, dressed in scruffy jeans and sweatshirts, with cropped hair and never any makeup. As her friends experimented with boys, drink, fashion, answering questionnaires in glossy magazines about 'How attractive to the opposite sex are you?', Mia had buried herself in books, or tagged after Johnny. She had played football with him and his friends, and computer games, tried to keep up with their musical tastes, was the youngest and quietest semi-member of a gang that had seemed impossibly grown-up and cool – and all the time her body was throbbing with her secret, shameful passion for Will. She took the bottle caps he left on the table after opening his beer and put them in her bedside table; she took a sheet of paper with his scribbled handwriting on it (Racing Demon scores after one evening spent playing cards at their house until late) and put it under her pillow. She never told anyone what she felt: while Maud and the rest of them were candid about hopeless fancies and happy flirtations, Mia felt that her feelings were too big for gossip.

She had told Isabel about having sex with Will in his mother's car and they had both cried. But she hadn't told her about all the other times, spread out over the next four years. She hadn't told her how violent they were with each other, clinging to Johnny by clinging to each other, punishing Johnny by punishing each other. Many of the thirty-one times she had confessed to Lucas had been passive, affectless encounters between her visits to Will or his to her. She thought of that Mia now as though she were a stranger. Even at the time she had been disconnected from herself: the swagger and bravado of the Mia who had lots of affairs and never seemed to get hurt faced the scared, lonely Mia across a great abyss of longing.

Nor had she told Isabel – or anyone, until now – about the time she had truanted from school and gone to York to find Will, waiting outside the library for hours until she saw him come down the steps, wrapped in another girl's arms, looking flushed and carefree. She remembered how he had glanced up and seen her and how the expression on his face turned ugly – furtive, hostile and scared. A chill had spread over her, like lead in her blood. She had stared and smiled, the smile freezing into a sneer, a jeering snarl, and watched him walk past as if she didn't exist.

Nor had she told anyone about how, upon eventually learning from Will during one of their violent arguments about Zoë's fling with Johnny, she had visited Zoë in Sheffield. She had arrived during the early evening and found out where Zoë lived, in a house in Nether Edge, with friends. She had knocked on the door and waited until it was opened by a young man with a shaved head and no fingers on his left hand. He'd told her Zoë wasn't there, but would probably come back any time. Mia had refused to come in. She had loitered outside the house, smoking roll-ups, wishing she'd put on a jacket at least because, although it was summer, the nights were still cool.

At last she had seen Zoë walking towards her, hand in hand with a handsome character wearing a hooped shirt and an earring, like a sailor in a Hollywood musical; Mia half expected him to burst into song and slap his thigh. She never discovered his name, or the name of the person who'd opened the door to her. The sight of Zoë's happy, guilt-free face, the memory of Will's cheerful face in York, made a mist rise before her eyes. She stood up, dropped her cigarette, and made her way slowly towards Zoë, who saw but did not recognize her until they were nearly upon each other. Her expression changed – grew surprised, then wary, and then, as Mia raised her fist, terrified. She was much taller than Mia, and more solid, but Mia had the advantage of surprise and an unbridled savagery, and Zoë didn't stand a chance. Mia had punched her in the face and split her lip, then in the stomach and watched her bow over, clutching herself, her face screwed up in pain. The man beside her had started yelling, but for some reason hadn't intervened. When he had at last tried to stop Mia, he had simply taken hold of her hitting arm, so she had kicked him in the shin and then the balls, and turned back to Zoë.

'That's for what you did!' she screamed. She was already ashamed of herself, which only made her angrier. Her voice splintered in the evening air. Doors opened. People came out. By this time Zoë's boyfriend had wrapped both his arms around Mia's torso and lifted her clean off the ground. She dangled in the air, still kicking out. She was pleased to see that there was blood dripping from Zoë's nose and lip and she was crying. Her mascara was smudged, her shirt was ripped, and she looked blowsy and fearful.

'Shall I call the police?' asked the sailor, putting her down at last. 'Who is she? Is she drunk?'

'I know her,' said Zoë, in a tremulous voice. She had pulled a tissue out of her bag and was holding it against her face.

'You don't know me,' said Mia. 'You've never known me. But I know you.'

'She's mad.'

Zoë's ineffectual protector had taken a step forward, ready to intervene if necessary.

'And I know what you did and I will never, never, never forgive you.'

Zoë took a step forward. 'It takes two to fuck,' she said quietly. 'Have you ever thought about that?'

'Don't you *care*?' asked Mia. 'You just want to make yourself feel better – but don't you even *care*? How can you live with yourself?'

'You think you're good enough to be my judge? The

precious Hopkins family. It's easier to blame me than look to yourselves.'

'That's true,' said Mia, surprising herself and Zoë. 'Yes. Quite right. You were just the straw. I'm off now. Have a good life.'

She had walked down the street, knowing several pairs of eyes were on her, then heard running footsteps and turned. Zoë grabbed her shoulder. 'I'm sorry,' she said. 'I'm really sorry. But you need help, you know.'

Zoë had been right: she had needed help. There were many ways in which she tried to alleviate her pain: every so often she cut herself (her arms still bore the faintest traces of those experiments); sometimes she followed Isabel's example and starved herself, so that her ribs and collar bones stood out starkly on her thin body; she had smoked too much and taken sleeping pills, so that oblivion came down at night like the executioner's axe. Just that once she had taken too many pills; she didn't know if it had been deliberate or just a hysterical mistake. Above all, she had given herself rules. Never see Will again – and she hadn't, not for almost three years. Never cry – and until Lucas had come along and sat her on his brown divan, she hadn't even felt close to tears. Never let yourself be vulnerable. Never look back. Never talk about Johnny. Be on your guard.

Mia finished talking. The sun had set now. Cars drove past in a blur of headlights; ahead of them, the lights of London flickered and glowed. Lucas took her hands in his and held them tight. 'Thank you,' he said.

'Oh, God, Lucas! Why? I'm just a head-case.'

'No. You're not. You're precious.'

'No one's ever called me precious before.'

'You are. To me.'

'Why are you so nice to me?'

'I fell for you the minute I set eyes on you.'

'Did you?'

'You didn't even notice me, but I noticed you.'

'I'm glad you did.'

'I was in a relationship at the time.'

'You never told me that.'

'After that first sitting, I went and ended it.'

'For me?'

'Because of what I felt about you.'

'You're too nice for me. I don't deserve someone like you.'

'Let's go home now.'

'Where's home? Yours or mine?'

'Home is where you are.'

'I think that's the nicest thing anyone's ever said to me.'

Johnny

Chapter Twenty-nine

'This is civilized.'

Lucas and Mia were at St Pancras International eating brunch: eggs Benedict for Lucas, and for Mia, granola with raspberry compôte. They sat at a table near the window of the café and watched travellers arriving and departing, dragging soft cases on wheels, carrying babies, holding hands with partners, waving farewell to those who were seeing them off or greeting those who had come to meet them. They had just taken the night train from Florence to Paris, and the early-morning train out of the Gare du Nord, but they didn't want their holiday to end yet, to return to their separate houses, to their stints in the bar, the shop, the market, the library, the classroom. They sat close together, thigh to thigh and shoulder to shoulder, occasionally leaning in to kiss the other on the cheek or the head.

'We can stay here all day if you want.'

'We should just get the next train out again. Brussels, in thirty-five minutes.'

'I wish.'

'What are you doing this evening?'

'Coming to yours?' Lucas suggested.

'I'm working, remember. Six until midnight.'

'I'll wait in your bed.'

'All right.'

They smiled at each other, dazed. He put his hand over hers and she leant against his shoulder, breathing in his smell. His lips were on her hair.

'I don't want to be separated from you,' he murmured.

'Nor me from you.'

'Really?'

'Really.'

'Mm. Do you want more coffee?'

'No.'

'Orange juice?'

'No. I should go. I promised Vicky I'd be back this afternoon. Anyway, the flat will be a tip – I need to get ready for Monday.'

'OK. I'll let myself into yours later this evening. I'll be waiting.'

'Good.'

They stood up, picked up their luggage, scattered coins on the table, kissed each other once, lightly, on the lips and turned to go, Lucas outside to get a bus and Mia down into the Underground, both thinking of the other.

The following morning Mia rose before Lucas and had a long shower, then made coffee for them both. It was September, and already the leaves on the plane trees outside were beginning to turn, after the summer. Today was windless and close, as if a storm might be brewing. She pushed more holiday washing into the machine, then went into the bedroom.

'Coffee,' she said gently, looking at how Lucas's soft dark hair lay across his forehead in streaks, at how his lips were half open, puffing out slightly with each exhalation.

She moved away and went to the open window for her first cigarette of the day, watching the flow of people thickening on the street below. Later she would go to the library, she thought. She had let her studies slip, and her friendships too. It was time to return to real life, to footnotes and bibliographies, bills and the reality of her bank statements, answering machine messages, obeying work rotas, the clock and the calendar.

She stubbed out her cigarette and went and sat on the bed beside Lucas. With his eyes still closed, he put out a hand and pulled her towards him. She laid her head on his pillow and kissed his smiling mouth and stared into his opening eyes. You could drown in another person. He ran his hand along her leg and she heard herself give a small exclamation of desire. She pulled off her T-shirt and slid further under the sheets.

Then the doorbell rang.

For a moment they lay there, waiting to see if Vicky would go. The bell rang again, a single note.

'Maybe a delivery,' said Mia. 'I'd better go.'

Swinging her legs out of bed, she pulled on Lucas's baggy white shirt, doing up its buttons as she went to the door.

'Hang on, I'm coming,' she called, fiddling with the chain.

Chapter Thirty

There was a man. He didn't move or speak and his arms hung slackly by his sides.

She saw the sun behind his head, hazy yellow above the chimney pots. She saw the plane trees with their rusting leaves and patchwork bark. She thought it was Paul who walked past, head bent towards the pavement, carrying all his possessions in three bulging, splitting Tesco bags. But she couldn't be sure because the world beyond her door was wavering and distorted. It was hard to make out what was real.

The man was very probably five foot eleven and a half inches tall. Just above average; the pencil lines scored on the wall at home put him seven inches taller than her and six taller than Tamsin. But perhaps he had grown since then, or maybe shrunk. He was a stranger – beloved, abhorred and unknown.

Neither said anything. Mia held on to the door. Sounds came in from the ordinary streets. Cars, doors, music from windows, voices. The noises of everyday life. A woman stepped past, eating a doughnut. Mia saw sugar on her chin. A young man in an expensive suit talking into his phone. A kid on a skateboard. The world slid past. Time slid past in a blur of receding sights and sounds. How long did she stand like that? She heard the shower upstairs,

Lucas singing loudly; she pictured him, head tipped back, water streaming off his gorgeous face and his strong shoulders, in another world.

This man, standing in front of her so passively, was older than he should be. His hair was too brown. Someone had cut it with blunt scissors, and one side was far shorter than the other. His skin was a funny colour – tanned, yet with an underlying mushroomy pallor. A purple and yellow bruise flowered exotically on his right cheek. There was a scar on his chin that shouldn't have been there. There were freckles that should be there but which seemed to have dissolved into a smudgy stain on his forehead and over the bridge of his nose. Which was bleeding. His shirt lacked buttons. His boots, laces. He had a dirty yellow cotton knapsack over one shoulder. His eyes were cornflower blue and unblinking. He needed a shave.

Oh, but he needed a hug, a roar of welcome, a springing ambush of delight and tormented anguish, but there was an abyss between him and Mia, so wide and so deep that she didn't know how to get across it.

For seven years, she had wished for this. Beware of what you wish for. Her tongue had stuck to the roof of her mouth and her feet were locked to the floor. This must be like dying, she thought – when your life passes in front of you like an unravelling dream, or that's what they say. She saw Johnny as he had been, the golden boy. She saw herself beside him, skinny and monkey-faced, hanging on to his hand. Isabel's tender face, the loveliness she had lost. She saw Felix standing very upright in his study, his violin tucked under his chin, his eyes blazing. Despair.

Soon the dream would fade and Johnny could melt back into the ghost he had been for so long. With a supreme effort, Mia reached out, grabbed him by his shirt, and tugged him inside, slamming the door behind him, so that they stood together in the hall. She was gasping with the effort. Her eyes were stinging, as though she had stood for too long by a bonfire. The man standing there – just a few inches from her: she could smell him and, if she reached out, she could touch him, hug him, hold him, hit his weathered sunken face with all the force that was coiled up inside her – still didn't move or speak. He simply stood very still, his face expressionless, his eyes on her. He was waiting, Mia realized – but for what? What was she supposed to do?

She took one tiny step and put out a hand to touch his arm. He didn't dissolve. Her fingers were touching his bony wrist. She swallowed hard.

'Fuck,' she said at last.

The man's lips moved slightly. It was nearly a smile. There was still that dimple.

Mia took another step so that now she was almost upon him. She slid her fingers around his wrist, circling it.

'Are you real?' she whispered. 'Are you?'

'I don't know.' He was whispering too. 'You have to tell me.'

'Oh, Christ. Oh, dear God.'

'Please.'

'What?'

'Let me come in.'

'What did you do to us?'

'Be angry later. Let me come in.'

Mia, still holding his wrist, led him through into the little kitchen and pulled out a chair for him. 'Sit down.'

He sank into the chair and for a moment closed his eyes – looking, suddenly, like the boy he had been. His Adam's apple bobbed in his throat. He opened his tired blue eyes and said, 'Mia.' It was as if he was trying out the name again, after years of disuse.

'Yes?'

'Can I lie down for a bit?'

'Now?'

'Yes. Just for a bit.'

'Of course. I'll –' Lucas was up there, and Vicky. 'I'm going to run you a bath first. Then you can sleep for as long as you want.' Her voice was steady; they were talking of beds and baths. Seven years. She had been a child when he had gone away and he had been soft and sweet. She steadied herself on the back of his chair and, bending down, kissed his unbruised cheek very gently.

'You have no idea,' she said. 'Wait here.'

She turned on the bath taps, then leant over the toilet bowl and was sick, retching and coughing, her eyes stinging. When her stomach was empty, she stood up, flushed the lavatory twice, brushed her teeth vigorously and washed her face. She went into her room.

'I have something to tell you.'

Lucas was tying his shoelaces.

'Are you OK? I thought I heard –'

'The person at the door . . .'

'Mm?'

'. . . was Johnny.'

She heard how calm her voice sounded, matter-of-fact and almost casual. She watched Lucas's face, which remained blank for a few seconds. It was like pain, she thought: you slice the knife through your thumb and see the skin flap open, blood pumps and still you wait to feel the hurt.

'Johnny?' he said at last, standing up slowly.

'Yes.'

'Downstairs?'

'I'm running him a bath. He's pretty filthy.'

'Hang on.' He put his hands on her shoulders and she felt the world steady. 'Why are you being so calm?'

'I don't know.'

'Why aren't you crying or jumping for joy or shouting in anger?'

'I don't know. I feel a bit sick, though.'

'Sit down.'

'No. I need to turn off the bathwater.'

'Shall I go and say hello?'

'Say hello?' Mia started to laugh, putting her hand over her mouth so that it came out in snorts.

'Are you OK?'

'Yes. No. Meet him later, when he's had a bath and a lie-down. Wait there.'

She ran out of the room and downstairs into the kitchen, where Johnny sat with his hands folded on the table in front of him and his eyes staring out of the window.

'Your bath's ready. I've put a towel out. My room is

directly opposite, so just climb into bed afterwards and sleep as long as you like.'

Johnny stood up obediently. 'Where will you be?' he asked.

'Here. I won't go anywhere.' For a moment, she felt a spark of anger: she would wait for him; she had waited for seven years.

She led him up the stairs and into the bathroom.

'Lock the door in case Vicky tries to come in and gets a surprise.'

'Vicky?'

'I share the flat with her.'

'Oh.'

He looked so helpless, standing by the steaming bath in his shabby clothes.

'Do you need me for anything?'

'No. No.'

Mia closed the door and stood outside it, listening. After a minute or so, she heard a ripple and a faint splash. She went back to Lucas. 'He's going to have a sleep after his bath,' she said.

'Right. Coffee?'

'Is it too early for a drink?'

'It's ten o'clock.'

'OK. A cigarette, then.'

She smoked two cigarettes and drank two cups of strong black coffee – Lucas wanted to add sugar, for shock, but she refused. 'Look. My hands are steady,' she said, holding them up.

'Tell me what you're thinking.'

'I'm not, I can't. He's Johnny and he's a stranger. I don't know him, but he's Johnny. Up there, in the bath. What can I think or feel? There's too much. I've dreamt about this. I've imagined him standing in my doorway like this. I've never thought about what happens next. I haven't even hugged him. Shouted. I've just put him in a bath.' She laid a hand over her eyes.

Lucas waited.

'Isabel and Felix,' she said. 'What shall I tell them? Shall I phone them? Go and see them? Take him with me? What shall I do?'

She stood up abruptly, wrapped her arms tightly round her body, then sat down once more, shivering in spite of the heat. Upstairs, there was the sound of the water running out of the bathtub. A door opened and closed.

'I don't know,' said Lucas, slowly. 'But listen, Mia.'

'What?'

'This is good news. Your brother has returned. You thought he might be dead. It's *good*. It's better than that – it's wonderful, like a miracle.'

'Yes. You're right. I know. You say miracle – and I've even prayed for this – me, who doesn't believe in God or miracles, but I've literally knelt by the side of my bed and begged him, whoever he is, to send my brother home to us. I just feel – oh, fuck. I don't know what I feel. I feel it can't be true. He can't be here. In my bedroom, lying down on my bed, his face on my pillow where I've just been. Do you want to go?'

'What?'

'It's not fair on you. You've walked into the middle of

a family psychodrama. I'll understand if you don't want to stay.'

'Hang on – do you mean go now, for the day, or are you talking about going for good?'

'I don't know.'

'Don't you ever listen to anything? I'm not going anywhere, do you hear? Except to my life-drawing class in about fifteen minutes. If you want me to stay away for the next twenty-four hours or so, tell me and that will be fine. If you want me to come straight back after my class, that will be fine too. If you want me to cancel it, I can do that.'

'Thank you,' said Mia, in a small voice.

'You hate to feel beholden, don't you? When will you get it? You're not bloody beholden. There aren't any debts here. I *love* you.'

'Oh!'

There was a silence. Mia gave a small sob. 'This day has got too huge for me.'

'I know, I know. I shouldn't have said that, not now.'

She dragged her sleeve – the sleeve of his white shirt – across her nose, sniffing. Then took a deep breath, half shutting her eyes.

'I love you too.'

'You don't have to say it.'

'I want to say it. I've never said it to anyone before, except my nephews and nieces when they were tiny babies and nobody could hear me.'

'Really?'

'I don't think I have, anyway.'

'Great.'

'I've never said it and meant it.'

'And you mean it?'

'I do. Now go to your life class.'

'When shall I come back?'

'I'll call you.'

'Mia, I'm really glad. About us. And about Johnny. Everything's going to be all right.'

'Go.'

Chapter Thirty-one

She stood in her bedroom and looked at Johnny sleeping. The sun streamed in through the window and she went over to it and drew the curtains. His face fell into shadows, and she sat on the floor and studied it intently. The bath had removed some of his grime and his drying hair looked softer and lighter. He was slightly less of a stranger than he had been when he had stood slackly on her doorstep. His mouth was half open and Mia could see that he was missing a tooth. The bruise on his right cheek was puffy, and there was another, darker, bruise now visible on his naked shoulder. Had he been in a fight, she wondered. She couldn't imagine the Johnny she used to know ever being in a fight. She had a sudden picture of him standing quite still and letting someone punch him, accepting any punishment. He had tried to shave but had missed several patches, and nicked himself just below the ear. A tiny trickle of blood had dried there. His face was thin, parchment over bone, and his collar bone jutted out sharply.

She stood up, careful to make no noise, and crept from the room. Vicky was in the kitchen, covering a piece of soda bread with raspberry jam.

'Morning,' she said thickly, through a large, crumbling mouthful. 'I am *so* late.'

'I thought I should warn you. My brother's just turned up,' said Mia, casually.

'Which one?'

'Johnny.'

'Johnny? I don't remember a Johnny – there's Ben and Rory, but I've never heard you talk about Johnny.'

'No, well, he's been away for a bit, but now he's back.'

'That's nice,' said Vicky, cheerfully. 'Will he be here this evening?'

'Probably.'

'Great. I'll meet him then.' She ruffled Mia's hair affectionately. 'You look a bit peaky this morning. Are you ill?'

'I'm fine.'

'Good.' She stuffed the last of the bread into her mouth and took a large gulp of Lucas's unfinished cold coffee to wash it down, wincing. 'Must fly.'

Mia waited until she was safely gone, then picked up the phone. Her hands were trembling. She hesitated, frowning, then dialled a number.

'Hello?'

'Tamsin. It's me, Mia.'

'Mia. No, Seamus. Put that down . . . Because Mummy is telling you to, that's why. Sorry. Yes, are you OK? I said, put it down. OK, come and sit on my lap then. There.'

'I have something to tell you.'

'That sounds ominous.'

'No. It's good, but – are you ready?'

'Now it really sounds ominous.'

'Johnny's come back.'

There was a pause at the end. Mia could hear Seamus muttering something to himself, in his lisping, gap-toothed voice.

'Say that again.'

'Johnny's come back. He's here.'

'With you?'

'Yes. He's asleep in my bed.'

'My God! My God, Mia! That's – that's completely – that's –' There was a gurgle and a shriek and sounds of Tamsin comforting her son. 'Sorry. I let go of him. I don't know what to say. I just – I never thought. What's he like? What's he saying? Where's he been?'

'I don't know.'

'Mum and Dad – have you told them?'

'Not yet.'

'You have to tell them *now*. At once. Oh, poor things – they're going to die of the shock.'

'That's the thing – should I tell them on the phone or go and see them?'

'You can't hold something like that back.' There was a pause. 'Can you? I don't know. I mean – I don't know. Shall I come over?'

'Now?'

'Yes. Though I'd have to bring all the kids. I could wait till Jed gets back and then come. I have to come. I have to see him. You're sure it's him? Not some imposter? Christ, I think I'm going to explode with excitement. He just turned up?'

'Yes.'

'Did you recognize him?'

'Yes. Kind of. Yes, of course I did.'

'Phone Ben and Rory. No. I will. I have to tell someone or I'm going to pop. You phone Ben and I'll phone Rory. They'll know what to do. I need to tell Jed as well. Shit. Are you all right?'

'Yes. Are you?'

'I don't know what I am. Oh, darling Mia. Fuck. Does he know what he did?'

'I don't know.'

'No, sorry. I'm burbling. I don't know what I'm saying. When's he going to wake up?'

'I don't know.'

'Go. Ring Ben. Then tell me what he said and I'll tell you what Rory said and we'll make plans. I can come this evening. I've made a chocolate cake I can bring.'

'A cake?'

'You don't want to know about me bringing a cake, do you? No. 'Bye. 'Bye for now. Call me. Shit.'

Mia called Ben at work. He was in a meeting and would call back. She put the phone on the table and wandered from room to room. What was she supposed to do while Johnny slept? She opened the fridge door and looked critically inside – it was a depressing mixture of empty and a mess. She should buy food so that when he woke she could make him something. An English breakfast, perhaps – except she fancied he might be a vegetarian. Maybe a vegan. She should buy eggs, at least, and fresh bread – Vicky had eaten the last of the old loaf. And the house needed flowers.

She crept back into her room and took a random selection of clothes – jeans from the floor, a red T-shirt and pull-on ankle boots with a hole in one of the soles. She dressed in the bathroom, stopping halfway through to look at herself in the mirror that was still misted over from Johnny's deep hot bath. What had he thought when he'd seen her? Had he recognized her at once, or had she changed as much as him? When he had left she had been an underdeveloped teenager with braces, a flat chest, and the self-conscious ungainliness of someone who feels awkward in their body. Now she was a woman. She'd lost her braces, spiked her hair, pierced her nose, slept around, swallowed pills. Had he been disappointed by what he'd seen? Had he understood that what he had seen had been partly formed by what he had done? His absence was written on her face, and her life was shaped around the hole he had left behind. She blinked at herself in the mirror, lifted her chin.

She left a note on the table, just in case – 'Gone to the shops, back in a few mins' – then left, pulling the door shut firmly. But he might escape! She halted just outside, considering, then double locked the door. Now if he wanted to run away he would have to leave the house naked, out of a window.

A dozen eggs, a wholemeal loaf, spreadable butter, Marmite – he'd always loved Marmite – grapes, as if he was ill, clementines, bacon, mushrooms, tomatoes. A random assortment – too many things, but they didn't add up to anything. She stopped at the small florist and bought a bunch of dark crimson dahlias. There were several ladybirds on their leaves and she carefully picked them off, one by one, and settled them on the flowers in the buckets before hurrying on. Her mobile vibrated in her pocket.

'Ben? . . . Yes. Thanks. Johnny's here.' It came out in a tumble of words. 'Yes. He's asleep in my bed.' She started to feel like Goldilocks talking about Baby Bear. Porridge! That was what she should have bought. Porridge and milk and demerara sugar. She turned, mobile pressed to her ear, and ran back to the shop.

'OK, Mia. Listen. Is he all right?'

'Yes. I don't know. He's physically OK. I think, anyway. But I don't know. We haven't talked. He just was there on my doorstep. Ben?'

'It's OK. I'll come over – I can leave in an hour or so.'

'Shall I tell Isabel and Felix?'

'Don't do anything yet. I'll come over. Does Rory know?'

'Tamsin's calling him.'

'All right. Sit tight and I'll be there as soon as I can.'

'I don't know. What if he doesn't want everyone all at once?'

'You think I shouldn't come?'

'I don't know.' She stood in the aisle of cereals and closed her eyes, recalling the way he had looked as he stood in her doorway. 'I think he's so ashamed he can hardly bear it,' she said. 'Perhaps it took all of his courage to ring my bell. One of us is hard enough. He mustn't run away again.'

'Mm.' The lovely thing about Ben was that he never got offended. 'You could be right. OK. Talk to him when he wakes up, and then call me again. Just remember I'm here.'

'And will you liaise with Rory and Tamsin?'

'Sure.'

She remembered what Lucas had said. 'It's good, though. Right?'

'It's bloody amazing.'

Her mobile rang and she looked at the caller's name. Isabel. No. She couldn't talk to her mother. She would hear it in her voice. There was no one like Isabel for hearing what lay between the lines, in the throbbing silence. She ran back to the house, the bag of shopping jolting against her leg, terrified that he would be gone.

She made porridge, half milk and half water, just as Isabel always made it, adding a tiny pinch of salt, and stirring it over a low heat, watching the oats soften and the mixture gradually thicken. Porridge is comforting; lightly scrambled eggs on buttered toast are comforting; cigarettes are comforting. She opened the kitchen window and lit a cigarette; she'd lost count of how many she'd smoked since she had opened the door. She'd lost count of today, and control of it and sense of it. It pounded in her head and thundered in her heart; she felt dizzy with it. She also knew that this was only the first tremor of the quake and that what she was feeling and perceiving was like staring at the sun through layers and layers of gauze, its terrible brightness dimmed.

His yellow knapsack sat on the floor, beside the table, a toothbrush poking out of its side pocket. She lifted the bag and found it was surprisingly heavy; she poked its soft sides and felt hard objects inside: books, perhaps. Was this all he owned?

At last, there was the sound of a door, a loo flushing, footsteps on the stairs. She readied herself. There he was, wrapped in the towel she'd put out for him. His chest was hairless, concave and white. She could tell the shape of his T-shirt from the pale upper arm and the brown lower.

'It sounds stupid,' he said, 'but I don't have anything to put on.'

'I threw away your clothes.'

'Oh. They were pretty rank.'

'At least without clothes you won't be able to run away,' she said, narrowing her eyes at him. He flinched.

'I'll get you a dressing-gown. It's Lucas's. You can wear that for now. Sit down.'

She ran upstairs, yanked the robe that Lucas kept at hers, returned to the kitchen and chucked it at him.

'Put that on. Tea or coffee?'

'Tea. Please. Thank you.'

'I've made porridge. Do you still like porridge?'

'Yes.'

'I've got eggs as well. And bread and things.'

'Porridge is good for now.'

She poured some into a bowl and put it in front of him, with the packet of demerara sugar and a spoon. He ate very slowly, as though it was painful to swallow. His wrists were so thin it hurt her to look at them.

'Have I seen you?' she asked, once he'd finished.

'I don't know. Perhaps.'

'Like a ghost,' she said. 'I saw you and then you were gone. Have you seen me?'

He met her eyes, although she could see what an effort it was for him to do that. 'Yes. Three, four times. But I found I couldn't –' And stopped.

'There's some more porridge in the pan. Do you want it?'

'Yes, please.'

'I haven't told them yet. I've told Tamsin and Ben and Rory, but not them.'

He stared at her with his sore blue eyes. 'I can't,' he

whispered. He covered his face with his hand; grazed knuckles, she saw. 'Please.'

'It's all right. You don't need to say anything. You don't need to do anything. I won't ask you. Eat your porridge. Drink your tea while it's still hot. I wish there was a garden here so you could sit in it. But we don't have a garden. Lucas does.'

'Lucas?'

'It doesn't matter. Not at the moment.'

Not for the first time, Mia wished she had something practical to do with her hands. She should cook, or draw, or make mobiles, or pots. Knit, sew, weave, carve – be one of those calming people who bent over the silk thread, the sliver of wood, stirred the pot or pummelled the dough, attentive but at the same time occupied. She sat at the table opposite Johnny and gazed at him, then looked away. He was too raw for her; words were too blunt and hard and he was already covered with bruises.

'What did they all say?'

'Things like "Fuck", and "Christ" and "Are you sure?".'

'Are you sure?'

'Ha! No. Of course not.'

'You look – nice. All grown-up.'

Mia bit back the urge to say that, yes, well, it has been almost seven years.

'Thank you.'

'I told you you'd be beautiful one day.'

Mia felt a rip in her chest. 'Oh, God, Johnny.'

'Sorry.'

'No. It's just that – where've you been? All these years, where were you? You don't need to answer that.'

'I will tell you.'

'But not now.'

He shook his head from side to side.

'I need to ring the others. What shall I say?'

'I don't know.'

'Do you want to see them?'

'Not all at once.'

'OK. I need to get you some clothes. If you promise . . .'

'I won't go. Not without saying.'

'You promise?'

'Yes.'

'I could ask Ben for some clothes. I think you're about the same size. Would you see Ben?'

'Maybe.'

'Just for a few minutes, if that's what you want.'

'OK.'

'You go and sit in the living room – you're shivering. Are you cold?'

'I am a bit. I don't know why.'

'Sit in the living room and I'll get a blanket, and you can – I'll put some music on. Just sit and have music. I'll call Ben.'

'Mia?'

She stopped in the doorway. 'Yes?'

'Just – I don't know. Words are no good.'

'It's all right.'

'I've thought about you.'

'Have you?' Not as much as I've thought about you.

'Not a day has gone by without me thinking of you.'

Then why, why, why? She nodded at him. 'Ditto,' she managed gruffly.

'Do you still hate lifts?'

'Yes.'

He sat slumped in a chair covered with a blanket and she put a CD on for him, hesitating over her choice and in the end selecting some old blues music. Then she rang Ben and arranged for him to come over. She emailed Rory and Tamsin and said she would call them later, when she knew better what was happening. She sat in the kitchen with a mug of tea and made a list of some of the things that Johnny had missed since being away.

Bernard had died.

Their next-door-neighbour had died, as had his soft-hearted dog.

Miranda had dementia and had become foul-mouthed and occasionally violent.

Tamsin had married a man he had never met or heard of.

Ben had married Gabriella, after years of separation.

Rory had lost his job and was a house-father while Helen worked.

Leah was dying of cancer.

He had six nephews and nieces.

His niece Lucy could read, write and do rudimentary multiplication and division.

Felix had had a nervous breakdown, and aged twenty years in seven. He had become a Quaker, though he still did not believe in God.

Isabel's hair was turning grey and she wore glasses most of the time.

*His uncle Graham had lost his hair but grown a wispy
    beard in compensation.*
There was a new government

– but he probably knew that.

*The old tree at the bottom of the garden had had honey
    fungus and been chopped down.*
*The sea had further eroded the coast so the place where they
    used to swim had now disappeared.*
His friend Alex had become a policeman.
His friend Will

– she scratched that out.

His friend Baxter had a son whose name was Johnny.

Ben took Johnny in his arms and hugged him. He gave
him a bagful of clothes he insisted he never wore, and
some new underwear he'd picked up on the way. Johnny
put on a pair of jeans that he kept up with a belt, a soft
blue shirt and a loose cardigan. He slid his feet into trainers that were a size too big for him. Ben took a stripy
cotton scarf out of the bag and wrapped it round his
neck. The three of them went for a walk round the block,
with Johnny in the middle. He was being protected and
guarded, a cosseted prisoner between his solicitous gaol-
ers, though he didn't look capable of making a dash for it.
It was a golden day, and every so often he stopped in his
tracks and gave a small sigh; Mia couldn't tell if it was one
of contentment or distress. They bought food for supper –
wild mushrooms, fresh coriander, assorted small salad
leaves that were still speckled with soil, risotto rice and

Parmesan – then slowly returned. Johnny stumbled as he walked; he was like a blind man feeling his way. Mia tucked her arm through his and drew close; there was such a heavy sadness in her, such a weight of anxiety and loss and love that she could barely move.

Chapter Thirty-two

'Will you come for supper?'

'Of course, if that's what you want.'

'I do.'

'How is he?'

'I don't know.'

They cooked together – Mia, Lucas and Johnny. Lucas, who loved to cook, instructed them all. He insisted that Johnny wear Vicky's brightly striped apron to protect his clothes, and sat him at the table with cloves of garlic and a large onion, telling him to peel and chop them; after that, he put him in charge of wiping the mushrooms and slicing them finely. Johnny seemed content or, at least, his face didn't seem about to crumble into an ash of despair. No one said anything, apart from a cheery few words about the job in hand. Mia stood over the saucepan and let the steam curl into her face. The rice fried in the onions, then melted into the stock that Lucas had prepared. Every so often, he would pause behind Mia and lay his hand on the small of her back in reassurance. His dark eyes were alert, flickering between brother and sister.

Vicky arrived as Mia was washing the leaves and Lucas was grating Parmesan. 'Hi!' she exclaimed. 'This smells good.' She screwed up her nose like an appreciative rabbit. 'Hello there, Lucas.' She pecked his cheeks. Over the past few months, Vicky and Lucas had become fast, unlikely friends. She turned to Johnny. 'Hello,' she said. 'So you're the brother.'

'I told her this morning that you'd been away and were staying for a while,' said Mia, swiftly.

Vicky thrust out her hand and Johnny took it in his, holding it for longer than necessary, as if uncertain of the etiquette.

'Where've you been?' asked Vicky, pulling back a chair and settling down for a chat. 'Anywhere interesting?'

'Oh – around,' said Johnny, squinting a bit. 'Scotland, some parts of Europe.'

Mia, standing at the sink, tried to look casual.

'Cool,' Vicky said. 'Did you go to Italy? I love Italy.'

'No.'

'Mia and Lucas were there recently, weren't you, Mia?'

'Yes.'

'Holland, Belgium, France, Spain,' said Johnny, in a mumbling rush. He threw a stricken glance at Mia and dropped his eyes again.

'Were you working?'

'Kind of.'

'Shall we eat?' asked Lucas. 'Here, Johnny, put out the plates, can you? And there are glasses in the cupboard behind you. I've bought a bottle of wine – I thought we deserved it.'

'No wine for me and I can only have a few bites of risotto,' said Vicky. 'Then I'm off out.' She looked at Johnny curiously, then turned to Lucas. 'You should paint his portrait. He's got the kind of face you like. He does these paintings,' she went on to Johnny. 'Watercolour sketches, really. He keeps saying he'll do mine but he never quite gets round to it, do you, Lukey? Maybe that's a good thing. They're not exactly flattering. They're very moody – washes of sombre colours. The ones he's done of Mia make her look quite wild.'

'You paint?' asked Johnny. He hadn't started eating yet, though he had at last lifted his fork.

'Not to earn a living by,' said Lucas. 'But yes. And I'd like to paint you one day – if you wanted me to.'

Johnny blushed, and Mia suddenly remembered how as a boy he used to blush readily, a flood of colour suffusing his freckled face. 'I'm not sure I'm ready to see myself as you see me,' he said quietly.

'There speaks a wise man,' said Vicky, standing up suddenly. 'Now I'm going to put my glad rags on. Sorry to rush. That was delicious. Mm.' She took a gulp of wine from Mia's glass, then kissed the top of her head. 'You're quiet,' she said. 'Are you all right?'

'Fine.' Although an extraordinary weariness had settled on her.

'Good. See you later. Or tomorrow, probably.'

After they had finished, Mia said, 'I have to talk about Isabel and Felix, Johnny.'

He turned to her, shielding his eyes with one hand as though he was looking into direct sunlight. 'Yes.'

'They have to know.'

'Yes.'

'I was thinking – we could go over tomorrow, Saturday. I think it's better than telling them by phone.'

'But –'

'I'll ring up and say I'm coming and we'll get a cab from the station and –'

'I just turn up?' he said. 'Just walk in? How?'

'Or,' said Lucas, 'how about if I borrow Alvin's car? I'm sure he won't be using it. Then I can drive you both. You can go in and tell them, Mia, and then I can bring Johnny in. Is that better?'

'I don't know. Johnny?'

'Yes,' he said. 'But –' He stopped, bending forwards across the table and covering half his face with the hand that had shielded his eyes.

'But?'

'I'm so ashamed,' he whispered. 'So very very very ashamed. Before I went away, I felt I was drowning, Mia – drowning in myself, in the black waters surging away inside me. I don't want to be melodramatic or sound as if I'm not facing up to what I did, but it's the only way I can describe it. Does it sound ridiculous to you?'

'It sounds depressed.' This from Lucas.

'Yeah. I guess that's one word for it.'

'But, Johnny, why couldn't you have come to us for help?' Mia heard her voice, high and accusing. She swallowed and said more soberly, 'We would have helped.'

'I know. I know that now – but then I didn't. I didn't know anything. I didn't even know how to breathe properly, or put one foot in front of the other, or make words come out of my mouth, stand upright. And the longer I stayed away, the more ashamed I became. I thought I'd never be able to come home because I didn't want to face it. It was eating me alive.'

'Well, you came.'

'Yes. Tomorrow, you say.'

'Will you be able to do it? If you can't, you have to say.'

'I'll do it.'

He stood beside her and listened to the conversation. She almost believed that Isabel would somehow be able to see him.

'Hello – Mum? Mama? It's me, Mia . . . Yes . . . No, I'm fine – but I wondered, are you and Dad around tomorrow? Lucas and I thought we might visit. Midday-ish? . . . Yes . . . No, honestly, nothing's wrong . . . Good. I'll see you then.'

She put the phone down: Isabel could always tell when she was hiding something.

That night, Mia and Lucas slept on the living-room floor on a double Lilo that slowly deflated. Mia told Johnny he had to get a good sleep, but the real reason was, she was frightened that in the small hours, on the threshold of his self-revelation, he would leave. She slept fitfully and woke often, thinking she heard a floorboard creaking, a footstep coming furtively down the stairs.

And then it was morning. He was still there. Lucas had gone to collect the car. She made Johnny have a bath and then she tried to tidy his hair a bit. His bruise was, if anything, more alarming than it had been the previous day; his lips were dry and cracked. She pushed tea at him, made him toast with Marmite. He would have to do.

Chapter Thirty-three

Isabel had known on the phone that something was up. Her first thought was that Lucas and Mia had separated – but Mia had said they were coming together. Perhaps she and Lucas had an announcement – that they were moving in together, that they were getting married, that Mia was pregnant. Any of those things would be wonderful: Isabel loved Lucas, and she loved the way he had changed Mia, softening her, restoring some of the trust she seemed over the years to have lost.

She picked chrysanthemums from the garden, and some late-flowering yellow roses. She dispatched Felix into town to buy bread and smoked mackerel and some of the creamy blue cheese to which Lucas was partial. She and Lucas sometimes exchanged emails about recipes, and he'd given chilli and aubergine plants to Felix for his allotment greenhouse, grown from seed on his kitchen windowsill. He'd painted a few quick portraits of her the last time they had visited, just before he and Mia had gone away on holiday together, in which her grief had seemed exposed. She had once even taken him into Johnny's room and shown him – *look, see how deranged we mothers can be* – the shirts hanging in the wardrobe, some of which she had bought only recently, the old photographs on the walls.

At ten to twelve, when Felix and Isabel were both in the

kitchen together, unpacking the shopping, Mia walked up the drive. Her chin was up and her face looked pale and stern. Isabel saw her from the window – yes, she had been right: her daughter was here to tell her something particular. But what? She couldn't work out if it was good news or bad she saw in her expression. Her heart fluttered. Drying her hands on a tea towel, she went to the front door and opened it.

'This is such a treat,' she said. 'Where's the car? Where's Lucas?'

'Is Dad inside?'

'Felix? Yes. Mia, what is it?' Now she felt scared.

'Let me tell both of you together.'

'What's happened?'

'I'll tell you inside.'

She had tried to rehearse these words. When Felix joined them, she looked from one to the other, drew a deep breath, and said, 'I'm not just here with Lucas.' Before she had finished she saw the terrible hope flare in Isabel's eyes. 'Johnny is here.'

It was like seeing a bizarre, choreographed dance – both Felix and Isabel, at the same moment, raised their hands and clutched at their hearts. Then Felix held on to the back of the chair and closed his eyes. He looked like an ageing priest at prayer. Isabel's mouth opened in a silent scream and her face seemed to collapse on itself; she was barely recognizable to Mia any longer. She looked haggard and terrifying.

Mia blinked away her tears. 'He's in the car,' she said.

Isabel ran. Out of the kitchen, into the hall, through the front door and down the driveway, barefoot over the sharp gravel, her hair streaming behind her. Mia stumbled after her. Isabel stood on the road staring in both directions.

'Johnny!' she yelled, high and keening. 'Johnny! Johnny! Johnny!' So loud that it must surely rip the skin off the back of her throat. 'Johnny! Johnny! Johnny!' The syllables bounced and rippled in the autumn air.

Down the road came Lucas, in Alvin's rusty car, drawing to a halt now.

'Johnny! Johnny!'

His face through the windscreen, blurring and shimmering with her tears. Like a spectre, he wavered. Isabel clutched her throat. Running, running, feet on fire.

The door was open now and she was holding him, his face in her hands, her lips on his hair, her voice in his ear. She couldn't bring him close enough. She held him off to make sure and then pulled him back to her.

'Mama?'

'I knew you'd come home, I knew you'd come. I knew. It was our fault, all our fault. You must remember that. Look at you, my lovely son, all thin and – oh, what's happened to your cheek?' She straightened up and stood, shining down on him. 'You are so very welcome,' she said, with a shaky attempt at pulling herself together. 'Thank you.'

A car drew up behind them, beeped its horn impatiently.

'We're blocking the way,' said Lucas. 'I'll just park in your drive, shall I?'

'Yes, yes. Of course.'

She hobbled after the car, as if she was scared it would

409

drive away again, and Mia ran to join her. As the car pulled up, she saw Felix standing at the front door, his face like a cliff against which too many waves had battered. Isabel pulled the car door open and helped Johnny out. He looked, thought Mia, like a convict with his badly cut hair and his bruised cheek, his grazed knuckles and his stricken face. She went round the car to Lucas and said urgently, 'He's not going to be able to bear this.'

'Look,' said Lucas.

Johnny was standing in front of Felix now, who stared at him for a moment and then opened his arms. His son stepped into them and they stood clasped together while Isabel stood near, wringing her hands and weeping.

'Shall we go for a walk?'

'Yes. Please.'

They drove to the coast – not the sandy, acceptable beach, but the shifting estuarine coast of salt marshes, mudflats and stilt-legged seabirds. It was deserted except for an old man down at the water's edge, looking for something – maybe samphire or whelks. Mia held Lucas's hand and they wove their way between rocks and shallow pools, past an old Martello tower that had tipped sideways, along the eroding cliffs. The sea was gradually withdrawing, leaving wet stretches of mud on which sun glinted, and small pools sucked and puckered its surface.

Mia felt enormously tired and anxious – and if she felt like that, what must Johnny feel? Gradually, he would have to meet everyone, all the people who'd searched for him, mourned him, given up on him, let him recede into a dim memory. Every time he saw someone for the first time, he would watch them measuring him against the eighteen-year-old he had been, and he would feel the insistent weight of their questions, even if they weren't articulated.

'I feel I've aged a decade in the last couple of days,' she said to Lucas.

'Or aged seven years.'

She smiled. 'Maybe. For the first time I can begin to understand why it was so hard for him to come back. As soon as he'd been away for a certain time, it must have felt like he was standing on the other side of a rushing river.'

'He'll need help.'

'They'll suffocate him.'

'Maybe not.'

'It would almost be better if they were angry with him. Forgiveness can be awfully hard to bear.'

Lucas regarded her wryly. 'For someone like you,' he remarked. 'But you're not Johnny.'

Chapter Thirty-four

Isabel concentrated on the physical fact of him. She touched his puffy bruise with her fingertips and asked him if it hurt – not how he got it. She noticed the missing tooth and said she should call a dentist on Monday to make an appointment. She thought he had lost weight but maybe grown slightly. She led him round the garden as though he were an invalid newly risen from his bed, pointing out the things he might not notice: the new flowerbeds, the stump where the tree had once stood, the crimson dahlias that were flowering well this autumn.

Inside the house, he looked dazed. His eyes flicked from the familiar to the new: he stopped in front of the array of photographs in the living room and put out a finger. 'Tell me,' he said, in a hoarse voice.

'That's Jed,' said Isabel, trying to sound neutral. 'He's a very nice man and he's made the world of difference to Tamsin. You'll like him, I'm sure. That's Meredith, that's Seamus and that's little Finn. She certainly did it all in a rush, but it suits her – you know Tamsin.' She faltered slightly, colouring, and then continued, 'And these three are Rory's lot – you remember Lucy, of course, but she's eight now. And here are Greta and Dan. Quite a handful . . .' Her voice trailed away.

'So you're a real granny!'

'Yes. Who'd have thought it? I don't feel old enough – who ever does?'

'My room.' Johnny stared out of the window. 'I mean, the room I used to have.'

'Your room is still your room.'

She had a sudden horrible vision of it as a frozen shrine. She had gone too far – she always went too far, never learnt from her multiple mistakes, seemed doomed to repeat her past over and over again. She had an urge to run up ahead of him and mess everything up a bit, scatter papers and books, gather armfuls of old clothes and stuff them out of sight.

'Can I go up there for a bit?'

'Of course. Do you want me to . . . ?'

'Maybe I could just be by myself for a while. If that's OK,' he added carefully.

'Yes. Of course.'

She wanted to say, *You're not a guest*, but stopped herself. Words felt dangerous, like barbed wire in her mouth, or like small bombs packed with hidden meanings. He was peeled and stinging: everything could hurt him.

She watched him as he made his way up the stairs. He used to take them two at a time, springing upwards; now he went slowly, his hand on the banister steering him.

Johnny hesitated for some time by the door, then pushed it open. He stepped just inside and looked around, taking in small segments of the room, like a camera focusing, clicking, recording. His old self was waiting for him here: in the books on the shelves, in the pens and pencils – the

very ones he'd taken off to university and Isabel, on collecting them, had carefully replaced them in the cracked
mug that had stood on his desk since he was fifteen or
so – and in the tennis racquet leaning up against the wall.
His shoes were lined up. The same shoes he had worn
when he was eighteen – some were old and shabby and
bore the shiny imprint of his feet on their insoles.

He shivered, feeling slightly sick. His folders and files
were stacked up neatly. There were his notebooks, his
writing on their pages. Formulae, scattered comments.
He'd been so busy and purposeful in this room, and now
he couldn't think for the life of him what he'd do in here
except sit with his knees drawn up to his chin, staring out
of the window at the garden full of autumn.

He took a few small steps further into the room, the
hairs on the back of his neck prickling, then reached out
and pulled open his wardrobe. He ran his hands through
the clothes that hung there, then saw that a few of the
shirts were new, with their price tags still on them. Isabel
must have bought them for him. There was a plastic bag in
the bottom of the wardrobe and he peered into it and saw
it was full of little presents, wrapped up in bright paper
and bearing his name. Happy birthday, Happy Christmas.
He pushed the bag to the back of the cupboard, shut the
door and closed his eyes. He had walked, run, got on trains
and buses and boats, stuck out his thumb for passing cars;
he had slept in ditches and huts and strangers' rooms, in
doorways and on lonely beaches – and he had ended back
here, after all, with his eighteen-year-old self.

There was a faint sound behind him and he froze. Then
turned. On the bed, curled neatly round himself in a nar-

row tortoiseshell ball, lay Digby, who opened his yellow eyes and stared at him. There was a tiny whimper, and Johnny couldn't tell if it came from him or his ancient cat, with his torn ear and his rickety bones. Digby lifted up one paw and licked it delicately, then swiped it across his face, his eyes still staring at Johnny, but without judgement. Johnny stepped forward and stood staring down at him.

'I thought you'd be dead long ago,' he said softly.

Digby yawned; Johnny could see the pink tunnel of his throat. He knelt down and put out a finger and the cat nudged at it.

'I'm so sorry I left you,' continued Johnny. 'I've thought about you. Often, at night, I'd wake up with a start from a dream and think you were there, like you used to be. My old friend.'

At last, tears stood in his eyes. His throat hurt and the terrible boulder in his chest loosened slightly. He put his forehead gently on Digby's insubstantial body.

'I can talk to you,' he went on, his foolish words muffled by the cat's fur, which smelt exactly as it always had, slightly musty. 'You're the only one I can talk to yet. You don't feel sorry for me, or angry with me, or scared for me, do you? I haven't broken your heart.'

He lifted his head and smiled. If anyone had been looking at him at that moment, they would have said he suddenly resembled the boy who had gone.

'What am I going to do?' he said. 'What on earth am I going to do now?'

Felix had taken himself off into his study with one fixed purpose – to hide his archive, which all of a sudden had struck him as a monstrous obsession, a vain and futile act of holding grief at bay and pretending he had control of an event that had rolled like a great unstoppable flood through their lives. As soon as he had set eyes on Johnny – his shy young son, his freckled child – his heart had ballooned in his chest with such violence that he had thought he must sit down on the gravel drive and weep. As Isabel, her face ravaged, had guided him from the car, he had had a vision of himself as such an arrogant and egotistical fool that he had tottered, held out his arms to his son in a gesture that begged for forgiveness, absolution. All these years of lying in bed with his eyes fixed on the ceiling, of sitting in his lair hoarding evidence he knew would lead nowhere, of neglecting Isabel, or turning away from his other children, of blindly running on his treadmill of lanes, of stolidly digging the soil in his allotment, of moving rigidly away from the outstretched hands of friends and colleagues, of steering himself along the tight little corridor of resistance to pure sorrow – just to avoid the pain that had carved itself into him, line by line, however he had armoured himself against it.

He had accumulated so much material that he didn't know where to start. He gathered up the scrapbooks in a pile on his desk, then started hurriedly to take the box files off the shelves. There was a chart pinned to the wall that showed how many people had been reported missing, year on year, and he tore it off, leaving the pins stuck into the plasterboard. He had to hide it all until he could put it in a box and take it to the dump, he thought. He couldn't risk leaving it out for the bin-men to recycle. He pulled open the large lower drawers of his desk and started pulling out bills and receipts to create space.

'Leave it, Dad.'

Felix spun round, knocking one of the box files to the ground. Its contents spread in front of them: Johnny's face stared up at them on yellowing paper; the faces of dozens of other young people that Felix had cut out over the years. 'I just thought . . .' he began, and then gave up. 'I think I went a bit mad,' he said. 'A compulsive collector of missing people. As if it would make any difference.'

'I'd like to see it.'

'No. Anyway, there's so much. Anything significant is lost in here – when you've got everything, you've got nothing. I tell my students that.'

'OK. But I'd still like to have a look.'

'Now?'

'No. But don't hide it away. Don't hide anything. Please.'

'You're sure?'

'Do you imagine it will make me feel better about what I've done if I don't confront it?'

'No.'

'And do you imagine if you don't mention it, if you try and shield me from things, that I won't think about it – that I haven't thought about it, day after day after day?'

'No.'

'So don't hide all that stuff. I don't want to be protected.'

'Did you see any of it?'

'What?'

'The posters, the leaflets and flyers, the newspaper coverage, the stuff I did for radio and local TV, the letters we

417

sent to you via the Missing Persons Helpline, the Facebook page.'

'No.'

'Nothing?'

'No.'

'Would it have made any difference?'

'I don't know.'

'Will you ever tell me why?'

'Yes,' Johnny said. 'I will. I owe it to you and to Mama. Not yet.'

'Of course.'

Johnny wandered over to the piano and pressed a few keys randomly. There was an odd little smile on his face. 'Did you hate me?'

'Hate you? Johnny –'

'Why not? I hated myself. I knew what you'd be going through. I knew what I was doing. The worse I knew you'd be feeling, the more impossible it became for me to come back.'

'Why did you, then?'

'I'm not sure. There were times when I thought I'd never be able to. I didn't have the courage, nowhere near. One thing I've learnt about myself over these years is what a coward I am.' He grimaced and pressed another note whose bright sound hung in the air for a few seconds. 'I had a friend who died.'

Felix didn't say anything or look at his son – he sensed that one gesture would shut Johnny up entirely.

'Ali. She went swimming one day and she never came back. I don't know if she meant to or not. You can't tell with people – you think you know them and then you discover you don't. We're all mysteries, to each other and to ourselves; that's what I've come to think. She had had a messy and sad life, always, but lately she'd seemed better, and then, just when no one expected it, she was dead.'

Felix went on looking out of the window, half turned away from Johnny. He wondered if this friend had been a lover, but couldn't ask.

'And I thought –' Johnny stopped dead; his face became blank. 'I just thought, It's now or never.'

Felix nodded and turned his eyes on Johnny. He felt he should say something in return, about himself. 'I have been going to Quaker meetings,' he said.

'Do you believe in God now?'

'No. But I believe in Quaker meetings. To sit among kind strangers and not have to utter a word.'

'Ah.'

'I have abandoned your mother to her own grief,' Felix heard himself say. It sounded faintly Biblical.

Johnny gazed at him. His pupils were very large, even though the room was filled with the lovely thick light of September. Then he sat down on the floor in front of the piano and pulled his knees up under his chin. He continued to regard Felix fixedly, and after a while Felix began to feel he wasn't being stared at, but stared into. He bent down and began to gather the scattered papers from the floor and put them back into their boxes.

'When I was away,' Johnny said, 'I didn't call myself Johnny, or not until the end. I called myself Michael. You would have thought I could have chosen a more interesting name, wouldn't you?'

'Michael?'

'Yes. I guess I just didn't want to be myself. I thought I could start over. You never can, though, can you?'

'I don't know,' Felix managed. 'I used to know things like that, but now I don't. All that awful certainty about life.' He hesitated, then lowered himself to the floor to sit beside Johnny, but didn't look at him, staring instead out of the window.

'I met Fergal,' he said. The name throbbed in the air, and he half wished he could take back the words.

Johnny didn't speak, just pressed his chin into his knees and waited.

'Twice. The first time with your mother. The second –' he swallowed. 'I went there alone. Your mother doesn't know. Maybe I can tell her now, I don't know.'

'What happened?' The question was quiet, like a murmur.

'Oh.' Felix made a vague gesture with his hand. 'That's not so important.' *A foul house, a filthy man swollen with other people's secrets; a fist in his stomach, a boot in his groin, spit on his face; a sense of such shame, such horror, that the pollution of it had never been washed away* . . . 'But I just felt so – so terrible for you, Johnny, that you had turned to him.'

'I'm sorry.' Johnny seemed to be shrinking beside him.

'No! No, that's not it at all. I just don't understand. He was so – so *horrible*. Why did you –' He felt his son flinch and stopped himself. 'Forgive me. You don't want to go through any of this now.'

Johnny closed his eyes. 'I was all at sea, Dad,' he whispered. 'I didn't know what to do. Everything was wrong inside me. I can't explain to you. I would wake in the morning and not know how to move, let alone get out of bed. Even the air felt heavy, pressing on me, pinning me down. Everything was so grey and dirty and dull, and I was grey and dirty as well, putrid. Nothing had meaning. Not even you and Mama. I didn't want anything or like anything or hope for anything. Except to stop the pain.'

Felix wanted to put a hand out and touch Johnny on the shoulder, to let him know that he understood. But he didn't move, stayed quite still, waiting for him to finish.

'I know it'll sound senseless to you, but Fergal offered me a way out. He said if I trusted him, he could help. I just gave myself up to him, I suppose. Put myself in his hands. I know what he's like. I know he's bad. He's got an ugly heart, Dad, and he knows exactly where your weaknesses are. It's like he can slide himself into your darkest places, like a stain.' Johnny gave a violent shudder, rocking forward, with his arms clutching his legs and his cheek against his bony knees. 'But he said he could save me and I wanted to be saved. I didn't know how else to go on.'

'It's OK, Johnny. It's OK.'

'It's not.'

'You could have come to us.'

'I couldn't. I couldn't do that.' He sighed. 'I probably should have gone to a doctor, though, something like that. It didn't seem possible at the time.'

'Here.' Felix wrapped an arm around Johnny's shoulders and Johnny curled into his father, lying against him with his cheek pressed into Felix's shirt. Felix kissed his son's damp forehead and tightened his embrace. He opened his mouth to say something, but there weren't words for this, so he simply waited until Johnny sat upright.

Then they both heard Isabel in the kitchen, the clatter

of pans. She seemed to be singing to herself, although her voice shook, kept missing the notes.

'She'll be cooking,' said Felix, standing up and holding out his hand to pull Johnny up too. 'It's what she does, always. If you're sad or tired or lonely or cross or guilty or confused, she cooks for you.'

'There must have been a lot of cooking in this house then,' said Johnny.

'Lots of cooking and not much eating. Eating's never the point – the point is making something. However bad things are, bread still rises in the oven. That's what your mother would say.'

'There are worse philosophies.'

'Indeed.'

In the kitchen, Isabel whisked eggs and sugar together until the mixture was pale and frothy. She weighed flour and sifted it, letting her fingers feel its silky fineness. *Now I can start my flower shop*, and *Now I can leave Felix if I want.* She didn't know if she would do either of these things. Her feelings, too, needed to be sifted and left to settle for a while.

She thought: *I can walk by the sea shore without keening. I can stand in a crowd without searching for his face. I can wake in the night and not have to go through the cruel process of remembering all over again. I can feel struck by gladness and not feel harrowed by my brief forgetfulness. I can pick up my grandchildren without wanting to weep into their squashy, sweet-smelling bodies. I can stop seeing ghosts. I no longer have to be haunted.*

She broke squares of dark chocolate into a glass bowl that she settled on top of a saucepan of boiling water.

Through the window, she saw Mia and Lucas arrive back, stepping out of the battered little car. She saw how they were talking intently to each other, and how, walking towards the house, they touched each other on the arm, the shoulder, for comfort. It had been such an arduous seven years for all of them, a journey through rocky, sunless places and no end in sight – just a blind, clumsy stumble into the unknown.

In the middle of the night, in its small fearsome hours, Isabel woke, as she always did, lying in her bed with her eyes wide open, straining for glimmers of light in the silent darkness. Felix slept beside her, his breathing uneven but deep. She slid from her bed and crept on to the landing, turning on the light. Then she silently made her way towards Johnny's room. She knew he had gone again and that the closed door would push open onto a void so black and deep that this time it would swallow her up for ever.

She opened the door and stared into the depths of the room. She took a few steps and stopped to listen but could hear no sound from the bed. She put out her hand and felt for his body and found it, motionless under the covers. Her eyes adjusted to the gloom and now she could make him out, the ragged head on the pillow, the uncurling fist near his bruised cheek and, beside it, Digby. If she bent very close, as she used to when he was tiny in his cot, she could hear the faint sound of his breathing. And just as she had when he was a defenceless baby, she thought what a miracle that was.

Chapter Thirty-five

He wrote by hand, in a fountain pen he had bought especially for the purpose, and on thick, cream-coloured paper with a watermark. On each sheet, he put his full address in the top right-hand corner, as he had been taught at primary school, and the date on the left. Each letter took him a long time, often hours. He sat at the table outside, in the warmth of the Indian summer, and would often pause to look down the garden to where Isabel worked. She was wearing a battered broad-brimmed straw hat that she had had ever since he could remember, and old canvas trousers, rolled up to her knees. She rose and dipped among the flowers. Sometimes she turned her head and glanced at him, reassuring herself that he was still there.

Johnny filled his pen with ink, wiped it carefully with a piece of kitchen paper, then began.

Dear Will,

Perhaps I should phone you, text you, Facebook you, come knocking at your door, instead of writing you a letter like this. I can't begin to tell you how many times I've thought of finding you over the years. I've had conversations with you in my head. I've talked to you out loud. I've dreamt about you, and sometimes they were horrible dreams but sometimes they were really good ones. Dream as memory, dream as hope. Football and poker and tennis

and music and playing up in science lessons with Mr Lowry,
arguing about politics, talking about girls, and mostly just sitting
around at your house or mine, in groups or just the two of us.
Knowing you were my best mate, would always be my best mate.
Johnny and Will. Growing up together, I guess – that's what we
did, isn't it?

I'm writing because I don't have the guts to talk to you straight
yet, let alone stand face to face and look you in the eyes. I'm scared of
what I would see there. I did a terrible thing to you. I know it was a
long time ago. Maybe it doesn't matter so much to you any more –
but it matters to me. I always thought I was completely trustworthy.
To be honest, I despised people who cheated on their girlfriends or let
down a friend. I thought I was better than them, deeper and truer or
something – and then it turned out I was just the same.

There are lots of reasons why I went away. Too many to write
in a letter, and I don't even understand them myself yet and
I don't know if I ever fully will. But one of them was because
I didn't want to be that person. I guess you could say I was running
away from myself and – surprise, surprise – I never quite
escaped. I followed me and now I've come home, and I'm still me
and I want to say sorry to you.

I am very, very sorry indeed for what I did, all those years ago.
And I am very sorry for not having the courage just to come and
tell you and face the consequences. And I am very sorry that you
spent so much time looking for me the way you did (Mum has told
me everything about it), and missing me. I am very sorry for all
the hurt I caused you. Usually when relationships go wrong, both
people involved are to blame but this was all me. You were the best
friend anyone could have, and (apart from the time you broke my
little finger) you never put a foot wrong. I put my whole life wrong.
I have regretted it every single day.

*If you want to see me, get in touch. I will completely under-
stand if you don't — and whatever, I wish you all good things in
your life.*

Love, Johnny

*PS I know about you and Mia — she's really fine about
everything now, and is happy in her life, but maybe you know that
anyway.*

*PPS I've probably forgotten how to play, but if you ever fancy
a game of tennis . . .*

*PPPS When I wrote 'Love, Johnny' I meant lots and lots of
love.*

He blew on the two pages to make sure the ink was dry,
then inserted them into the envelope and wrote Will's
address neatly on the front, gumming it shut before he
could change his mind. He turned to the next letter. It was
very short:

Dear Zoë,

*I hope this is still the right address for you. You might have
already heard that I am back. I have no idea how much what
happened between us has meant to you. But I want to tell you that
I never meant to hurt you, to drag you into my own chaos, to
make you feel disproportionately guilty, or disrespect you or cause
you harm in any way. We used to be close and I have happy
memories of us all together. I don't want to pollute that. I have
done a terrible thing, but you should not have had to suffer for it.
So I am sorry, Zoë. Good luck with everything, and take care,*

Johnny xxx

Dear Granny,

*I am going to come and see you soon, but I wanted to write to you
before that. Dad says you have been extremely angry with me, and
I think that of course you should be. I don't want to explain
myself really, and I certainly will never try to justify myself, but
I just want to say that I know I have done wrong to my parents and
I know how much they have suffered. I also know how much you
have supported Dad through all of this — he says that you were
the only person he could bear to have around sometimes.*

*To tell the truth, I was always a bit scared of you — you seemed
so indomitable. But I always thought you were an amazing
person. Now I know what an amazing mother you are as well.
A pillar of strength and love, Dad said. I wanted you to know
that.*

*I will call in a few days and I hope you will agree to see me.
I can't make amends, but I want to hug you again.*

*With lots of love,
Johnny*

She probably wouldn't be able to understand what he'd
written, he thought; perhaps she wouldn't even be able to
read the words. His pen was running out of ink, so he
refilled it.

Dear Mr Lowry,

*I know my mother told you I was back. I heard you helped look
for me. Thank you. Wherever I have been, I have looked up at the
stars and been comforted by them. I have you to thank for that —
and for so much more. I am applying to university again for next*

September — but you will always be my best teacher. All my mistakes were my own,

Johnny

Dear Leah,

Mum has told me that you are dying. I have hesitated for many minutes before writing that word. It seems too enormous and implacable, and you have always been so present and so very alive. But I know you have never shied away from truths, however big or hard. It is how I always remember you: speaking out, calling things by their proper name. A woman of courage.

Mum has talked to me about how you and Jenny have carried her through these years. I have brought her anguish, but you have brought her solace. You have shown what true friendship is. From the bottom of my heart, I thank you.

Johnny xxxx

Johnny put only Leah's name on the envelope, since Isabel was going to the hospice soon and would take it with her. He went into the kitchen to make a pot of coffee and took a mug to Isabel where she was working.

'All right?' she said.

He put an arm around her shoulders. 'I'm fine,' he said.

In truth, he still felt like a convalescent. The world was too much for him. He walked slowly and spoke carefully and sometimes he would have to remove himself from company and be alone.

'Really?'

'Really.'

'Good.'

'I can help you later, if you like. Rake up all the leaves or something.'

'That'd be great.'

'I've got a letter for you to take to Leah.'

'She'll be pleased. I'll leave in a few minutes, after I've changed into something less grubby. There's plenty of food in the fridge.'

'I know. I'll be fine.'

After she had gone, Johnny made himself a cheese sandwich and took it outside, with a tumbler of water. He ate slowly, watching the swallows line up on the telephone wires. All the way to Africa, he thought, and then all the way back again next spring. Which was home?

After he'd cleared away his plate, he started the next letter.

Dear Mr and Mrs Melrose,

You don't know me and you've probably never heard my name, but I knew your daughter well in the last few months of her life.

I am so very sorry for your loss. I don't have children, so I can't begin to understand what it must feel like for you. I do hope that you have people around you who can help you through. I know you have two other children; I hope that is some kind of comfort, and I hope that they will be all right.

I met Ali in the north of France, where we worked on a farm together for a while. She made me feel welcome there, and went out of her way to help me. She was not like anyone I have ever met before. She was a life force. To know her was to love her. Even though she found life difficult, she made other people's lives easier for them. She may have got angry sometimes, but she was never mean-spirited. I remember her laughing (throwing back her head and her hair flying out) and I remember her dancing and I remember her being happy. I hope that after a while you will also be able to remember all the good things in her life, as well as the way that it ended too soon.

Ali talked a lot about you both, and about her sister Janine and brother Thomas. I know there were arguments, but she loved you all a great deal.

I hope you do not mind me writing to you like this. I am just so sorry for all you have lost,

Johnny Hopkins

He walked down the garden, to where the guinea pig used to be. Digby was lying in a puddle of sunlight, his skinny flank rising and falling with his breathing. Johnny sat down beside him and looked out over the stubble and the rooks' nests. There were small white clouds in the sky, a chill in the air when the sun momentarily disappeared behind them. After a long while, he rose again and returned to his task.

I am sorry but I can't remember your name, if I ever knew it. But some months ago, you were very kind to me. You found me lying outside your house and instead of chasing me away you took me to the station and you gave me £40 to buy a ticket to London, which I enclose now, with my sincere thanks. It was more than the money – though that was very important – it was your act of kindness to someone who was so clearly out of luck and in a mess. It meant a great deal to me at the time, and it still does now. Thank you. I hope that if you are ever in trouble or in need you will find that a stranger is as kind to you as you were to me then.

With heartfelt gratitude and all best wishes,

Johnny Hopkins

He took a long drink of water and sat with the pen poised above the next sheet of paper.

Dear Wendell,

This four-leafed clover is for you. I found it this morning and you were the first person I thought of. It's to give you good luck at school. I know you are going to be just fine.

I am sorry I went without saying goodbye. This letter is saying goodbye, and hello, and lots of love,

Johnny
PS Keep practising your cartwheels!

Dearest Elsie,

I am writing this sitting in my parents' garden in East Anglia. I am sure I described it to you. It's very beautiful, very English. There are roses and apple trees here, and today the sun is shining, but gently. Sometimes I feel it is healing me.

So I am home. Or, at least, I have returned to my childhood home. I suppose I have to find my own home now. You were very generous with your home, Elsie. You took me in and you made me feel safe. I do not know what would have happened to me if I hadn't met you when I did. You didn't impose any conditions, you didn't ask any questions, and you shared your life without asking for anything in return. In truth, I didn't have much to give in return, did I? I was wretched, lonely and lost, and you made me feel stronger – and when I was strong enough, I left again and you never tried to make me stay or feel guilty for going. You are the most kind-hearted and good person I have ever met and I will never, ever forget you or cease to be grateful to you.

That sounds too formal. I wish I had the words. In the past few years, I have met some pretty nasty characters. I've been exploited, tricked, beaten up and robbed. When you're homeless, you become invisible to most people, and despicable: a thing, an object, sub-human. You gave me back my humanity. It's the greatest gift anyone will ever give me. I owe you my life.

I'm going to try and do things better this time. I'll go back to university, as you said I should, and before then I am going to do a gardening course near here. Grow things, get my hands dirty. Think, but not think too much.

Give Wendell a big hug from me.

I don't know how to end this letter. Thank you, Elsie. Always.

Johnny xxxxxx

Chapter Thirty-six

Johnny ran. Along the sea wall for mile after mile and then down on to the beach, half sand, half mud and grit. It was harder here. His feet sank into the ground and slid on trailing ropes of seaweed, crunched over oyster shells, sharp fragments of razor clams and metal bottle tops. Things that are washed up by the sea: driftwood and plastic bags, the sole of a shoe and the groping claws of a crab; feather of a bird and remains of a fish, brown glass and green, red toy car missing its wheels, rotting tennis ball once thrown out for a dog, half a Frisbee and a child's plastic tennis racquet, lacking its strings; a flowery shirt that must once have been smart, a single pink flip-flop whose strap was fastened by a small daisy shape that would slide between the toes. A desiccated starfish, a bottle without a message, a piece of rope with a knot in one end, a crumpled can, a wind-up toy that must have dropped from the hot fist of a toddler pulled along by his parent – how he would have cried when he discovered it was gone.

Johnny ran on. On one side was the gradually crumbling cliff. One day houses would slide into the sea; some already had. There were lost hamlets under the water; drowned villages. On the other side was the grey sea, which was slowly moving up the beach towards him, gathering up shells and wood and litter. On its curved horizon was a single ship, a dark shape against the haze. A man and a boy came towards him from a distance, their shape gradually focusing, becoming clear. A small dog ran between them, yapping, occasionally racing in a frenzy to the water's edge, then retreating at the small, slapping waves that licked away the distance between sea and cliff.

Johnny ran on. He saw the man, the child, the dog, the ship, the sea and the cliff, the starfish and the broken toy. But he also saw other things, which crowded in on him and pressed home. He saw his mother's face as she had waved goodbye to him all those years ago, full of love, and her face as she stooped down towards him in the car, all the years of missing carved into her. He saw the water streaming under the prow of a ferry as he stood in the cold wind, watching everything he knew disappear into fog and rain and nothing. And he saw his friend far out at sea, although he had not been there when she went, a face becoming a white blur, a shape becoming a dot becoming an absence, just the swallowing waters. He saw himself, digging beet out of the soil on a cold day, his hands as raw and earthy as the knotted roots he dragged at. And himself picking leaves in a poly-tunnel, surrounded by men and women speaking languages he didn't understand – but there was a common language of deprivation and of human solidarity, and the kindness of those more lost than yourself. He saw fists raised and flesh opening and blood – his? theirs? – pulsing out on to snow. He saw himself curled in a doorway and a man pissing on him, laughing. He had become detritus, rubbish, a soiled thing that people kicked at idly as they passed. He saw the empty blackness of skies at night, when he was the only person

434

left alive in a universe ringing with silence. He saw Zoë's face as he'd entered her; he watched his own face although, of course, he had not seen it then, convulsed in desire and self-hatred. He saw loneliness as though it was a tangible thing: a void, a vortex, a face meeting him from the round bottom of a well that was his face, drowned and staring; a face rising at him out of a mirror that was his face, supplicating.

He had been to a land of self-horror and knew that no view would ever look the same again. He had come home at last, but could never fully return. He had been reunited with friends, after a fashion, but they could never be his intimate friends again – too much lay between them, too much anger and shame. He would have to start over.

Johnny Hopkins ran. Winter, spring and summer, he ran. Until it was time to go again.

Chapter Thirty-seven

'Are you ready?'

'Yes.'

'Wallet, phone, keys, iPod?'

He patted his jacket pocket. 'Yes.'

'You don't seem to have very much.'

'I don't need very much. Whatever I've forgotten can't be important.'

It was so different from last time, when he had packed most of the contents of his room into the car: books, clothes, pots and pans, pictures and photographs, sports equipment and uncountable knick-knacks, as if he needed to carry his past with him. Now he had two moderate-sized bags and a small rucksack. Isabel would drive him to the station and she knew he wouldn't want her even to see him on to the train, let alone stand on the platform as it pulled away, his face dissolving into a moving blur, her hand lifted in farewell long after he had disappeared. He was going to spend the night in London with Mia and Lucas, and then get the train some time the next day. He didn't want any ritual. If it had been possible, he would have gone without saying goodbye at all.

'You put it in the boot and I'll call Felix,' said Isabel.

She knocked on the door of Felix's study and then, at his call, pushed it open and put her head inside. 'Ready.'

'Now?'

'Yes.'

He stood up and took his glasses off the bridge of his nose, pushing them into his top pocket. Together they went out to the car. Johnny was already sitting in the passenger seat. His face was quite calm, unreadable.

'I can drive him there, if you'd prefer,' Felix said hesitantly, to Isabel.

'It's fine.'

Felix had given up driving recently, unless it was absolutely necessary. Instead, he had bought a bicycle and travelled miles on it, his face stern under his cheerful yellow helmet. He would use it even in the pouring rain, with his waterproof cape billowing behind him, water dripping from the helmet on to his chin. He biked to the station and took a train to work, and every week he biked to his Quaker meeting, eleven miles away. Isabel had gone to a couple with him, trying to understand why they meant so much to him. She had seen how everyone there welcomed him, how he had found a new kind of family who didn't judge him and with whom he didn't feel a failure, and she was grateful to them. Perhaps they could make him better. She couldn't – but accepting that had been a melancholy kind of liberation. All her life, since her mother had died and her father had turned helplessly to her, she had thought she could take people's burdens from them and that that was her role in life – the thing she was uniquely good at. She could be their answer. Now she understood what she'd always known: that everyone had to be their own answer. Only Felix could rescue himself, accompanied by his impartial new friends and their silent ceremonies; only Johnny could help Johnny and untangle him from guilt. She had to let them go and attend to herself at last.

Johnny wound down his window.

''Bye, then, Dad,' he said casually, a funny little smile quirking his mouth.

''Bye, Johnny.'

Felix blinked several times, leant in and kissed the top of Johnny's head. 'You have a good time,' he said.

'Yeah.'

'And remember –'

'I'll remember. You don't need to worry.'

'OK.'

'You go easy on yourself, though.'

'Yes.'

'I'll see you.'

Felix tried to smile. 'Yes. Please.'

Isabel climbed into the car and turned on the ignition. 'Right. Off we go.' She raised a hand to Felix and, with a splutter of gravel, drove away.

It was only a twenty-minute journey to the station and they didn't talk a great deal, just chatter about arrangements. And when she pulled up and made to get out of the car, Johnny laid a hand on her arm. 'I'll just go. OK?'

'Of course.'

'Goodbye, Mama.'

'Goodbye, darling Johnny.'

'Trust me, all right?'

'I will. I do.'

'Good.'

He swung himself out of the car and went round to the boot to get his bags. Isabel twisted in her seat and watched

438

him. He put his rucksack on his back, hauled his bags onto the road, pulled shut the boot, then took a bag in each hand, all without looking at her. But at the entrance to the station he turned and, bags still in hand, made a small theatrical bow – just as he had done so many years ago. Then he disappeared and left her alone. Leaving home. For a moment, she sat quite still, staring at the space where he had stood. She turned her head to the passenger seat, still warm from his presence. She could scarcely breathe. The old anguish lodged in her throat and it took all her willpower not to hurtle out of the car and onto the platform, take him in her arms again, one last time, stop him going, drive him home and keep him safe – though she knew that safety had to lie within, and knew as well that she didn't want him to stay. *Let go*, she told herself. *Let go*.

She saw the train come down the tracks and disappear into the station. She waited, face leaning against the window, until it left again, and only then did she climb out of the car and walk out onto the platform. She half expected to see him still there, with his bags at his feet, but it was quite empty, now that all the passengers who had disembarked had gone, except an old woman with a flowery holdall on wheels, standing at the far end. Johnny had left. She imagined him looking out of the window at the familiar buildings and meadows flowing by. What was he thinking? She remembered all those days and nights of concentrating so hard on him, believing that somehow she must be able to find him simply through the force of her will and the power of her love.

At last, she drove from the station, but she didn't go

straight home. She went instead to the sea. It was late September, cool and windy with grey swirling clouds low in the sky. She stopped in the small empty car park, got out and walked down a path lined with gorse bushes to the beach, where she sat down beside a branch that must have been washed up by a particularly high tide. It was twisted, like a snake, and had a piece of seaweed wrapped around it. Isabel stared out to sea, then took off her shoes, putting the car key into one of them. She lifted her skirt high and walked down the sand into the cold water. She could feel the ground beneath her shifting, gravel curling away under her toes, bits of grit whirling round her calves. She walked in further, up to her thighs, tasting the salt spray on her lips. And further. Her skirt was soaked through now so she let it spread out in the water around her. To her waist, to her breasts. It would be so easy not to turn back. It would be so much easier.

At last she went back to the beach, wading through the surf with her sandy, sodden skirt flapping against her legs and her wet hair slapping her stinging cheeks. She was suddenly freezing cold; her limbs shook and her teeth chattered. She found her shoes and the key and made it back to the car, although it was hard to insert the key into the lock with her thick, numb fingers. Home, down narrow lanes.

The lights were on downstairs and Felix must have lit a fire because smoke was curling out of the chimney into the sky that was fading towards dusk.

Isabel went to the front door and opened it. Leaving wet footprints on the floor, she padded into the living room and stood in front of the large painting there. She stared at her mother and her mother stared back at her with the odd little smile that never changed.

'Mama?' she said aloud. 'Mama, have I done well?'

What should she do now? Where should she go and who should she be? What should she do with her life?

She turned and walked from the room, stepping out of her skirt as she went, pulling off her shirt, collecting a towel from the kitchen and rubbing her chilly flesh dry.

The door to the study opened and Felix came out. He looked at her for several moments, not speaking but gazing at her as if he was trying to make something out, and she saw in his face the man she had fallen in love with all those years ago; the fineness in him, the restraint and the longing. Then he held out his hand and, after a hesitation, Isabel stepped forward and took it in hers and held it against her cold cheek. She smiled at him, and he smiled back.

'Well,' she said. 'Our Johnny's gone.'

NICCI GERRARD

THE WINTER HOUSE

When Marnie receives a phone call that summons her to the side of a once-beloved friend, she is wrenched from her orderly London life and sent back into a past from which she has fled but never escaped.

Ralph, Marnie and Oliver once knew each other well and are still inextricably bound by ties of love and betrayal. Now they meet again in Ralph's secluded cottage in the Scottish highlands to spend the precious days that Ralph has left with one another.

As they reminisce, Marnie is taken back to the summer years ago when everything changed between them, and heartbreak and desire broke up their little group. Will Ralph have the chance to say what needs to be said before it's too late? And can they put to rest the devastating events of twenty years ago and rekindle the intimacy they once shared?

'Beguiling, poignant, wonderful' *Sunday Express*

'Acutely observed and beautifully written' *Woman & Home*

'Subtle, poignant and tremendously skilful' *Observer*

He just wanted a decent book to read ...

Not too much to ask, is it? It was in 1935 when Allen Lane, Managing Director of Bodley Head Publishers, stood on a platform at Exeter railway station looking for something good to read on his journey back to London. His choice was limited to popular magazines and poor-quality paperbacks – the same choice faced every day by the vast majority of readers, few of whom could afford hardbacks. Lane's disappointment and subsequent anger at the range of books generally available led him to found a company – and change the world.

'We believed in the existence in this country of a vast reading public for intelligent books at a low price, and staked everything on it'
Sir Allen Lane, 1902–1970, founder of Penguin Books

The quality paperback had arrived – and not just in bookshops. Lane was adamant that his Penguins should appear in chain stores and tobacconists, and should cost no more than a packet of cigarettes.

Reading habits (and cigarette prices) have changed since 1935, but Penguin still believes in publishing the best books for everybody to enjoy. We still believe that good design costs no more than bad design, and we still believe that quality books published passionately and responsibly make the world a better place.

So wherever you see the little bird – whether it's on a piece of prize-winning literary fiction or a celebrity autobiography, political tour de force or historical masterpiece, a serial-killer thriller, reference book, world classic or a piece of pure escapism – you can bet that it represents the very best that the genre has to offer.

Whatever you like to read – trust Penguin.